"HOW DARE YOU PRESUME TO JUDGE ME?"

Juliet's voice trembled with outrage. "You know nothing about me. I am as honest a woman as any you'll ever meet!"

Amos glared back at her. "I don't know whether you are or not. But I can see the way men are around you. You could tear a man's heart right out of him if he was foolish enough to fall in love with you."

His words were bitter and harsh, but there was an odd note of longing in his voice. He drew a sharp breath and turned away.

Also by Candace Camp

Rosewood
Light and Shadow
Analise
Bonds of Love
Bitterleaf
Crystal Heart
Rain Lily

Published by
HarperPaperbacks

ATTENTION: ORGANIZATIONS AND CORPORATIONS

Most HarperPaperbacks are available at special quantity discounts for bulk purchases for sales promotions, premiums, or fund-raising. For information, please call or write:
**Special Markets Department, HarperCollins Publishers,
10 East 53rd Street, New York, N.Y. 10022.
Telephone: (212) 207-7528. Fax: (212) 207-7222.**

Harper Monogram

CANDACE CAMP

HEIRLOOM

HarperPaperbacks
A Division of HarperCollinsPublishers

Special edition printing: February 1994

HarperPaperbacks *A Division of* HarperCollins*Publishers*
          10 East 53rd Street, New York, N.Y. 10022

Cover photograph by Herman Estevez
Quilt courtesy of Quilts of America, Inc., N.Y.C.

First printing: September 1992

Printed in the United States of America

HarperPaperbacks, HarperMonogram, and colophon are
trademarks of HarperCollins*Publishers*

❖ 10 9 8 7 6 5 4 3 2 1

ACKNOWLEDGMENTS

Of great help to me in the writing of this book was the biography of growing up on a Nebraska farm, *No Time on My Hands* by Grace Snyder and Nellie Snyder Yost.

And, as always, I wish to thank the Austin Public Library, without whose excellent resources my job would be much more difficult.

HEIRLOOM

One

The noise out front was getting worse. Lily pulled back the heavy curtain a fraction and put one eye to the crack. "They're getting restless. Bunch of hayseeds! Who wants to play in Steadman, Nebraska, anyway? Why did James book us into here?"

"You mean the Steadman Opera House?" Juliet tossed back wryly. "Didn't you know it's the cultural mecca of the West?"

Lily grimaced. "Yeah, and my name's Sarah Bernhardt." She took another peek at the audience, then let the curtain fall back into place and glanced around in irritation. "Damn! Where is James, anyway!"

"Probably off on another bender," Mrs. Fairfax commented dryly. She was a veteran of the stage and had weathered too many such crises to be dismayed at the fact that their leading man was missing. "I'll be in that closet the locals laughingly term a dressing room—in case James should turn up."

She turned and swept away dramatically, as usual.

Lily turned to Juliet, her blue eyes round with fright. "What if she's right!" she gasped. "What'll we do then?"

She cast a nervous glance toward the curtain, beyond which the murmurings and shifting were rapidly turning into loud grumbles.

"Bring on the show!" someone called loudly from the audience, and there was a chorus of whistles and stamping.

"Oh, dear." Juliet's stomach sank. "Why are you asking me? I don't know what to do."

"But you've been on the stage all your life! Surely you must!"

Juliet looked from Lily's uncertain face to that of Hamilton, the man who played the piano for her songs and took on the minor male roles in the plays the Westfield Company performed. Juliet sighed. "Why did Mrs. Fairfax leave? She knows more than I do. I've never been in a production where Hamlet didn't show up for the last act."

She stepped over to the curtain herself and peered out. Several men were out of their seats, looking around with belligerent expressions, and nearly everyone in the audience was talking, their voices growing louder with each passing second. They appeared anything but happy.

Juliet wished herself a thousand miles away. No, two thousand. She wished she were back in New York, or perhaps Philadelphia with her sister Celia. *Never again*, she vowed to herself. Never again would she take a job with a troupe touring the western states. It was asking for trouble—ceaseless traveling over unending miles of nothingness, playing to rural audiences to whom they might as well have recited nursery rhymes as Shakespeare, enduring heat and wind and dust. And now this: a Hamlet who had doubtless gotten drunk and who had disappeared during the last intermission—and an audience that looked as if it had no intention of gracefully accepting a play that had no ending.

Right now she wished fervently that she hadn't taken this job. She wouldn't have, knowing how little she liked touring through the West, except that she had needed the money and James Westfield had been the only manager of a troupe willing to give her a position without her having to grace his bed, as well. Since her father's death two years ago, she had had a difficult time finding work without giving up her virtue, and she had realized just how much her parents had protected her all these years. But with both her parents dead and her sister married to a theater manager in Philadelphia, she had had to fend for herself, and she had taken many jobs that once she would have deemed beneath her talent as a singer. This one was turning out to be the worst.

"Where's the fight?" somebody roared.

"Yeah, I thought somebody got stabbed!"

"Oh, dear." Juliet chewed nervously at her lower lip. It looked to her as if a riot was brewing.

She let the curtain fall and looked back at her companions. They were all gazing at her expectantly, even Joseph, who was older than she and played much bigger parts. Why did they all think she would know what to do? But she knew the answer to that; it was because her entire family was composed of actors—both her parents and her sister—and she had grown up backstage in hundreds of theaters. It didn't matter that she hadn't much acting skill and even less authority, that her primary contribution to the shows were the songs she sang between the acts while the props and costumes were being changed. To the others, she *knew* the theater.

Juliet drew a breath. "All right. Let's see . . . Joseph, do you think that you could do James's lines?"

He cocked an eyebrow. "You mean, have a sword fight with myself?"

"No. Of course, you can't play both Hamlet and Laertes. What was I thinking? Then, let's see . . . I guess there's nothing for it but to tell them the truth."

"The truth? That Hamlet's probably down the street in the saloon?"

"Well, no." Juliet smiled, a dimple popping into one cheek. "I shan't be quite *that* veracious."

She walked to center stage and parted the curtains, stepping out onto the apron of the stage. At the sight of her, the audience erupted into cheers and clapping. Juliet smiled and made an elegant curtsey. They had liked her songs and had been quite vocal in their approval; she only hoped their goodwill would last through her announcement.

She held out her hands for quiet, and at last the audience settled down. Gravely she began, "I am so sorry." Though she discounted herself as an actress, she had a lovely, well-trained voice that she could make roll out majestically when she chose, giving her small frame an air of dignity and authority. The rich crimson velvet dress she wore made her seem older than her twenty-four years—and the soft white shoulders it revealed and the bright red-gold of her hair were enough to catch any man's attention. The last few stray murmurs in the crowd hushed, and they all looked at her expectantly.

"I am afraid that I have sad news for you," she went on. She injected her voice with sincerity and sorrow, and by biting the inside of her cheek hard, she caused tears to spring into her vivid blue eyes. "Mr. Westfield has become suddenly ill. Terribly ill. He will be unable to continue this performance despite his brave attempts to do so."

Her voice shook on her words, but it was less because of her acting skill than because of the black looks that were directed at her and the immediate mutterings of discontent. Obviously the people of Steadman were not moved by pity to forego their entertainment.

Quickly Juliet held up her hands. "Wait! It is but a poor substitute, I know, but, if you will be so kind as to listen, I will sing a few songs to try to make up, at least in some part, for Mr. Westfield's absence."

The mutterings quickly turned to a loud roar of approval. One man cheered, and in another corner of the room, another loudly called, "To hell with Hamlet! I'd rather see you, sugar!"

Oh, Lord, Juliet thought. She felt like a singer in a saloon. Her mother would probably turn over in her grave if she could see Juliet singing popular songs in front of a rowdy crowd of Nebraska farmers and cowmen.

But there was nothing for it but to sing and hope that it would appease the crowd. Holding one hand toward the side of the stage in an elegant gesture, she said, "Mr. Blaine? If you will accompany me?"

Hamilton hurried out to the piano, looking flustered.

Juliet walked over to him and murmured the names of a few songs to him. Then she folded her hands demurely and began to sing, "Green grow the lilacs, all covered with dew. . . ."

As it turned out, Juliet had to sing far more than the three or four songs she had planned before satisfying her audience, who repeatedly shouted and whistled for her to continue. By the time she finally left the stage, she was exhausted. The rest of the players—the cowards!—had left the theater during her performance, seizing the opportunity to slip away. Hurriedly, she wiped off most of her stage makeup, but she found the theater eerie with only her and Hamilton in it, and she decided to leave without changing out of her red velvet costume.

Throwing on a cloak over her low-cut dress, she walked the three blocks back to her hotel room. Hamilton walked with her part of the way, but when they passed the saloon, he left her and went inside for a drink. Juliet trudged the rest of the way, mentally condemning James Westfield every step of the way.

As she neared the hotel, she saw that a man was seated on the top step, his folded arms resting on his knees and a pipe in his hand. His coat was off, slung carelessly across the porch railing, his sleeves were rolled up, and he was staring straight ahead, lost in contemplation. At the sound of her footsteps, he turned toward her, and surprise flitted across his face, followed swiftly by a grin.

"Miss Drake!" He jumped to his feet.

Juliet stopped at the foot of the steps and looked at him uncertainly. *Had she met this man today and had forgotten it?* She couldn't imagine that. He was too large a man to be overlooked—tall, with the heavy shoulders and arms of a man who worked hard—and too handsome for a woman not to remember. His hair was black and his eyes darkly mysterious in the dim light, and the lines of his face were strong and compelling.

"I'm sorry." Juliet smiled tentatively. "Do I know you?"

The stranger looked abashed. "Oh, no. I'm sorry." The words came a little stiffly from him, as if he were uncomfortable. "I shouldn't have—I mean, I just saw you perform, and I guess I felt as if I knew you." He shrugged and, amazingly, Juliet thought that he blushed.

"I'm sorry," he said again.

"No, there's no need to apologize." Juliet smiled. "I understand."

"You were beautiful," he blurted out. "That is, I mean, your singing was beautiful."

"Why, thank you."

"I didn't much care for the rest of it, frankly. I was relieved that fella didn't come back."

Juliet had to smile at his honesty. "I suspect there were a few others who felt the same way."

He smiled again, and his face shifted in a way that did funny things to Juliet's stomach. "I reckon you're right about that."

For an instant, Juliet thought wistfully of what it must

be like to live an ordinary life, to meet a man like this and know that one would run into him again as the weeks went by, to hope that he might come to call on her . . . .

Firmly she pushed the thought out of her mind—that simply wasn't her life, and it never would be. She held out her hand to him and said briskly, "Good night. It was nice to meet you."

"Good night, Miss Drake." He took her hand in his large rough one. His skin was hard and callused, and the touch of it against her own smooth skin was oddly intriguing. "God, you're lovely," he breathed, staring down into her eyes.

Juliet gazed back up at him. There was an odd tightness in her chest, and she found it difficult to look away.

"I'm sorry," he said, abruptly dropping her hand and stepping back. "I shouldn't have said that. I didn't mean—" He broke off with a noise of irritation. "You must think that I'm an idiot."

"No, of course not," Juliet demurred. It was, in fact, rather flattering to think that she could rattle a mature, handsome man. His frank, unstudied compliment set up a fluttery feeling in her stomach that never happened with the smooth, suave flattery of the men who called on her backstage, certain that either their charm or their money would lure an actress into their beds. It was infuriating always having to fight the popular image of an actress as little better than a prostitute, and it was balm to her spirit to have a man apologize for being too forward.

She was tempted to linger on the porch and talk to him. Strangely, exhausted as she had felt walking home, she no longer felt tired at all. But, of course, she couldn't stay here with a strange man, chatting, or she would be acting just as brazenly as people always assumed actresses did.

"Good night." She turned away.

"Good night."

With an inward sigh, Juliet opened the door of the hotel and walked inside. She climbed the stairs, aimlessly trailing her hand along the polished wooden balustrade, thinking about the man she had left behind on the porch. It wasn't until she stepped into the second-floor corridor that she finally became aware of the low, but excited chatter of voices. She glanced down the hallway. There was a small knot of people huddled together at the end of the corridor, conversing in agitated whispers. Juliet wasn't surprised to see that they were several of the people from her troupe; no doubt they were discussing James Whitfield's propensity for drinking.

"Juliet!" Lily caught sight of her and swung around to face her.

She looked, Juliet thought, far more agitated than their leader's being passed out in his room would warrant. Juliet hurried toward her, a chill of real fear running through her. "What? What's happened?"

"You won't believe it!" Lily exclaimed. "He's run away!"

"What? Who?"

"James Westfield!" Joseph stuck in impatiently. "His room is vacant; he's taken all his bags and things. And Amanda's gone, as well." He named a curvaceous blonde who had played minor female parts on stage.

"What?" Juliet stared. "But—"

"That's not the problem," Mrs. Fairfax snapped, scowling. "The problem is: he's taken all our money with him!"

"Our money! No! All of it?"

"All of it. The strongbox is gone, and the desk clerk says he saw Westfield walking out of the hotel with it earlier this afternoon. He's absconded with our receipts, including tonight's take."

The blood drained from Juliet's face. "But that means—"

"Exactly." Mrs. Fairfax bobbed her head decisively. "He took the money he was supposed to pay us with tomorrow. We're stranded in this hick town in Nebraska, and we haven't got a penny!"

It wasn't the first time that Juliet hadn't been paid her salary or had been stranded somewhere when a company abruptly folded. But it was the first time that her father hadn't been with her when it happened. Somehow Alexander Drake, with his optimistic approach to life and his years of experience in the vagaries of the theater, had usually managed to land on his feet. He had always seemed to have some object to sell or pawn or he would use his elegant charm to sweet-talk the proprietress of their boardinghouse or hotel out of charging them or he would manage to convince someone that he was worthy of a loan. If worse came to worst, he would even do physical labor to earn the money that they needed.

But the situation was different with Juliet on her own.

They had used up most of their valuable assets during her father's long illness before his death two years ago; all she had left was his engraved pocket watch, and she could never sell it. It was her only link to her father. Nor had she been able to save any money in the time since her father died. It had been a shock to discover how much less she had had to live on when she was the only one bringing in money. Her payment for the songs she sang was far less than what her father had made. So she had nothing to sell and very little money with her. It wasn't enough to even pay her hotel bill for longer than a day or two, let alone purchase a ticket on the train to Omaha and points east.

Early the next morning she went to the one millinery shop in town to look for employment. A tall, thin woman glanced up at her entrance, and the smile on her face immediately died. "Yes?" she inquired, her voice as icy as an arctic blast.

Juliet forced a smile. "Hello. I'm Juliet Drake."

"Yes, I know. You're with that acting troupe." The woman invested the words with scorn.

"Yes. Could I speak to the owner, please?"

"*I* am the owner. Miss Aurica Johnson." She looked forbiddingly at Juliet.

Juliet's heart sank. She knew she wouldn't have a chance with this woman, but she had to try, anyway. "I am looking for employment. I have some experience with millinery work. I decorated this hat myself."

She gestured toward the one on her head, a shallow-crowned felt hat decorated with ostrich feathers and turned up jauntily on one side and pinned with a paste jewel brooch. Juliet knew that it looked quite fetching on her. But Aurica Johnson's steely eyes swept over the hat in question with disinterest.

"I have no positions open now," she said flatly, then continued, "and even if I did, I would not allow the reputation of my shop to be damaged by hiring an *actress*." She said the word much as she might have said "thief" or "prostitute." Her opinion of Juliet's profession was obviously much the same.

Juliet flushed. "I'm sorry to have bothered you," she said shortly, whirling and almost running out of the store.

Juliet stood on the street for a moment, collecting her composure, then continued with her job hunting.

By the time she returned to her hotel room late that afternoon, she was weary, bedraggled, hungry, and depressingly close to tears. The last thing she wanted to find was Mrs. Morgan, the shrewd-eyed proprietress of the hotel, standing behind the desk, but that was the sight that greeted her when she stepped inside the door.

"Oh, Miss Drake?" the woman called in her carrying voice and came out from behind the tall counter. She was an imposing woman despite her relatively short stature. She was fully corseted and packed into her plain brown dress; her bosom jutted out above her corset like the prow of a ship. Her jaw thrust forward in much the same way, and there was determination and will in every line of her strong features. But her mouth was full and generous, countering the sharpness of her face, and her firm voice was not unkind.

"Good evening, Mrs. Morgan." Juliet tried to smile, but found it difficult to do. She could feel tears welling up in her eyes, and it was all she could do to hold them back. The last thing she wanted to do right now was face Mrs. Morgan's questions about paying her hotel bill.

"Could I speak to you a moment?" Henrietta Morgan took Juliet's arm and steered her toward the back of the hotel.

"Of course." Resigned, Juliet went with the woman to a small, cramped office past the front desk.

Mrs. Morgan closed the door behind them and pointed toward the only chair in the room. "Sit down. Sit down. You look as if you could use a little rest. I've been in a chair all day adding up figures."

"Thank you." A little surprised, Juliet sank down onto the chair. It felt heavenly to be off her feet.

"Mrs. Fairfax and her companion left the hotel this afternoon. They took the train to San Francisco, I believe."

"Did they?" It didn't surprise Juliet that the leading lady and her dresser cum wardrobe mistress had enough money stashed away to buy a train ticket out of town.

"They told me about the dreadful thing that Mr. Westfield did." Her brows knit together darkly. "That man ran off without paying for his room, either."

Juliet nodded. "I'm sorry."

"No reason for you to apologize. It was none of your doing."

"I know. But I guess Mrs. Fairfax told you about his taking the money box, too."

"Yes. She said that she imagined the rest of you would be stranded here."

Juliet nodded. "I'm afraid so. Lily and Hamilton went over to the saloon to look for work."

"Mmm." Henrietta looked noncommittal. "My husband, Samuel, sent the older man over to the livery stable, where they need a hand."

"Mick?" Juliet smiled. "That's good." Mick, who had moved their scenery and carried their trunks and done other odd jobs for the troupe, was a nice man, and she was glad to hear that he had found something. Of course, he was no doubt qualified for all kinds of jobs—unlike her.

"That Joseph Campbell took off last night, it looks like," Henrietta went on with a sniff of contempt.

"He didn't pay you, either?" Juliet's heart sank. Between Westfield, his paramour, and now Joseph, that was three people who had cheated the Morgans. Juliet was sure that Mrs. Morgan wouldn't be inclined to give her the benefit of the doubt.

"No." She shrugged. "Well, that's always a chance you take. You can't outsmart all the crooks of this world."

"No, I suppose not." Juliet looked down at her hands. "I'm sure you'll have a hard time believing this, but I promise that I will pay you what I owe you. I only have enough for last night right now, but as soon as I find employment, I'll give you the rest. I promise."

"I'm sure you will, dear." Henrietta patted her shoulder kindly. "You have a good, honest look about you. And Mrs. Fairfax recommended you as a fair, responsible person. She said that she was sorry she couldn't help you, as she had known and respected your father, but she only had enough money for the two of them, she said."

"It was kind of her to think of me." Juliet looked up at the older woman with dawning hope. "Does that mean you'll let me stay here then? Until I can find work and a place to stay?"

Henrietta nodded. "But that's not why I called you in here. I think I might be able to help you with both problems."

Juliet's jaw dropped. "You what?"

"Have you found work yet?"

Juliet shook her head. "No. I'm afraid not. I—well, there aren't many jobs for women in this town. I went to the general store and looked at the advertisements posted inside their door, but there wasn't anything for a woman. Two seamstresses had notices up that they took in sewing, so I guess there isn't much call for another seamstress. That's something I do quite well. I make most of my clothes."

"Do you?" Henrietta looked astonished, and she glanced over Juliet's outfit with a judging eye. "Why, you're quite good, my dear. You look very fashionable."

"Thank you. Unfortunately, Miss Johnson wasn't impressed."

"The milliner?"

Juliet nodded. "I asked her for work, and she turned me down flat."

Mrs. Morgan made a dismissive gesture with her hand. "Oh, she's a prissy one. No, I wouldn't think you'd get very far there."

"I looked through the newspaper, too, and I couldn't find anything."

"I'm sure they would hire a singer over at the Golden Cage."

"The saloon?" Juliet's eyebrows shot up, and for a moment she looked as haughty as a Boston *grande dame*. "I'd never work in a saloon. They expect far more of one than singing."

"A commendable attitude," Henrietta murmured.

"But not one you'd expect from an *actress*?" Juliet retorted scornfully. She was weary and disappointed, and the last thing she wanted to hear was another sneering comment about the morals of actresses. "I know what everyone thinks of any woman in the theater, but some of us do have morals, you know. My parents were both in the theater, and they raised me in it, but they were firm in my moral upbringing, as well. My mother was the daughter of a country parson in New Hampshire, and she never forgot where she came from. She raised Celia and me to be ladies, and I wouldn't think of compromising myself by working in a saloon any more than you or any of the ladies of this town would!"

"My." Henrietta chuckled and clapped her hands together. "You're better than I imagined. What luck!"

Juliet's eyes widened in surprise. "What? What are you talking about?"

"Why, the job, of course . . . at my brother-in-law's farm."

Juliet stared at her. "You mean you're offering me employment?" It was so far from what she had thought when Mrs. Morgan had called her into the room that she couldn't quite comprehend it.

"Yes—well, I'm telling you that there is a job available. I suppose that Amos will have the final say, of course. However, he did put me in charge of finding a housekeeper for him."

"A housekeeper? That's what you need?"

"Yes. I presume that you are able to cook and clean house, of course."

"Oh, yes, of course," Juliet lied evenly. The truth was that, though she was more than handy with a needle, she had had little experience cooking and taking care of a house. After her mother had died when Juliet was twelve, she and her father and sister had stayed in boardinghouses, where the meals were part of the charge. She had rarely done more than make coffee and take care of her and her father's room. Even their clothes had usually been taken to a laundress, as there was no way to wash and dry clothes in the hotel and boardinghouses.

But how hard could keeping house be? she rationalized to herself. After all, most women were able to do it, so surely she would catch onto the chores quickly enough. And she desperately needed this job. There was no work for her in the town except at the saloon; she was convinced of that. So surely she would be forgiven for just a little lie.

"Good. Well, my husband Samuel's younger brother, Amos, is desperately in need of a housekeeper. Frances is getting too sick to do it anymore. It's pitiful." She shook her head. "Yes, truly pitiful." Her voice lowered. "I'm afraid it won't be long now."

"Frances?"

"Yes, that's my husband's sister. She's always stayed on the farm with Amos and kept house for him and his son."

"And now she's—she's—"

Henrietta nodded. "Dying. I'm afraid so. She's lost so much weight she hardly looks like herself. She was always a big woman, like all the Morgans, not fat, mind you, but tall and big-boned. Well, she's positively frail now. It's sad."

"I'm sorry."

"Well, that's neither here nor there; there's nothing we can do about it. The fact is, Amos needs a woman to do the housework and help with Frances. I've been looking for someone for weeks now, and no one's willing." At the doubtful look on Juliet's face, she added hastily, "Not that he's an ogre, you understand. He's, uh, well, he has a sort of gruff and silent way about him. And his standards are high."

A qualm ran through Juliet. Perhaps it was foolish even to think of working for this man who had a reputation for high standards, when she wasn't sure of all the basics of housekeeping, let alone the finer points!

But Henrietta didn't allow her time for doubt. "But I'm sure that you'll do fine. Why don't you come upstairs to the family's quarters and meet Frances and Amos? They're in town for the day. Frances has been to see the doctor, and they'll be heading back to the farm tomorrow. That way, if Amos accepts you, you can ride out there with them."

"All right."

Juliet rose and followed the other woman up the stairs to the third floor. Henrietta walked toward the back of the hotel and opened an unnumbered door. She stepped into a parlor that was richly furnished, and Juliet followed.

"Amos!" Henrietta called, walking across the room and looking into the next one. "Come here. I've hired you a housekeeper. Come meet her."

Juliet heard the rumble of a masculine voice. A moment later, there were footsteps across the wooden floor, and a large man walked past Henrietta into the room. He saw Juliet, and his jaw dropped. Juliet stared back, sure that she must look equally amazed. Henrietta Morgan's brother-in-law, the man who needed a housekeeper, was the man she had met on the front porch last night!

Two

$\mathcal{A}$mos Morgan stared at Juliet without speaking for a moment. In the daylight, he looked even larger than he had last night, his shoulders broad and his arms heavy, his hands wide and long-fingered, sinewy. His hair and his eyes were both dark as coal, his face weathered by the elements, though handsome, and Juliet thought that he looked much harder and fiercer—especially now that his look of astonishment was being replaced by a scowl!

He swung his head to Henrietta. "Is this some sort of joke?"

Henrietta opened her eyes innocently wide. "Why, Amos, of course not. Whatever are you talking about?"

"What am I talking about?" His voice vaulted upward in exasperation. "Are you telling me that you hired her—" he swung his arm in Juliet's direction, pointing his finger at her in a way that reminded Juliet of Calvin Knox accusing a scarlet woman—"to keep my house?"

"Yes, Amos." Henrietta's voice was patient. "That's exactly what I'm telling you."

"But she's—she's—" he sputtered, turning back to look at her, "she's an actress!"

Juliet planted her hands on her hips and glared back at him. "I am not an actress; I am a singer."

"I saw you on the stage last night."

"I take a few minor roles, as is necessary in a small, traveling company. But I can assure you, as the daughter and sister of actors, that I do not qualify."

He looked at her oddly. "Well, it doesn't matter what you call it. The fact is, you perform onstage."

"What does that have to do with anything, may I ask?"

"You are not a housekeeper."

"Actresses have to live someplace, like anyone else," Juliet pointed out, her voice heavy with sarcasm. "We have to eat and keep our homes clean and take care of our clothes, like anyone else."

"Of course they do," Henrietta put in. "Amos, I don't understand why you're being so exasperating. Just because a woman is an actress doesn't mean that she isn't capable of taking care of a household as well. Why, Miss Drake sewed this dress herself. Isn't she clever?"

"I'm sure she is." His voice was tight and angry, and he shot his sister-in-law a furious look. "I don't see how that qualifies her to be a housekeeper. Besides, that isn't the point."

Henrietta assumed a puzzled expression. "Her qualifications aren't the point? Then what is?"

"Henrietta!" he roared. "Damn it, woman, be sensible. She's an actress! Think of the talk! Think about Ethan!"

"Ethan! What does he have to do with this?"

"He's only sixteen; he's at a very impressionable age.

To have an actress in the same house with him!"

Henrietta laughed. "Oh, Amos!"

"I won't have an actress corrupting my son!"

"Corrupting your son!" Juliet blazed. "How dare you! You know nothing about me! You have no idea—"

"I know enough!" he retorted.

"Why, you pompous, narrow-minded—"

Hastily Henrietta said, "Really, Amos, that's ridiculous. What could happen? Why, you are in the house with them, and if anyone could put a damper on a budding romance, it would be you."

"I'm sure you think that's very amusing, Henrietta, but I don't find my son's welfare all that funny. He's young; a beautiful woman like her could turn his head so fast you wouldn't believe it. He wouldn't know what hit him until it was too late."

"What possible interest could I have in turning your son's head?" Juliet asked scathingly.

Amos gave her a scornful glance. "You may think I'm a country bumpkin, Miss Drake, but I assure you that I'm no fool. The real question is what possible interest could a woman like you have in coming to a farm as a housekeeper unless it involves hooking a man and squeezing money out of him? I can't imagine you wanting to scrub pots and floors or cook meals. A woman who looks like you has other, far easier wares to sell."

Juliet let out a wordless shriek of rage and started toward him, her hand curling up in an instinctive urge to hit him. Henrietta, looking a little shocked, intervened, stepping in between the two and facing Amos, her arms folded sternly across her chest. "Amos, really! I'm surprised at you! Even you aren't usually so rude. You have no call to insult Miss Drake. I won't have you questioning the morals of a guest in my house, especially one about whom you know absolutely nothing. Now, apologize." Amos set his jaw mulishly, and Henrietta prodded, "Right now."

"Oh, all right!" He glared at Henrietta, then, gazing at a spot just below and to the left of Juliet's ear, he mumbled, "I'm sorry. I should not have said that." Juliet drew a deep breath. She thought about telling the boor that his apology was not accepted. *How could she have found this man intriguing last night?* He was the rudest, most insufferable man she had ever met—well, no, she admitted honestly, there had been others far worse than he, men who had groped and leered and suggested lewd things to her. But this man, somehow this man had offended and hurt her worse than any of them. She would have liked to tell him to forget his job, to inform him roundly that she hoped she would never set eyes on him again, let alone be in the same house with him.

But Juliet was well aware of the reality of the situation. She couldn't afford to let her hurt feelings speak for her. The only thing she could do was take this job—no, persuade him to give it to her, rather.

Juliet sighed. "I accept your apology," she said primly. "Unfortunately, I have to admit that there is some reason for the way many people think of women who perform onstage. Some of them do care little for their craft but are only interested in—in attracting the attentions of a wealthy man, as you say. However, I assure you that I have no ulterior designs on your son . . . or anyone else. I wish only to work. I need to earn enough money to pay for my train fare back to New York City, or at the least to Chicago, where I might be able to find decent employment singing. Yours is the only position I have found open here; I am willing and capable of keeping house in order to get enough money together to leave!"

Amos crossed his arms and took a step back. Henrietta shifted from in between them, and Juliet drew back to where she had been standing.

"Now," Henrietta said. "Do you think we could sit down and discuss this like rational people, Amos?"

"Well, I'm still not hiring her," Amos said belligerently, moving toward the sofa but not sitting down.

"Mr. Morgan," Juliet began, forcing her voice to sound calm even though her stomach was quivering inside, "I don't think you've given me a fair chance."

"You're all wrong," Morgan responded irritably. "You're too young, too small. Fragile. I need someone who's strong. A farm woman has to work hard."

"Mr. Morgan, I am hardly fragile. I'm quite healthy and strong, and I'm accustomed to work; I've worked since I was fifteen. I have survived worse hardships than living in a farmhouse, believe me. I'm never sick. Perhaps I am younger than what you envisioned for a housekeeper, but it isn't as if I'm a child. My mother died when I was young, and I took care of my father and my sister and me well enough. Why don't you let me prove myself? Let me work there for a week or two, and then if you aren't satisfied with the job I'm doing, you can send me back. You won't have lost anything."

"She's right, you know," Henrietta stuck in. "What harm would it do for Miss Drake to keep house for a few weeks? Then you'd know whether or not she could do the job. It's not as if you have any other choice. No one else has wanted to take it on."

"Well, we don't need a housekeeper, anyway," Amos remarked irritably. "Frances does it just fine."

"Mr. Morgan," Juliet protested, "you do need a house-keeper. Mrs. Morgan tells me that your sister is quite ill."

"Frances'll be fine before long." Amos dismissed Juliet's statement. "She's simply having trouble getting over a winter illness."

"For mercy's sake, Amos, it's a lot more than a winter illness. The doctor told her today that she doesn't have but a few months to live."

"Nonsense! What does he know?" Amos whirled on Henrietta, and his eyes snapped with anger. "He's from the city. He doesn't understand what farm women are like. Frances is tough as whip leather, always has been. She'll be well by summer."

Henrietta stared at him. "Amos! She has cancer. The doctor said it's spreading all through her abdomen."

Amos glared at her and his hands knotted into fists at his side, but he said nothing.

"If she recovers," Juliet put in, trying to smooth over their disagreement, "it will certainly take time, Mr. Morgan. I imagine she won't be up to cleaning pots and pans for weeks."

He grimaced. "You don't know the first thing about it."

"And you do?" Juliet retorted, her hands returning to her hips. She found it very difficult to stay reasonable and calm around this man. *What was the matter with him?* It sounded obvious from Henrietta's words that his sister was dying.

"Frances is getting better!" he roared. "She'll be well soon. You don't know her. We don't need a housekeeper."

"Oh, yes, Amos," a quiet voice said behind them. "You do."

All three of them jumped, startled, and whirled to the doorway, where a woman had entered without any of them noticing. She was tall and spare, bony beneath too little flesh. Her hair was graying at the temples and pulled back tightly in a braid wound in a coronet at the nape of her neck. Her angular, strong features were appealing, if not precisely pretty, and her large dark eyes were intelligent and warm, but her face was tired and lines feathered around her eyes and mouth.

"Frances!" Amos and Henrietta exclaimed, almost in unison, and Henrietta bustled over to take her arm. "Here, come sit down on the sofa with me, dear. We were just discussing hiring Miss Drake to keep house for you."

"So I heard," Frances admitted with a wry smile and a glance at the others.

Amos looked abashed. "I'm sorry. Did I wake you?"

"No. I wasn't able to sleep, anyway. I heard what you were saying, and I had to come in." She looked at Amos with clear, kind brown eyes. "My dear brother . . . I love you very much for trying to pretend that I'm going to be all right. But we both know that every day I get weaker. I've tried, but I can't take care of the house properly anymore. Some days it seems as if I can hardly make it out of my bed."

Amos's mouth opened, but no sound came out, and he closed it again. Finally he said, with a mulish set to his mouth, "You'll be better soon."

"I won't." Frances's voice was quiet and it trembled slightly, but there was no doubt in her tone.

"Frances, no. . . ." Amos looked away.

"I've been hiding from it long enough, and so have you. Henrietta's right. I'm dying."

"Doc Hempstead's a tippler; everybody knows that. You can't take what he said for gospel."

"It's not what the doctor said—at least, not only that. I can feel life slipping out of me, Amos. I can feel that thing inside me, eating me up. You're just too blamed stubborn to admit it."

Amos thrust his hands into his pockets and turned away. He started to speak, then cleared his throat and began again, "All right. If you want a housekeeper, then you'll have one." He turned toward Juliet. "It's time to begin planting, and I can't waste time looking for someone else, so you'll have to do. But it's only as a trial, you understand. If you can't handle the work, then I'm bringing you back. Is that understood?"

Juliet nodded. "Yes. Thank you for giving me the opportunity. I'll make sure that you don't regret it."

Without another word, Amos turned and stalked out the door. Juliet let out a sigh of relief, and her tight muscles relaxed. She had managed to get the job. Now all she had to do was figure out how to do it so well he wouldn't send her back in a week—when she didn't know the first thing about housekeeping!

Juliet pulled her eyes from the monotonous landscape stretching around them in all directions and glanced at her companion. Amos, sitting as far from her as he could on the other end of the long, benchlike wagon seat, had not said a word to her the whole trip. He hadn't even said "hello" that morning when she came out of the hotel. He had only nodded while giving her a hand up onto the high seat. Juliet suppressed a sigh and looked behind them into the bed of the wagon.

Amos had put a feather mattress in the long flat wagon bed, and his sister lay upon it, a light quilt covering her. Her eyes were closed, and her face was tight, the lines around her mouth etched deeply into her flesh. Juliet suspected that despite lying on the mattress, the constant jolting of the wagon was causing Frances a great deal of pain. However, she hadn't offered a word of complaint. Perhaps farm women like Frances were a tougher breed than she was, she thought, and a little ripple of unease passed through her. *What if Amos were right, and she could not stand up to the rigors of the life?*

Amos clicked to the mules and twitched the reins, and the animals turned off the road onto a narrow path.

A few minutes later, a plain two-story farmhouse came into sight. A row of fir trees lined the drive, uniformly bent a little by the wind. A single hickory tree stood beside the house, but other than that there was no vegetation to soften its spare, sharp lines. Beyond it was a pen and a large barn and two or three other small sheds, and from there the land rolled on the horizon, barren of trees. It looked, Juliet thought, utterly desolate, and tears welled unexpectedly in her eyes. *How could she live alone out here with a dying woman and this silent, disagreeable man?*

Hastily she blinked back her tears. She wasn't about to give Amos Morgan the satisfaction of showing weakness. The mules moved faster now as they approached the farmyard, heading for the barn, and Amos hauled back hard on the reins to stop them in front of the house.

A young man emerged from the barn at the noise of their arrival and loped across the yard toward them, grinning. "Pa!"

A smile creased Amos's impassive face, and his dark eyes brightened as he gazed at his son. "Ethan."

Ethan was tall, still with the lanky, awkward look of youth that indicated he had not yet finished growing. His hair was a light brown and his eyes were hazel, and his thin face was attractive though still rather unformed. When he caught sight of Juliet, his jaw dropped and he came to a dead stop.

Amos's smile turned to a frown as his son gaped at Juliet. "Ethan, this is Juliet Drake. She's going to be our housekeeper—at least for a while."

"Our housekeeper?" Ethan repeated in astonishment, then a smile broke across his face like sunlight, and he moved forward, removing his hat and nodding to her. "I'm pleased to meet you, Miss Drake. I never expected a house-keeper like you."

His naive admiration was balm to her spirits after his father's gruff disapproval, and Juliet smiled at him, daz-zling him even more. "Hello, Ethan. It's nice to meet you. I'm surprised you didn't come to town with your father."

"Somebody has to stay and look after the animals," Amos told her flatly and jumped down from the wagon.

"Unfortunately, it was me," Ethan continued, stretch-ing up a hand to help Juliet down.

Juliet climbed down a little stiffly and followed Frances into the house. Amos set her trunk and carpet-bag down on the porch, then got back into the wagon and drove it to the barn, leaving Ethan and Frances to show Juliet the house. Frances, pleading tiredness, went up the stairs to her room, but Ethan was happy to show her around.

"This is the parlor and the dining room," he said, ges-turing toward the closed doors on either side of the dark hallway inside the front door. Past the stairs was another room, this one standing open and obviously more used, which he termed the back parlor. A short hall crossed the longer one like the top of a T, and Ethan gestured down it to the left. "Kitchen's in there, and the other way's a guest room. I reckon you'll sleep in it."

Juliet went to the kitchen, wanting to see the room

where she would be spending much of her time. It was large and, she was relieved to see, quite sunny, with two sets of double windows. A large wooden table and chairs sat in the middle of the room, and she had a quick impression of cabinets and a sink with a pump handle. Dominating the room was a large black stove that sat against the far wall, squat and ugly, a box of wood beside it.

Looking at the room and its furnishings, Juliet knew that it should have been a sparkling, well-stocked kitchen. Everything in the room was of good quality and bespoke pride and money expended. It was obviously the room in which the Morgans spent most of their time. Normally it would have been well cared for.

But the kitchen, though nominally clean, was not as it should be. The dishes had not been cleared from the table or the table wiped. Pots and pans were piled in the sink, dirty. The floor needed to be swept, and needed even worse to be mopped and waxed. The windowpanes were dirty, and there were cobwebs in the high corners of the room. The pans that hung from the hooks by the stove were not gleamingly polished, but dull. Juliet was sure that this was not the state in which Frances had kept the kitchen in the past. Even though she barely knew her, Juliet was positive that Frances Morgan was a meticulous housekeeper. But it was clear that lately she had been able to do no more than the most necessary cleaning and cooking.

Well, at least she knew what she had to do here, Juliet thought, as she untied her cloak and hung it on the peg near the back door. She smiled at Ethan. "I suppose I might as well get started, hadn't I?"

He grinned back. "I'm glad you came," he blurted out, then blushed and ducked his head shyly. "I reckon I better get back to work, too." He nodded at her in good-bye and went out the side door.

Juliet watched him walk across the yard toward the barn. She wondered how that stern, unlikeable Amos Morgan had raised a son as nice, open, and friendly as Ethan was. She also wondered about Ethan's mother. Obviously she wasn't around; Juliet presumed she must have died. *Living with Amos Morgan would probably be enough to kill anyone.*

As she watched, Amos came out of the barn and started toward the house, meeting his son halfway. They talked for a moment, or, rather, Ethan talked and Amos listened, watching his son with an indulgent smile. His whole face changed when he looked at Ethan, Juliet realized; it was obvious how much he loved the boy. He threw back his head now and laughed, and Juliet thought how much more handsome he looked when there was love and laughter on his face. He looped an arm around Ethan's shoulders, giving him a sort of sideways hug, and they ambled back to the barn together.

Juliet turned to the kitchen and set to work. She swept the floor and climbed on a chair to sweep the cobwebs from the corners. She cleared the table, pumped water into the metal basin beside the sink, and washed and rinsed the dishes. Afterward, it was time to start supper. Henrietta had sent a picnic lunch with them, which they had eaten beside the road, but it had been light, and Juliet knew that she would have to prepare a full meal for that evening.

This was what she had been dreading. Cooking was her weakest point. She wasn't even sure what to prepare, let alone how to do it. As she cleaned, she had found a large pot that Ethan must have set out earlier. It was filled with beans, soaking in water. Now she located the breadbox and opened it. Good. There was a loaf of bread in it. She had the beginnings of a meal. But what else should she fix? And how should she cook the beans?

She knew that one usually boiled beans for a long time. Perhaps she should put them on now. Juliet turned and looked at the big black stove. It was, she thought, an ominous thing. Carefully she approached it, almost as if it were a live creature. She stretched out a hand toward it. She could feel no heat. She touched the metal; it was cold.

Juliet sighed. She had been afraid of that. What few times she had been allowed to heat up something on a stove in one of the boardinghouses, it had already been hot, and she had had only to put the pot on it and stir. She hadn't the slightest idea how to get the stove started.

She opened the various doors in the front of the stove; inside the largest door she found ashes, so this must be where the fire should be built. She considered going upstairs to ask Frances what she should do. But she hated to awaken Frances—almost as much as she hated to reveal her ignorance. Juliet decided to try to muddle through on her own.

Taking a few pieces of wood out of the box beside the stove, she piled it in the large compartment. She had no idea how to arrange the wood or whether she had put in enough—or too much. Juliet shrugged, piled some kindling on top, took a match from the holder on the stove, and lit the fire. When it was burning well, she closed the door and waited. After a while, she noticed that the kitchen seemed smoky. Juliet coughed. It was growing more smoky by the moment. Her heart began to hammer in panic. Something was wrong.

She hurried to the outside door and flung it open to let the smoke escape the room. She turned back worriedly and gazed at the stove, chewing at her bottom lip. What had she done wrong? She thought of fireplaces and the damper in them which, if not opened, sent the smoke pouring back into the room. Perhaps stoves had dampers, too. She ran to the stove and searched frantically for something to pull or twist or push that might operate a damper. She coughed repeatedly, and her eyes watered from the acrid smoke. Finally, on the left-hand side, near the stovepipe that vented the air outside, she found a lever. She pulled on it, and there was a pop.

"Eureka!" she exclaimed and fell into a fit of coughing. She ran to the door to pull in fresh lungfuls of air.

When she had finished coughing and wiping the tears from her eyes, she turned to look at the room. The smoke had stopped pouring out of the stove, and it seemed to her that the air was not quite as thick with it. Juliet sat down on the doorsill with a sigh, setting her feet out on the stoop. So far, she was not excelling in her cooking efforts.

"Miss Drake?" Juliet turned to see Frances standing in the doorway. "What's the matter? I thought I smelled smoke."

Juliet hopped up and came back into the kitchen, forcing a smile onto her face. "I'm afraid you did. It was terribly silly of me; I lit the stove and forgot to open the damper."

"Oh." Frances nodded, giving her a slight smile. "I've done that myself sometimes." She walked over to the table and sat down at one of the chairs.

Juliet felt more cheerful now. Perhaps she could manage to extract a few helpful cooking hints from Frances. "I found a pot of beans soaking on the table, so I was about to put it on the stove to cook."

Frances nodded. "Good. I told Ethan to do that; I'm glad he remembered." She smiled. "Sometimes boys his age are so scatterbrained."

"Uh . . . I wasn't sure exactly when I should have supper ready."

"Usually Amos and Ethan come in from the fields around sunset. When it's planting season, sometimes they stay out even longer. Today I imagine they'll be in on time. Henrietta's little lunch probably won't stay with Amos too long."

"Was there anything else you planned to cook?"

"Oh. Yes. I have some leftover ham in the icebox. I was going to cube it and put it in the beans. And there are sweet potatoes in the root cellar; you could fix them."

Juliet beamed, one of her problems answered. She set the pot of beans on the stove and went to the icebox to pull out the ham. She cut it into chunks and dumped them into the pot with the beans. The beans were now boiling rapidly, she noted, and she wondered if they were supposed to cook this hard. She vaguely thought that beans just simmered. She cast a sideways glance at Frances and decided not to ask. Cooking a pot of beans was one of the most elementary things a cook would do; if she had to ask questions about it, Frances would be sure to know that she was not qualified for the job.

Juliet was glad that Frances had suggested sweet potatoes, which even she knew one had only to pop into the oven and let bake for a while. She had eaten them frequently that way. Frances directed Juliet outside to the cellar, a small, dark room, dug into the ground under the house, where they kept their vegetables and fruits for long periods of time, packed in straw. Juliet found the orangish tubers and brought several back into the kitchen, where she scrubbed them clean and stuck them into the oven.

Frances gave her an odd look. "You're putting the potatoes in already?"

Juliet knew that she had taken a misstep.

"How careless of me," she said lightly, picking up a hot pad and going to the oven to take them out. "It's too early, isn't it? I don't know what I was thinking of. I must be a little nervous about this job." *Now, how was she going to know when it was the right time to bake them?* She racked her brain, trying to remember if she had ever heard any kind of reference to the time it took to cook a sweet potato. It wasn't the sort of thing that came up frequently in conversations among performers.

"There's no need to be," Frances assured her. "You'll do fine. Don't worry about Amos; his bark is always worse than his bite."

Juliet's expression must have shown her disbelief, for Frances laughed and went on, "Truly. He's a wonderful man. He's just . . . very protective of both me and Ethan. He doesn't want to admit that I'm dying, that there's nothing he can do to stop it. And he's . . . well, he isn't good with strangers."

"I'm sure he is a good man." Juliet certainly wasn't going to argue with a man's sister about his good or bad qualities. She sat down at the table beside Frances. "But Mrs. Morgan told me that he has high standards, and I'm afraid he'll find me lacking. Cooking isn't my forte."

That was the understatement of the century, she thought. She felt bad about prevaricating to Frances—she seemed so nice, and Juliet already liked her—but she couldn't admit to Frances that she had obtained the job under completely false pretenses!

"Don't worry," Frances replied calmly. "No one expects you to be a great cook. After all, you are an actress; I don't imagine you've spent too much of your time taking care of the house."

Juliet smiled. She didn't know what to say; she didn't dare confess to exactly how little caretaking she had done.

"You probably won't continue keeping house for long."

"Oh, no," Juliet agreed heartfeltly. "I need to earn enough money to go back home, that's all."

"And where is home?"

Juliet hesitated. "I'm not sure, exactly. New York City, I suppose. That's where I've lived most of my life. But Papa and I traveled around a great deal; we never really had a permanent home, and now that he's gone, I don't have any relatives in New York. My sister moved to Philadelphia."

"Your sister acts, too?"

"Oh, yes. She's a much better actress than I. I was always a severe disappointment to my parents; they both acted, you see, and then Celia followed in their footsteps, but I . . . well, I can get by, but no one would mistake me for a good actress."

"I imagine it must be wonderful and exciting," Frances said, resting her elbow on the table and propping her chin on her hand. Her eyes were dreamy as they regarded some personal vision in the air. "To sing so beautifully like you do, and have all those people applaud you. To travel, go all kinds of places, do so many different things. I've never been farther than Omaha, and that was probably the most exciting thing in my life."

"I enjoy the singing," Juliet admitted. "And it's grand when you hear everyone clapping and cheering, like they did the other night. I've done it forever, it seems; I can't imagine not doing it. But the travel—well, I don't know. I've traveled all my life, mostly from city to city in the East, and, frankly, I'm tired of it. You know what I've always dreamed of having? A house of my own. Just a pretty little home that I could take care of and stay in forever. A place I'd know I wouldn't have to leave the next day or the next week or the next month. Where I could do what I wanted." She gave Frances a self-deprecating smile. "Pretty foolish-sounding, I guess."

"No. It sounds lovely, something anyone would want." Frances smiled back. "It is funny, though, don't you think, that here I wish I could have traveled and seen someplace else, whereas you've done all that and you would like to have a home and stay in one place."

Juliet chuckled. "I suppose that's the way it is; a person wants what she doesn't have."

"Yes. I suppose." Frances gave a small, weary sigh. "If you don't mind, I think I'll sit in the parlor for a while. These kitchen chairs get so awfully hard after a while; it's difficult to get comfortable in them."

"Of course not. Go ahead." Juliet suspected that anywhere Frances sat these days would not be comfortable. She felt sorry for the woman.

Frances stood up, and Juliet had to resist the urge to take Frances's arm and help her. She sensed that the other woman would regard having to be helped as a defeat. There was something about this family that bespoke an enormous, prickly pride. It was obvious in the stern set of their mouths and their arrow-straight backs; they expected the world to be hard, and they expected themselves to be even harder.

"If there's anything I can do for you . . . ," Juliet offered.

"No. That's sweet of you. But I'll be all right. Just go ahead with supper."

After Frances left, Juliet set the table and checked on

the pot of beans. It had boiled down a good bit, so she added water and wondered if there was a seasoning she should put in to make them more flavorful. She searched the pantry for something to use for dessert and was delighted to find a jar of applesauce. She poured it in a pan and added brown sugar and cinnamon and heated it. It stuck to the bottom of the pan, but she carefully picked out the burned bits when she turned it out later into a bowl. She added a dollop of butter and sprinkled cinnamon across the top.

The beans were beginning to look altogether too done, Juliet thought as she added more water to them. At least the fire in the stove had died down, and they had finally stopped boiling. She remembered that she hadn't put the potatoes in the oven, so she hastily stuck them in, hoping that she hadn't waited until too late.

As the light outside faded, Juliet found a small glass kerosene lamp on a narrow table in the hall and lit it. Not long after that, the men came trooping up the back steps and into the kitchen. Mentally Juliet squared her shoulders. It was time for her first test, her trial by fire. She wondered whether after supper tonight, she'd still have a job.

Three

The back door opened and Ethan came in, followed by his father. Juliet turned and smiled at them with what she hoped was a confident expression. "Hello."

Ethan's face lit up when he looked at her, and he swept his hat off. "Hello." He continued to look at her, grinning broadly and twisting the brim of his hat between his fingers. "Can I do anything to help?" He glanced around the room, and his eyes fell on the half-empty wood box. "How about some more wood? Would you like for me to bring in some wood?"

"Yes, that would be nice, thank you."

Behind Ethan, Amos hung his hat on the hook beside the door. He said nothing, but his eyes traveled from Ethan's face to Juliet and back, and his mouth tightened. Juliet saw his expression, and she was certain that he didn't like the eager way Ethan looked at her.

Juliet sighed inwardly. Doubtless Ethan had become somewhat enamored of her. It wasn't surprising. Young men always fell easily into and out of love, and she was probably one of the few women he had ever met. Living out here like this, with such a gruff man for a father and no one else but his ailing aunt, he was no doubt starved for companionship, and probably naive and utterly untutored in the art of social intercourse as well. He would probably be attracted to any woman who wasn't downright painful to look at and who was of an age anywhere close to his.

Ethan wasn't the first young man to develop a boyish infatuation with her. It was a hazard of being on the stage. She had become adept at discouraging them without hurting their feelings. She could do it with Ethan, too—as long as his father didn't clumsily interfere.

Ethan went back out to fetch the wood, and Amos clomped over to the washstand. He picked up the pitcher and carried it to the stove, where he took the large ladle that hung on the wall beside the stove and started to dip it into the deep well at the back of the stove. He stopped and leaned over, peering into the well.

"Why is there no water in the reservoir?" He grumbled.

So that was what that was for! Juliet had wondered about it. The water would be warmed by the heat of the stove, and then she wouldn't have to heat it up everytime someone needed to wash. Juliet had spent enough time in rooming houses to know how unpleasant it was to wash in cool water.

"I'm sorry," she said quickly. "I should have checked it when I started cooking dinner."

Amos's glance told her that she certainly should have, but he said nothing, just went back to the washstand with his pitcher and began to wash his hands and face.

Juliet turned away, uncomfortable at witnessing a stranger doing something as personal as washing. In the theater, the men had always had a separate dressing room, and in the boardinghouses, she and her father had had a washstand in their room or she shared one only with the other women. Though she had spent a great deal of time in close confines with the other members of the troupe, both men and women frequently sleeping sitting up in railroad cars and stagecoaches, she realized that this situation was more intimate.

She would be living in the same house with Amos Morgan for weeks, maybe even months, cooking his meals, cleaning his room, washing his clothes. It was a situation that was disturbingly similiar to being married, and the thought of it made Juliet feel a little nervous and embarrassed. Thank heavens his sister was living here.

Not that she feared that Amos Morgan would make untoward advances to her. The way he felt about her, she was certain that that was the farthest thing from his mind. It just wouldn't be proper for them to live in the same house without another woman around. And Juliet was always careful not to flaunt society's rules.

When he finished washing up, Morgan strode to the back door and tossed the dirty water outside. Juliet glanced at him. The hair around the edges of his face was wet and curling just a little. His face was smooth and tanned, the firm skin softer around his eyes, where tiny squint lines fanned out. Her gaze dropped down to his hands. His sleeves were rolled up, and she could see a bare expanse of brown skin, the black hairs clinging damply to his flesh.

An odd sensation twisted through her abdomen.

Hastily Juliet returned to the pots on the stove. She found that the beans had thickened yet again and were turning mushy. As she stirred them with the long-handled wooden spoon, she felt some thick substance at the bottom of the pot which scraped off as she stirred. Pulling up her spoon, she found a skin of blackened sludge stuck to the end of the spoon.

Quickly she grabbed a hot pad and lifted the pot off the firehole, setting it on the blank space above the oven, where the metal top was warm but not hot. Then she bent down and wrapped the hot pad around the oven handle, opening the oven door to check on the sweet potatoes. She hadn't worried about them overcooking because she had put them in so late. But now she saw to her horror that the potatoes were all much darker on one side than on the other. There was, in fact, a strip of black running down one side of each of them.

The fire box was to the left of the oven, so the heat on the left side of the oven would naturally be fiercer, she realized. The two potatoes on the left were almost half black, whereas the two on the right were blackened only a little. With a sigh, she pulled the potatoes out, and laid them, too, atop the oven. Surely they must be done, given their appearance.

Ethan returned to the kitchen with a load of wood and dumped it in the box beside the stove. Frances came in and helped Juliet dish up the meal and put it on the table while Ethan made his ablutions at the washstand. As Juliet ladled the beans out into a bowl, several pieces of char came with them, and she carefully picked them out. She turned the sweet potatoes so that the blackened sides were not visible, putting the worst ones on the bottom, intending to take one of them for herself. The meal at least looked good. All the table needed was a vase of flowers or a small centerpiece in the middle to brighten it up. It was early spring, so flowers ought to be blooming soon.

The four of them sat down at the table. A little to her surprise, the others immediately bowed their heads, so Juliet hastily did the same. Frances said a terse prayer, then they raised their heads and began to dish food onto their plates. They ate with concentration, saying little other than to ask that something be passed. Juliet, used to the camaraderie among the acting company, found the silence almost unnerving.

The beans had turned out worse than she had thought, Juliet realized when she took her first bite. They had boiled so much that they were of the consistency of lumpy flour paste. She glanced up worriedly at Amos. An odd look crossed his face as he chewed, and Juliet noticed that he had to chew rather hard for a moment before he swallowed. She knew that he must have found one of the bits of hardened, burned beans that had escaped her search. He looked at her, his expression puzzled. A flush rose in Juliet's cheeks.

Quickly she turned her attention back to her plate and cut her sweet potato in half. One side was hard as a rock, but the other wasn't too bad. She noticed that Amos and Frances left part of their potatoes, too, though Ethan managed to down all of his. She wasn't sure whether he was being polite or was just, like many boys his age, capable of eating anything that would stay on his plate.

Fortunately, Amos made no comment about the quality of the food. He talked to Ethan a little about the farm and what had happened in his two days' absence and asked Frances how she was feeling after the trip. Juliet felt his gaze on her once or twice, but he said nothing to her. Frances went up to her room as soon as she finished eating, but Ethan lingered after the meal, thanking Juliet for the food (though he wasn't untruthful enough to tell her it had been good) and asking her about the places she'd been and the things she had done. Amos stayed too, though he added nothing to the conversation, just sat and smoked his pipe, watching Ethan and Juliet.

Finally he stood, saying, "Ethan, there are still the evening chores to do."

"Oh." Ethan's face fell, but he stood up, too. "All right. Good night, Miss Drake."

"Good night, Ethan."

Dispiritedly, Juliet scraped the plates and washed the dishes. By the time she finished, she was exhausted, and her back felt as if it might break in two. She couldn't remember the last time she had been so physically tired. And she hadn't even worked a whole day! She hated to think what the next day would be like, with two more meals to prepare.

She dragged off to the room that Ethan had indicated would be hers. Amos had set her trunk and bag inside the door. She stood for a moment, looking around her. It was a small, cheerless room, bare except for a small, plain oak bed, washstand, and chest of drawers. There was no fireplace or stove, and the air, musty from months of being closed up, was chilly on this spring evening.

She told herself that it would look much homier once she had unpacked her things but it was hard to keep the tears from coming. At the moment, everything seemed bleak. Juliet was so tired that she considered just lying across the bare mattress and sleeping on it as it was without putting on the sheets and cover.

But she could not let herself do that, even as tired as she was, so she pulled herself together and went out to the linen press in the hall. She took sheets and a quilt and went back to her room, but as she walked inside, heavy footsteps sounded in the hall behind her and she heard Amos say, "Miss Drake."

What now? She looked back at him, bracing herself for whatever was to come. He followed her into her room and stopped, looming over her. Juliet was sure that he was trying to intimidate her, and the flash of anger she felt at the thought gave her added strength. She stood her ground, staring back at him.

"Mr. Morgan?" she tossed back coolly.

"I want to make something clear to you. I let you come here because Frances wanted it. But I will not allow you to bewitch that boy. If you lead him on, if you hurt him, I swear I'll—"

"Don't be ridiculous!" Juliet snapped, her nerves frayed.

"I'm not being ridiculous. You already have him half

under your spell. I saw the way he was staring at you tonight at supper; I saw the way he was mooning around all afternoon."

"That's not my fault. I didn't *do* anything. All young boys develop infatuations. Believe me, it will pass."

"Oh," his voice was heavy with irony, "you know so much about sixteen-year-old boys?"

"I know about their foolish crushes on older women. I've found more than one boy like Ethan hanging around the stage door."

"I'm sure you have."

"What is that supposed to mean?" Juliet flared.

"That you have experience, what else?" Just the way he said the word was an insult.

"How dare you presume to judge me?" Juliet's voice trembled with outrage. "You know nothing about me or the life I've led. Well, let me tell you something: I am as honest a woman as any you'll meet. I had a family, a mother and father, who taught me right from wrong. And I don't have to excuse or justify myself to you! You have no right to come in here and accuse me of trying to ensnare your son!"

Amos glared back at her. "I don't know whether you would or not; you're right. But I can see the way Ethan is around you. I know how quickly he could fall in love with you . . . how easy it would be for you to entrap him. It isn't difficult for a beautiful woman to deceive a young boy just off the farm."

She spread out her hands toward him in a gesture of sincerity. "Mr. Morgan, I assure you, I won't do anything to harm Ethan. I hope you will believe me."

Amos hesitated, looking down into her eyes. "I——it's very easy to believe you," he said in a husky voice. "That's what's so dangerous."

"Me? Dangerous?" Juliet chuckled.

"Yes, you. You could tear a man's heart right out of him if he was foolish enough to fall in love with you." His words were bitter and harsh, but there was an odd note of longing in his voice. He drew a sharp breath and turned away. "If I've wronged you, I'm sorry. But I can't let anything happen to Ethan."

Juliet replied calmly, "Ethan does seem to be a trifle sweet on me right now. But that will pass. I'll do my best to make sure it does. But I have to do it easily; I don't want to hurt him."

He turned to give her a final searching look. "Make sure you don't."

With those words, he was gone.

Juliet relaxed with a sigh. The energy her indignation had sparked suddenly drained away, and she felt limp and weak. Wearily, she made up the bed, then changed into her nightgown and crawled into bed, not even bothering to take down her hair and brush it thoroughly, as she usually did. She sank into the soft feather mattress and was asleep almost immediately.

A noise brought Juliet awake. She blinked her eyes, still half-asleep and confused, uncertain even where she was. She heard the heavy sound of footsteps past her door and the low rumble of a man's voice. She sat up, pulling her fuzzy thoughts together, remembering where she was and why. But that didn't explain what Amos and Ethan Morgan were doing up talking in the middle of the night. She wondered if something had happened to Frances.

She slipped out of bed, shivering as her feet hit the cold wooden floor, and went to the window. It was black outside, with only the glitter of faraway stars. She looked northward toward the barn. Two men, darker shapes in the night, were walking toward the barn, carrying buckets. Amos and Ethan weren't up because of some emergency. They looked as if they were setting out to work!

Juliet let out a groan of disbelief and flopped back on her bed, closing her eyes. She was used to the hours that actors kept, working until late at night and arising equally late the next day; it was the way she had lived her entire life.

But if Amos and Ethan were up and working, no doubt they would expect breakfast soon—and Juliet would be expected to prepare it. Gritting her teeth, she pushed herself out of bed and unbuttoned her nightgown. She dressed slowly, yawning so wide she thought her jaw would crack and struggling to keep her eyelids from drifting closed. Finally she was clothed, though unaware that she had buttoned the multitude of tiny buttons down the front of her shirtwaist wrong, so that her shirtwaist was awry, one side of the collar sticking up higher than the other.

She sat down on the edge of her bed to put on her stockings and shoes and lace them. Halfway through the first stocking, she began to tilt to one side, and the next thing she knew she was jerked awake by the sound of the back door closing.

Oh, no! She had fallen asleep! Juliet jumped up from the bed, hastily pulling on the other stocking and thrusting her feet into her shoes, tying them only as far as her ankles.

"Miss Drake?" She heard Ethan's puzzled voice in the kitchen. She was grateful that it was he and not his father who had come in and found the kitchen dark and the stove cold.

She bolted out her door and down the hall to the kitchen, frantically trying to repin her hair into some kind of order. She hadn't taken it down the night before, and she was sure it was sticking out all over the place, but she hadn't the time right now to brush it out and pin it back up.

Juliet burst into the kitchen. Ethan had lit the oil lamp and set it on the counter and was standing uncertainly by the back door. He looked relieved when he saw her.

"There you are!" He smiled. "I gathered the eggs for you." He gestured toward a basket that sat on the counter.

"Thank you. I'm sorry. I'm not accustomed to getting up this early." Her hand went instinctively to her hair to smooth it.

"We keep farmers' hours," Ethan explained. "'Specially when we're planting, we need every hour of daylight we can get."

"Of course."

"You want me to light the fire for you?" Ethan offered.

"Would you?" Juliet was flooded with relief. That would be one less thing to do before Amos returned, ready for his breakfast, and perhaps Ethan would build it correctly, as she obviously hadn't last night.

Ethan went to the stove and cleaned out the ashes, then built the fire and lit it. Juliet, still feeling foggy with sleep, moved much more slowly about the kitchen and pantry, getting out the coffeepot and a pan, pumping water, searching for the coffee and oats in the pantry. She decided to make something that she had cooked before, oatmeal porridge. That way, there wouldn't be any mistakes.

Ethan stood up, dusting off his hands. "Fire's going." He glanced at Juliet, then around the room, and continued reluctantly, "Well, I better go back to the barn. Pa'll be mad if I don't get the rest of my chores done."

Juliet smiled at him, thinking what a nice young man he was, so unlike his father. "Thank you."

"Anytime."

Juliet put the coffeepot on the stove, then pumped water into a pot for the porridge. It had been some time since she had made porridge, and she added too much water, so that when Ethan and Amos came in twenty minutes later, ready to eat, the oatmeal was too thin.

Ethan shrugged out of his jacket and hung it on one of the hooks beside the door, sniffing the air appreciatively. "Mmmm. The coffee smells good."

Amos also started taking off his jacket, then stopped abruptly and looked down at his chest. He wore no shirt;

beneath the denim bib of his overalls was only his long-sleeved undershirt, a faded red. Obviously he wasn't used to dressing completely when he got up to do the chores; he just pulled on his overalls and threw his jacket over them.

He cleared his throat and let his short coat fall back into place. "Ah, I'll go upstairs and wash up," He started toward the hall. "Come on, Ethan."

Ethan looked at him, puzzled. "But why—"

His father shot him one brief glance, and Ethan didn't finish his sentence, just shrugged and followed his father out of the kitchen.

Juliet turned back to the stove to stir the porridge, willing it to thicken. At least she had a few more minutes for it to cook while the men washed up and put on their shirts. As she stirred, she thought about Amos's embarrassment at his attire, and she smiled. But then she recalled exactly how disheveled she herself must look. She reached up to her hair, and as she did so she glanced down at her dress. She noticed that her buttons were fastened up wrong, pulling her blouse crooked, and heat rose in her face.

Hastily Juliet unfastened her buttons and did her shirtwaist up again, then hurried over to the small mirror over the washstand to smooth and pin back her hair as best she could.

She turned from the mirror, frowning, noticing an odd smell in the air. With a start, she realized that the source of the burning odor was her untended pan of oatmeal, and she hurried back to the stove. Well, the oatmeal was no longer too thin, she thought dryly. The bottom was stuck to the pan, and the rest had turned thick as paste.

Quickly she pulled the pan from the stove and dumped the porridge into bowls. She set the bowls down on the table just as Ethan and Amos returned to the kitchen, now wearing shirts under their overalls.

The men sat down at the table. Amos cast a jaundiced eye at the bowl of thick porridge in front of him, but he said nothing, merely picked up his spoon and began eating. She poured coffee for them all, then sat down at the table, too. By the time she sat, the two men were already through eating.

Amos looked up from his bowl and glanced around the table. "What else are we having?"

"Having?" Juliet repeated, dismay rising in her.

"For breakfast. To eat," he explained impatiently, looking at her as if she were slow-witted.

"I—well, that's all I prepared. I didn't realize you'd want more . . ." Her voice trailed off as she began to think frantically about something else they could eat.

"I'm full," Ethan assured her helpfully, smiling at her. "Don't worry."

Amos stared at him suspiciously. "That's the first time I've ever known you to get full on one bowl of mush."

A dull red rose in Ethan's cheeks, and he shrugged, not meeting his father's eyes. "I'm not very hungry this morning."

His father let out a grunt of disbelief and turned back to Juliet. "Frances usually fixes eggs and bacon or sausage. And biscuits."

Juliet's face brightened. "Would you like some bread? I could slice some."

She jumped up and pulled out a loaf and set it on the table, adding a jar of plum preserves she found in the pantry and a small pot of butter from the icebox. Amos took a slice of bread, buttered it, and ate it. Juliet noticed that Ethan, despite his avowed lack of hunger, managed to consume three pieces.

Amos took a sip of coffee and looked surprised. "Why, this is good!"

"Thank you." He needn't act so astonished, she thought. After all, it wasn't her fault that on a farm people apparently ate like horses, as well as got up in the middle of the night to go to work. You'd think they could have warned her, at least.

He poured himself a second cup of coffee and drank it down quickly, then stood up. "Time to go, Ethan. The fields aren't planting themselves while we sit here."

Ethan stood. "I'm coming, Pa." He nodded to Juliet. "Good-bye, Miss Drake."

"Good-bye, Ethan."

Amos gave her a nod. Then he stood, waiting, looking at her. Juliet looked back.

His eyebrows went up a little. He glanced at the counter and the table, then back at her. "Our lunch?"

"Your lunch?"

"We take a basket of food to eat in the fields. Saves time."

"Oh. I'm sorry. I—uh, I'm not used to working on a farm. What—what would you like to take with you?"

"Usually Frances gives us biscuits and sausage or

bacon sandwiches from the leftovers at breakfast," Amos told her.

"Oh." Panic began to rise in her.

"Is there any ham left over from last night?" Ethan volunteered helpfully. "Maybe we could have some of that and a few slices of bread. That'd be good, wouldn't it, Pa?"

Gratefully Juliet rushed to the icebox and pulled out the remainder of the ham. There was enough for a meal. Amos cut it while she got out more bread and searched the pantry for something else to stick in the lunch basket. She found a small jar of pickles and another one of what looked like spiced apples, so she put them in along with the bread and ham and covered the whole thing with a spread-out napkin. Ethan poured water into an earthenware jug and stopped it with a cork. Amos picked up the basket, and the two men left the house.

Juliet sank down onto one of the chairs with a sigh of relief. *Thank heavens they were finally gone!*

After Amos and Ethan left, Juliet considered going back to bed. There was nothing she would like better than to pull the covers over her head and sink into the blissful oblivion of sleep. However, there were dishes to be washed, and then she had to mop the kitchen floor. After the fiasco of breakfast this morning, she better do something to make Amos Morgan believe that she was a housekeeper.

So Juliet pulled herself up from her chair and carried

the dirty dishes from the table to the sink, where she washed and dried them. When she had finished, she took a bucket and pumped water into it until it was almost full and so heavy she could hardly lift it. She stood for a moment looking down at the bucket of water. Surely that wasn't right, Juliet thought. She ought to use something more than plain water to wash the floor.

She took the thick bar of lye soap from the kitchen sink and put it into the water, working it up into a lather with her hands. When the bucket was foamy with suds, she dipped a scrub brush into it and began to work her way across the floor on her hands and knees. She found that using the brush was tiresome and slow, so she scrubbed only the worst patches of dirt or stain with it and afterwards covered the rest of the floor with a rag mop on a long handle, which she found just inside the pantry door. By the time she was through, the floor was thoroughly wet—*next time she would remember to squeeze out the mop better*—and covered with soapy bubbles.

Juliet tossed out the dirty mop water and refilled the bucket with clean water. She dipped the mop into the water and began to rinse the floor. But, strangely, it seemed as if the bubbles grew with the additional water she put on the floor, and after a few swipes, the water in her bucket was as soapy as that on the floor. She had to toss out the bucket of water and fill it again.

Frances came downstairs and paused at the kitchen doorway. She glanced in a puzzled way at the floor, still covered with bubbles. Juliet felt a flush of embarrassment rising up her throat.

"Would you like some breakfast?" she asked Frances, ignoring the issue of the floor in front of her.

"No. That's all right. My stomach's a little queasy this morning. I—uh—thought we might start on the spring cleaning today. You're right; the kitchen floor should be done first. After you've finished, perhaps we can begin on the floors in the other rooms."

Juliet nodded, forcing a smile onto her face. *More rooms? Oh, Lord, she'd never get through!* "All right. Just let me rinse this clean."

"I'll be in the front parlor."

After Frances left, Juliet attacked the floor furiously, dumping out several bucketsful of clean water on the floor and sweeping it out through the back door with the mop. What didn't go out the door simply seeped down through the cracks between the boards. Then she took a towel and crawled around the room drying away whatever was left of the standing water and bubbles. Her arms ached as if they would fall off. She almost wished they would.

Wearily she went in search of Frances. The other woman was in the front parlor, one of the closed-off rooms along the hallway. Frances was on a stool, taking down the heavy green velvet curtains, and sunlight was flooding into the room.

It was a lovely room, filled with elegant mahogany furniture. The couch seat and back were covered in plush dark green velvet, as was one heavy chair. Two other straight-back chairs had painstakingly embroidered cushions. There was an embroidered footstool, as well. The chairs and couch sported crocheted antimacassars, and lace runners adorned the small tables. Someone had once taken a great deal of care with this room—and spent a lot of money, as well. Juliet wondered who it was. Amos Morgan's wife, perhaps? What had happened to her? And why did they now keep the parlor closed off and unused?

"I dusted the furniture," Frances told her. "It gets terribly dusty in here. I try to go over it at least once a month, but lately . . ." She shrugged, her voice trailing off.

"It's a lovely room." Juliet went to help her with the drapes. "Why do you keep it closed?"

"We don't use it," Frances replied shortly. "Why try to keep it warm?"

It was a practical answer, of course, but Juliet couldn't understand why one would want to have the room with the lovely furniture in the first place if one wasn't going to use it.

After they hauled down the heavy draperies, they hung them outside on the clothesline to beat the dust from them, then rehung them. Next, Juliet took the two large rugs in the parlor out one by one and beat them free of dust, also. Leaving them hanging on the clothesline, she swept and mopped the floors of the dining room and parlor.

It was heavy work, and Frances was quickly tired, so Juliet insisted that Frances rest while she continued to work. Later, after Frances had napped, Juliet heard her in the kitchen preparing supper. Juliet was relieved. Cleaning the formal rooms might be physically taxing, but at least it was something she could do.

Once she had the floors clean and the rugs back on them, she started to work on the furniture in the dining room, polishing the rich mahogany table and china cabinets until they gleamed. It was a beautiful room, she thought, from the elegant glass chandelier to the porcelain plates and glass goblets on the open shelves of the china cabinet. It seemed ridiculous to keep such beauty closed off from the rest of the house. Obviously Amos Morgan didn't have any appreciation of beauty, or he wouldn't do so.

When she opened a door in the bottom of the mahogany sideboard, she found a jumble of items that made her draw in her breath sharply. The sideboard contained a veritable treasure trove!

At the back was a silver tray and tea service, badly tarnished but obviously of excellent workmanship. In front of them were two elegant, highly detailed glass candlesticks, the bases of which were formed into the shape of dolphins. There was a small ormolu clock, an exquisitely drawn miniature portrait, a little shellwork basket, and a glass millefiori paperweight containing a dazzling burst of tiny pink and blue flowers in its depths.

Carefully she drew out the pieces one by one and set them on the sideboard. She smoothed her fingers over the glass candlesticks and the paperweight, her soul answering to their beauty.

She was so wrapped up in them that she didn't even hear the heavy tread out in the hallway until the loud, angry voice broke in on her reverie: "Damnation, woman, what the hell are you doing!"

Four

Startled, Juliet jumped, snatching her hand back from the paperweight as though it had burned her, and whirled around. Amos Morgan loomed in the doorway, scowling ferociously at her, his dark eyes snapping with anger. He looked so menacing that Juliet unconsciously raised her hand to her throat and took a half step back.

"Mr. Morgan," she said a little shakily. "You frightened me."

"What do you think you're doing?" he repeated, ignoring her words. "Don't touch those. Put them back."

"What?"

"I said, 'Put those things back.' Then leave them alone."

"But, Mr. Morgan . . ." Juliet spread her arms in a gesture of bewilderment. "They're lovely. They shouldn't be locked up in a sideboard. They should be out where they can be seen and appreciated."

"It's hardly your place to tell me what I should or should not do with my possessions. I want them put away."

Juliet blinked. "But why? This tea set needs to be polished; then it would look perfect here on top of the sideboard. And the paperweight is beautifully done."

"And you, I'm sure, are an expert on the subject," he replied with heavy irony.

"As a matter of fact, I *do* know something about art. My father appreciated art. He taught me—" she began, but he cut her off.

"I don't give a damn if you're the foremost connoisseur on the subject. Those things are not yours, and you have no right to be in here prying and peeking—"

"I wasn't prying!" Juliet retorted hotly. "I was cleaning, and when I saw these, I took them out because they were so lovely and I thought they should be seen."

"Snooping," he said flatly. "You were simply snooping. I won't have it. Those things will stay in the sideboard, and that's an end to it."

Juliet stared. "What possible reason could you have to hide such lovely pieces? Art isn't meant to be hidden away."

"It's none of your business. Now do as I said and put them up."

He was her employer, and Juliet knew that she had to obey him. The things were his, after all, and he had every right to keep them hidden if that was what he wanted. But his reaction infuriated her, and she couldn't keep herself from continuing to argue against his command. "I don't understand why—"

Then it came to her, and she broke off. "Of course. They must have belonged to Ethan's mother."

"Ethan's mother!" He roared, his eyebrows shooting up. "What in the hell are you talking about?"

"That's it, isn't it?" Juliet felt a trifle smug at having guessed it. It made Amos's bizarre actions much more sensible. "It hurts too much to see her things about the house. Isn't that why?"

"No!" The word was so loud, so explosive, that Juliet thought it was a wonder that the entire house didn't shake under the force of it. "What is the matter with you? What makes you think you have the right to dream up wild fantasies regarding me or my son? Ethan's mother has nothing to do with it. With anything! She is dead to him."

Dead to him. What a bizarre way to put it! Juliet wondered what he meant by the statement.

Juliet braced herself to face his wrath. "That is no reason for you not to put her things out. Surely Ethan deserves to see the objects that his mother treasured."

"They are not *hers*!" he spat. "She wouldn't have the taste to treasure them. They belonged to my mother, since you insist on knowing everything."

"Your mother? Then surely you would want to see them. I would think it would give you comfort and happiness to see her things, especially such lovely things."

"It doesn't matter what you *think*, Miss Drake." He looked as if he were about to burst. "The fact is, they have nothing to do with you, nor does my mother or anyone else in my family. You had no right to come in here and take things out of the cabinets. You had no right to open up these rooms."

"I was under the impression that I was here to take care of this house," Juliet shot back. "I was cleaning them, that's all. But, frankly, I don't see why you don't keep them open. What's wrong with it? It lets in light, opens up the place. And they're beautiful, the loveliest rooms in the house!"

"It makes the house too hard to heat," he growled. "And the sun ruins the furniture if you open the drapes."

Juliet gaped at him. "So in order to preserve the furniture, you want to shut the drapes and close off the room. What use is it to preserve the furniture, then, if it's never seen and enjoyed? As for heating, well, perhaps that's a valid argument in the dead of winter, but it's spring now."

"Damn it!" he exploded. "Can't you follow an order? I told you to leave the rooms closed. That's the way I want it. And I want those knickknacks put up. Do I make myself clear?"

Juliet seethed. But she knew there was nothing she could do about it. She did, after all, work for the man, and it *was* his right to decide what should be done with the rooms in his house and with his possessions.

"As you wish," she said coldly and turned back to the sideboard, opening the door and replacing the things she had found.

"I'll do it," Morgan said shortly and came across the room. "You need to see to supper. Frances is in there cooking it, and I believe you came here to save her work."

Juliet stepped back, stung by the injustice of his statement. She'd been slaving over this house all day, and now he acted as if she were shirking her duty! She was too angry to speak, so she just turned on her heel and stalked out of the room.

She stormed into the kitchen, where Frances was sitting at the table, peeling potatoes for supper.

"Honestly!" Juliet exclaimed. "I simply don't understand that man!" She plopped down across the table from Frances. "I know he's your brother, but—how do you stay so calm? Doesn't he ever make you angry?"

"Amos?" Frances grinned. "My goodness, yes. He's always had that knack. Amos and I have had so many arguments, it isn't worth counting. But he tip-toes around me these days. And I don't find much now that seems worth being at odds with my brother. Besides, you're here to take up the slack for me."

"Well, thank you very much." Juliet picked up the bowl of potatoes Frances had peeled and carried it over to the sink, setting it down with a thunk. "I'm so glad that I have the honor."

Frances chuckled again. "You're much better at it than I ever was, anyway. Amos and I are too much alike. Bull-headed. All the Morgans are."

"I don't understand him." Juliet shook her head in bewilderment as she began to wash the potatoes. "I found the most exquisite things in the sideboard, but he made me put them back. Why would he not want them out where they can be seen? Does he dislike beauty?"

"No. I think he likes it a great deal," Frances replied, shifting in her seat and frowning.

"Then why did he make me put back the tea set and everything?"

Frances sighed and shifted a little in her seat, a twinge of pain crossing her face. "I think—somehow, to get back at our father. Amos was only twelve when Mama died. He loved her very much; we all did. She was a sweet, gentle woman. Too fragile for this life, I think. She shouldn't have tried to have another child. She'd already had two that she couldn't carry to term."

"That's how she died? In childbirth?"

Frances nodded. "Yes. Amos blamed Pa for it. Pa wanted more children—you can always use more hands on a farm—but Ma wanted the baby, too. We had a little sister that died when she was about four, you see, and Ma was heartsick for a baby after that."

"How sad."

"The life out here is hard." Frances's mouth thinned into a grim line. "'There's no place here for weaklings.' That's what Pa used to say. Pa was a hard man. He and Amos used to fight something terrible. Amos cried about Mama, and Pa told him to hush, that that was what a weakling would do. Pa told him he had to stand up and be strong, be a man. And Amos told Pa that he hated him. Anyway, after that he put Mama's things away in the sideboard. I think he didn't want Pa to be able to see any of the things she'd loved when she couldn't." Frances shrugged. "'Course, it didn't bother Pa any. He never noticed them anyway. He always thought Mama's heirlooms were foolishness."

"But why does he still hide them?"

"I'm not sure. I think it's the memories they bring back. Amos doesn't like to think about the past. He— well, it's easier if you don't think about those things. You have to go ahead with your life and not dwell on what's happened, or you'd just give up."

Frances's hands lay motionless on the table, her fingers slowly letting go of the potatoes he had been holding, and she stared vaguely across the room, as though she wasn't really seeing it, but something else, something from long ago. Then she shook herself and looked up at Juliet, giving her a half-smile. "There. See? I got to thinking about the past, and I forgot what I was doing."

Juliet frowned. "I wonder—isn't there anything that makes your brother smile? Anything that makes him happy?"

"Happy?" Frances looked at her in faint surprise, as if that was something she hadn't ever considered before. "I—I don't know." She paused, then said slowly, "This land, I guess. He's always loved it. And Ethan."

"No. I don't mean people or things he *loves.* Just anything that makes him smile. Or laugh. Something funny. Or sweet. Something—I don't know, *special* that simply brings him pleasure."

Frances gazed back at Juliet for a long moment. "I'm not sure. We, well, I guess we weren't brought up that way."

How sad. Even in the midst of her anger at Amos, Juliet couldn't help but feel sorry for him. He lived a life without joy. She couldn't imagine living like that. It was no wonder he was a sour person. She told herself that she would try to be more understanding of him.

That evening when he came into supper, she smiled and set his supper down in front of him, just as if they hadn't argued this afternoon. He gave her a wary glance or two, she noticed, but she ignored them, too. Frankly, it wasn't very hard not to appear angry. She was too exhausted to carry a grudge today. All she wanted was to get through the meal, wash the dishes, and fall into bed. This had been the most tiring, strange day of her life, she thought, and she would be glad never to have another one like it.

Two hours later, at a time that in the past she would never have dreamed of going to bed, Juliet was sliding beneath her covers with a sigh of pure bliss. She had never realized before how wonderful it could feel just to stop and stretch out full length, to close her eyes and slide into the velvet nothingness of sleep. Her last thought before she drifted off was to wonder how long it would be before she would have enough money to leave this place. She knew it couldn't be soon enough!

The next morning Juliet was again pulled from sleep far earlier than her mind and body wished to function. This time, however, she was awakened earlier by the sound of footsteps in the room above her, and by the time the men came downstairs, she had managed to brush out her hair and put it up, as well as fasten up her skirt and blouse correctly.

She hurried into the kitchen and set about making the kind of breakfast Amos had requested, slicing bread and toasting it as well as frying sausage and scrambling eggs. She let the sausage slices cook too high too long, until they looked like lumps of coal. The eggs, on the other hand came out a trifle runny. The toast was the best thing she made, only slightly blackened around the edges (though it was the second set, the first one having been completely burnt.)

Juliet cast an anxious glance at Amos as he sawed away at one of the pieces of sausage with his knife. She felt relatively sure that this wasn't the breakfast that he had had in mind yesterday. She would never have thought that cooking could be so complicated—getting the temperature and the time just right, making everything come out at the same moment, without burning some things and undercooking others. And to have to do it first thing in the morning, when it was still night, was simply too much to ask!

Amos laid down his knife and fork and took a final sip of his coffee. He folded his napkin, set it on the table, and stood up. He turned to Juliet. "I think you better stick with porridge."

As Juliet was clearing away the breakfast dishes, Frances came downstairs. She was wearing a dark green dress which, though severe in cut and lacking ornamentation, was of good quality. She carried a small black bonnet and a pair of black gloves in her hand. Juliet looked at her blankly.

"Today's Sunday," Frances said in explanation of her dress.

"Oh. My, I'd completely forgotten what day it was."

"Will you be attending church with us?"

"Why, yes, I think I'd like to, if you have time for me to change."

Juliet's father had been a freethinker, not given to ceremonies or traditions, and that attitude had extended to church, so Juliet had rarely gone when she was young. But as she had gotten older, she had learned that she found a certain peace and comfort inside a church, and she had often attended one wherever she happened to be, though she was enough her father's daughter that she wasn't overly concerned with which denomination the church belonged to.

She hurried back to her room and quickly pulled on one of her best day dresses, a stylish blue skirt trimmed around the bottom with three rows of ruffles and a matching bodice with leg-o'-mutton sleeves. She fastened the bodice at the top with a small cameo and quickly grabbed her gloves and hat.

When she returned to the kitchen she found all of the others sitting at the table waiting for her. Amos looked up and saw her, and he rose slowly to his feet, almost as if drawn against his will. Ethan grinned broadly and jumped up without hesitation. "Hoo-wee! You look beautiful, ma'am!"

Frances turned and smiled also. "Yes, you most certainly do. What a lovely dress."

"Thank you."

Juliet noticed that there was no compliment from Amos, but she told herself that that was what she had expected.

"Ours is probably a far simpler church than anything you're used to," he said, coming around the table toward her.

"Oh, I've visited a few churches that weren't cathedrals," Juliet returned lightly.

Unexpectedly a smile touched Amos's mouth, and his dark eyes were for a moment warm as he looked down at her. "I'm sure that they looked far grander with you inside."

Juliet's eyes widened a little in surprise at his compliment. He seemed suddenly to realize what he had said, and the smile vanished, replaced by a frown. "I mean, you're much more elegant than anything we're used to around here."

Juliet raised her eyebrows. Apparently a gracious compliment was something he avoided at all costs. "Indeed?"

She swept past him, fastening on her hat as she went. The rest of them filed out behind her and climbed up into the two-seat surrey.

The Morgans' church was only a few miles away at a crossroads. It was small and made of white clapboard, with a squatty steeple. It was plain and clean, both inside and out, almost to the point of barrenness. But Juliet liked the simple building. There was something about its spartan sturdiness that was reassuring. It would last forever, it seemed to say.

Before church began, Juliet noticed that a young girl a few rows in front of them and to their left glanced back. She did so several more times during the course of the service. Juliet realized that the girl was looking at Ethan.

Juliet shot a curious glance at Ethan, beside her in the pew. He was staring steadfastly at a hymnal, but she caught him sneaking a peek back at the girl. Juliet smiled to herself. She had been wondering how to wean Ethan away from his crush on her, and now she knew. A girl of his own age, small, blond and freshly pretty, was interested in Ethan, and he was obviously aware of her. Juliet suspected that it wouldn't take much encouragement for him to transfer his youthful affections to her.

"Who is that family that sat about three rows back from the front?" Juliet asked innocently as they filed out of the church after the service was over. "A man and a young woman and a couple of boys."

Ethan glanced at her, and a faint color crept into his cheeks. "You mean Ellie Sanderson? I mean—that's the daughter. John Sanderson's her father. And there are two younger boys. I forget their names."

Juliet hid a smile. Obviously the boys weren't as important as the daughter. Amos looked at Juliet, then at the Sandersons, walking up the aisle some distance ahead of them, and back at Juliet, and he frowned. He said nothing, just strode ahead in his usual abrupt way. Juliet repressed a sigh. Did Amos resent her even speaking to Ethan? It seemed absurd to her, but, then, she was able to understand little about Amos. He was such a silent, angry man.

She dismissed Amos from her mind. Whatever was wrong with him, it wasn't important. The issue at hand was getting Ethan together with the pretty Ellie.

"Do you know Miss Sanderson?" Juliet asked, keeping

her eye on the family in question. They had stopped in the vestibule, near the front door, and the father was talking to someone. That was good; maybe they would stay there until the Morgans reached them.

"Oh, yes, we went to school together. Until this year, that is; she didn't come back last fall. 'Course, I stopped when the planting started. I don't know; I probably won't go back next year, either. We're getting too old."

Too old? Juliet didn't think that either one of them could be more than sixteen. But she supposed that in this farming community, when one was grown physically and planning to spend one's life following in the footsteps of a father or mother, farming or taking care of a farmhouse, formal education didn't seem necessary. There wasn't much she could say, anyway, since she herself had rarely attended a school for longer than a few weeks.

Her father had seen to it that she had received an excellent education, of course, teaching her himself. He had taught her far more than she would normally have learned in school about history, philosophy, government, and art, and they had read daily from the classics in literature and discussed them. He had even gritted his teeth and waded with her through arithmetic books (though she had seen the relief in his eyes when at twelve, she had told him she had no interest in learning algebra). Hers had been a liberal education, and as a result of it, she had grown up with a deep respect for knowledge and learning, but she could hardly say that it was a result of her attending school.

They were nearing Ellie and her family now, and Ellie

smiled at Ethan, then lowered her eyes demurely. Ethan grinned back and nodded shyly.

"Why don't you introduce Miss Sanderson to me?" Juliet whispered. There was no reason to, of course, and it would probably be considered impertinent of a house-keeper to suggest that she be introduced to an acquain-tance of her employers, but she was sure that Ethan wouldn't think of that.

"Really?" Ethan's face brightened. "Would you like to meet her?"

"Of course. She looks like a nice young girl."

"All right." Ethan crossed the space to where Ellie stood beside her father, who was talking to another mem-ber of the church. Aunt Frances and Amos continued outside.

"Good morning, Ellie," Ethan said, and the girl dimpled.

"Good morning, Ethan. It's nice to see you."

"I've missed you," Ethan continued. "I mean—your not being at school and all."

Her dimples grew. "Why, thank you. I've missed . . . school, too."

Ethan looked so thoroughly tongue-tied after that admission that Juliet thought he wouldn't be able to get anything else out. For a moment he was silent, grinning and blushing, but then he blurted out, "This—I—I'd like you to meet somebody. This is Miss Drake. Juliet Drake."

Ellie eyed her curiously. "It's nice to meet you."

"Thank you. It's a pleasure to meet you, too."

"Oh—" Ethan realized belatedly that he hadn't fin-ished the introduction. "Juliet, this is Ellie Sanderson.

They live down the road from us." He turned toward Ellie again. "Miss Drake's keeping our house now."

"I see. How nice."

The conversation died, and they all stood looking at each other awkwardly. Juliet searched for something to say to keep the two young people talking to each other, but she couldn't come up with anything more original than a comment about the weather, to which both of them nodded eagerly, but had nothing to add. Juliet sighed inwardly; they weren't helping her a bit. If only she could get them talking to each other, then she could withdraw from the conversation and leave, giving them a chance to be alone together—or at least as alone as they could be with an entire church population milling about the vestibule and front yard.

"Well, Ellie," a deep voice said behind Juliet, and she turned. Mr. Sanderson had stopped talking and turned back to his daughter. He was speaking to Ellie, but he was smiling at Juliet. "I see you've made a new friend. Won't you introduce us?"

"Of course, Papa. You know Ethan Morgan, and this is their new housekeeper, Juliet Drake."

"How do you do, Miss Drake? I am John Sanderson."

"It's so nice to meet you." Juliet held out her hand and smiled, grateful for his intervention. If she could keep him talking to her, it would provide a natural separation from the younger couple, and surely without an adult listening in, they would manage to come up with something to say!

John Sanderson smiled back. He was tall and wiry,

with light-colored eyes and blond hair, lightly tinged with gray at the temples. He was a nice-looking man with a pleasant manner. "So, you are the Morgan's housekeeper? I thought you are such a pretty lady, that Amos must have brought him home a town wife."

Juliet blushed. Imagine thinking of her as Amos's wife! If only he knew how Amos felt about her . . .

"No. I am from town. But Miss Morgan needed a little help with the housework."

"Of course." His face sobered, and he shook his head. "Such a sad thing . . . Miss Morgan is a good woman. That house is too much for her alone. My wife was lucky she had our Ellie to help her." He sighed and shook his head. "But now that Anna is gone, it is a lot of work for Ellie. The boys help her some, but a young girl should not have to work so hard. And she can no longer go to the school-house."

His wife must be dead, then. "I'm sorry," Juliet said.

He shook his head. "It's been over a year now; it gets easier. But"—he shrugged—"it isn't good for a man to live alone, I think."

"I'm sure not," Juliet murmured.

Suddenly John's eyes took on a twinkle. "Perhaps I, too, should find myself a housekeeper. What do you think?"

Juliet realized, with some surprise, that Ellie's father was flirting with her a little. She hadn't meant for *that* to result from her move to push Ethan and Ellie together. Of course, he was rather nice-looking, she thought, and he smiled, which was a welcome change after being in

Amos Morgan's company. It wouldn't be hard to flirt back with him. No doubt the dour Mr. Morgan wouldn't approve of his housekeeper flirting with anyone; it was too frivolous a thing to do.

Juliet sneaked a glance around the vestibule, empty now of most of the churchgoers except for small clusters of people talking. Amos had apparently walked his sister to the wagon, then returned, for he was standing stiffly just inside the door, his back against the wall and arms folded across his chest, watching her and Ethan grimly. Juliet felt childishly like sticking out her tongue at him. *What did it matter what he thought?* He could hardly think any worse of her than he already did. Anyway, it was none of his business whom she talked with or whether she flirted a little. It had nothing to do with the work she did for him; he didn't run her life just because she lived in his house.

She turned back to Sanderson, raising her chin defiantly and flashing a particularly brilliant smile. She refused to be intimidated by that man's bad moods. Her father had contended that no one had power over you unless you gave it to him, and Juliet believed that. She wasn't about to give Amos Morgan power over her.

"Perhaps you should get one," she agreed. "Although I hope that you are pleasant to yours."

Her companion chuckled. "Amos can be a hard man."

"So I've found," Juliet murmured.

They continued to talk for a few more minutes. Juliet could see out of the corner of her eye that Ethan and Ellie were now standing closer together, talking in low voices and smiling at each other. Good. They had broken the ice at last. Juliet's goal was accomplished. Next Sunday she'd make sure that they were thrown together again. Surely there would be some occasion coming up before long, a dance or a church social, that would give the two young people a better opportunity to get to know each other. She was confident that it wouldn't be long before Ethan had entirely forgotten Juliet and was singing Ellie Sanderson's praises.

Juliet was engrossed in her own thoughts, only half listening to John Sanderson. She didn't even notice when Amos walked up behind them until he spoke.

"All right," he said abruptly, without greeting or preamble. "We have to go home. Frances is getting tired, sitting in the surrey."

All of them turned to look at him. He looked thunderous, though Juliet couldn't imagine why. He stood stiffly, his hands shoved into his pants pockets. He seemed old-fashioned, out of sorts, and generally at odds with the world. Juliet smothered a smile as she gazed at him; he appeared so patently disagreeable that it was, peculiarly, almost endearing. She didn't understand the feeling, but for once he aroused amusement more than irritation in her.

"Hello, Amos," John greeted him. There was a twinkle in his eyes that told Juliet that he, too, found Amos's bad-tempered bluntness amusing. "How are you today?"

"Fine," Amos responded shortly. His eyes slid to Juliet and quickly away. "We have to go now."

"Aw, Pa." Ethan grimaced, reluctance written on his features. "Already?"

"Already?" Ponderously Amos pulled his watch from his vest pocket and opened it. "I've been standing around waiting on you for twenty minutes. It's time we went home. Some of us don't have the time to waste gabbing. Ethan. Miss Drake."

He turned and strode away, pushing through the front door and on outside. He didn't even look back to see if the others followed him.

Well, Juliet thought, at least he was as rude to everyone else as he was to her. She turned and gave Mr. Sanderson an apologetic smile. "I'm sorry. It looks as though we have to leave now."

"I understand." As she started away, he reached out and touched her arm. "Wait. Let me ask you: Would it be all right if I came by to see you some Sunday afternoon?"

Juliet looked at him blankly for a moment, surprised by his words. She had been more intent on giving Ethan and Ellie a chance to talk than on her own conversation with Mr. Sanderson. But he, apparently, had had more interest in it. Or, at least in her.

She hesitated. He was a nice enough man, she supposed, but she wasn't particularly interested in him. However, perhaps if he came, he might bring his family with him, and Ethan could see Ellie again. Even if he didn't, what was the harm in a little socializing? Heaven knows, she didn't get much chance for a decent conversation in the Morgan household. She didn't have to want to marry the man just to let him come calling a few times.

"Of course, if you can't, I understand," he went on quickly. "I know how Amos can be."

"Mr. Morgan has nothing to do with whether or not I receive callers, " Juliet flared. He had touched her on her sorest spot, her independence. "I make such decisions. And I would like very much to see you again. Feel free to call some Sunday afternoon."

"Good." He smiled.

Juliet nodded and hurried to follow Ethan out the door. It would be just like Amos to drive off without her.

The others were already waiting in the carriage, and she quickly clambered up onto the wide seat beside Frances. Ethan sat up with his father, and they both looked disgruntled. Amos clucked to the horses and slapped the reins to get them started.

"I don't know why we had to hurry off like that," Ethan complained sulkily. "We never do much on Sunday, anyway."

"Frances is tired," Amos said tersely, keeping his eyes on the front. "Besides, I don't see what's so all-fired entertaining all of a sudden about talking to the Sandersons."

Ethan shrugged. "Ellie's a nice girl. I like her."

"Yes, she seemed very sweet," Juliet added.

Amos made a short noise of disbelief in his throat. "Looks to me like you were talking to John, not Ellie."

Juliet glanced at him, her eyebrows lifting in surprise. What did it matter whether she talked to the father or the daughter? Beside her, Frances, looking straight ahead, muttered, "Dog in the manger."

"What?" Amos swung his head toward her, scowling.

Frances made her face exaggeratedly blank and gazed off into the distance.

"What's that supposed to mean?" Amos persisted.

Frances shrugged. "You know."

His mouth twisted, and his only reply was a noncommittal grunt. Amos clucked to the horses again, and they picked up speed. Everyone was silent the rest of the way home.

Five

*A*mos smoothed his thumb across the piece of wood, feeling for the slightest roughness that would need to be sanded. As soon as they returned from church, he had retreated to the barn to work with his wood, as he always did when he was feeling troubled. Somehow, as the figures took shape beneath his hands, the thoughts or pain or whatever was hounding him gradually slipped away.

Today his thoughts were taking a much longer time to leave. He'd felt twisted up inside ever since they'd walked out of the sanctuary and Juliet had started flirting with John Sanderson. To make it worse, he knew that he was acting like a fool, but he couldn't stop himself. Juliet Drake had a perilous effect on his control.

The first moment he'd seen her onstage, it had been like a punch in his stomach. He thought she was the most beautiful woman he'd ever seen, her red-gold hair a glory of femininity, her blue eyes glowing like sapphires, her gently rounded form that beckoned a man's hand. And her voice was so rich and sweet, it sent shivers through him.

When Henrietta had trotted Juliet out the next morning and proposed her as his new housekeeper, he had been at first stunned, then dismayed. He had feared Ethan would fall in love with her; he didn't see how any man could help it. But, in truth, that hadn't been his primary reason for not wanting her as his housekeeper. What he had feared was the way her beauty would disturb his own peace. And he'd been right—he had been in a state of turmoil from the moment she arrived.

"Pa?" He heard Ethan's voice and turned.

"Back here, son."

"Oh. There you are." Ethan ambled back to the small work area where Amos kept his wood-working tools. "What are you working on?"

He craned his head to look at the piece of wood in Amos's hands. A woman's head was carved into the wood. Her face was tilted slightly and she was smiling; she seemed almost alive.

"Pretty," Ethan commented. "You know, she looks kind of like Miss Drake."

Amos scowled. "You see Miss Drake everywhere you look."

Ethan chuckled and settled himself on the floor, leaning back against the wall. He had sat this way many times, watching his father work and talking to him. It was always easiest to talk to Amos when he was working at his hobby; he seemed freer and looser.

"Pa . . . ," Ethan began slowly. "How can you tell if a girl likes you? I mean, really likes you."

Amos glanced at him, his brows drawing together. "You mean Miss Drake?"

Ethan looked surprised. "Miss Drake! Heavens, no."

"You seem to be getting pretty sweet on her."

Ethan chuckled. "Oh, she's awfully pretty. It's kind of amazing to think that she's actually right there in our kitchen. You know?"

"I know," Amos replied grimly.

"But she's not real. I mean, obviously she's real. But she's not anyone that I could ever—oh, you know what I mean. She's too beautiful, too perfect; heck, she's older than I am. I wouldn't ever expect her to have any interest in me. She's someone you'd dream about."

That was true enough, Amos thought, but he said only, "Then who are you talking about, if not Ju—Miss Drake?"

"Ellie Sanderson." Ethan looked at his father as if he'd gone daft. "Didn't you see her today at church?"

"Oh. Of course." Amos hid a smile. Obviously Ellie was all Ethan had seen. "She's a pretty girl."

"Isn't she?" Ethan's face lit up.

"Yes." Amos smiled at him fondly. "And you're wondering if she's interested in you, too."

Ethan nodded. "She talked to me and seemed real happy to see me and all. But, then, she's always nice to everybody. How do you tell if she especially likes you?"

Amos shook his head. "I'm the wrong person to be asking about something like that. What I understand about women you could put on the head of a nail. Most of the time they seem . . . unfathomable to me."

"Oh, Pa . . . you must know something about them. You were married to my mother, after all."

"Your mother," Amos said slowly, turning his attention back to the piece of wood in his hands. "Actually, I think I understood her least of all."

Ethan sighed. "I guess you weren't together all that long before she died."

"No." Amos hesitated, then went on, "I guess you know if she's really interested in you by the way she looks at you and talks to you. It's hard to judge. But, say, with Ellie, did she talk to you the same way that she talked to Miss Drake?"

"No. She was nice to Miss Drake, but she just said a little bit to her; Ellie and I talked most of the time." He looked up hopefully. "You think that means something?"

"I wouldn't be surprised."

"Do you think it'd be all right if I called on her sometime?"

"I don't see why not." He gazed seriously at Ethan. "You're a good, hard-working, fine-looking young man. I can't see why any girl wouldn't be proud and happy to have you come calling on her."

Ethan blushed a little. "You don't usually say things like that."

Amos shrugged. "That doesn't mean I don't think them. You go ahead and call on Ellie if you want. Just—just don't get too serious too young. You've got years and years in front of you. There'll be other girls to come along."

Ethan grinned and jumped to his feet. "Thanks, Pa. Can I have the surrey to go to her house next Sunday?"

Amos laughed. "I reckon so." He set down the wood and sandpaper and laid his hand on his son's shoulder.

"Now we better get back to the house. Frances will have our hides if we spoil her Sunday dinner by coming in late."

Juliet was grateful for the day of rest that Sunday provided. She wasn't sure her aching muscles could have done any more chores. Even the meals didn't go too badly because Frances seemed to be feeling better that day and helped her with them.

But Monday the grind started all over again. Frances came downstairs briefly in the morning, but after doing a few chores, she returned to her room to rest. Juliet continued doggedly with the spring cleaning despite the soreness of her muscles, which protested every move she made. When Juliet looked at her hands, she wanted to cry. Her lovely hands were turning red and chapped from the time they spent in water and strong lye soap. Even worse, there were blisters forming on her palms!

Before she went back to bed, Frances had started stewing a chicken in a pot on the stove, and she suggested that Juliet make chicken and dumplings. Juliet knew that to make the dish, one made bread dough and dropped it in lumps into the boiling chicken broth. Of course, she didn't know the proportions, but she was lucky enough to find a file box of recipes in the pantry, and though there wasn't one for chicken and dumplings, there was one for biscuits, and she reasoned that it would be much the same.

Her other dishes were limited by what was in the

larder. She picked out a few wrinkled brown potatoes from the root cellar, and, of course, the inevitable winter fare of dried beans or peas. There were some dried apples, so she decided to make apple cobbler. A good dessert ought to sweeten up even Amos Morgan, and since there was a recipe in the box for cobbler, too, she would be able to make it.

With determination she set to work. She made the biscuit mixture and set it aside while she took the boiled chicken and shredded it from the bones. Her confidence grew as she went along. The biscuits hadn't been hard, with the recipe, and she thought she was beginning to understand how to work that contrary stove. She wouldn't cook the beans as long, and after they had boiled, she would take them off for a while and set them back on to heat later. And she would remember to turn the cobbler in the oven periodically so that it wouldn't burn on one side as the sweet potatoes had done. Juliet smiled to herself as she put the beans on, thinking how surprised and pleased everyone would be by the meal. It would make up for that disastrous breakfast yesterday morning.

She put the deboned chicken back in the broth and brought it to boil again. She wasn't sure what seasonings to put in, so she threw in a little salt and pepper. Then she made the dough for the apple cobbler, working it and rolling it out again and again until she had it just right. By the time she had the filling made and the cobbler put together, the chicken had been boiling merrily for some time, and she hastily threw in the dumplings. She set the cobbler in the oven, stirred everything again, and began to set the table.

When Ethan and Amos came in from the fields, the meal was ready and sitting on the table. Juliet was particularly pleased with the cobbler, which had a deliciously golden-brown crust, though it did seem strangely thicker than when she had put it in the oven and some of the juice had slid over the side of the pan and down the oven, creating black streaks of burned syrup and an awful smell. Juliet sat down at the table with great expectations.

It took only one bite of the chicken to prove her wrong. The broth was too thin, and the chicken had cooked too long, so that it had almost disintegrated. Worst of all, it was bland, even tasteless.

Then there were the dumplings, not at all light as they were supposed to be, but heavy and sodden. The potatoes, which she had mashed, turned out too dry; they were difficult to swallow. The lima beans were all right—or at least as all right as lima beans could be. But the cobbler, which was to have been her pièce de resistance, was the worst thing on the table. The crust was tough, and the filling was sour. It was also too thick, chock full of apples, with almost no syrup.

Juliet took a bite, then put her fork down, forcing herself to swallow what was in her mouth. *What had gone wrong?* She had been so careful! Then it struck her—the recipe had no doubt been intended for fresh apples, and she had used dried ones. She had put in the cupfuls called for, but that would have been a fewer number of apple slices than the dried apple slices. They had soaked up all the syrup, swelling as they did; that was what had caused the cobbler to grow so and to spill over. And there hadn't been enough sugar for that number of apples, making it too sour!

Tears pricked at the back of Juliet's eyes, and she wanted to put her head down on the table and cry. She had ruined dinner.

At the end of the table, Amos, too, laid his fork aside after taking a bite of the cobbler. Only Ethan gamely continued to eat it. "Miss Drake . . ." Amos's voice was chilling.

Juliet didn't want to, but she had to look up at him. "Yes?"

"This is a most unusual cobbler."

"Yes. Well, I, uh . . ."

"You don't know how to cook," he finished for her.

"It's not that bad, Pa," Ethan protested. "Just a little tart."

"I—I forgot that the apples were dried and I put in too many of them and not enough sugar and—"

"The reasons aren't really important. The fact of the matter is that I have never in my life eaten meals quite as terrible as the ones which you have fixed the past few days."

Juliet lowered her eyes, color flooding her cheeks. It was humiliating to have her charade exposed this way, to have to listen like a wayward child while Amos Morgan lectured her in his cold, cutting way.

"I don't know what you are, but it is obvious that you

are no cook—and I would guess no housekeeper, either."

Juliet drew a shaky breath and forced herself to look up at Amos. She was in the wrong, she knew, but, still, she refused to let herself be intimidated by this man. Perhaps she hadn't been exactly honest with him and the other Morgans, but it wasn't as if she had committed a crime.

"I am trying to earn a living," she replied, managing with some effort to keep her voice even. "You are right. I was not . . . precisely truthful. I was desperate for employment. So I—I stretched the truth."

"Stretched the truth!" He repeated, his brows vaulting upward. "I'd say you damn near broke it!"

Juliet gritted her teeth. "I assure you that I had no intention of defrauding you. I did not expect the work to be as . . . difficult as it has been. I thought I would catch on quickly. Nor am I entirely devoid of skills; I am an excellent seamstress. I haven't shirked my duties; I've done my best to give an honest day's work for my wages."

"That's true," Frances put in. "She is a hard worker."

"Thank you." Juliet gave the other woman a small smile. "I am sorry that I so overestimated my ability to learn what I needed to in the kitchen."

"It's harder to cook than most people think."

"I am learning," Juliet added hopefully.

"I have no desire to pay you housekeeper's wages while you 'learn' how to cook! I am terminating your employment as of right now."

Juliet's stomach twisted with fear. She needed this job,

however hard it was. "When you throw me out, what are you planning to do for a housekeeper? You need one, you know. Miss Morgan is not strong enough to care for the house herself."

"We'll get another housekeeper," Amos replied flatly.

"Are you so sure of that?" Juliet retorted. "I was given the definite impression that I was the only candidate for this position. I was the only woman who knew so little about you that I was willing to work for you."

Amos gaped at her, amazed by her temerity. "Is that so?"

"Yes. Now that I have been around you for awhile, I can understand why that's true. Who would want to work like an ox *and* put up with your bad temper? Frankly, I don't think you'll find anyone except someone who has no other choice, like me."

"It couldn't be much worse having nobody than it is having to eat what you prepare."

"No doubt you can say that because you are not the one who will have to fix the meals if I leave," Juliet pointed out sharply. "It is your sister who will be burdened with that. She is the one who will suffer."

Amos's eyes flickered guiltily to Frances, so Juliet pressed home her point. "It isn't only that she'll have to prepare the food, either. There's all the housecleaning that will fall on her shoulders again. The washing and ironing. Maybe I'm not a good cook, but I'm smart enough and I can learn to do it better. And I can wash the dishes and sweep and clean."

"I can teach her how to cook," Frances put in. "And

whatever else she needs to know. I'm strong enough to sit here and give directions. I would have done it today, but I didn't realize . . ."

Amos's mouth twisted. He looked away, then back at Juliet, then over at his sister, obviously torn. He sighed. "Oh, all right. Damnation! I don't like it! But I haven't the time to drive you back now, anyway. I need every minute of the day to get the crops in. I ought to kick you out and let you find your own way back. However, that would be tantamount to murder; a greenhorn like you would never make it to Steadman. So, much as it goes against my grain, I'll let you stay."

A smile broke across Juliet's face. "Oh, thank you, Mr. Morgan. I promise you, you won't regret it. I'll—"

"I already do that," Amos informed her ungraciously. "And remember, it's only until we get the planting done. Then I'm taking you right back to Henrietta's doorstep. Am I clear?"

"Perfectly."

Amos gave her a final scowl and left the kitchen. Juliet sat back down in her chair with a thump. Now that the confrontation was over, her legs were suddenly like water. Frances glanced at her sympathetically.

"You should have told me you didn't know how to cook," Frances told her mildly. "I could have helped you."

Juliet smiled. "I know. Thank you. But I—you see, I didn't know what your reaction would be. I was afraid you would send me back to town, and then I didn't know what I'd do."

"I understand. Better than Amos. It's hard for him to imagine how difficult it would be for a woman to have to make her way in the world." Frances's voice was gentle, and for a moment, sadness tinged her face. But then she shrugged and put a smile on her face. "But now—what we have to do is turn you into a cook."

The next morning Frances was waiting in the kitchen when Juliet walked in, yawning widely. Juliet knew that Frances's illness had made her so tired that she rarely managed to struggle out of bed before eight o'clock, and she was touched that Frances had made this special effort just for her.

Frances led Juliet out to the chicken coop. "Your first job every morning is gathering the eggs," she explained as they walked across the bare yard toward the small wooden henhouse. A couple of hens were scratching listlessly through the yard, heads bobbing up and down. A rooster perched on top of the low house, and he crowed and turned his head to fix a bright eye on them as they approached. When they drew close, he swooped down and planted himself in the middle of their path.

"That rooster!" Frances exclaimed, making a shoo-ing motion with her arm. "He's a mean one. I never have liked him. If you aren't careful, he'll try to jump on your back and spur you."

Juliet stared at him in astonishment. She had never thought about something like a chicken being nasty or dangerous.

Frances caught her surprised look. "You ever been on a farm before?"

"No," Juliet confessed. "I haven't. I've always lived in a city, except when we were traveling."

"I've been right here my whole life. I was born in the front bedroom. My father and his parents settled here when he was about Ethan's age. Over there's their original sod dugout." Frances pointed to a low, small earthen building between the barn and the fields. "Amos uses it for a smokehouse now."

Frances stooped to go inside the low henhouse door, and Juliet followed her. The acrid smell, which had been noticeable outside, was almost overpowering in the small, dim hut. Juliet tried to cover her nose unobtrusively as she glanced at her companion. Frances didn't seem to notice the smell.

"This is the chicken coop," Frances told her, "where the hens lay their eggs." She made a gesture toward the wooden boxes stuffed with straw on shelves along the walls. Hens sat in several of them. Some were asleep; others were watching the women with jerky movements of their heads. "We reach in and get the eggs out." Frances demonstrated, pulling out a small brownish egg. She showed it to Juliet, then laid it in her basket. "Now you try."

Juliet hesitated, glancing around at the hens. "They don't mind?"

"They're used to it, I reckon."

Tentatively Juliet stretched out her hand and slipped it into one of the boxes, delving under the hen until her fingers ran into something hard and smooth. She closed her fingers around it and cautiously pulled it out. The hen paid no attention to her. Juliet relaxed, sighing.

"There. That's not so bad, is it?"

Juliet gave Frances a small grin, a little embarrassed at her uneasiness. It seemed silly to be afraid of something no bigger than a hen. "No. I guess not. It's just that I'm not used to them."

"You'll get that way soon enough."

Juliet wasn't so sure. However, she was rather pleased with herself for what she had done as they walked back to the house through the crisp dawn air. Gathering eggs was completely outside her realm of experience, but she had done it. Perhaps she could learn how to do the other things she needed to, as well. It occurred to her that the world was nice at this time of day—once one got accustomed to awakening this early. The air was invigorating, and everything looked clean and new in the pale wash of light. She glanced at the eastern sky, streaked with pink and gold. The dark shapes of the cottonwoods down by the creek were etched sharply against the horizon. It was the first time that Juliet had ever thought that this flat, forbidding landscape was appealing. But she saw in it now a stark, spare beauty, the kind that made one's heart ache to look at it.

Inside the kitchen, Frances explained to Juliet how to stack wood in the firebox of the stove and how much to put in to cook the sausage at a low temperature. Juliet sliced the sausage and laid it in a skillet, then set it on top of one of the lids of the stove and covered it to let it cook while she went about making coffee. At least *that* was something she knew how to do.

Next Frances taught her how to make biscuits, kneading the dough and rolling it out, then taking a small drinking glass and cutting the biscuits out. She directed Juliet to grease and flour the flat metal sheet on which she laid the biscuits. After she popped the biscuits into the oven, she broke the eggs and whisked them, adding a little milk, salt and pepper. When Juliet took the sausage out of the pan, she scooped up the remaining bits of meat from the grease, as Frances directed, and poured some of the grease out in a tin can kept for that purpose, then scrambled the eggs in the remaining grease.

The meal was done when the men came in from their chores, and Juliet laid it out proudly on the table. Amos glanced around the table. Juliet suspected he was searching for something to gripe about, and she had to suppress a smile when he couldn't find anything wrong. He sat down in a grumpy silence, and they began to eat.

Juliet noticed that Amos gulped down the food she had made and took a second helping of the sausage and her biscuits. Finally, when he pushed back his chair and stood up to leave, he said, not looking at her, "That was a good meal." He glanced at her and away. "Thank you."

"You're welcome." Juliet smiled. It seemed to her that she shouldn't feel so good just because he had paid her the merest of compliments, but she couldn't seem to help it.

He looked at her again, and for an instant it seemed as if he would say something else to her, but then abruptly he turned away and headed for the door. "Come on, Ethan. Time's a wastin'."

Ethan jumped up at his father's words, casting a grin

Juliet's way. "I'm coming, Pa. Thank you, Miss Drake. Aunt Frances."

Frances and Juliet cleared the dishes from the table and washed them. Then Frances began Juliet's lessons on household chores. She taught Juliet how to skim the cream from the milk and how to churn butter, then mold it. Next she walked her through the baking of bread, from mixing to kneading it just the right amount before she left it to rise, then punching it down and letting it rise again before finally baking it.

Juliet was wrung dry by the end of the day. She wondered if she would ever reach the point where she knew what she was doing—or where she wasn't bone tired by the end of the day, her arm muscles aching.

As she was setting the table for supper, the back door opened and Amos clumped in. Mud clung to the soles of his shoes, and Juliet watched in horror as he tracked mud across the floor that she had so painstakingly cleaned the day before!

"What are you doing?" she shrieked.

Amos came to a standstill, looking at her as if she had suddenly taken leave of her senses. "What?"

"Your boots!" Juliet waved her hand at his feet. "You're tracking mud all over my clean floor. Go back out and take those boots off at once!"

He blinked, obviously surprised at her audacity in telling him what to do, but he only nodded shortly and retraced his steps to the door.

"And in the future I'd appreciate it if you would leave your boots outside when you come in. I spent all morning cleaning up that floor, and I'd just as soon not have it ruined by your carelessness."

Amos cast her a sardonic glance as he sat down on the doorstep and removed his boots, setting them down carefully on the small stoop. "You don't exactly hold back your opinion, do you?"

Juliet felt a stab of uneasiness. What she had said wasn't any way to talk to an employer; she had been incensed by the sight of mud on her clean floor. But she wasn't about to kowtow to some petty tyrant, either, just because he was used to it.

"I see nothing wrong with speaking my mind," she replied stiffly. "I take it you aren't used to anyone daring to question you?"

"Question? Is that what you'd call it?" Again the odd half-smile played across his mouth. Juliet noticed how much more attractive he was when he smiled. "I'd have said you were raking me over the coals."

Juliet hesitated. She didn't know what to say. Obviously she wasn't accustomed to being a servant. She had grown up an equal among equals, and her father, moreover, had always encouraged free thinking and free speech in his daughters. Such an attitude, she realized, was not what one looked for in a cook or scrubber of floors.

"I—I shouldn't have been so abrupt," she said carefully, looking away from him.

"No." He held out a hand. "Don't worry. You were right. I—it's nice. For you not to be scared of me, I mean. Some people are."

Juliet smiled, relieved.

"I shouldn't have teased you," Amos went on.

Juliet glanced at him, surprised to hear that he had been teasing her. It seemed too lighthearted a thing for Amos Morgan to do. Amos had a slightly startled expression on his face, as though he, too, was surprised to find himself acting so uncharacteristically. Then his face shut down again, before he turned away. Juliet stood for a moment uncertainly, wondering what had broken the slender thread of connection that had stretched between them for that brief time. Then she shrugged and went back to work. It was useless trying to understand Amos.

After that first morning, Juliet handled breakfasts on her own. She became more at ease with gathering the eggs, too, although she still felt a healthy distrust of that rooster, who was wont to come darting at her, screeching and squawking, from out of nowhere. As Frances had suggested, she carried a dish towel with her, which she would flip at him when his mock attacks seemed too menacing. She was soon able to distinguish one hen from another, and she often talked to them, even naming them, as she scattered their feed in the evening or retrieved their eggs in the morning.

A great deal of the time Frances spent teaching Juliet was devoted to the kitchen and various aspects of cooking. Frances would sit in the afternoon and write down recipes that she knew by heart and had learned the same way from her mother. As they worked together, they talked. Frances was eager to hear about Juliet's life in the theater and the places she had lived, and though she thought her own life dull in comparison, Juliet enjoyed her anecdotes about life on the farm. She found the Morgans, with their silent, stoic strength, intriguing, and the way they lived was a whole new world to her. Frances was entertaining, in her own quiet, droll way, and every day Juliet grew fonder of her.

Juliet often sang as she worked, for it made the job easier. One morning, she was singing as she washed the dishes after breakfast, and she happened to glance over to where Frances sat at the table. Frances was leaning back against her chair, her eyes closed, a beatific look on her face.

Feeling Juliet's gaze, Frances opened her eyes and smiled, a little chagrined at being caught. "Your voice is lovely. I could listen to it for hours. Our mother used to sing sometimes. She couldn't sing like you; she had only an ordinary voice. But she loved music. She had a music box that her father had given her, and when you lifted the lid it played the most wonderful tune, so graceful and delicate. I used to think it sounded like little silver drops." She sighed. "It's upstairs in my bottom drawer. I put it away; it hurt too much to listen to it."

Like her brother, Juliet thought.

"Mama loved beautiful things," Frances went on reminiscently. "Her family were city people, you know, and well-to-do. That furniture in the parlor and dining room was her family's. She brought those heirlooms, the candlesticks and all, with her when she married Pa. I remember, she used to sit sometimes and look at them or touch them, and I'd ask her what she was thinking. She'd say, 'I'm remembering, that's all.' I don't know why she married Pa; he wasn't like her a bit. Except he was a handsome devil when he was young. There's a picture of them when they got married, and he was good-looking. Kind of like Amos, but colder."

Colder than Amos? Juliet thought he was like ice most of the time when he looked at her. Well, no, now that she thought about it, Juliet decided that Amos was really more hard than cold. His eyes could blaze like fire when he was angry.

"Go ahead and sing," Frances went on. "Don't mind me. I love to hear you. Especially when I'm lying up there in my bed. Somehow your singing makes it more bearable."

Tears clogged Juliet's throat; it was difficult to accept the fact that Frances was dying. Juliet swallowed hard and began to sing.

Frances's next lesson was in doing the laundry. She sent Juliet upstairs to strip the sheets from the beds. Juliet felt a little strange, almost guilty, going into the others' rooms, as if she were an invader. It made her especially uncomfortable when she walked into the large bedroom that belonged to Amos.

It was sparsely furnished, with only a bed, a chair, and a single dresser, all made of sturdy oak, plain in design. The counterpane was equally simple, and the folded quilts across the foot of the bed were faded with many washings. There was little evidence of the occupant of the room, except perhaps in the very simplicity and plainness of it. On one wall hung a daguerreotype in a metal frame; it was the only decoration. Curiously Juliet went over to it, wondering if perhaps this was a picture of Ethan's mother. No one ever mentioned her, and Juliet often wondered what had happened to her. She supposed that Amos's wife must be dead since she plainly was not there, but it was a mystery when and how she died.

But the daguerreotype was a portrait of a family, the father seated, hands on his knees, holding his hat in one hand, the mother standing behind him, hand on his shoulder, two little boys on either side of the bench on which the father sat, a small girl standing in front of the taller boy, and a baby, sexless in its cap and long white gown, on the father's lap. All of them stared stiffly in front of them.

Juliet was intrigued. She thought that this must be Amos Morgan's family. The stern-looking man with the mustache and thick sideburns would be his father, the pale, slender woman his mother. She looked a little frightened, probably at having her picture taken by this newfangled contraption. Henrietta had said that Amos was younger than her husband, so Amos must be the smaller boy or even the baby. It was hard to imagine him as either. The girl, of course, would be Frances.

Juliet pulled herself away from the picture and went to the large bed. She laid the quilts on the trunk at the foot of the bed, then pulled off the counterpane and folded it, setting it on top of the quilts, and started stripping the sheets from the bed. It made her feel a little embarrassed to be doing this to Amos's bed, as if she were doing something she shouldn't. It seemed too intimate a thing to do for a stranger. It should be the province of someone who knew him better, of a woman who shared his bed and life.

Hurriedly Juliet finished her task and left the room. She went briskly through Ethan's and Frances's rooms, doing the same thing. Those rooms didn't make her feel as nervous. They were as bare and functional as Amos's, with almost no knickknacks or ornamentations to make them cozier and more personal.

She had thought her room plain because it was just a spare room; no one lived in it. But there was little difference between her room and those of the family. In fact, now that Juliet had set out her things around her bedroom, it was more welcoming than theirs.

The Morgans seemed to make no attempt to soften the world in which they lived or to add color or beauty. Juliet couldn't understand it. It was too different from her own life.

There had been times when Juliet had wished that her father were more practical and less driven by his artistic nature. When he used the money set aside for food to buy her a scarf of fine lace, as delicately spun as cobwebs, she had wanted to cry, then to shout at him. But even then she had understood what had prompted the gesture, and she had loved the scarf. She could not conceive of not wanting to gather pretty things around oneself.

Juliet dragged the dirty clothes downstairs and outside to the yard. There she and Frances washed and scrubbed in a big tub with a washboard, rinsing them out in another large tub. Then she hung the sheets and clothes on the lines to dry in the afternoon, taking them in before nightfall and folding them. It was backbreaking work, and when she was done, she still had to iron them and put them away.

There were a multitude of other chores, as well—the spring cleaning as well as the daily duties of sweeping and dusting and polishing furniture. It seemed to Juliet as though the list of chores was unending, and as soon as she finished one, she had to start another.

She was beginning to think that it would never get any better. Every night she fell into bed exhausted. Muscles she had never known existed ached now. Everything seemed to take her longer than it should, and she was frustrated by her clumsiness at many of the tasks. And still she made mistakes. She scorched one of Amos's dress handkerchiefs when she was ironing, putting a plain brown imprint of the sadiron on it. She put too much starch in the tablecloth and napkins, and they were stiff and hard. A batch of bread came out small, heavy, and flat-tasting because she left the baking soda out of it. Everyone at the table ate it—there was no other bread to eat!—but as Juliet watched them chewing away grimly, she felt like sinking through the floor. Would she never get everything straight?

One morning, after she gathered the eggs and was walking from the chicken coop toward the house, she spotted one of her hair pins lying on the ground. She squatted down to pick it up, and suddenly something heavy hit her in the back. She heard a crow and the whir of wings flapping. Startled, Juliet dropped her basket and jumped to her feet, letting out a scream. The rooster was attacking her!

She batted backward with her hands, and the rooster dug in, spurring her through her clothes. She shrieked again, panicked, flailing awkwardly at the bird.

Amos came running from the barn. He grabbed her Juliet's arm with one hand and with the other knocked the rooster halfway across the yard.

"Goddamn! Crazy old bird!"

Juliet burst into tears, shivering. Suddenly it was all too much. Her fright and the pain in her back where the rooster had cut her skin combined with the exhaustion and frustration she had been feeling for days, and her emotions boiled over into a storm of tears.

"Are you all right?" Amos asked, grasping her arms and turning her so that he could see her back. "Damn! He's cut clear through to your skin. Good thing you were wearing that cape, or it would have been deep."

Juliet continued to cry, unable to stop herself. She raised her hands to her face, trying to hide her tears from him.

"Miss Drake? Juliet?" His voice sounded worried. "Are you all right? What's the matter?"

"What's the matter!" Juliet repeated in gasps as she cried. She scrubbed angrily at the tears that wet her face. "How can you ask what's the matter? That bird attacked me!"

"Well, yes, I know." He frowned down at her. "But you seem awfully upset . . ."

"No doubt a real farm woman wouldn't cry over something as measly as a rooster attacking her!" Juliet jerked away from him, and, to her embarrassment, her tears poured out harder than ever. "Well, I'm not a farm woman! That's obvious! I'm just a silly scared city girl, and I wish that I had never come to this godforsaken place!"

She started back to the house, seeking a place where she could cry her heart out in privacy. Amos hurried after her and grabbed her arm, pulling her to a stop.

"No, wait, I didn't mean—ah, hell! I wasn't saying you were weak or anything; I just thought, maybe you were hurt someplace else I didn't see."

"Yes, I am!" Juliet snapped back. "I hurt all over. From the top of my head to my toes. Every night when I go to bed, I feel like one big ache!" Her words came out in jerky bits and pieces, interrupted by her tears. She felt as if she were choking; she couldn't stop the words from rushing out of her, like a volcano erupting. "You were right! I'm not cut out for a farm. I can't do it. I make mistake after mistake. Even that stupid bird realizes that!" She gestured wildly toward the rooster. "He knows I don't belong. He senses how hopelessly outmatched I am." Juliet drew a long, shuddering breath, struggling to regain some hold on herself.

"No. You're making too much of it. That rooster hates everyone."

"But he attacked *me!*" Juliet pointed out. Her sobs had gradually slowed down, and now she sighed and wiped the tears from her face as a gloomy sort of calm descended on her. "After all the effort Frances has put into teaching—I know she must be horribly disappointed in me. I thought I'd be able to pick it up. I thought it'd get easier. But it doesn't."

"That's no way to talk," Amos told her gruffly. "Frances doesn't think that."

"How could she not?"

"She doesn't. She told me so."

"She did?" Juliet looked up at him in surprise. Her eyes were still moist with tears, her lashes stuck together in dark spikes like the points of a star around her eyes. Crying had intensified the blue color of her eyes and given them a vulnerable look. It had also made her mouth seem softer and fuller, eminently kissable.

Amos cleared his throat and pulled his gaze away, fastening it on the house. "Yes. Of course. Why else would I say so?"

"I don't know. I thought perhaps you were trying to make me feel better." Her voice hardened. "I should have known better."

Amos's mouth pulled into a tight line, and he folded his arms across his chest. "She told me a couple of days ago that she thought you would work out fine. That she didn't want you to leave. She said you were catching on real quick, and you had a lot of heart."

"Really?"

"Yes, really." He turned an annoyed gaze on her. "I said so, didn't I?"

Juliet fished in her pocket and found her handkerchief. She wiped her eyes and blew her nose, pulling herself together. "I thought—it seems like I'm always doing something wrong."

"Everybody makes mistakes. Spring's always hard. There's a lot of work—spring cleaning and everything. Frances doesn't want you to leave."

Juliet's breath caught in her throat. A moment earlier she would have sworn that nothing would please her more than getting off this farm immediately. But the thought that Frances liked her and wanted her to stay warmed her. Maybe the worst was over. Maybe if she stayed, it would get easier.

"What about you?" she asked softly. "Do you want me to stay?"

Amos shifted uneasily, avoiding her eyes. He shrugged. "I reckon it'd be easier than trying to get another housekeeper. You're doing fine. I—I was wrong to jump on you the way I did. Everybody deserves a chance."

A smile played across Juliet's lips. "Then I guess that means that I ought to give you a chance, too."

He glanced at her in surprise, and then, amazingly, smiled. Juliet was disconcerted by the way the smile lit up his eyes and softened his features, making him almost handsome.

"Come on," he said gruffly, "let's get you into the house and put something on those cuts."

"All right."

They went into the kitchen, and Amos pulled a small brown bottle down from one of the cabinets. Juliet took off her light cape. Amos turned toward her with the bottle and a small piece of cotton and stopped.

"We need to clean the scratches."

Juliet's shirtwaist opened down the front. She realized that for Amos to reach the cuts on her back, she would have to take it off. A flush rose in her cheeks. She couldn't do that in front of a man. But it was impossible for her to reach the wounds herself, and she hated to wake up Frances for such a small thing.

"Uh—perhaps I should wait until Frances gets up."

Amos frowned. "I don't know. Cuts like that can go bad on you awfully quickly." He went closer to her and put his hands on her shoulders, turning her so that he could look at her back. "He ripped your shirt up good. I think maybe I could clean it through the holes. Then Frances could put on a bandage later."

"All right." Her voice was a trifle unsteady. The touch of his fingers on her shoulders was unnerving—and yet it felt good, too. She wasn't used to a man touching her. Because it was difficult to retain her virtue in the looser world of the theater, Juliet had solved the problem by simply avoiding all contact with the men who tried to pursue her. So there was a certain forbidden quality to Amos's touch that was exciting. His hands were firm and warm, reassuring, making it easy for her to relax and entrust herself to him.

Amos wet the cotton at the washbasin, then carefully separated the two sides of the shirtwaist at one of the gashes. He dabbed at the long red streak on her skin beneath, and Juliet flinched.

"I'm sorry."

"No, it doesn't hurt much. It was more the cold water."

"Oh." He cleaned the wound, his touch so gentle and light she could hardly feel it, only the cold dampness of the cloth. Juliet thought of Amos's blunt, rough fingers, his big frame, and she wondered how a man as big as he could have such a gentle touch.

"It's not deep," he told her. "You shouldn't have much of a scar." His hand moved on to a new tear in the blouse, another raw red line. Neither of them spoke as he continued to wash the narrow wounds.

She felt a tremor in his hands as he brushed along a cut, and he stopped abruptly and stepped back. "There. That's all of them." His voice sounded hoarse, and he cleared his throat.

"Thank you." Juliet started to move away.

"Wait. I need to put on the medicine."

Juliet stopped, waiting patiently, her head curved down. Behind her she heard Amos shake the bottle, then uncork it, cursing under his breath when the stopper wouldn't come loose easily. Finally it popped, and he began to dab at her cuts again. Juliet kept thinking about him working on her back through the torn shirtwaist, looking at the bare patches of her skin. It made her a little breathless. She wondered if he felt anything or if he was utterly indifferent to her. He had called her beautiful, she remembered, and she wondered if he felt any of the excitement that quivered through her when he touched her bare skin.

"You aren't the first one that rooster's attacked," Amos said suddenly. "He went after Ethan's dog once when he started poking his nose around the coop. After that, the dog stayed away; we never had to worry about him sucking eggs."

Juliet smiled faintly. "I can believe that."

"He usually goes for smaller things than people."

"Well, actually," Juliet admitted, "I was bending down to pick something up."

"That's probably it. He thought you were smaller. Or maybe he saw that bow in your hair; something like that can startle an animal."

"Oh." Juliet clapped a hand to the nape of her neck. She had been late this morning, and she had just hastily pulled her hair back and tied it with a big floppy calico bow. "That never occurred to me."

"Not that it doesn't look nice." Juliet thought she felt something touch the long tail of hair hanging down her back, but it was so brief and so light that she wasn't sure. "Roosters aren't the brightest creatures." There was a pause, and he said, "I haven't seen you wear your hair that way before."

"I don't usually." Juliet felt embarrassed. It wasn't proper to wear one's hair down around a man, even if it was tied back or braided. "I hadn't time this morning to do it up."

She felt his hand leave her back; he had finished applying the medicine. He stood behind her for a moment longer, then whirled away and walked over to the cabinet, putting the bottle back on its shelf.

Juliet turned toward him. "Thank you," she said softly. He nodded, not even pausing or glancing back at her, and strode out of the door.

Six

John Sanderson came to call the following Sunday afternoon after church. Everyone in the house sat awkwardly together in the rear parlor. Frances was obviously tired, and Amos said almost nothing, just sat there looking at Juliet and Sanderson stonily. Even Ethan was rather tongue-tied, overawed by the presence of Ellie's father in their midst. Juliet tried to make up for the others' silence by chattering. After a while, she, too, ran down, and finally John stood and took his leave. Juliet walked him to the door.

He opened the door, then turned back to her, taking her hand and gazing meaningfully into her eyes. "I hope I may come back again to call on you."

"Yes, of course." Juliet kept her voice as noncommittal as she could. Personally, she would rather not endure another afternoon such as this one. John was nice enough, but he didn't set her heart to fluttering.

Sanderson smiled at her and gave her hand a squeeze, then left. Juliet closed the door and leaned back against it with a relieved sigh. Then she walked back to the back parlor to retrieve her mending and take it to her room to do. The mending basket was always full, and it seemed that she never had enough time to finish it; she worked on it whenever she was sitting down and resting.

Frances and Ethan had escaped from the parlor, and only Amos was there, slumped down in his chair, his long legs stretched out in front of him. Juliet tiptoed into the room, but Amos raised his head and looked at her.

"I'm sorry. I was trying not to disturb you." Juliet gave him an apologetic smile and started backing toward the door.

"I was waiting for you," he told her, and Juliet stopped and stared at him.

"You were what?"

"I was waiting for you. I need to talk to you."

"Why?" His tone made Juliet uncomfortable. She suspected that he was about to give her another moral lecture.

"It concerns you. And Sanderson."

Juliet raised her eyebrows coolly. "Yes?"

"I don't know how to say this except flat out. You may not like it." He paused again.

Juliet crossed her arms defensively in front of her and waited.

"I'd think twice if I were you about seeing John Sanderson."

"What?" His words weren't exactly what she had expected, and Juliet was momentarily confused. "I don't understand. What are you saying?"

Amos squirmed in his chair, then got up and walked over to the set of shelves against the far wall. A pipe stand and humidor were there, and Amos took out a pipe and began a production of filling it with tobacco. Not looking at her, he went on, "I'm saying that it might not be a good thing for you to see too much of Sanderson, that's all."

Juliet set her hands on her hips. "What are you talking about? I've never known you to beat around the bush before. Why shouldn't I see Mr. Sanderson? Do you think that I'm trying to ensnare him, too?"

He swung around, gaping at her in astonishment. "No! What kind of a fool thing is that to say? I'm talking about it for your benefit, not Sanderson's. You shouldn't see him, that's all."

"Why not?"

"Can't you take my word for it?"

"I don't see why I should. I don't know what you're talking about, and you've given me absolutely no reason for not seeing him. I'm not in the habit of following orders blindly." Juliet's mouth twitched in irritation.

"You're right about that," Amos agreed bitterly. "You're stubborn as a mule."

"Thank you very much. Now, if you're through evaluating my character, may I leave?"

"No, you may not!" He whirled around. "Not until I tell you what I started out to say."

"I believe you've already said it. You warned me away from Mr. Sanderson, but you refuse to say why. I see little point in continuing this—"

"Because he doesn't respect women, that's why!" Amos snapped.

Juliet stared. "Doesn't respect women?" This was so far

from anything she had expected him to say that she could not quite take it in.

"Is that not clear enough for you? Let me say it this way: he's a womanizer."

Juliet's jaw dropped open. "What? No, you must be mistaken."

"Mistaken?" His eyebrow quirked up. "I might have known it; you figure I'm the one that's lying."

"I didn't say that."

His answer was a disbelieving grunt. "You didn't have to. Well, you may not like me or want to believe what I'm saying, but it's the truth. He's had that reputation for years, even before his wife died."

"A reputation isn't necessarily based on the truth. How do you know it's true?"

Amos grimaced and swung back around to continue working on his pipe. "You'll believe whatever you want. There's nothing I can do to stop you. I'll tell you this, though: You may think that man is interested in marrying you, but he's not. I promise you."

"I didn't assume he wanted to marry me!"

"Well, good, then you won't be disappointed when all he does is try to maneuver you into the hayloft alone."

Juliet barely suppressed a gasp. His words hit her like a slap in the face. That was the only way Amos thought of her, she realized; he didn't consider her a woman about whom a man might care or whose conversation was enjoyable or whose personality pleasant to be with. He couldn't imagine any other man thinking of her that way, either.

"Mr. Morgan," she said, unable to hide the quiver of outrage and hurt that ran through her voice. "That seems to be all you ever think about. First it was *I* who you feared would entice your son into my wicked bed. Now it is Mr. Sanderson who has designs on me. You see seduction in the simplest word or gesture. But not everyone thinks like you, thank goodness. I enjoyed talking to Mr. Sanderson this afternoon, and I think he enjoyed visiting with me. Perhaps we are interested in something other than what you are. I refuse to let you taint our perfectly ordinary, perfectly nice afternoon with your nasty innuendos. If Mr. Sanderson wants to see me again, I will see him, and what you want or don't want doesn't matter."

"That's obvious." Amos's mouth was tight and pale, his eyes set. "Go ahead and believe whatever you want to. I won't try to interfere again. I was a fool to have said anything. Women want something else entirely in a man, not steadiness or devotion."

He walked past her and out of the room. A moment later Juliet heard the kitchen door slam. No doubt he had gone out to the barn. He seemed to spend most of his spare time there; Juliet couldn't imagine what he found to do.

Juliet stalked down to her own room and sat down on her bed with a disgruntled sigh. She didn't have any interest in seeing John Sanderson. Yet here she was, planning to let Sanderson continue to call on her, just because Amos had told her she shouldn't! Juliet shook her head. She didn't know whether to laugh or cry. It seemed as though no matter what she did, Amos Morgan interfered with her life.

The weeks passed by, and Juliet's work grew easier—or rather, she grew better able to do it. Taking care of the house was a big job, but it was no longer frustrating, and it went much more quickly. Her hands flew over the familiar tasks. Juliet now knew how much starch to use so that Amos's and Ethan's Sunday shirts no longer came out stiff enough almost to stand by themselves. She knew how big a fire to build in the stove and when to stir it up or let it subside into hot coals. She was even getting to where she could judge the temperature of the oven by sticking her hand in it, as Frances could. Though she wouldn't go so far as to say that she was an expert housekeeper, Juliet was satisfied that she was no longer a novice.

Amazingly enough, she found satisfaction in the work. She took pride in looking around the kitchen at the end of the day and seeing each gleaming surface. She enjoyed hearing Ethan brag about her cooking or seeing Amos take a second helping of something. There was satisfaction, too, in seeing the clothes neatly pressed and folded in the drawers of the bureaus and in the snap of freshly washed clothes hanging on the line. It was rewarding to take a garment from the mending basket and make it whole again.

But Juliet wasn't content to stop with just the housework. She wanted to make the house prettier, as well. She picked handfuls of the wildflowers that were coming to life along the roadway and in the meadow north of the farmyard and arranged them in vases and bowls, which she set in the kitchen and around the house. She kept the vase in Frances's bedroom full, hoping that the flowers would brighten up her days a little. She made new curtains for the kitchen windows, using a cheery yellow cotton cloth she found in the attic. The house seemed brighter now, more pleasant. It would have looked lovely, she thought, if only Amos would agree to open up the two formal rooms and set out his mother's elegant bibelots. But she didn't have the nerve to ask again.

Much to her surprise, she found that she was starting to like the farm. She had grown accustomed to the utter quiet of the place. She especially liked the hushed stillness of the evening, after the sun had fallen and before the landscape plunged into blackness. She often went out into the yard then, having finished the evening dishes, and walked around, looking up at the stars and moon, tired but content.

A few flowers and trees would be nice, she thought, but she was coming to appreciate the grandeur of the open country, the untamed vastness. In the evening sometimes, when the sun set in a red blaze of glory, Juliet would simply stand outside and gaze at it, lost in the wonder of its wild beauty.

Best of all were the baby animals. One evening Amos came into the kitchen. "Come here," he said, sticking his head inside and smiling, motioning for her to join him.

"Why?" Juliet asked, though she untied her apron and

left the dishes readily enough. She was intrigued by the expression on his face, light and happy.

"You'll see."

He looked almost like a little boy, she thought as she followed him across the yard to the animal pens. They drew close to the foul-smelling pigsty, and Juliet wrinkled up her noise expressively.

He chuckled at the face she made. "It's worth the smell." He went up to the wooden fence and peered over it. "Come here. You'll love it, I promise."

Juliet couldn't imagine what she would find lovable in a pigpen. Cautiously holding up the hem of her dress to avoid any stray muck, she stepped up to the fence beside him and looked over.

A weary mother hog lay on her side in the pen, a mass of squirming little piglets pushing and shoving to suckle at her teats. Juliet laughed aloud. "They're darling!"

Amos grinned, watching her delight. "I told you you'd like it. She just had them today."

"I never knew that pigs could be cute!" Juliet leaned against the fence, gazing down at the greedy little creatures, forgetting about the odor of the pen and the fact that her back ached from bending over a washtub all afternoon.

"Almost anything's cute when it's a baby. Even a hog. But you should see the calves. They're the best."

A few days later one of the cows dropped a calf. When Juliet heard Ethan and Amos talking about it, she insisted on going down to the barn to look at it, too. As Amos had said, it was darling, all big, sad eyes and knobby knees, clumsy and sweet and completely endearing. Juliet fell in love with it at once. "I want to name it! May I?"

Amos chuckled and shook his head. "Go right ahead. But you don't name calves."

"Whyever not? They have personalities. They ought to have names."

After that came the new chicks and the goslings and still more calves. Frances said that the mare would foal, too, before much longer. Suddenly it seemed as if the farm was teeming with life. Juliet loved it; her soul soared in response whenever she saw one of the babies. Her favorites were the chicks. The bouncy balls of yellow fluff never failed to amuse her. She loved to watch them run across the yard on feet so tiny one could hardly see them, scattering wildly when she or someone else came near them, or just bobbing along behind their mother in a comical line. Sometimes her heart felt so full, it seemed as if it would burst. At times like that she felt like singing. Sometimes she did, especially if she was working. It seemed to make the tasks go more quickly.

The only thing that spoiled her happiness in her current life was the fact that Frances grew sicker daily. She spent more and more time in her bed, until after a few weeks, she was lying in it all day long, coming down only for an hour or two at a time. She lost weight steadily; she could keep very little food down. And she was often in pain.

It saddened Juliet terribly to see her this way. She had grown quite close to Frances while she'd been there, until

Frances seemed almost like part of her own family. Juliet could only imagine how much worse Amos and Ethan must feel when they saw her suffering.

Amos and Ethan finished the planting, including the vegetable garden near the house. The next Saturday, Amos drove the wagon into town to buy supplies, and Juliet went with him, leaving Ethan at home to look after Frances. The spring day was sunny and warm, and Juliet looked around her happily. She felt excited and eager, and she had to laugh at the thought that going into Steadman, Nebraska, would be enough to get her excited.

When they reached the town, Juliet walked around, looking in storefronts while Amos bought his supplies at the lumber store. She paused in front of the millinery shop, gazing at the hats on display in the window. She would have loved to buy a new hat, and she had some of the money she had saved from her weeks of salary. It wouldn't matter if she didn't save *all* her money, she thought; it would just mean having to wait a little longer to leave for the East, but that prospect no longer filled her with dread.

She started to go inside the store, but then she thought about the shop owner and the contemptuous way she had spoken to her the time Juliet had come in asking for a job. Juliet turned away. She didn't want to face Miss Johnson again.

Juliet walked to the general store, where she was to

meet Amos, and gave her order for foodstuffs to the clerk. A few minutes later Amos came in and paid for the goods, adding a few things for himself. As they waited while the clerk carried their supplies out to the wagon, the front door opened and Aurica Johnson came in. Juliet's stomach tightened. Aurica glanced around, trying to look casual, but Juliet had the feeling that she was looking for something. When her eyes fell on Amos, her face brightened, and Juliet realized that Amos was the something she was looking for.

Aurica walked toward them, smiling. As she reached Juliet, she ostentatiously swept her full skirt aside so that it did not brush against Juliet's, and spoke to Amos, without glancing toward Juliet. "Why, Amos Morgan," Aurica simpered up at him. "It's so nice to see you."

Juliet moved away to a display of work gloves, staring down at the counter unseeingly, her cheeks flushing with embarrassment at the other woman's slight.

Aurica cast a glance toward Juliet, standing a few feet away, and lowered her voice, "Are you here with . . . *her?*"

Amos looked over at Juliet, then back to Aurica. "Why, yes. Miss Drake is our housekeeper, you know."

Aurica's eyes widened expressively. "Really! I'm surprised. Have . . . well, this is hard to put delicately . . ."

Amos's eyes narrowed, and he folded his arms. "Why don't you try putting it bluntly, then? I've never been noted for my delicacy."

Juliet would have been amused by Amos's words and tone toward the interfering woman at any other time, but today her sense of humor was suppressed by the embarrassment rising in her. It was obvious that Aurica Johnson was about to denigrate Juliet to Amos, and while Juliet had endured slights before, somehow suffering one now and here, in front of Amos, seemed far more hurtful than any she had received before. She wished she could reach out and snatch Aurica away, just grab one of those long, stiff curls that lay across her shoulder and drag her bodily from the store.

Aurica started to bridle, but then thought better of it and leaned forward confidentially, laying her hand on Amos's sleeve. "Haven't you heard what she was? It's quite scandalous. She was an actress."

She paused meaningfully, waiting for a reaction from Amos, her eyes fixed on his face. Juliet thought with longing of slapping those long white fingers off Amos's sleeve.

Amos simply looked at her. "Yes?"

"Well, an actress . . . you know what they are like."

"No, what are they like? I have never been acquainted with many actresses," Amos replied blandly. "I take it you must know some well."

Juliet covered her mouth to hide her smile at Aurica Johnson's shocked expression and turned around to watch them openly. Amos was definitely not reacting the way Miss Johnson had assumed he would.

"Of course I don't know any actresses!" Aurica exclaimed. "Not at all!"

"Oh." Amos appeared puzzled. "I assumed you must since you spoke so knowledgeably of them."

"Mr. Morgan, really, that's an insult to suggest that I would associate with actresses!"

"Is it? You mean that you were insulting my house-keeper a moment ago when you told me that she was an actress? That hardly seems like a lady of your stature, Miss Johnson."

A bubble of laughter escaped Juliet at Amos's pointedly ingenuous words.

Bright red spots of outrage blossomed on Aurica's pale cheeks and she stepped back from Amos, her body stiff. "Mr. Morgan! I'm sure I don't understand your sense of humor. You have taken an actress into your house, and everyone knows that they're scarlet women! How can you live with yourself knowing that your young son is exposed to that kind of influence? I would think you would be concerned about the way everyone is talking about you and that woman. The rumors are rampant all over this town!"

"I'm sure you have done your share to keep them flying."

"Well, really! I won't stand here and accept that kind of—of—"

"Insult?" Amos suggested. His brows drew together fiercely, and his voice grew louder. "Yet you seem to think it is all right for you to stand not four feet away from Miss Drake and insult her—not even directly, but to another person."

Aurica twitched back her skirts and started to walk around Amos, but he stepped squarely in her path. "Mr. Morgan! What are you doing?" Aurica hissed. "People are watching!"

"You mean you are ashamed to hear what you've been saying? Good, you should be. But you are the one who began this conversation, and I intend that you stay and finish it."

Aurica glanced around at the other occupants of the store, all watching them now, gape-mouthed, and her face turned chalky, her cheeks flaming redder than ever. Juliet felt a twinge of sympathy for the woman, despite Aurica's remarks about her. It was not pleasant to be on the receiving end of Amos's ire, even when there weren't several people watching.

"I am no gossipmonger, unlike you," Amos said flatly, in a loud, clear voice. "Therefore, I have not been privy to whatever rumors are flying around this town concerning me or Miss Drake or my son. But I'm going to tell you, so that everyone's curiosity will be satisfied. There is not and never has been anything even the slightest bit scandalous in Miss Drake's stay at my house. She is my housekeeper, and an excellent one, I might add, and that is all. It would be obvious to anyone of sensitivity and understanding that Miss Drake is not remotely a scarlet woman. She is a virtuous, hard-working, up-standing young woman and a good friend to my sister. I will not hold myself up as any paragon of virtue, but I think everyone in this town knows that Frances is a true and proper lady. For anyone to suggest that Frances would condone an immoral liaison under her own roof would be an insult to Frances herself!"

"Well, of course not . . . everyone knows . . . Frances is a wonderful . . . perfect lady," Aurica gabbled frantically, backing up from him. "It's only that . . . well, she's sick, and . . ."

Amos's expression turned thunderous, and his voice boomed out, "Then you are saying that I would carry on an affair under the same roof where my sister lies dying, knowing that she is too weak and ill to realize it or do anything about it! If you were a man, I'd call you outside for that!"

"Amos!" Juliet hurried over to stand between Amos and Aurica, who had turned so pale and wide-eyed that Juliet was afraid she might faint on the spot. "Please! I'm sure that Miss Johnson didn't mean to imply anything like that. Did you, Miss Johnson?" She turned toward Aurica questioningly.

Silently Aurica shook her head, her mouth opening and closing like a fish but no sound coming out.

"There. You see?" Juliet swung back around to Amos, smiling sweetly. "No one would ever question Frances's virtue or your devotion to her."

"No," Amos said with heavy irony, "just the virtue of a woman whom she knows nothing about. That, I'm sure, is much more proper." He executed a bow toward Aurica, mocking in its briefness. "I apologize, Miss Johnson. I am afraid I tend to get somewhat fierce when the virtue of my family and friends is questioned. Please excuse me."

He turned to Juliet, holding out his arm for her to take. "Miss Drake? I believe it's time to go."

"Yes, I think you're right." Juliet smiled back and took his arm, and they walked out of the store.

They climbed into the wagon outside. Amos clicked to the mules, and they started off. Juliet supposed she ought to feel embarrassed and upset by what Aurica

Johnson had said about her, but the truth was she wanted
to smile. Those minor feelings were drowned in a flood of
warmth and pride. *Amos had defended her*. Juliet wanted
to laugh; she wanted to hug him. *Amos had defended her*.

Seven

Juliet looked up from the table, where she was kneading dough. Strangely, the room seemed darker than it had earlier. She glanced out the window. The sun had disappeared behind masses of dark gray clouds. As she watched, a gust of wind sent dust and bits of plants swirling across the yard. A storm was brewing. Juliet punched the dough once more and left it to rise, tossing a cotton dishcloth over it. She washed her hands and walked to the front door to see what the sky looked like in the west.

As she opened the door, a blast of wind whipped it out of her hands and slammed it against the wall. The western sky before her was almost black, and, as she watched, lightning crackled through the clouds. A primitive fear clutched at her heart. She couldn't remember when she'd seen the sky look this dark and ominous. It was still afternoon, but one wouldn't have known it from the increasing gloom. Thunder boomed, and lightning forked across the sky again.

Juliet grabbed the door and shoved it to, locking it as though that could keep out the storm. She went back into the kitchen and peered anxiously out both windows. Where were Amos and Ethan? It looked as if there would be a real downpour in a few minutes. She saw the black-and-white cat streaking into the barn, and Jupiter, Ethan's dog, came into the yard and stood stiffly, alternately sniffing the wind and barking ferociously. The thunder cracked again, and the dog whirled and ran for the barn, stopping in the doorway to turn and bark again. Juliet smiled at his false bravado.

"Juliet!" The word was faint, and Juliet turned, listening. Had Frances called her?

She left the kitchen and went up the stairs. Frances called her name again, and Juliet hurried the last few feet to her room. Frances was sitting up in bed, her brow wrinkled with worry. She looked frail and wan; it struck Juliet how much weight Frances had lost in the short amount of time that Juliet had been there.

"Hello." Juliet pasted on a smile to cover her anxiety. "There's a storm brewing."

"I know. That's why I called you. It looks like twister weather to me. We better get down to the storm cellar."

Juliet's smile faltered. "Twister?" She hadn't thought of that.

"Yes. A tornado. They come in the spring. Have you ever seen one?"

"No. I—I've heard of them. But I've never been in one."

"They're terrible. They can tear a house to pieces." Frances pushed aside her covers and got out of bed, putting her feet into her slippers and reached for her robe. "That's why we need to go to the storm cellar."

"All right." Quickly Juliet helped her on with her robe, casting a nervous glance out the window. The roiling clouds were moving toward them rapidly, and the sky was growing darker every minute.

She put a hand under Frances's arm and walked with her out of the room and down the hall toward the back staircase. Frances moved with agonizing slowness, and with almost every step she leaned more and more heavily on Juliet. Soon Juliet had her arm around Frances's waist and Frances's arm around her shoulders. Frances was tall, like all the Morgans, and despite the weight she had lost, she was still as heavy or heavier than Juliet.

At the top of the stairs Frances sagged as she looked down. "Let me sit for a minute," she said, her breath ragged, and she grabbed the banister and lowered herself to the floor with Juliet's help. She leaned against the banister, eyes closed. After a moment, she said, "We're supposed to open the windows. That's what Ma always did. That way there isn't such pressure."

"All right. I'll do that while you rest." Juliet was glad for something to do.

She ran to the end of the hall and made her way through each of the bedrooms, flinging up every window. The wind whooshed through the rooms, so chilly and strong that it raised goose bumps on her skin. It was as dark as dusk out there now, and rain had started to fall in fat drops. As she hurried back to join Frances on the stairs, thunder broke overhead, so loud that it made her jump.

Juliet helped Frances to her feet again, and they continued down the staircase. Frances clung to the railing with one hand, and her other arm was heavy on Juliet's shoulders. She had to pause to catch her breath on the landing, and by the time they reached the bottom, her breath was labored.

"I'll open the windows downstairs while you rest a minute," Juliet suggested.

"No. You better go on. I'll follow when I can."

"Don't be silly. The windows need to be opened; you said so yourself."

Juliet left before Frances could raise any more argument and rushed through the first floor, flinging open the doors and shoving up the windows. The rain was coming down in torrents, and the wind had become enormously strong. In the distance, along the road to the highway, the windbreak firs tossed and twisted in the wind, and bits and pieces of them went flying past along with dust and straw. Juliet's heart thumped with fear. Even the worst moment of singing on stage hadn't been scary in this way; she had never before faced such a wild, strong natural force. Never had she feared that she might actually be killed.

"Frances, get up!" She ran back to the other woman. "You have to get up. We have to go!"

Frances took a breath and hauled herself up by the banister. "I'm sorry."

"Don't waste your breath. We have to hurry."

Juliet looped Frances's arm over her shoulders and took a firm grip around her waist. Cradling her against her hip, she took as much of Frances's weight as she could and walked through the back hall and the kitchen to the outside door. It seemed to take an eternity. The doors and windows rattled under the force of the wind. It shrieked around the corners, drowned only by the frequent bursts of thunder.

When Juliet at last reached the door and turned the knob, the wind flung it open. The rain poured in, borne by the wind, and splattered them with its chilly drops. Juliet struggled against the wind out onto the stoop. Their skirts were whipped around wildly, and the wind jerked strands of their hair from their neat buns. Juliet, half supporting Frances, pushed her way down the steps, fighting the wind every inch of the way.

It wasn't far from the kitchen to the low, flat door to the storm cellar, but against the wind, with the rain beating down on them, it seemed like miles. Frances grew heavier with each step, and finally, halfway to the cellar, she collapsed, her legs folding under her, and sank down to the ground. Juliet bent over her, trying to pull her up.

"Come on! We have to keep on!" She screamed over the noise of the storm.

Weakly Frances shook her head, and Juliet had to bend her head down to her lips to hear her answer, "I can't. I can't walk anymore. You go on. Let me rest."

"You can't rest now," Juliet told her firmly. "And not in the rain. You have to come with me. Please, Frances, please, stand up."

She shook her head. "It's useless. Go on."

"I can't leave you here!" Juliet shrieked. "You have to come! I can't leave you!"

Frances said nothing else, only leaned wearily against the side of the house, her eyes closed, her breath coming in gasps that shook her frail body. Juliet glanced desperately around her. The rain and wind were almost blinding, but it was obvious that there was no help for her anywhere around here. Ethan and Amos hadn't come back, and there was no one here except her and Frances.

Overhead the sky was almost black, lit now and then by the crackle of lightning. The wind was bending the firs almost to the ground. As she stood there, in the distance a cloud seemed to dip and elongate. In horror she realized what that dark funnel was as it moved down to the ground and then back up. A twister!

Fear shot through her, bringing a strength she wouldn't have guessed she had. Juliet bent and grabbed Frances by the waist, hauling her to her feet. Frances swayed, leaning against the house, and Juliet stepped in front of her, pulling Frances's arms forward over her own shoulders and crossing them at the wrist in front of her chest. Then, firmly gripping Frances's opposite arm in each hand, she bent over, taking most of Frances's weight on her back, and dragged her across the stretch of ground separating them from the storm cellar door.

The wind fought her at every step, and she could scarcely see for the fierce, needlelike rain. Her heart was pumping as if it would burst, but Juliet was seized with determination, filled with strength. She refused to die out here in the middle of nowhere. She would save herself and Frances.

She reached the door at last and pulled it up. The wind caught it and flung it back, ripping it from its hinges. A noise like an enormous train bearing down upon her filled Juliet's ears. She fell to her knees, cracking them sharply against the wooden frame of the door, and Frances's weight bore her forward. They tumbled awkwardly into the dark pit of the storm cellar.

The cellar was shallow, and Juliet did not fall far, but, with Frances's weight atop her, it knocked the wind from her. For a moment she was aware of nothing but the pain inside her, the terrifying inability to draw a breath, while above her the tornado thundered across them. Dust and leaves, pieces of the fir trees pattered down upon her and Frances, as did the rain.

At last Juliet was able to breath again, and she lay, drawing in shallow gasps of air, still weighted down by Frances's body, while outside the storm swept onward. Finally she rolled over, pushing Frances off her, and staggered to her feet. The cellar was so shallow that she couldn't stand upright except in the hole where the door had been ripped away. She looked out at the farmyard, the rain pelting down on her head. The tornado had passed. The darkest clouds were now toward the northeast of them, and the sky was beginning to appear again in the southwest. The wind was still fierce, whipping her hair around her face, but it wasn't the uncontrollable force it had been when she had staggered to the cellar door.

She sank down onto the floor of the cellar and leaned back against the wall, trying to pull herself together. They had survived the storm. She lowered her head. Suddenly she felt weak and almost sick. It was all she could do not to cry.

Juliet looked across at Frances, lying on the floor in the dim light from the open door. She was pale, her eyes closed, soaked to the bone just as Juliet was. Juliet couldn't hold back the tears any longer; they began to stream down her face.

She thought of Amos and Ethan, somewhere out in the open during this storm, and her tears flowed faster.

"Juliet?" Frances's voice was weak, barely more than a whisper.

"Yes?" Juliet's head snapped up. Frances's eyes were open and she was looking at her. Hastily Juliet wiped her arms across her cheeks and eyes and gulped down her sobs.

"What happened?"

"I—I'm not sure. We got to the cellar somehow." Juliet swallowed hard and pushed the hair back from her face, straightening herself both mentally and physically. This wasn't the time to give way to hysteria. She still had to see after Frances; it was even more imperative that she be in control if something had happened to Amos and Ethan.

She crawled across the floor to Frances's side. "Are you all right?"

A small smile flickered over Frances's bloodless lips. "As all right as I can be, I think."

Juliet felt herself blushing. *What a clumsy thing to say!* "I'm sorry. I mean, I was afraid maybe you had broken a bone or something in the fall."

"No. I can move everything." She sighed. "I don't want to, though. I'm sorry, but I'm so tired."

"Of course you are. It's miraculous the way you managed to make it downstairs and out here."

"I was barely conscious the last part of the trip," Frances said slowly. "You got me here all by yourself."

Juliet shrugged. "Sort of. I'm not sure exactly how I did it." She laid a hand on her arm. "But you're freezing lying there in those wet clothes."

"There're blankets down here." Frances's voice was barely a whisper, and her eyes began to flutter closed.

Juliet glanced around the small room. It was the root cellar, too, and there were small piles of potatoes and onions against the walls, as well as a barrel and several shelves full of canning jars, most of them empty. In the corner, she spotted a small metal trunk, and she made her way over to it and opened it. Inside were blankets, a lantern, candles, and matches.

"Hallelujah!" she exclaimed joyfully, pulling the treasures from the trunk. "We've got everything we need right here."

She lit the lantern to dispel the gloom and set it on the ground. Then she crawled back to Frances and helped her into a sitting position. Juliet peeled down Frances's wet nightgown and robe and wrapped a blanket around her shoulders, leaving enough of it above her body to curl up over her wet head. Frances lay back down, and Juliet discreetly threw the other blanket over her legs before she pulled down the sodden garments and dropped them in a pile. She tucked the blanket in all around Frances.

Finally, satisfied that Frances was as warm as she could make her, she sat back with a sigh and considered her situation. Outside the storm was almost gone. The wind had died down, and the rain had stopped, and it was growing lighter by the minute inside the cellar. She stood up and looked out at the farmyard again. The clouds were moving away, the sky reappearing sunnily.

The farmyard had survived the storm largely intact. There were branches scattered around, and two of the shutters had come loose and were dangling. The weather-vane atop the house had snapped and fallen, and several shingles had come off the roof. But the barn and house were still standing, as were most of the fences around the pens. Even the chicken coop had only partially collapsed. The hens were free and squawking about the yard, smoothing their feathers and pecking for fresh worms in the aftermath of the rain.

Juliet glanced back at Frances and gnawed worriedly on her lower lip. Frances needed to be back in bed, warm and cozy. But Juliet knew that she could never get Frances up the little ladder and outside. She would have to wait for Amos and his son to arrive.

Provided that they did arrive.

Provided they weren't dead.

A shiver ran through her. Juliet rubbed her arms vigorously. She needed to get out of her wet clothes. She was soaked clear through to the skin, and the sodden mass of skirts and petticoats lay cold and heavy upon her.

With one final look at Frances to make sure she was sleeping comfortably, Juliet climbed the short ladder and crawled out onto the wet ground. She stood up awkwardly, pulling her heavy skirts out of the way, and started down the side of the house to the door.

As she walked she glanced toward the barn, then out into the fields. There she saw two men hurrying toward the house. Her heart leapt into her throat. Amos! Amos and Ethan were all right!

"Amos!" she cried, waving her arm wildly. "Amos!"

She picked up her skirts and began to run toward them.

"Juliet!" Amos dropped the hoe he was carrying and broke into a run, also. Ethan followed on his heels.

"Thank God, you're all right!" Juliet cried.

Amos reached her and his arms went out and wrapped around her, lifting her off the ground. He squeezed her to him so tightly she could hardly breathe, and for an instant she felt the touch of his head against hers. It was wonderfully warm and secure in his arms, as though his strength and size could protect her from everything bad, and Juliet clung to him, burying her face in his chest.

"Are you all right?" he asked hoarsely, and Juliet nodded without saying anything.

Ethan came up beside them. "Juliet! Are you okay? Pa, is she hurt?"

"No." Amos set her down abruptly and took a step back. He looked away. "Where's Frances? Is she all right?

Did you make it to the storm cellar in time?"

"Yes. She's in the cellar."

Amos's brows rushed together. "You mean you just left her down there alone?"

Why did he always assume the worst about her? After all that had happened and the emotions that had buffeted her for the past few hours, his suspicion was simply too much. A swift anger swelled up in Juliet.

"I couldn't get her up by myself!" she snapped. "I was going into the house to put on some dry clothes. I'm sure you think that's very selfish of me. But, frankly, at this point, I don't care what you think! I don't know why I even worried about you. No mere disaster could be your match in meanness."

She knew that she was on the verge of tears, and she wasn't about to let him see that he'd made her cry, so Juliet whirled and ran for the house.

"Pa, why'd you have to say that?" Ethan asked, giving him a reproving look. "You know Juliet wouldn't have left Aunt Frances if it wasn't all right."

Amos shot him a dark look. "I don't need you reprimanding me, thank you. It just came out wrong. It always does with her." He started toward the cellar. "Come on, let's get Frances out of there."

As they drew closer to the storm cellar, they saw that the door to it had been ripped from its hinges. Amos exchanged a look with his son.

Ethan let out a whistle. "That must have been some wind to pull it right off like that! Do you think the tornado we saw going up in the clouds actually hit here?"

Amos's mouth tightened. "I don't know. The house and barn weren't hit. But it must have come awfully close."

He climbed down into the cellar. Frances was sleeping, wrapped in the cellar's blankets. Her wet clothes lay in a heap a few feet away from her. Amos felt a pang of guilt as he saw how Juliet had taken care of his sister, undressing her and making sure she was warm before she went into the house to get warm and dry herself.

"Frances." He knelt beside her. "Fanny? It's me, Amos."

Frances's eyes fluttered open, and she gave him a small smile. "Amos. Thank heavens you're all right. And Ethan?"

"I'm right here, Aunt Frances." Ethan stuck his head down into the cellar, grinning at her. "We're fine. You know Pa—Miss Juliet said he's too mean to die, and she's right."

"Juliet . . . how is she?" Frances asked, frowning in concern. "She was so good to me." Tears sparkled in her dark eyes. "Oh, Amos, I was so weak I couldn't get down here by myself. I almost didn't make it at all. I wouldn't have except for Juliet's help. She carried me the last few yards; she wouldn't leave me, even though we could see the twister coming. If she'd been hurt, it would have been my fault."

Chagrin and regret twisted more deeply into Amos at her words. He didn't have the nerve to look at his son, knowing the expression that would be on his face.

"Well, she's all right, so you needn't worry about it,"

he told Frances gruffly. "It isn't your fault that you're feeling weak. You'll be stronger soon."

Frances gave him a fond look. "No. It's sweet of you to tell me that, but we both know I won't. It wasn't worth her risking her life to save someone who probably won't be here by the time harvest comes."

"Don't say that!"

"One of us might as well face the truth, don't you think?"

"It's not the truth. You're going to get well, damn it."

"Oh, Amos." Tears formed in Frances's eyes again, and she reached up to pat his cheek. "I'm so weak I don't think I can even climb that ladder out of here."

"Of course not. You don't need to climb it, anyway. I'll carry you out."

Gently he lifted her to her feet, keeping the blankets wrapped around her, and helped her over to the open doorway of the cellar, where they could stand upright without having to crouch. He picked her up and handed her up to Ethan, kneeling on the ground above. Then he climbed out himself and carried her in his arms like a baby into the house and up the stairs to her room. It made his heart hurt to feel how light she was in his arms.

He laid her down in her bed and pulled the covers up. "I'll ask Juliet to come up and help you into a dry gown."

"That's all right. Don't bother her; I'm sure she's tired. I can't imagine how she managed to carry me that last bit."

The thought boggled Amos's mind as well. "There's more to her than I guessed."

Frances nodded. "I know. I misjudged her, too, when she first came here. But she's a strong, good woman." She hesitated, looking at her brother. She wasn't given to saying this sort of thing, any more than anyone else in their family, but she felt compelled to say it now, "You know, she'd make you a good wife, Amos. She's terribly pretty, and she has lots of heart."

A flush rose in Amos's cheeks, and he looked away. "What kind of talk is that? I don't need a wife; I've done fine without one all these years."

"Have you?" Sadness tinged her voice. "I'm not sure I've done so well without a husband. I look back at my life now, and it seems wasted. Dying gives you a different way of looking at things."

"Don't say that. You're life's not been wasted, and neither has mine. We've done well with the farm; we've done what we should."

"But what about what we wanted? Did we ever do that?"

"Sometimes what you want isn't what's best." He gave her a bleak look. "I know."

"But just because it's what you want doesn't necessarily make it wrong, either. Amos, I know how much that woman hurt you, but—"

He turned aside abruptly. "There's no point talking about this."

"Yes, there is!" The sudden strength in her voice surprised them both, and Amos turned back to look at her. "I want you to be happy," she told him fiercely. "I want to die knowing that you will be happy. Please, Amos . . . just promise me that you won't close yourself off to Juliet."

"Frances . . ."

"Please? Promise me that?"

He grimaced. "All right," he told her grudgingly.

"All right, what?"

"I promise I won't close myself off to her."

"You'll think about what I said? You'll give her a chance?"

"Yes! Yes, I'll think about it!"

"Good." Frances smiled weakly.

"Now will you go to sleep?"

"Yes. I feel much better."

She smiled at him, and Amos left the room, closing the door gently behind him.

Amos walked down the steps and paused outside Juliet's door. Taking a deep breath, he rapped sharply on her door and opened it before he could change his mind and run. Inside the room, Juliet whirled around at the sound of his entrance. She stared at him, shocked into speechlessness. For an instant Amos could do nothing but stare back at her, equally frozen.

Juliet had taken off her wet clothes, dried and begun to dress again, but she had gotten no farther than her stockings, underpants, and chemise when Amos unceremoniously opened her door. A flush rose up Amos's neck into his face, and his mouth opened and closed without uttering a sound. Finally Juliet came out of her shock and grabbed the petticoat lying on her bed, pulling it up to her chest to cover her. Her movement seemed to break Amos's own paralysis, for he hastily backed out of the room and closed the door.

Almost running, he hurried down the hall and into the kitchen. He jerked open the back door and went outside, and there he really did begin to run. He dashed across the yard to the barn and didn't stop until he was inside its familiar, warm dimness. He stopped and leaned against one of the stalls, bracing his arms against it, and closed his eyes.

Lord, but he'd really done it this time! He had gone to Juliet's room to apologize. But then, like a fool, he'd barged into her room, not even waiting for her permission to enter. He had been so intent on what he had to say that he hadn't even thought about knocking. Now, he knew, she would think him not only rude and unfair, but a lecher as well!

She wouldn't be far off about that, he had to admit. He could still see in his mind's eye exactly the way she had looked: her eyes wide, color tinting her cheeks and the sweet soft, curves of her body barely hidden beneath the thin cotton chemise. Her breasts were high and round, their deep rose tips visible through the cloth. He could imagine how warm and soft they would feel beneath his hands, how tantalizingly hard the buds of her nipples would turn.

He sighed as the heat stole through him, thinking about her. He was honest enough to admit how much he wanted right now to kiss her, to hold her, to run his hands over her delicately rounded body. Just the idea of it was making him hard.

His father had always told him he was too driven by

lust, that it would get him into trouble. He had been proven right, of course, by Helen. He had been so blinded by his youthful lust that he hadn't seen what she really was. Over the years, though he had carefully stayed away from most women, he had been driven to seek out the company of loose ones, unable to curb his desires.

But Juliet Drake didn't fit into that category. Marriage, of course, was unthinkable, no matter what Frances said. He had long ago realized that marriage wasn't for the likes of him, and, besides, given the way Juliet felt about him, he knew that she would never consider it. Yet anything other than marriage was equally unthinkable. Juliet was his housekeeper, a woman living under his protection, and he could not take advantage of that. Even if Juliet would consent—which he thought highly unlikely—it would be utterly unscrupulous of him. She was young and vulnerable.

The desire that had surged in him that afternoon must be curbed. He simply had to put out of his mind the picture of Juliet in her chemise. He would steer clear of her, as he had for the whole time she had been there.

He occupied himself until it was dark by working on the collapsed side of the chicken coop. When he went inside for supper, he assiduously avoided looking at Juliet, and the only words he spoke to anyone were short requests to be passed this or that item of food on the table. As soon as supper was over, he left the table and went to his room.

Because he never looked at her directly, he didn't see the small smile that touched Juliet's lips when she realized what he was doing. The last thing he expected her to do was to initiate a conversation with him. But that was exactly what she did when he came downstairs later to take a stroll around the yard before turning in. She was wiping off the last countertop in the kitchen, finished with her chores, when he passed through to the back door. She followed him outside.

"Mr. Morgan," she called to him softly from the stoop.

He jumped, startled, and turned around. Fear clutched his heart, for he was suddenly certain that she was telling him she was leaving, after what he had done that afternoon.

He tried to answer, but he had to clear his throat before he could get out a word. "Yes?"

"You never did say what you wanted to tell me this afternoon. The reason you came into my room."

Heat flooded Amos's face, and he was glad of the covering darkness. Even so, he looked away from her. "I'm sorry. I shouldn't have barged in like that. I didn't think. It was . . ." He couldn't think of the right word to describe what he had done.

"Rude?" Juliet suggested, her voice light with amusement.

"Yes." He nodded. "Worse than that. But I didn't mean anything wrong by it. I—sometimes I get an idea in my head, and I don't think about anything else. I hope you weren't too embarrassed." *I hope you won't leave because of it.*

"It was something of a shock," Juliet admitted. She didn't add that after the surprise passed, she had been left with a warm feeling in the pit of her stomach, a kind of anticipation and excitement.

"I hope you will forgive me," Amos continued stiffly, addressing the wall beside her.

"Of course. I know it was simply a mistake." She grinned. "I didn't think you had any evil designs on my virtue."

"No! Of course not!"

The haste and emphasis with which he denied any designs on her was not precisely flattering, she thought—*not*, of course, that she wanted any such attentions from him.

"So you needn't keep avoiding me," Juliet went on. "Let's forget the whole incident, all right? I think it will be much more comfortable in this house if you and I can look each other in the eye and talk. Don't you?"

"Yes. Naturally." He felt like a fool. Why was it that this slip of a girl always acted with such poise, while he, a steady, solid man at least ten years her senior, seemed to regress into a schoolboy around her?

"Good. Then why don't you tell me why you came into my room? You must have had something you wanted to discuss."

"Yes." Amos grimaced. "The truth is, I came to apologize."

"Apologize?" Juliet stared. "Truly?"

She came down the steps of the stoop. Her face was pale in the light of the moon, and her eyes were huge and mysterious, shadows in her delicate face. Amos could not take his eyes off her.

"Yes." It was an effort to talk. He wanted only to look at her. No, that was a lie, he knew. He wanted to kiss her, as well. "About what I said to you this afternoon. I shouldn't have said you were wrong to leave Frances in the cellar by herself. I—it was simply that I was worried. I was afraid something had happened to her, and I took it out on you."

"I understand. I was worried, too, about you . . . and Ethan, of course."

"Frances told me how you helped her down to the cellar, how you risked your own life to save hers. I should have thanked you, not barked at you."

Now it was Juliet's turn to feel embarrassed. "I couldn't just leave her."

"There are those who would have when they saw a twister headed straight for them."

Juliet chuckled. "It scared me, sure enough. I grabbed her and ran as hard as I could."

"You've got pluck."

Juliet shrugged. "Is that what it's called? Usually I think it's only necessity. What else can you do when it's staring you in the face? You can't just lay down and die."

"It's not something you'd do," he agreed. "But that's why you're strong."

She looked at him, startled. "Do you really think that?"

"Of course. Why else would I say it?"

"I never thought of myself like that. I certainly never would have guessed that *you* thought I was."

"I didn't, at first. I didn't reckon you could last out

here. Maybe you didn't know how to do a lot of things, but I can see now that you had the grit. That's what's important. You've stuck to it and learned what you had to. You haven't given up."

Pride swelled Juliet's chest. She didn't stop to wonder why it was so important that this man had decided that she had grit. A smile flashed across her face. "Does that mean you aren't going to drive me back to town now and dump me on your sister-in-law's doorstep?"

He grinned a little shamefacedly. "You mean you hadn't figured that out yet? I could have taken you back weeks ago."

"I know. But I wasn't sure."

"Well, now you know. I'm not planning to take you back. I—you're doing just fine." Amos knew that being around this woman was going to be a trial by fire for him. But he could hardly tell her to leave just because he was afraid of his own weakness.

"That's wonderful." Juliet couldn't stop beaming. She stuck out her hand. "Let's shake on it."

Reluctantly, he took her hand. It was small and fragile in his. But there was warmth and strength in it, too. He found that he wanted to close his hand around hers and keep on holding it.

"You won't regret it," Juliet promised cheerfully.

But he already did.

Eight

The next day, Amos inspected the crops and found that the storm had done little harm to them, no doubt because the shoots were still small, barely pushing above the ground. Then he and Ethan set out to repair the damage that had been done around the farmyard. First they replaced the fallen fence rails in the animal pens. They boarded up the window in Ethan's bedroom that had been broken by a limb torn from the hickory tree. By nightfall they had also repaired the boards that had been torn from the barn walls.

The next day, Amos sent Ethan into town to fetch the lumber and shingles that they needed to complete their repairs. After Ethan left, Amos leaned a ladder against the house and climbed up onto the roof to start repairing the roof.

Some time later, Juliet, working in the kitchen, was surprised to hear the sound of a horse outside in the yard. Wiping the flour from her hands onto her apron, she walked down the hall to the front door and opened it.

John Sanderson was tying his horse's reins to the

hitching post in front of the porch, and he looked up and smiled at her. "Juliet!"

Juliet sighed inwardly. She had no time for John Sanderson right now. He had come to call on her twice more during the past few weeks, though she had tried to be quietly discouraging. Obviously she was going to have to be more direct and simply tell him that she didn't wish to see him anymore. It was the height of silliness to have let him come to call just because it annoyed Amos.

"I wanted to drop by and see how you had weathered the storm," John said, coming up onto the porch.

"We got through it all right. No one was hurt. Just a little damage to the buildings." Juliet felt a little ashamed of her uncharitable reaction to his visit, given his concern for her. To make up for it, she smiled and motioned toward the wooden chairs on the porch. "Won't you sit down? Could I get you something to drink? Or eat?"

"No, I'm fine. Knowing that you're all right is tonic enough. I was worried about you."

Juliet forced another smile. John's sweet words always rubbed her the wrong way. She sat down in one of the two chairs, and John sat beside her, pulling his chair closer to hers.

"I saw the Morgans' wagon going into town," he told her, his voice low and soft, confidential. "I knew it was my chance to see you alone."

"Indeed?" Juliet turned to face John, her eyebrows lifting. "Why would you want to see me alone?"

He grinned, reaching over to take one of her hands. "I

can see that you are an actress. You deliver that line like a lady of the manor."

"I'm not sure I know what you're talking about."

She started to pull her hand away, but Sanderson held on fast to it. "Come now, Juliet, why pretend? I think you know how I feel about you. It must be obvious."

He lifted her hand to his mouth and kissed her palm. His mustache tickled her skin. "You're a beautiful woman," he went on, his voice growing husky. "I know you've had men want you before."

Juliet snatched her hand back as though it had been burned. Color flooded her cheeks. Amos was right about this man!

"I'm afraid you've made a mistake, Mr. Sanderson," she began coldly. "This is hardly the proper topic for a conversation."

"Oh, hell," he said scornfully, "don't tell me you're going to start in about your loyalty to Morgan."

"I beg your pardon?"

"He'd do, I suppose, when you're suddenly dumped in Steadman, penniless. But now that you've been around him for awhile, you couldn't want to stay here." Sanderson reached over and took both her hands, standing up and pulling her up with him. "I assure you, you'll find it much more pleasant with me."

He ran his hands insinuatingly down her arms, smiling into her eyes. There was no mistaking the sexual intent of his words and smile.

Juliet jerked her arms away from his hands and stepped back. Fury swept up her, making her voice shake.

"Exactly what are you saying? Do you think that I—that Amos and I—" Her words stumbled to a halt; she was too angry to be coherent. She took a deep breath. "You think that I am his mistress? And you're offering me the same position?"

Sanderson looked puzzled. "Juliet, what's the matter? Come now, we're adults. There's no need to be coy. We both know what you're doing here. I'm simply offering you a cozier bed than the one you share with Morgan."

Juliet's hand lashed out and cracked across his cheek. "How dare you! I am Mr. Morgan's housekeeper, nothing else. Why, his sister and his son live in the house with us! How can you think that he and I—what kind of opinion do you have of me that you would think I would do something like that!"

Sanderson's face hardened, shock replaced by a cold, dark anger. "Why, you little bitch!"

He grabbed her arm at the wrist, squeezing so hard her hand went numb. "You think you can hit me and get away with it? I don't take that from anybody, least of all some strumpet off the streets. You think you're the Queen of Sheba because you're bedding down with Amos Morgan?"

He twisted her arm back so hard that Juliet let out a cry and tears sprang into her eyes. "Let me go!"

"No, goddammit! Not til I've taught you—"

Overhead there was a crash, then several heavy thuds across the porch roof. Both Sanderson and Juliet glanced up at the roof, startled. Then Juliet remembered: Amos! Amos had been up on top of the house, fixing the roof!

Had he heard everything they'd said? Humiliation flooded her, wiping out even the pain in her arm from Sanderson's cruel grip.

As if in answer to her thoughts, there was a final, heavier thud, and Amos swung down from the porch roof. He hung for an instant by his hands, then dropped, with surprising lightness and agility for a man his size, to the ground.

"Let go of her." Amos's voice wasn't loud, just deadly cold; it sent a chill through Juliet. His face was equally hard, and there was no mistaking the threat of his huge hands balled up into fists at his side.

"Morgan!" John stared at him in amazement, and he quickly dropped Juliet's arm. "I—I didn't realize you were here."

"Obviously. Now I suggest that you apologize to Miss Drake, then get off my porch and don't ever step foot back on it."

"Apologize!" Sanderson went bug-eyed with astonishment. "What in the hell—look." He turned his hands out, palm upward, in a placating manner. "I shouldn't have encroached on your territory. I'm sorry. I admit I was wrong. But I got carried away. You of all people should know how very enticing she is. It's not the first time a woman's caused a man to make a fool of himself."

"What!" Juliet let out a screech at Sanderson's implication that it was somehow her fault that he had acted the way he had.

"You don't need any help to make a fool of yourself," Amos replied stonily. "And I didn't say to apologize to me. It's Miss Drake's forgiveness you should be begging; it was her you slandered."

"Slandered?" Sanderson's tone was derisive, but he turned and made a mocking bow toward Juliet. "Oh, I beg your pardon, *Miss Drake*. How could I have been so mistaken?"

His mouth twisted bitterly, and he whipped back around and trotted down the steps toward his horse. Amos's hand lashed out and grasped his shirt at the collar, jerking him over in front of him. He stared down into Sanderson's eyes.

"Damn you. Half the town knows what you are, Sanderson. You're an adulterer, and now I've seen that you're a bully as well. But only with women, isn't that right? Someone weaker than yourself. Well, I don't fit into that category, so you better listen to me goddamn good and well: If I hear that you've said one word about this incident to anyone, that you've spread even a single rumor about Miss Drake, I'll come after you. And I won't stop until no woman'd look at that face of yours twice. Do you understand?"

Sanderson's mouth thinned into a bitter line, but he nodded his head shortly.

"All right."

Amos released the man, and Sanderson hurried away to his horse and got on it, riding out of the yard as if the hounds of hell were after him.

"Oh, Amos." Tears filled Juliet's eyes, and she pressed her hand against her mouth. She had never been so filled with shame in her life. She had accused Amos of being in the wrong, of being a prude; she had defended Sanderson when all the time Amos had been right. He must think she was a fool, so easily charmed by flattery and a handsome face that she had paid no attention to John Sanderson's true character, even after she had been warned.

That was bad enough, but worse were the things that John had said to her, the implications he had made about her position as Amos's mistress. Aurica Johnson had implied the same thing. Was that what everyone in town thought? Did everyone despise her? And had she ruined Amos's reputation, too, just by working for him? Sanderson's words had made her feel dirty and ashamed, as if she had indeed done something wrong. The fact that Amos had been a witness to the whole humiliating scene made it even worse.

Juliet's face flooded with red, and she whirled and ran back into the house, where she busied herself with putting together a lunch for Frances. She arranged the buttered bread and thin soup—about all that Frances could get down anymore—on a tray and added a spoon and a napkin, artfully folded into the shape of a rose to perk up Frances's spirits a bit.

When she climbed the stairs to Frances's room, however, she saw that for once nothing was necessary to bring Frances out of her lassitude. There were faint spots of color in her cheeks, and her eyes were bright.

"What was all that ruckus I heard out there?" she asked as soon as Juliet stepped through the doorway.

"Oh, my!" Juliet stopped and looked at her. "I'm sorry.

I didn't think that you could have heard it, too."

"I don't know how I could not hear it," Frances returned a little peevishly. "It sounded like a herd of horses ran across our roof."

Juliet had to giggle at the description. "No. It was only Amos."

"What in the world was Amos doing running around on the roof? And what was that yelling? Was someone else here?"

Juliet nodded. "Yes. It was John Sanderson. I'm sorry it disturbed you. I should have come up and put your mind at ease, but I didn't think you'd heard."

"John Sanderson! What was he doing here? Mighty odd time to come calling, right after a twister."

"He said he wanted to see if we had come through it all right. He seemed concerned."

"Oh. He must be awful attracted to you." Frances frowned.

"I think he came because he saw the wagon going into town and he thought both Amos and Ethan were in it. He thought I was alone, well, except for you."

"And a lot of help I'd be," Frances concluded disgustedly. "Did that man make an indecent proposal to you?"

Juliet gaped at her. Did everyone know what Sanderson was like except her? "Yes," she said, her voice low.

Frances sighed. "I should have warned you about him."

"Amos did," Juliet told her glumly. "But I didn't believe him."

"Whyever not?" Frances gave her an odd look. "Amos

is always truthful. Fact is, he's truthful to the point of being downright annoying."

"I should have known that, I guess. I should have at least checked it out to see if it was true. Obviously, all I would have had to do was ask you."

"So that noise I heard must have been Amos coming to your rescue."

Juliet nodded, blushing and glancing away. "I was happy to see him, I'll tell you."

"Yes, it's a good thing he was there." Frances was sipping from her cup of broth as she talked, and Juliet was glad to see that in her interest in the subject she was eating more food than usual.

"Yes." For the first time, embarrassment wasn't Juliet's only emotion when she thought about the scene. She remembered how heart-stoppingly fierce Amos had looked. How he had stood up for her. "He sent Mr. Sanderson away, even made him apologize to me."

"Exactly right. You can always count on Amos."

"Can you?"

"Of course." Frances gave her a quizzical look, as if she must be lacking in brains to question the fact.

Juliet wondered what it would be like to know, unquestioningly, that one had a man like Amos to rely on, no matter what happened. It had been a long time since she had had anybody except herself to rely on. Even when her father was still alive, she had been the one on whose shoulders most of the burden of decisions and actions fell.

"I didn't even thank him," Juliet murmured.

"What?" Frances glanced at her curiously.

"I didn't thank Amos. After what he'd done for me. I was so embarrassed I came back into the house." Her forehead wrinkled in consternation. "He must think I'm awfully rude."

Frances shook her head, smiling. "Don't worry about it. Amos probably didn't even notice. He wouldn't expect you to thank him."

"But I should have."

That thought nagged at her over the course of the afternoon. Lunchtime came and went, but Amos did not come down to eat. Later in the afternoon, Ethan came home. He dropped into the kitchen to tell Juliet the news from town about the tornado and the damage it had done, then he went out to help his father on the roof. They stayed there, hammering, until the sun went down.

It was easier to face Amos with Ethan around, and Juliet managed to get through supper without either blushing or having to speak directly to Amos. He looked at her as little as she looked at him, and he did so in the same way, with uncertain sidelong glances.

After she had washed the supper dishes, Juliet went out to the barn to find Amos and thank him for what he had done that morning. It was embarrassing, and she hated to do it, but she knew she had to.

She stepped inside the wide doorway of the barn and peered around. "Amos?"

She walked toward the back of the barn, where light poured from the lantern. She hadn't been this far inside the barn before. Against the far wall there was a tall counter with a high stool on which Amos now sat. A wooden chest stood to one side, opened. There were tools inside it and more tools hanging on the wall. There were also several shelves below the tools, and it was to these that Juliet's eyes were drawn.

The shelves were filled with cunning figures carved of wood. Some were statues and others were pieces of wood left in their natural state, with figures carved in bas relief, looking as if the creature was coming out of the wood itself. There were animals, people, and strange, unreal creatures, things that looked like elves and fairies and sylphs, trolls and monsters. Whatever they were, each was well done, life-like and evoked an immediate response in the viewer, whether of amusement, fear, or liking.

Juliet gasped, coming to a halt and staring at the pieces. Amos, hearing her gasp, whirled, and an expression of chagrin went across his face.

"Amos!" Juliet forgot what she had come here for in her fascination with the wooden pieces behind Amos. "Did you do these?"

He nodded, shrugging. "It's kind of a hobby. I started whittling when I was a youngster."

"Why haven't you ever mentioned it? They're wonderful!" She went up to examine them more closely, while Amos looked on in an uncomfortable mixture of pleasure, embarrassment, and anxiety.

"You like them?" He sounded uncertain.

"They're delightful!" Juliet walked up and down, peering at the figures on the shelves. She would never have dreamed that these fanciful creatures were made by Amos. He seemed so stolid and practical. Yet these pieces spoke of a fertile imagination, as well as skill.

Juliet glanced at him again, feeling as if she were seeing him for the first time. "You're quite good," she told him.

"Thank you." He couldn't meet her eyes. "Some of them seem pretty foolish, I guess, but . . ."

"Oh, no! They aren't foolish at all. I love them."

"I started out copying people out of a book of fairy tales my mother had," he explained. "And I liked them—the creatures that weren't real."

She pulled her eyes away from them and smiled at him. "I always loved fairy tales."

For an instant there was a closeness between them, as if some sort of recognition had passed between the two of them. Then Amos stepped away, and the brief bond was broken. Juliet was reminded of why she had come.

"I didn't mean to disturb you," Juliet began almost formally. "I came out here because I wanted to thank you for what you did this morning."

He shrugged. "It was nothing."

"It was quite a lot to me, I can assure you. I—it was very kind of you, and I should have told you so at the time. It was rude of me not to."

His teeth flashed whitely in a rare smile. "Rudeness is something I'm quite at ease with. Don't you think?"

Juliet had to smile. *Why, Amos Morgan was actually joking!* It was hard to believe.

"I have to tell you something else," she continued, emboldened by his easy manner. "You were right when you told me about Mr. Sanderson. I should have listened to you. I'm sorry."

He shrugged. "There's nothing to apologize to me for. You're the one who was hurt. I could see you were . . . mighty attached to him; you didn't want to believe it. I didn't want to cause you any pain. I'm sorry. I guess you must have cared for him a lot."

Juliet stared at him. Then she giggled. Amos frowning, puzzled.

"I'm sorry." She pressed her fingers to her lips to quell the laughter bubbling up. "It just struck me as funny."

"Funny?" It was obvious from the look on his face that he thought she had lost her mind.

"I mean, that I cared a lot about him. I didn't give a hoot about John Sanderson."

"You didn't?" He looked disbelieving.

"I didn't!" she reiterated.

"Then why did you refuse to believe me? Why did you insist on continuing to see him?"

"Oh." She gnawed at her lower lip. "Because you told me not to," she explained in a small voice.

"What? *That's* why you let him call on you? Because I didn't want you to?"

"It sounds awfully contrary when you put it that way, but . . . well, yes. It got my back up when you told me I shouldn't see him. I really wasn't interested in seeing him again; I was hoping he wouldn't come back. But when you told me that I *couldn't*, then I had to."

He shook his head, but a slow smile crept across his features. "I'll be damned," he said softly.

Juliet giggled. Her actions had been silly, but for some reason she felt more amused than embarrassed by them now. Perhaps it was because Amos had reacted with humor rather than anger.

"Could I watch you work?" she asked.

Amos seemed surprised, but he nodded and jerked his thumb in the direction of the wooden chest. "You can sit down if you want. Just close the top of that."

He returned to the figure in his hands, and Juliet sat down to watch him. His hands moved slowly and expertly over the wood, never hurrying. Her eyes strayed from his hands to his face. From this angle, she could see one side of his face and his dark, thick hair. His hair needed cutting; it was too long, and he was forever shoving it back impatiently behind his ears. Juliet could have trimmed it; she had often cut her father's hair. But she wasn't bold enough to suggest it. It seemed too personal an act. She looked at the clean line of his nose and brow, the thick sweep of his lashes over his eye.

"We got the roof fixed," he told her. "Soon as I make a new shutter for Ethan's window, the house'll look good again."

Juliet hesitated, then said, "You know what I would like?"

"What?" He glanced back at her, and his eyes lingered for a moment on her face.

"Flowers in front of the porch. Maybe some rose bushes. Daisies or something pretty. It'd make the house look nice. More homey, you know."

A faint smile touched his face. "And then you'd have more things to stick in all those little pots of yours."

Juliet chuckled. "Yes. It would brighten up the inside, too."

"My mother always liked flowers," he went on reflectively. "She had rose bushes in front of the porch. She had ivy, too, that she was training to climb up the columns. But after she died, nobody took care of them. You have to water plants, baby them a little out here. The ivy died, too."

"That's too bad." Juliet didn't know what to say. There was still a lingering trace of sorrow in his voice.

He shrugged. "Way life is, I reckon."

"Not always."

Again he looked at her. "You've lived a different kind of life than me, then."

"Yes, I suppose I have." Juliet paused. "People probably think it was a rough-and-tumble way to live, not very certain nor very genteel. And I guess it wasn't. But we were happy. My parents. Me. Celia."

"Celia?"

"Oh. She's my sister. She's married now and lives in Philadelphia. She's an actress, a real actress, I mean, not just a casual one like me."

There was a pause. "Sometimes I hear you singing."

"You do?" Juliet looked a little surprised.

"Yes. When I'm sitting out on the back stoop, smoking my pipe in the evening, and you're working in the kitchen, sometimes you sing."

"Oh. I didn't think." Juliet felt a blush rising in her

cheeks. She wasn't sure why. She had sung in front of thousands of people, and she knew that her voice was excellent. It seemed ridiculous to feel embarrassed just because one man had heard her. Yet it did but it made her pleased and proud, too. "I—I hope I didn't disturb anyone."

"How could you disturb anyone?" Amos raised his eyebrows in astonishment. "You're beautiful. I mean, that is, you sing beautifully. Well, of course, you're beautiful, too, but I didn't . . ." His voice trailed off, and he looked back down at his hands. Juliet saw, amazed, that his cheeks were stained red.

For a few minutes both of them were silent. Then Amos said, "My mother would have loved to hear you. She was musical."

"Frances told me."

"Both of you like beauty, you and Mama. You have it. I mean, the two of you understand it. Does that make sense?"

"Yes. But anyone can understand beauty."

"No. Some of us just aren't—well, it's foreign to us. We can see it. Appreciate it. But we don't know it. Not deep inside, the way I know the land. I can feel the earth, see? It's part of me. I feel at home when I'm working in the fields. When I look out at the dirt turned over and laid out in rows, or see the shoots coming up out of the ground, or watch the sun setting over the fields as I'm walking back to the house—" He stopped and grinned at her wryly. "I suppose that sounds crazy."

"No. It sounds to me like you're talking about beauty

again. It's just beauty in the land, that's all that's different. And these figures that you make, that's beauty, too."

"Maybe. It seems different to me. But that's not what I wanted to say. I wanted to tell you . . . about those geegaws of Mama's . . . you can put them out if you want to. Wherever. It doesn't matter."

Juliet's jaw dropped. She couldn't believe that he had just given her permission to put those lovely objects out. (And *geegaws!* Only Amos Morgan would refer to an Italian millifiore paperweight as a geegaw.) "Why, thank you."

He shrugged. "No reason for them to sit in there just gathering dust. I always hated to see anybody else touching them. But I reckon you know what to do with them."

Juliet thought that Amos had just paid her a compliment. With him, it was hard to tell. "Thank you."

He nodded, looking ill at ease.

Juliet stood up. "I guess I better go inside now." She paused. "See you tomorrow."

"Good night." He nodded without turning around.

But after she began to walk away, he turned and watched her go until she was swallowed up by the darkness beyond the barn.

Nine

The following Sunday Henrietta and Samuel came to call. Henrietta bustled in, talking a mile a minute, and her husband followed more quietly and slowly. Samuel shook his brother's hand and Ethan's and nodded at Juliet politely. First they went upstairs to see Frances. A few minutes later Amos led them back down to the front parlor, which Juliet had opened up and decorated with his mother's bibelots the day after Amos gave her permission.

Samuel was shaking his head and saying, "Poor Frances, she looks—" when suddenly he stopped and stared around him in surprise at the room.

"Well, well," Henrietta commented, sitting down on one of the velvet chairs with a great rustling of her skirts. "The parlor looks lovely, Amos. Whatever made you decide to open it up?"

Amos frowned. "It's a parlor, isn't it? Why wouldn't we use it?"

Henrietta widened her brown eyes expressively. "I'm sure I wouldn't know, dear. But I must say this is the first time I've known you to sit in it unless there was a funeral."

She stopped suddenly and colored. All their minds went to Frances upstairs in her bed, already so wasted by her disease. "I mean—oh, dear, I—" She glanced around desperately, looking for something to change the topic. "My goodness, there are those candlesticks!"

She got up and went over to the table on which Juliet had placed the two glass dolphin candlesticks. "These are so lovely." She turned toward Juliet. "It must have been you who convinced Amos to set them out. He likes to hide the most beautiful things in the house. It's sheer perversity."

Although Juliet liked Henrietta and was grateful to her for giving her this job, she bristled at the woman's comments. "Amos was quite pleasant about setting out his mother's objets d'art," Juliet lied blandly. "He realized their beauty, of course."

Amos turned an astonished face her way, and Henrietta said skeptically, "Amos?" She smiled almost slyly. "Well, well. How nice to hear that. I have to admit, Amos, that I am somewhat, well, surprised."

Amos looked back at her and shrugged. "That's something, at least—being able to surprise you. Usually you know everything in town before it happens."

Henrietta's smile grew wider. "That's true," she admitted lightly.

Juliet went to the kitchen to make a pot of coffee and slice a pie for their visitors. When she returned, Henrietta was in the midst of an accounting of all the damage done to every house in Steadman and most of the farms around town.

"And Oscar Metz's barn blew down. Did you hear that?" she was saying as Juliet entered the room with her tray.

Amos shook his head, and Juliet could see from the glazed look in his eyes that he was only half listening to his sister-in-law. She suspected that his mind was busily turning, looking for an excuse to slip out of the parlor.

"Mr. Stanfield told me," Ethan joined in. "There's going to be a barn raising for the Metzes next Saturday."

"A barn raising?" Juliet repeated. "What's that?"

Ethan stared at her in amazement. "You never heard of a barn raising?"

"No."

"Remember, she's a city girl, son," Amos put in, but there was a trace of a smile on his lips that took the customary sting out of his words.

Henrietta's eyes went to Amos, then to Juliet and back, and Juliet could almost see the rapid calculation going on behind them.

"A barn raising is exactly what it says," Henrietta explained. "Neighbors get together and put up a barn. Doesn't take nearly as long with everybody working on it. People out here have to help one another."

"How nice."

"'Course, all the womenfolk bring food, and there's a picnic."

"Lots of times there's a dance afterward," Ethan added, his eyes turning brighter.

"Oho." Juliet smiled at him teasingly. "I know what interests you, then."

Ethan blushed. "Nah . . ."

"Don't tell me that. You aren't thinking about how Ellie will probably be there, and how you might ask her to dance?"

"Ellie?" Henrietta perked up at the hint of gossip. "Ellie Sanderson? Are you interested in her, Ethan?"

"Ah, Aunt Henrietta," Ethan groaned.

Henrietta laughed. "You just answered my question, I think. Well, if you want to dance with Ellie, you better get in line quickly. I know lots of young men who would like to take a turn around the floor with her."

"I'm not going to dance with Ellie," he protested.

"Why, Ethan, whyever not?" Juliet asked. "I'm sure she'd say yes."

He shrugged. "I don't know how to dance."

"What?" Juliet could hardly believe her ears.

"I don't know how to dance," he repeated, his voice sinking even lower. "I've never done it."

"Well, that's no problem. Dancing can be learned. I'll teach you."

Ethan sat up straighter, light beginning to dawn on his face. "Really? You mean it?"

"I'd love to."

"In that case," Henrietta put in dryly, "you'll have to teach Amos, as well. None of the Morgans know how to dance."

Ethan chuckled and looked at his father, who was glowering at Henrietta in a way that would have frightened anyone less indomitable than that woman. "Yes, Pa, why don't we let Juliet teach us?"

"I don't need to know such folderol," Amos said gruffly.

"Don't be such an old grouch," Henrietta told him. "I taught Samuel to dance, and he enjoys it now. Don't you, dear?"

She turned toward Samuel expectantly, and for the first time, he contributed to the conversation, nodding his head shortly and saying, "Yep. I reckon I must. We go to pretty near every dance around. 'Course now Henrietta don't want to dance with me. She just sits in a corner and gossips."

"You do enough dancing for both of us. And don't try to pretend that you don't enjoy dancing with all those pretty young girls."

A slow, teasing smile creased Samuel's face. "Maybe I do, at that."

"See, Amos?" Henrietta directed a pointed look at him.

"Let Samuel get out there and make a damn fool of himself, then. I'm not."

Henrietta rolled her eyes. "Amos, you're incorrigible."

"Probably. But you aren't getting me to dance."

Henrietta made a noncommittal face. "I'm sure *I* won't."

Juliet decided it was time to change the subject, before Amos and Henrietta got into a full-fledged argument. "Well, what else was damaged in town in the tornado, Mrs. Morgan?"

"The sign in front of the livery stables was knocked down, and—"

She was off on a further description of the various disruptions and inconveniences the wind had caused. Amos settled back in his chair, arms crossed. He lasted about ten minutes before he stood up abruptly and suggested that the men might like to go down to the pens to see the new livestock.

When the front door closed behind the men, Henrietta breathed a sigh. "Well, they're finally gone. I thought they were going to stay around forever."

Juliet looked at her blankly. "You wanted them to leave?"

"Of course. How can women have a good, cozy gossip with a bunch of men hanging around looking sour? The Morgans are good people, but they're death to conversation."

Juliet couldn't help but chuckle.

"There. You know what I'm talking about." Juliet nodded, and Henrietta went on, "Lord knows, I love my Sam, but he's too quiet. You might think I'd like that, given how much talking I do—no competition that way!" She laughed merrily, her little brown eyes twinkling. "And maybe I do, most of the time."

She stood up, stripping off her gloves. "Well, what are we doing here? I'd guess you have a lot of housework that you could use some help with. Especially with Frances laid up like that." She shook her head sorrowfully. "I hated to say it in front of them, but I don't think she's long for this world."

"I don't know. She's strong. Her will, I mean, is strong. She's trying her best to fight."

"Some things you can't fight, though. Selfishly, I'd like for her to hang on, but when I see how thin she's getting and how drawn her face is, I can't help but wonder if it wouldn't be a blessing for her to go quickly. Not that she will, of course. The Morgans are the stubbornest lot of people imaginable."

As they talked, Henrietta pulled the pins from her hat and set it aside, then started walking toward the kitchen, unbuttoning and rolling up the sleeves of her silk Sunday dress as she went. Henrietta put on an apron when they reached the kitchen and tackled the dinner dishes, which Juliet had been in the process of cleaning when Henrietta and Samuel arrived. It didn't take Juliet long to understand why Henrietta had volunteered to clean. The woman was a dynamo. Juliet realized that probably the hardest thing for her to do was to sit still in an elegant room and merely talk. She whirled through the dishes, talking all the while, skipping without reserve between comments on the weather, gossip about people in Steadman, and a discourse on the nature of the Morgan family.

"They're a moody bunch," she told Juliet confidentially as she handed her the last plate to dry and turned to grab a broom and begin sweeping the floor. "Everyone of them I ever met, 'cept their mother, of course, but then she wasn't a true Morgan. Frankly, I don't know how she stood it. It's old Mr. Morgan's fault. Sometimes I wish I could get my hands around that man's neck and throttle him, the way he treated his children. Stern and righteous as John Calvin, that's the way he was. Never gave those children a bit of slack. Amos hated him, and Sam didn't like him much better, I'll tell you. He had a free hand with the belt, and he didn't brook any misbehavior. He didn't like foolishness or frivolity. He figured life was earnest and real and we were all put here to work.

"Now, I don't mind a bit of work; why, I wouldn't know what to do with myself if I didn't have plenty to keep my hands occupied. But what good is it if you don't leaven it with a little fun now and then? Life wasn't meant to be all gloom and doom. But the Morgans find it hard to laugh. I've straightened Samuel out, mostly. He likes a good time now as well as the next man. But, then, he left this house early, went into town when he was only sixteen and started working in the general store. But Amos stayed here and worked and put up with their pa until the old man died, oh, ten or twelve years ago. I think he had it a lot worse. Him and Frances."

Juliet listened to the flow of words, eagerly picking up every morsel of information Henrietta gave about Amos and his life. She didn't stop to examine why she had so much interest in what Henrietta said about him.

At another point, after the kitchen was cleaned up, and Henrietta had turned to polishing the silver, she asked Juliet, "How are you and Amos getting along?"

"All right. Well, honestly, at first it was a little difficult."

Henrietta snorted indelicately. "That's an understatement, I imagine. Amos is prickly as a porcupine."

"It wasn't his fault," Juliet said quickly.

Henrietta shot her a disbelieving look.

"Well, it wasn't," Juliet insisted. "I'm afraid that I wasn't quite honest with you when you hired me. I—well, I was not an expert housekeeper."

The other woman laughed, and her eyes lit up with amusement. "Do tell."

Juliet stared. "You mean you knew I wasn't?"

"It didn't make much sense, did it? Someone who spent her life touring around the country, making money by singing and acting? It didn't seem likely that you were an excellent cook and housecleaner."

"Why'd you hire me?"

"I figured you'd catch on quick enough; you seemed a sharp girl. And there wasn't much selection; not all that many women looking for positions around here, and nobody who knew Amos was eager to work for him. Besides, I thought you seemed like exactly what this house—and Amos—needed."

"What do you mean?"

"You're pretty and lively. I figured if anybody could sweeten Amos Morgan up, it'd be you. How many chances like that come along?"

Could she possibly mean what she had said? Juliet could hardly believe it. Henrietta sounded as if she had chosen Juliet for something more personal than housekeeping, as if she had wanted her to become romantically involved with Amos. "Are you serious?"

"Of course I'm serious. Amos needs to marry. If he waits much longer, he'll be so set in his ways, nothing could ever help him."

"You hired me because you hoped that Amos and I—that we would get married?"

"Not entirely." Henrietta shrugged. "After all, he really did need someone to look after the house and help with Frances. But if there was a possibility that something might develop between the two of you . . ." Henrietta smiled, casting Juliet a sly glance. "Well, so much the better."

Marry Amos! Juliet had never thought of the possibility. But now, after Henrietta's words, she couldn't keep from thinking about it. She tried to imagine being in front of a minister with him, their hands clasped, pledging her life to his. Sitting across the table with him every day of her life. Sharing her bed with him. Coming to know him as she would never know anyone else. Feeling his lips on her mouth, his hands on her skin. Being *his*.

Heat flooded up her throat at the images that passed through her mind, and Juliet knew that Henrietta must see that she was blushing with embarrassment. Juliet turned away, her nerves jumping.

"I don't think that's possible," she said softly.

Henrietta sighed. "I know it may not seem too likely. But Amos isn't a bad man. Underneath all that gruffness, he's good. He would never hurt anyone, least of all a woman. I was hoping that maybe if you were around him, you would come to see what he's really like, that you might even come to care for him. He would provide well for you. He lives simply, but he's one of the wealthiest men in this area. His farm is the largest in the county."

Juliet whirled around, drawing herself up proudly. "I

wouldn't marry a man for that reason!"

"You're a fool if you don't think about it," Henrietta said practically. "After all, who's going to look out for you if you don't do it yourself? Look at the position you found yourself in before you came to the farm. However"—she raised a hand as if to stop Juliet's coming words—"I'm not trying to talk you into marrying him. I only wanted to let you two have the chance. I hope you won't close your mind to it, or him."

"I—I wouldn't do that. I mean, I've come to realize that Amos isn't what he seems at first. He is kind; he didn't throw me out when he discovered how completely incompetent I was at cooking. He's quite wonderful to his sister. And he's treated me with respect. But I—well, I really don't think that Amos has any interest in marriage. With anyone, least of all me."

"You *are* a fool if you think he wouldn't be interested in you. Why, look at you; any man would be. Amos may be standoffish, but I've never heard anything to indicate that he wasn't normal in that regard. Believe me, he wouldn't have let you set out his mother's things if he didn't have some feeling for you. Sure, he doesn't think about marriage. What man does? That's why we have to give them a push to help them along the way."

"Mrs. Morgan! What are you suggesting that I do?"

"Don't look so scandalized. I'm not talking about anything improper, I assure you. But it wouldn't hurt to let him see that smile of yours sometimes or to go out of your way to draw a conversation out of him."

Henrietta set down the silver tray she was polishing

and leaned forward, laying one hand on Juliet's arm. "I am fond of Amos. I'd like to see him happy. It would do him a world of good to have the love of a good woman."

Juliet smiled wryly. "But how do you know that that's what I am? You barely know me. And I was an actress."

"Oh, that." Henrietta made a dismissive gesture with her hand. "If you were that sort, you'd have been like the others and gone straight over to the saloon to earn money. I knew you had quality because you didn't."

Juliet blinked. "I don't know what to say. I'm stunned."

"No need to say anything." Henrietta went busily back to rubbing the tray with the silver polish. "Just think about what I said. Promise me that you'll give Amos a chance."

"Yes, I will. But I can't imagine Amos wanting a chance. He's . . . well, there's my reputation. I'm glad that you don't think that way about me, but lots of other people do. Apparently there are rumors all over town about Amos and me."

"What?" Henrietta put her hands on her hips pugnaciously. "Who's talking about you, I'd like to know?"

"Aurica Johnson told Amos that—"

"Oh, her." Henrietta waved her hand dismissively. "Everybody knows that she's just a sour old maid who's had her eye on Amos for years. She's never gotten anywhere with him, and I'm sure she's jealous as all get-out that a pretty girl like you is out here with him. Nobody else in town is talking about you. They wouldn't dare; I'd set them straight quick enough. And if you think Amos cares about gossip, think again. He does exactly what he wants to."

Juliet laughed. "I'm sure that's true."

"Of course it is. Just don't you give up on him."

Satisfied that she had accomplished what she'd set out to do, Henrietta set into work, humming.

"Juliet." Ethan carried the last dish from the table to the counter beside the sink and set it down, then looked at her with the earnest, beguiling face of a young boy begging for a treat.

"What?" Juliet was already smiling, just looking at him; she suspected that he would soon wheedle whatever it was he wanted out of her.

"You said yesterday that you could teach me to dance. I was thinking, why don't we start?"

His request surprised Juliet; she hadn't thought again about their half-joking exchange yesterday afternoon. She glanced around the kitchen. Frances, whom Amos had carried down to supper tonight, as he had done several times the past two weeks, was sitting at the table, leaning back wearily against her chair. Amos was seated at the table with her, and he regarded Juliet and Ethan with interest.

"Right now?" Juliet asked. "Here?"

"Sure. Why not? There's plenty of space." Ethan gestured toward the large empty area between the table and the pie safe. "I need lots of practice, so you better teach me as soon as possible. The dance is only five days away."

"All right." Juliet smiled at the young man and reached back to untie her apron. "You're right—why not? I can finish the dishes afterwards."

A smile split his face. "That's wonderful! What do we do?"

"Well, first you have to ask the girl to dance."

"How do I do that?"

"Go over to her and bow very politely and say, 'Miss Whatever, may I have the pleasure of this dance?'"

Ethan copied her slight bow from the waist. "Miss Drake, may I have the pleasure of this dance?"

"Why, certainly, Mr. Morgan," Juliet replied, smiling coyly at him like a marriageable young maiden and wafting a pretend fan. "It would be my pleasure."

"Then I offer my arm," Ethan contributed smugly, sticking out his elbow. "I've seen that."

"That's right." Juliet took his arm and walked with him into the middle of their 'dance floor.' "Now you turn to her and you take up the position of the waltz."

She showed him where to place his hands and then led him through the steps. Ethan kept his eyes on their feet as they moved clumsily about and tried to match his steps with hers. Amos watched them, his mouth twisted into a grimace, his expression clearly stating that he considered the whole thing a bunch of nonsense. After several minutes Ethan's hands were damp with nervous sweat, and his face was contorted in frustration. Finally he broke away from her, exclaiming, "It's no use! I can't do that!"

"Of course you can," Juliet responded bracingly. "It just takes practice."

"Music would help," Frances offered softly.

"I know. But I can't play the piano and show him the steps, too."

"There's my music box. Mother's music box." Frances turned to her brother. "Amos, would you go up and bring it down? It's in my dresser, the second drawer."

Amos hesitated, looking as if he would like to refuse, but he couldn't say no to his sister, so he nodded shortly and strode out of the kitchen. Frances smiled at Juliet. "Go on. I suspect it'll be easier to learn when Amos is out of the room."

She was right about that, Juliet found. Without his father's disapproving presence, Ethan was able to concentrate on the steps much better, and several times in a row he moved correctly, if rather heavily.

Amos returned with a beautifully carved wooden box and set it down on the kitchen table. He wound it up carefully, opened the lid, and a delicate waltz began to drift out. It was easier to dance with music, and Ethan began to move more naturally. They shuffled around and around the small vacant space, Ethan frowning horribly as he bobbed his head in time to the three-count music.

When they stopped, Juliet glanced over at Amos, and some imp inside her prompted her to say, "Now it's Amos's turn."

"What?" Amos looked poleaxed.

Ethan chuckled. "Yeah, Pa, now Juliet can teach you."

Amos shook his head vigorously. "Absolutely not."

"Why not? How else are you going to have fun at the barn raising Saturday night?"

"I'm not going there for fun. I plan to help put up the barn and then I'll spend the evening resting, thank you. I sure as thunder am not going to get out on a dance floor and make a spectacle of myself."

"You won't make a spectacle," Juliet promised. "Do you think that I'm that poor a teacher?"

"No," he growled, scowling at her. "It's not that."

"Then what is it?"

"I can't dance!"

"That's why I'm going to give you lessons," Juliet countered with exaggerated patience.

Ethan laughed. "She's got you there."

Amos shot his son a black look.

But Ethan was undeterred. "Come on, Pa, if I can do it, so can you."

"But you wanted to. That's the difference. I didn't ask for this."

"I'd like to see you dance," Frances spoke up. "Go ahead, Amos, it'll be fun. I'm having a good time."

Amos looked at his sister. Her cheeks were tinged faintly with color for the first time in weeks. "Yeah, you'll have a wonderful time laughing at me stumbling around like a three-legged dog," he grumbled, but his tone was considerably softer, laced with love and resignation.

"Please, Amos." Frances's smile was a heartrending contrast to her drawn, thin face.

"Oh, all right."

Amos stalked over to where Juliet stood waiting. She was smiling broadly, and her blue eyes twinkled with laughter. She looked more beautiful to him than any woman had a right to be, and Amos didn't know whether he was filled more with fear or excitement at being close to Juliet.

He stuck his hands out stiffly at approximately the positions Juliet had shown Ethan. But Juliet clicked her tongue reprovingly. "You forgot something."

Amos looked puzzled, and Ethan stage-whispered, "You gotta ask her first, Pa."

He heaved a tremendous sigh to show his opinion of such foolish play-acting, but he sketched a little bow and said, like a schoolboy reciting by rote, "May I have this dance, Miss Drake?"

Juliet swept him a curtsey so deep that she dipped almost to the floor, spreading her skirts out wide beside her. "Why, certainly, Mr. Morgan."

Ethan laughed his approval of their show, and Frances smiled.

"Now. Put this hand here." Juliet took his left hand and turned it palm-up facing her and out to the side, elbow bent. She put her own hand in it, and Amos's fingers curled around hers automatically. "Your right hand goes here."

She picked it up and clamped it against her side. His hand was hot; she could feel it through the cloth of her dress. Her stomach gave a peculiar little jump. Suddenly the teasing impulse that had impelled her left, and Juliet was very aware of how close together they stood and of Amos's hands on her.

"Now what?" Amos asked.

"Uh, well, you move your feet." She demonstrated the

simple steps. "I go backward, and you go forward. You see?" She counted out the beat, "Step, two, three. Step, two, three."

Juliet lifted her skirts a little so that he could see her feet as they moved, and her dark-stockinged ankles came into view, slender and lithe. Ethan rewound the music box, and its tinkling sounds floated through the air again. Juliet moved gracefully, and Amos followed her as best he could, his eyes on her feet. As she moved a flash of her leg showed, the beginning of the soft curve of her calf.

Juliet looked at Amos's face. His eyes were intent on her feet, but she could see the sudden warmth in their black depths, quickly suppressed. There was no disguising the heat, however, in his hands. Being this close to her, holding her in the dance position, aroused him, she realized, and the thought made her own breath come faster in her throat. There was something alluring in the heat of his skin and the flash of his eyes, and his quick, only partially successful attempt to disguise it made it even more exciting. He found her attractive; he wanted her, despite his own battle against the feeling, and Juliet thought how strong the need must be to break through the barrier of Amos's will.

She hastily turned her eyes down toward the feet, afraid that something of her thoughts would show in her face, but then she could not keep herself from looking up at his face, and the same shimmer of excitement ran through her again. Amos's fingers dug into her waist more tightly. Juliet realized that they had moved unconsciously closer together. She was having difficulty controlling her breathing.

Juliet broke away from him, searching for something to say to cover her own peculiar reactions. "You've been leading me on."

"What?" Amos looked at her, confused, as though he was having difficulty concentrating on her words.

"You already know how to dance. You're catching on too quickly."

He shook his head. "I don't. Well, I did dance, a little, a long time ago. It was—I never was any good."

Juliet swallowed. She felt confused and betrayed by her own sensations. "Don't be silly. You did quite well. I'm sure in no time you'll be dancing like an expert." Her smile was brief and more a grimace than a smile. She turned toward Ethan. "And Ethan, too."

"Can we practice every evening?" Ethan asked eagerly.

"Yes. I don't see why not. But right now I'd better get back to the supper dishes."

They dispersed then, Amos carrying Frances back upstairs to her bed, Ethan going outside, and Juliet returning to her work. Amos came back downstairs later and passed through the kitchen to the outside door. He said nothing, and Juliet carefully kept her attention focused on the sink and her hands in the soapy water, not turning around to look at him.

Juliet found herself jumpy all through supper the following evening, and as she carried the dishes to the counter when the meal was through, her attention was focused on the back door, waiting for Amos to slip through it on his way out to the barn. But he remained sitting at the table. A knot formed in Juliet's stomach.

He was still there while she and Ethan danced, watching them. The music from the carved box tinkled through the air like crystal, clear and sweet and beautiful. When she and Ethan stopped, Juliet hesitated, and her eyes went to Amos of their own accord.

He rose slowly and walked over to her. Juliet could read nothing in his dark eyes. Without a word, he reached out and put his hand on her waist and took her other hand in his. Her palm tingled where it lay against his. They began to dance. They moved more easily this time, more in tune with the music. He was overwhelming in his nearness, his size and strength very obvious. Yet it wasn't frightening to Juliet; in an odd way, it was reassuring. Amos was like a rock, steady and strong, and there was more protection than intimidation in his presence. It would be, Juliet thought, amazingly easy to lean against him and let him support her, to let him wrap his strength around her.

Juliet came to a halt and pulled back from Amos. "I think you have the steps down well enough."

For a moment he didn't answer. Then he said, "There must be more steps to learn. Aren't there?"

"Of course. There are turns, if you'd like to try them."

He looked at her. "Yes," he said finally. "Let's go on."

Ten

"*H*ow pretty you look!" Frances clapped her hands together in delight as Juliet pirouetted in front of her. Spots of color on Frances's cheekbones blazed brightly against her pale skin. Juliet was glad that she had come in to show Frances how she looked before they left for the barn raising. Frances seemed more excited about Juliet's going than Juliet herself. "Are you taking another dress for the dance?"

"Yes, just as you told me." Juliet smiled. Frances had made certain that she was fully prepared for the social event. "Are you sure you wouldn't like to come, too? Amos could carry you to the wagon, and I'd fix you a pallet in the back. You could sit in the shade or lie down in the Metzes' house, and that way you could see everybody." Frances had had Amos carry her downstairs every evening this week to watch their dance lessons, and she had enjoyed it so much and seemed so interested in this party that Juliet wished Frances could at least go to it.

Frances shook her head, her smile wistful. "No. I couldn't. It sounds lovely, but I'm too tired. Besides, I'd hate for everyone to see me looking like this."

"Why, you're looking good this morning," Juliet protested, a pang of grief piercing her as she said the words, for she knew that they weren't true.

"Thank you. You've seen me every day; you know how bad I've looked for weeks. But the others haven't seen me since I was well. I couldn't bear the looks of pity."

"I understand. But I think your neighbors would love to see you."

"Thank you."

There were footsteps in the hall and Amos stuck his head inside. He wore overalls and a plaid shirt, and carried a small bundle of clothes with him.

Amos glanced at Juliet, and his eyes lingered for a moment, sweeping down the pale blue cotton dress she wore, prettier than her everyday skirts and shirtwaists. Juliet wondered if he, too, thought she looked pretty in it. She wished she had a clue to Amos's thoughts. They had practiced dancing each evening this week, just as she and Ethan had, and though Juliet had been nervous and a little excited each time they danced, she hadn't been able to tell whether it had had any effect on Amos. There had been times when his hands had seemed abnormally hot or there had been a brief flash of something in his eyes, but it had never been enough to be certain.

"About time to go, Juliet. They'll start early."

"All right. I'm ready. I was saying good-bye to Frances. The food we're taking is downstairs on the kitchen table."

"Ethan's loading it into the wagon." He walked over to the side of Frances's bed and took her hand. "You sure you'll be all right here by yourself for awhile? Gladys Snipes said she'd be here by eleven or so, and she'll look after you this afternoon."

"I'll be perfectly all right," Frances told him with some asperity. "You'd think I was a child, the way you act. As if I can't make it for one morning and one evening by myself! Why, I don't see why I have to have Gladys here all afternoon just to watch me sleep. Juliet's left me a glass and a jug of water by the bed and a little cold luncheon, in case Gladys doesn't get here by noon. I'll be fine."

Amos grinned, pleased by his sister's spirited attitude. "All right."

"Now, I want you to forget about me and have a glorious time. I want you to dance; promise me you will."

"All right. I'll dance."

"Good. I can just see you." Frances smiled, the color staining her cheeks even more brightly, and her eyes glowed. She seemed almost uplifted. "I always loved to dance."

Amos looked surprised. "I didn't know you danced."

"Only if Pa wasn't around. Actually, it was Henrietta who taught me."

"That figures."

"I enjoyed watching you two dance this week. I wish I *could* go. I'd love to dance one more time."

The look on Amos's face made Juliet's heart ache. Suddenly he bent down and lifted Frances out of her bed. "Then you shall."

"What? You're joking."

"No, I'm not. Juliet, where's that music box? Wind it up."

The box was sitting on Frances's dresser. Juliet hurried to do as he bid. As the notes spilled out of the box, hanging in the air like crystal drops, Amos began to dance with his sister. Her hair hung down her back in a loose braid, and she wore only a nightgown, her feet bare. She was far too pale and far too thin, and they moved slowly, Amos supporting her more than leading her through the steps. But it was a beautiful sight to Juliet. Tears filled her eyes.

Amos lifted Frances off the ground completely after a few moments, carrying her weakened body as he danced. He ended by twirling around in two grand turns. Then he laid Frances gently on her bed again and pulled the covers up to her waist. He turned and strode out of the room without saying anything or looking at either of the women.

"Good-bye. I'll come up to see how you are as soon as we get home." Juliet took Frances's hand and squeezed it gently.

Frances nodded at her, smiling, looking terribly tired, but happy. Juliet left the room and hurried down the stairs. She discovered Amos in the hall below, his arm braced against the tall newel post and his head resting on his arm, face hidden. The lines of his body were eloquent with sorrow.

Without thinking, Juliet reached out and put her hand on top of his where it lay on the stair railing, trying to give him some measure of comfort. She heard him sniff, and he looked up, wiping his eyes surreptitiously on his sleeve as he lifted his head.

"I'm sorry," she whispered, her throat choked with emotion.

He nodded, and the bleakness on his face was painful to see. Amos gripped her hand briefly, then let go. "Come on. It's time to leave."

Juliet was a little surprised by her eagerness to get to the barn raising, as well as by the almost joyful gladness she felt when she stepped down from the wagon when they arrived and spotted several women she knew. She had met them at church, but other than that she had had no contact with them, and she could hardly call them friends. But it was wonderful simply to see other women and know that there was a full day of visiting ahead of her. She realized how isolated she had been for the past weeks on the farm. At the time, with the work she had to do and with Frances there to talk to some of the time, she hadn't felt lonely. But now it struck her full force how little she had seen any other people and how pleasant it would be to chat to her heart's content all day long.

She felt a moment's hesitation. The women she had met and talked to at church had seemed friendly, but after her experiences with Sanderson and with Aurica Johnson in town, she couldn't help but wonder what everyone really thought of her. Perhaps in church they felt that they could be nothing but polite, but in a social setting like this, they might turn away from her contemptuously as Miss Johnson had done. They might not want to associate with her.

As she stood beside the wagon, debating what to do, Ellen Case saw her and waved. "Juliet! Come this way. I'll show you where to put your food."

Smiling, Juliet moved toward her. As she walked into the house, all the women she knew greeted her, and she responded cheerfully. Before long, she was chatting away as she and Ellen stored the mountains of food everyone had brought for the day-long occasion. When they were done with that, there was no question of them simply sitting around idly. Quilting squares were brought out, and the women sat down in several groups to piece them together while the children played outside. They talked as they sewed, tongues moving as rapidly as the silver needles that flashed in and out of the material. Juliet had never put together a quilt before, but she was an excellent seamstress and she had little trouble following what the others were doing.

They paused to lay out a luncheon on long tables beside the house, and the men stopped their work to sit down with them and eat. Afterward, when the dishes were clean, the women resumed their quilting. The windows were open, and a breeze played through the house, lifting the curtains gently. The sound of the children's laughter and shrieks as they played came in through the open windows, as well as the continuous hammering of the men building the barn.

Later there was supper, once again at the trestle tables. The barn loomed in the background, the outside almost completed. Afterward, the younger children were put down to sleep on pallets in the house or on the flat beds of the wagons. The single women and childless wives used this time to change their clothes inside the house. There was much giggling and chattering and primping in front of the few mirrors as the women slipped into their simple party dresses.

Juliet had brought a white dress with a wide bertha of eyelet embroidery, dainty cap sleeves, and a lavender satin sash. Around the bottom the hem was drawn up every foot or so to reveal white eyelet ruffles, each arch decorated by a small lavender ribbon. It was by no means her most elegant or beautiful dress. In fact, it was years old; she no longer wore it, deeming it too girlish. She had had it in her trunk only because it was perfectly suited to one of her small roles in the play. She had decided that its simplicity would be more suitable to this evening than a dress she would have worn dancing or to the theater in a city. As she put it on now, glancing surreptitiously around her at the others, she saw that her judgment had been correct. The other women were wearing cotton dresses, too, usually with the lower scoop neckline that befitted a party and spruced up with satin ribbons and bows, lace, and ruffles, but still rather plain and simple compared to many that Juliet had seen.

She waited her turn to get a chance at one of the mirrors, taking down her hair and brushing it to a sheen while she waited. When she finally got to the mirror, she sat down on a low chair in front of it and quickly put up her hair in a smooth, soft pompadour style. Another woman stood behind her, taking advantage of the mirror higher up. Juliet finished and gave herself a last inspection, pleased with the results of her toilette.

Juliet went outside onto the porch and waited with several of the other women, reluctant to go across the yard to the barn, which had during the day become male territory. While the women had been in the house, the men had been behind the barn, washing up at the stock tank below the windmill and changing into their dress shirts and suits.

But as the crowd of women on the porch grew and was joined by the older, married women, the lure of the lanterns in the barn and the scraping sounds of fiddles tuning up, of the mellow, deep laughter of men, drew them off the porch and toward the barn. In the same way, more and more of the young men had spilled out of the barn and were standing in front of it, talking and smoking cigars or pipes or the newfangled cigarettes, leaning back against the wall of the barn, and casting frequent looks toward the house. Mrs. Metz finally set it all in motion by calling to her sons to come fetch the table for the refreshments. Several men jumped to help, and the two groups began to mingle and drift into the barn.

Inside, the barn was stark and new, still smelling strongly of wood. The interior loft and stalls had not been built yet, so that it was huge and open. Straw had been scattered across the ground to help keep down the dust kicked up by dancing. Lanterns hung at either end and on several of the supporting posts, but it was not enough to completely dispel the cavernous darkness. There were shadows in the corners, and the roof was hidden. The light was warm and yellowish, glowing, and it added a soft golden touch to everyone's faces.

Juliet glanced around, looking for Amos, yet trying not to be too obvious about it. She found Ethan almost immediately, standing with a bunch of other boys his age in an awkward cluster, laughing loudly and making large gestures, filled to bursting with the energy of the young. She also saw that Ethan's attention often left the group as he glanced around the room, his eyes searching, and Juliet was certain that he was hunting for Ellie Sanderson.

Ellie's father was here. Juliet had seen John almost as soon as she had stepped into the barn, but she had managed to keep from looking at him directly. She didn't want to see him face-to-face and be forced to give him a polite nod or to raise questions by cutting him directly.

She sighted Amos at last, standing against the back wall beside Mordecai Hamilton, a member of their church. Amos's hands were thrust into his pockets, so that his arms pushed his suit coat back, exposing the wide snowy expanse of his shirt. It struck her anew how handsome he looked.

The fiddles were tuned up now, and Henry Armstrong had joined them with his harmonica, and the three men began to play. Almost immediately several couples whirled out onto the floor in front of the musicians and began to dance. By the minute more and more couples joined them on the floor. Ethan came over to Juliet and asked her to dance. Juliet thought that he probably was working up his courage to ask Ellie by starting with a sure thing. But she was happy to oblige him; it made it easier for her to join the group, too.

After Ethan, several other men asked her to dance. Some were young, like Ethan, and one or two others were white-haired; she didn't even know the names of two of them. But it didn't matter. Neither she nor they were dancing as a part of the courting ritual. They simply enjoyed dancing for its own sake, loving the chance to cut loose and have some fun after a hard day—hard weeks!—of work.

All the while she danced, Juliet was conscious of where Amos was. He didn't dance with anyone, she noticed. He talked a little, got a glass of punch from the refreshment table, and wandered back to the wall to stand, stopping to say hello to a couple of people on the way.

She saw that Ethan had finally gotten up the nerve to approach Ellie, and the two of them danced several times. She also caught sight of Ellie's father during one of those dances; his arms were crossed, and he was directing a black look at the young couple on the dance floor. Juliet sighed inwardly. It appeared that John Sanderson was going to hold a grudge against everyone in the Morgan household because of what had happened between him and her. Later, her fears were confirmed when she glanced across the room and saw Sanderson talking to Amos. Fortunately there was so much noise that their voices couldn't be heard, but Sanderson's face was flushed and angry, and Amos's expression was stony. As Juliet watched, she saw a sudden flare of anger light Amos's face and his hands balled into fists at his side. He said something to Sanderson, leaning closer. In another minute, Juliet suspected, they would come to fisticuffs.

Quickly she crossed the room to where they stood, circling the dance floor. She didn't know quite what she was going to do to stop their argument, but she knew that she had to. If the two men actually got into a fight, it would be the end of any hopes Ethan might have of courting Ellie.

"Amos!" she called when she was close enough for him to hear her, and the two men turned in surprise. Amos's brows snapped together when he saw her. Quickly, before he could tell her to mind her own business, Juliet smiled sweetly at him and said, "I believe you promised me a dance, didn't you?"

Amos's mouth set in grim lines, and for an instant Juliet was afraid that he was going to thunder out that he hadn't. But then he turned toward her and said tersely, "Yes. Certainly."

He took her arm in a viselike grip and walked with her onto the dance floor.

"Amos!" Juliet hissed. "You're hurting me!"

"What?" He glanced down at her. "Oh, sorry." He released her arm. "I didn't mean to. I was thinking of something else."

"Obviously."

A reel was playing when they reached the dance area, and they took a place at the end of the line of couples, clapping along with the others. The dance was fast, and by the time it finished both of them were breathing hard. But it had burned off some of Amos's anger, and the fierce look was gone from his eyes. He paused at the edge of the dance area, his hand still around Juliet's.

"Thank you," he said. "I think I was about to commit a grave social error."

Juliet smiled. *Did it only seem that way or was Amos actually beginning to joke more?* "You're welcome. I thought I spied a disaster looming."

A waltz started up. Amos glanced back toward the dance floor. "Would you—shall we try again, just for dancing's sake this time?"

Juliet smiled. "I'd like that."

They moved closer to the musicians, and Amos took her in his arms. They began to circle the floor with the other couples, but Juliet didn't notice anyone else. She looked up into Amos's face, and she could not look away. He seemed equally oblivious. He drew her closer to him. The other couples swirled around them, but they didn't infringe on their world, suddenly shrunk to the space encompassed only by the two of them. Juliet felt as if she were under a spell of enchantment, as if a magic veil of gossamer had been wound around them.

They danced on and on, Juliet wasn't sure how long. It seemed as if it went on forever, the music filling the air around them, unending, and Amos's arms around her, the heat from his body warming hers. Yet, when at last they stopped, it also seemed as if the dance had passed too quickly, as if it had barely started. Slowly Amos released her. Juliet felt cold apart from him, and she barely suppressed a shiver. She came back to reality with a thump. They were Amos Morgan and his housekeeper, and they were in the midst of a crowd of people.

She glanced away and a blush rose in her cheeks. She couldn't look up into his face, afraid that her expression would reveal too much of how their dance had shaken her composure. "I—uh, thank you for the dance."

"Thank you." Amos's voice was low and sounded shaken. Juliet wondered if he had felt the same strange sense of isolation from the others, the same intensity of emotion, as if life had crazily jumped onto another path altogether.

Amos took a step back. Juliet wondered if everyone at the dance was staring at them. Had anyone noticed how absorbed in each other they had been? She didn't dare look around for fear of what she would see on the faces of the others.

Amos cleared his throat and said brusquely, "It's time to go, don't you think? I'm tired."

Juliet nodded. "Yes. Me, too."

She wasn't, actually. She felt as if life were rushing up inside her, as if she could accomplish anything. But she didn't want to stay here. She wanted to be alone, to let herself feel the new and wonderful sensations that were sweeping through her, to examine the mix of emotions inside her.

"I'll find Ethan, and we'll go." Amos started off, and Juliet turned to find Mr. and Mrs. Metz and take their leave of them, certain that Amos would never think of doing such a task.

She said a pleasant good-bye to them—and a much longer one than she really wished. But eventually she pulled free of Mrs. Metz's effusive thanks and slipped out of the barn. She walked across the farmyard to the Morgan wagon, where she found Amos harnessing the mules to the wagon.

"Where's Ethan?" Juliet asked, glancing around.

Amos shrugged. "Go ahead and get in. He's not coming with us. He wanted to stay, and Mo Cunningham said they'd drop him off on their way home."

"Oh." Juliet thought of riding home alone with Amos, sitting beside him on the wagon seat, and excitement tickled inside her.

She climbed up into the wagon, using the big wheel and the step on the side above that. She sat down beside Amos and folded her hands in her lap, composing herself. Juliet found that it was more difficult to do than she would have imagined. She kept wanting to glance over at Amos, to study his features, to smile at him and see his answering smile.

It was a long ride home. Amos never talked a lot at any time, and tonight Juliet couldn't think of anything to say, either. She was too aware of Amos's physical presence beside her: the muscled strength of his thigh; the long, supple fingers that held the reins; his sharply cut profile, pale in the moonlight. Her breath came shallowly, and her every nerve was alive. It seemed as if all her senses were sharpened. She could smell the scent of sage from beside the road and hear the night hum of the insects. She could feel the brush of the air over every inch of her skin like a caress as they moved along. There was something scary inside her, something daring and exciting and nervous. Juliet clasped her hands together tightly in her lap and braved a brief look at Amos.

What was he thinking?

They reached the farmyard, and Amos pulled to a stop in front of the barn. He climbed down quickly from the wagon and walked around to Juliet's side. She started down, reaching blindly behind her with her foot for the wooden step, but Amos reached up and grasped her by the waist, swinging her down. He set her on the ground, and Juliet smiled up her thanks at him. Amos looked at her, his eyes slowly trailing over each feature of her face, lit by the white moonlight. His hands remained at her waist, his fingers pressing lightly into her flesh. His chest lifted and fell in a long sigh.

Unconsciously Juliet moved half a step toward him. Amos closed the gap, pulling her to him. She felt the impact of his hard body, his arms closing around her, wrapping her in his warmth and strength. His hand went to the back of her neck, fingers splayed, and held her head firmly in place, as if she might move away from him.

But Juliet had no intention of moving. She wanted this to happen, wanted to find out. She waited, wide eyes open, soft and dark, watching as his face loomed closer and closer. Her eyes fell to his mouth, firm and full, lips slightly apart as the air rasped through them. She could feel the faint tremor in his hand, the bands of heat where his hard arms crossed her back, the unyielding plane of his chest against which her breasts were pressed. His heat shimmered around her: his face filled her vision. She felt surrounded by him, and the sensation sent a wild liquid fire surging through her. She knew that she wanted to feel his arms even more tightly around her, that she ached to push her body against his until there was no telling where he left off and she began.

The wildness of her desires stunned her. The heat in her loins was fiery and pulsing, insistent. Juliet imagined rubbing her body against Amos's and hearing, *feeling* his response.

He hesitated, his mouth only a breath away from hers, and Juliet wanted to cry out in frustration. Then something seemed to break inside him, and he let out a smothered groan, and his mouth came down hard on hers. His hand clenched in her hair, pulling it a little, but Juliet didn't even notice the tiny flash of pain. Amos ground his lips into hers, separating them. Juliet went up onto tiptoe, her mouth eagerly answering his; her arms slid around him, squeezing him tightly. She felt as if she had been ignited; every inch of her flesh suddenly burned as if in flames. She wanted to taste him, to touch him, to be consumed by him. Never in her life had she known anything this wild, this strong. His tongue slipped into her mouth, startling her, but she did not pull away. She savored the new, exciting sensation, and after a moment, her own tongue tentatively touched his.

Amos groaned, and suddenly he jerked away from her. "Oh, God, Juliet!" He turned away, shoving his hands into his hair. His voice was rough and low. "Go on in the house. Please! Go!"

Juliet hesitated for an instant, then turned and ran for the house.

Eleven

Juliet went up to check on Frances. She was glad to find her asleep, since her feelings were in such a turmoil that she would have had trouble making any sort of polite conversation. Then Juliet went back downstairs to her room and went straight to bed, but the emotions churning through her made it impossible for her to go to sleep for hours.

The next morning she awoke feeling hardly rested. She was excited, eager, scared—a vast jumble of emotions. She didn't know how she would face Amos after what had happened last night. On the other hand, she was eager to see him.

She hurried into the kitchen to prepare breakfast, her stomach aflutter with nerves. When the outer door opened, she jumped and whirled around, only to find that it was Ethan coming in. He looked a trifle tired, but he beamed broadly at Juliet and gave her a buoyant "Good morning!"

The next time the door opened, Juliet knew that it had to be Amos. She was more prepared this time, and she did not jump, but turned slowly and deliberately. He was watching her, but as soon as her eyes met his, he glanced away. Nodding vaguely at the room in general, Amos went over to the washstand.

Juliet dished up the food and put it on the table, turning Amos's behavior over in her mind. It occurred to her that he must want to ignore the kiss they had shared last night. She wondered if that would be easy for him; it was impossible for her.

Juliet had always been very much a creature of her emotions, and it was difficult for her now to place logic and propriety above them. Obviously it wasn't as difficult for Amos. She was hurt by his apparent eagerness to ignore her. *Did he wish that it hadn't happened?* That thought scored her heart.

Amos continued to avoid her throughout the day, indeed, for the next several days, until at last Juliet gave up on ever knowing the truth. Sternly she tried to quash her own tumult of emotions. After all, what did it matter how she felt about Amos when it was so obvious that he had not felt anything for her?

She would have been surprised to learn that Amos did not consider it at all easy to hold back from her. His desire for Juliet had been growing every day she was in his house, and after the passion had flared into life between them in that kiss, his desire and consequent frustration had become almost unbearable. He tossed and turned at night, unable to find any way to sleep, tormented by lustful images of Juliet in his bed, her body white and soft beneath his hands. He wanted her so desperately that the only way he could keep himself from grabbing her and kissing her was to stay as far away from her as he could. If he talked to her, if he even looked at her for long, the same fierce desire would flame up inside him until he wasn't sure that he could control himself. But he found that he missed talking to her, missed seeing her, missed hearing her laugh and sing.

The only thing he could do was hold on for as long as he could, staying away from Juliet as much as possible and savoring the moments when he was able to look at her, to be around her, until the desire became so fierce that it drove him away. There was no way that it could end well for him, he knew. He was caught, and there was nothing he could do about it.

Two weeks passed, and with their passage came the advent of summer. Almost overnight, it seemed, the days went from mild to hot, though the evenings did have a blessed coolness. With the hot weather Frances's health went precipitously downhill. She was constantly in pain and so weak now that she needed Juliet's help to do almost anything, even sit up in bed or eat or use the chamberpot. There was a bell on her bedside table to ring whenever she needed Juliet, but Juliet was afraid that sometimes she might be too weak even to get the bell and ring it, so she made sure to look in on her every hour. Despite her weakness, Frances gave Juliet instructions about canning and preserving and all the multitude of tasks that would come with the harvest, her forehead creased with anxiety, as if she knew that she would not be there when those occasions arrived.

Juliet had to let some of the housework slide because of the extra time she now spent helping Frances. She also hoed weeds in the vegetable garden, which she had learned was considered the domain of the woman of the house. The men were busy weeding in the corn and wheat fields, with little time to spend on the vegetables.

"As if they weren't important," Frances told her with a weak smile. "I wonder what they'd think if they didn't have any vegetables to eat all winter."

Juliet grinned. "I can guess."

One evening after the supper dishes were washed, Juliet was in the vegetable garden, hoeing weeds. She had found that it was more pleasant to do the heavy outdoor work in the evenings, when it was cooler. The vegetable garden was close by the chicken yard, and now and then as she worked, Juliet glanced over at the fuzzy yellow chicks hopping along behind their mothers, their heads bobbing down to the ground. She smiled to see them.

Juliet went up and down the rows, wielding the long-handled hoe against the weeds which had cropped up (overnight, it seemed) among the tidy lines of beans, peas, squash, and tomatoes. The shadows stretched longer as the sun began to set, and the evening grew cooler.

Suddenly the air was split with an awful shriek, and Juliet jumped and whirled around, her heart pounding. There was a commotion among the chickens, and from them came a cacophony of shrill cheeps and squawks and the wild fluttering of wings. The hens and chickens were scattering everywhere. It took Juliet a moment to realize what was going on.

Two of the baby chicks lay still; several other little yellow balls were scurrying around in terror and confusion. The mother hen was dancing wildly in the middle, jabbing with her beak and scratching with her claws. Juliet recognized with a gasp exactly what the hen was fighting: a long, brown-patterned snake, its jaws wide apart and fangs sunk into the hen's side.

A rattlesnake! A rattlesnake had killed two of the chicks and was now in a deadly battle with their mother. It wouldn't be long before she was dead, too; her sharp claws were no match against its venom.

Anger flooded Juliet. *Those darling baby chicks!* They were hers! She had raised them, had cooed and giggled over them, cuddling the little balls of yellow fuzz in her hands. All the chickens were her animals. She threw out their feed and kept their pan of water full; she gathered their eggs. And no snake was going to destroy her chickens!

She didn't stop to think, just gripped her hoe tightly and ran toward the scene of the attack. When she reached the battle, she raised her hoe above her head and swung down with all her strength, cutting the snake in half. Both ends of the snake writhed. The hen flopped to the ground, and Juliet swung the hoe again and again, severing the vicious triangular head from the remainder of its body. The hen shook all over and finally went limp in death. The pieces of the snake stilled.

Bile rose in Juliet's throat. She rested her hoe upon

the ground and leaned against it, swallowing against the blackness that suddenly rose up inside her. Lights sparkled at the backs of her eyes, and her stomach flip-flopped.

"Juliet!" Amos was screaming at her, his voice raw and tight, as he ran across the yard. "What the hell—"

His words died in his throat as he got close enough to see the pieces of snake and the dead chickens in front of Juliet, and he closed the gap between them in an instant, grabbing Juliet around the waist just as she began to slide toward the ground.

"Are you all right? Did he get you?" He swung Juliet up into his arms and ran toward the house.

"No," Juliet whispered. The faintness was receding, but she shivered, suddenly cold, and clung to Amos's neck, grateful to have his strong arms around her.

"Are you sure?" He reached the back steps and sat down, cradling her in his lap, and shoved her skirts up, checking her legs for the sign of a puncture.

"Yes, really." Juliet leaned against his chest, too shaken to even protest at the indecent position of her skirts and petticoats.

Amos slid his hand up and down each of her arms, turning them so that he could see all sides. "Oh, God, Juliet! When I saw what you were doing!" He shook his head. "Are you insane? What were you thinking of?"

"I couldn't let him kill all my chickens."

"To hell with your chickens! *You* could have been killed! Didn't you think about that?"

"No," Juliet confessed. "I didn't. I just thought that I couldn't let that snake kill them." Her eyes filled with tears. "Those poor little chicks! Oh, Amos! He killed two of them. Did you see them? I raised them. They're—they're my pets." Tears spilled over and ran down her cheeks. "I love them."

Amos looked down at her, and his angry expression softened. "I know you do." He curved his hand over her cheek. "You're too tenderhearted. I've told you that before. Animals aren't pets on a farm."

"Maybe not. But that's no reason to stand back and let them be killed. Wouldn't you have rushed in and killed it?"

"Of course I would have. That's exactly what you should have done: call me and let me kill it."

"I didn't think of that. Besides, there wasn't time. By the time I called you and you came, he would have taken care of another hen and gotten her chicks, too."

"Better them than you. There are only so many chicks a rattlesnake can eat."

"Amos! How can you be so callous!" Juliet leaned away from him, looking up at his face in irritation.

He smiled and shrugged. "It comes naturally to me. Didn't you know?"

Juliet rolled her eyes, and he chuckled. His chuckle grew into a full-grown laugh. "Lord! If only I'd had a picture of you out there!" He leaned his head back and cackled at the memory. "A little city girl, afraid of the chickens when you first came, wouldn't even get near a cow—"

"That's not true! It was that stupid boar of yours I was scared of."

"And there you were, chopping that rattlesnake up

with a hoe!" He laughed so hard that tears seeped out of his eyes, and Juliet couldn't help but join in, nerves and fear dissolving in the laughter. "Remind me never to get you mad, lady. You can really swing a hoe!"

"You better remember that next time you start arguing with me," Juliet teased back.

Then, surprising them both, Amos squeezed her tightly to him for a moment, and he dropped his head to hers, burying his face in her hair. Juliet felt the warmth of his breath against her head, the taut strength of his muscles wrapped around her. She thought of their kiss after the dance, and even in the midst of her shaken state, she felt an upsurge of the same physical longing that she had experienced then. Heat lanced through her abdomen, and shivers of delight ran out all over her body.

Finally Amos's arms relaxed around her and he let her go, raising his head. Reluctantly Juliet stood up and stepped away. She looked back down at Amos.

He was gazing up at her, his dark eyes intent, and an odd, soft, almost longing expression upon his face. He seemed on the verge of saying something, doing something, and Juliet waited tensely. But he did not move or speak. Juliet wanted to throw herself back down into his lap and hold onto him forever. But, of course, she could not do that, not when he gave her no encouragement. Instead, she turned and walked shakily back into the house.

Ethan slammed into the kitchen. Juliet was standing at the counter peeling potatoes for their supper, and she turned in surprise at his noisy entrance. It was Sunday, and Ethan had gone over to the Sandersons to call on Ellie, the first time since the dance. He had been eager and excited when he left. The last thing Juliet would have expected was for him to return like this. He looked thunderous, and his lean young body was taut with anger.

"Ethan? What's the matter?"

He looked at her. His lips tightened, and she thought he wasn't going to answer, but then, as if he could not hold it back, the words burst from him, "He told me not to come back! He told me I couldn't see Ellie anymore!"

Juliet stared. "What? Who told you? Mr. Sanderson?"

"Who else?" Ethan spat.

"But why?" Surely Sanderson wasn't punishing the boy because of what had happened between Sanderson and her! That would be too cruel!

"He said—he thinks I'm not good enough for her. He says he doesn't want her to get too serious about me." Ethan flung up his hands in a gesture of frustration. "He's sending me away because she likes me!"

"But where's the harm in that?" Juliet asked reasonably. "I realize that Ellie is young, but so are you. It isn't as if you're about to marry any day simply because you like each other. There're years ahead of you to decide if your feeling for each other is—"

"I don't know. I told him that we weren't serious yet, that we weren't planning to jump into marriage. But he said that's what worried him, that he didn't figure marriage was on my mind."

"What!" Anger rose in Juliet's chest. What a hypocrite John Sanderson was! She dropped the potato and knife she was holding and rushed to Ethan. "How could he say such a thing?" She took his arm and looked up into his face. His dark eyes were bright with a mixture of pain and fury. "You're one of the nicest people I know. I've never seen you act like anything but a gentleman."

"I told him I would never think of harming Ellie in any way! He made me furious. I felt like hitting the old buzzard." His voice was rough with unshed tears. "But I didn't. Why would he think I'm like that?"

Juliet grimaced. She knew why. It was because it was what Sanderson himself would do; he was judging Ethan by his own conduct. "He's a fool."

"He told me I would taint her."

"Taint her! Why, the nerve of that man!"

"Why would he say that? Why would he think that just being around me would ruin her? I mean, I know that I—" A blush stained his cheeks. "Well, that I feel things for Ellie that aren't proper. But I would never do anything like that to her!"

"Of course not." Juliet sighed. It hurt her to see Ethan looking so woebegone. "I'm sorry. I'm afraid—oh, it's my fault. Mr. Sanderson is angry with me and your father, and he's taking it out on you."

"Angry with you?" Ethan's forehead wrinkled in confusion. "But why would he be angry with you?"

At that moment Amos appeared in the doorway from the hall. "What the devil's going on out here? I could hear you clear into the sitting room, Ethan."

Ethan cast a glance toward his father and mumbled, "Sorry, Pa."

"Well, isn't anyone going to tell me what the commotion's about?" Amos looked from one to the other in a disgruntled way.

Ethan shrugged. He looked at the floor and said in a low voice, "Mr. Sanderson forbade me to call on Ellie anymore."

"Oh." And odd expression touched Amos's face. Juliet, watching him, thought that it looked almost like fear, but that was ridiculous, she knew, so she dismissed it. "I see. What—what did he tell you?"

"Nothing, except he doesn't want me keeping company with his daughter anymore. I'm not good enough for her, it seems."

"I hope you don't believe that damn fool."

"I don't know. I don't understand it. I thought he liked me well enough." Ethan might be a man in height, but there was a little-boy look of hurt in his eyes as he said it.

"He did, I imagine. It's me he hates," Amos said calmly.

"You? I don't understand. First Juliet says its her Mr. Sanderson's mad at, and now you say it's you."

"It's probably a little of both," Amos conceded. "But more me than Juliet. I'm the one who made him back down in front of her. Made him look bad. That's what he can't forgive."

"Made him back down? Why? You mean you had a fight with him?" Ethan stared at his father, nonplussed.

"And what did Juliet have to do with it?"

Suddenly understanding dawned on his face, and he looked at Juliet. "You mean—they fought over you?"

Color rose in Juliet's cheeks. "No! They didn't fight over me! It was just that, well, Mr. Sanderson and I parted company a few weeks ago in less than an amicable way."

Amos snorted. "That's an understatement. You had bruises on your wrist the next day; I saw them."

Juliet shot him a quelling look. "There's no need to make it anything more than what it was. Mr. Sanderson made an improper advance toward me, and I told him that he had misjudged me. He became rather upset."

"He grabbed her arm," Amos amplified Juliet's statement, "and wouldn't let go."

"He hurt you?" Ethan looked astonished. "Why didn't you tell me?"

"I didn't think it was necessary, and I didn't want to cause any trouble between you and Ellie's father. Your father helped me out of the, uh, situation, and, well, it was over and done with. I saw no need to bring it up with you. The whole thing was very embarrassing, and I didn't want to talk about it. I never dreamed that he would be so petty that he would exact revenge on you."

Ethan turned back to his father, and a satisfied grin popped onto his face. "You booted him off the farm, huh?"

"I told him he had to leave. I guess he felt I humiliated him in front of the woman he . . . wanted. Obviously he wanted to get back at me."

"That son of a bitch!" Ethan spat.

"Yes." Amos didn't reprove his son for his language. "I'm sorry, Ethan, but there wasn't anything else I could do."

"Of course not." Anger sizzled in Ethan's eyes. "But how does he have the gall to accuse me of tainting his daughter, when he's the one who goes around accosting innocent women?"

Amos shook his head. "I don't know. But that's the way John Sanderson is. Always has been. I didn't like him when we were in grammar school together."

"It's not fair!"

"No, it's not," Amos agreed quietly. "But there's not anything you can do about it, son. Ellie is his daughter, and he has the right to set rules for her and for her suitors."

Ethan cast an anguished look at his father, then turned away. "No. I guess there's not. But I'd like to tell him what I think of him."

Juliet was surprised to see that same odd, almost panicked look flicker across Amos's face. "I know. But what good would it do?"

"Probably none. But it'd make me feel better."

"Maybe he'll calm down after awhile," Juliet put in. She sensed that it was important to Amos that Ethan not talk to Sanderson again. She wasn't sure exactly why, but the look on Amos's face when Ethan mentioned it made it clear that it was not something he wanted to happen. "In time he'll forget how angry he was with me. Then you could see Ellie again. But if you go over there and get into a big row with him, tell him what a scoundrel you think he is, it's certain that he'll never allow you to call on her."

Ethan wavered. "I guess you're right." He sighed and looked down at the floor, as if he would find some solution to his problem there. "I think I'll take a walk down to the creek. Cool off some."

He turned and went back outside. Amos watched him go, then plopped down in one of the kitchen chairs and propped his elbows on the table, heaving a great sigh, and dropped his head into his hands. "Damn that man."

"I feel terrible about this," Juliet told him. "Maybe if I went over and talked to Mr. Sanderson, he'd change his mind. Perhaps I could make him see that this has nothing to do with Ethan."

"Don't bother. It isn't just the incident on the porch. That does have something to do with it, since he was willing to let Ethan come around as long as John was seeing you. But now . . ."

"I don't understand. What else is there?" When Amos didn't say anything, she went on, "Does it have something to do with you two arguing at the dance?"

"Not really. At the dance Sanderson was telling me that he didn't want Ethan coming around anymore. I was hoping he'd cool off, that he'd think better of it and wouldn't say anything to Ethan. Obviously my hopes were unfounded."

"But how could he have anything against Ethan?" Juliet persisted. "He's a good, sweet boy. He'd never do anything to hurt Ellie."

"Sanderson doesn't want his daughter falling in love with him. He would never let her marry Ethan, and he's afraid she's getting serious about him. He doesn't want it to go that far. So he's barring Ethan from the house now." He grimaced. "Well, at least he didn't tell Ethan the reason. I was afraid he would." He looked up at Juliet, and his expression was bleak. "Ethan's illegitimate. Sanderson doesn't want his daughter marrying a bastard."

Juliet sank down into a chair across the table from Amos, too stunned to speak. Amos Morgan had fathered an illegitimate child! She had wondered several times about Ethan's mother—why no one ever spoke of her, whether she had died, or if she had been unable to take living with the dour man and had fled. But it hadn't even entered her mind that Amos might not have been married to the woman. It didn't surprise her that Amos had had relations with a woman without the benefit of marriage. Juliet had been raised in too worldly an atmosphere to be shocked by that aspect of human nature. Besides, she had kissed the man, and it was obvious that there was plenty of passion bubbling beneath Amos's quiet exterior.

However, she also knew that Amos was a good man. She would never have imagined that he had gotten a woman pregnant and then callously cast her aside, refusing to marry her when she became pregnant with his child. She remembered how he had come to her aid with Sanderson, how he had warned her that Sanderson did not respect women. Juliet could not believe that Amos himself had had so little respect for a woman.

"But I—" Juliet faltered.

"Don't look at me like that," Amos growled. "I might have known you'd think the worst of me."

"No, I don't! That's just it. I can't believe you would abandon his mother."

"Abandon! Ha!" There was no mirth in his tone. Grim lines bracketed his mouth. "That's a rich one. It was she who—hell, I wanted to marry her. I begged her to marry me. She just laughed. 'Marry a farmboy?'" He mocked a woman's contemptuous tone. "She didn't want any of me or of a baby, either. The only reason she had Ethan was because she was too scared to try to get rid of him."

The color drained from Juliet's face. "Oh, Amos . . ."

"I loved her," Amos confessed, his voice as dry as sand. "I assumed we would marry. I—I worshipped her. I thought she was a goddess, an angel. Cleopatra and Helen of Troy rolled into one."

An ache speared Juliet's chest as she looked into his face, the old, wounded love written clearly on it. How much he had loved that woman! No wonder he had never married.

The words came pouring out of him now, rusty from their long secrecy, but unstoppable. "For months she was the only thing I thought about, dreamed about. I was young and naive, completely inexperienced. I had no restraint; I was consumed by love and desire. Then she told me she was tired of me. I was . . . destroyed. Later she showed up here, handed me the baby, and left. I kept him, of course. Pa gave me holy hell about it. He wanted me to give him up to an orphanage, called him the product of my lust. But I couldn't do that; he was my own flesh and blood."

"No, of course not!" Juliet spontaneously reached across the table and laid her hand over his in sympathy. "Of course you kept him. How could you do anything else?"

He gave her a wry smile. "Lots of people thought I could have. Old lady King turned her back on me the first time I walked into church with him. For a long time after that, I refused to set foot inside the place again. Pious bunch of hypocrites! Frances stood by me, of course. She kept right on going to church, facing those people, until finally I realized what a coward I was being, so I went back, too. Eventually people forgot about it or came to accept it. Probably because after Pa died, I became the wealthiest farmer around."

"Don't be so cynical."

He shrugged. "Henrietta helped, too, I have to admit. She and Samuel accepted Ethan without a word. And Henrietta's a force to be reckoned with."

Juliet smiled a little. "I know."

"I never thought about anything like this happening. I mean, once it all quieted down. I didn't think about people holding it against Ethan when he was older."

"He doesn't know?"

"Of course not! What would I have said to him, 'Look, son, you're a bastard'?"

"No, of course not." Juliet grimaced at him. "But don't you think he has the right to know?"

"The right? Maybe. But he doesn't need to know. He doesn't want to. What good would it do him to learn that his mother didn't even want him, that she would have left him on a doorstep if I hadn't taken him in?"

"What did you tell Ethan about his mother?"

"I lied through my teeth whenever he asked me about her. I told him she was good and sweet and loved him and that she'd died right after he was born. And if he didn't ask, I kept my mouth shut. Frances, too. And no one else had the nerve to say anything to his face. Most folks are scared to cross me."

"With good reason, I suspect."

He looked at her without expression. "I set some people straight once or twice about it."

"But what about now? Don't you think he's bound to find out sooner or later? Won't he be upset about your lying to him all this time?"

"Not if everybody keeps their mouths shut." Amos fixed her with a hard stare.

"Don't glare at me! *I'm* not going to tell him. But he's going to get interested in some other girl sometime, and their fathers—"

"Not everybody's as big an ass as John Sanderson. There are plenty of people who wouldn't mind having their blood linked with a bastard's, as long as that blood brought the biggest farm in the county with it."

"Maybe you're right." But Juliet didn't believe her words. Secrets were too hard to keep; the only reason Amos had been able to keep it from Ethan this long was because they lived in such an isolated manner. But Ethan would not be satisfied with the solitude that Amos preferred. He was a sociable young man; he would be going to picnics and barn raisings and church bazaars. He would go into town. He'd dance with girls and go calling on them. Somewhere, someone was bound to inform him of the truth.

And then what would happen to him? Juliet hated to think of the possibilities. Ethan would be crushed, not only at finding out that his mother was far from the sweet creature his father had described to him, but that his father had lied to him for years, as well.

Juliet sighed. It was no use trying to convince Amos of her fears, and she doubted that it would serve any purpose anyway. If Amos were to tell Ethan now, it would have the same effect on him. Better to let sleeping dogs lie, as they said, she thought. But she was afraid that Amos and Ethan were on a dark road to disaster.

Twelve

Juliet awakened and sat up stiffly, blinking as she tried to orient herself. She realized that she must have fallen asleep as she sat up watching Frances, for she was sitting in a chair beside Frances's bed, her head resting on her crossed arms on the bed itself. It had been a cramped and uncomfortable position to sleep in, and she felt it in her shoulders and neck. She put her hand against the back of her neck and rolled her head from side to side to ease the stiffness. Then she stood, stretching, and moved to the head of the bed.

Frances was asleep, her face as pale as the sheets beneath her. Juliet sighed, and tears pricked at her eyelids. It hurt her to see Frances slipping away so inevitably, bit by bit every day. Frances had completely stopped eating a few days ago; her stomach rebelled against anything that she tried to put in it. It was just as well, Juliet knew, for Frances was tired of the fight. She would be better off to slip away than to endure more of the constant anguish she had been suffering. But knowing that didn't ease the pain of those who would be left behind.

As she stood there, watching her, Frances's eyes opened. She smiled weakly at Juliet. "Hello."

"Good morning." Juliet was careful not to ask how she felt. "Would you like some water?"

Frances shook her head. "No. I'm fine."

"How about if I sit with you awhile?" She ought to be downstairs getting breakfast for the men, but she knew they would understand. As she had to care more and more for the bedridden Frances, they made do much of the time with their meals.

Frances nodded and lifted her hand to take Juliet's in hers. "I always wanted a sister. Or a particular friend. Another woman I could talk with, share secrets. I never had one. The farms are too far apart—and I reckon we were never ones to mingle, either." She squeezed Juliet's hand; her clasp was pitifully weak. "But I guess I got my wish finally. They say the Lord works in mysterious ways."

Tears sprang into Juliet's eyes. She couldn't speak. She smiled, swallowing the lump in her throat.

"I'm glad to have another woman with me when I go. It'd be hard having only men, even if Amos is my brother. He loves me, but it's not the same."

"Of course not. I'm glad I'm here for you, too." Juliet pulled her chair closer and sat down, still clasping the other woman's hand.

"I was dreaming about my mother," Frances said softly. "It was so real, I could have sworn I could see her. Do you suppose she was here?"

"Maybe. In spirit. I've heard that things like that can happen."

Frances nodded and closed her eyes, drifting back into sleep. Juliet eased her hand from Frances's grasp and went downstairs with a heavy heart to fix Amos and Ethan their breakfast.

When the men came in to eat, Amos glanced questioningly at Juliet, but didn't say anything. The look on Juliet's face told him all he needed to know.

The rest of the day Juliet went through her chores as quickly as she could, doing only what was absolutely necessary to keep the household going. Every few minutes she went upstairs and tiptoed into Frances's room. It was reaching the point where each time she came into the room, there was a clutch of fear in her stomach that this time she would find Frances no longer breathing.

Late in the afternoon, as Juliet was sitting beside Frances's bed, her hands busy with mending socks, Frances began to talk about her father. "Pa hated Malcolm."

"Malcolm?" Juliet's voice was puzzled. She had never heard of anyone named Malcolm. Had there been another child?

"Yes. The boy I liked." A sweet smile of reminiscence crept across Frances's face. "But Pa said he wasn't good enough for a Morgan. I don't know. Maybe he was right. But I cried for weeks when Pa told me I couldn't see him anymore."

"He forbade you to see him?"

Frances nodded. "Amos told me later that Pa did it because he didn't want to lose a housekeeper. Amos said I should have gone against Pa, but I couldn't. Besides, it wasn't as if Malcolm had asked me to marry him. We were just sweet on each other."

The words sat oddly on the lips of this woman, who looked twenty years older than she was, her face pale and lined with pain. Juliet's heart twisted with pity.

"Amos was in Omaha then, so I didn't have anyone to stand up for me against Pa. I was afraid he'd throw me out of the house if I defied him. Where would I have gone if he had?" She turned her bleak eyes on Juliet. "You know how hard it is for a woman on her own. If everybody knew that your own father had put you out . . . well, it would have ruined my reputation. Everyone would have figured I'd done something wicked. What kind of future would I have had?"

"I know." Juliet nodded, her own eyes filling with sympathetic tears. "How awful for you."

"I cried and cried, till I thought I didn't have any more tears left. I reckon I didn't, cause I've never cried much since then." Frances sighed. "I feel awfully tired. I wonder why I started talking about Pa? It was all so long ago. You'd think a body would forget those things."

"Some things you can't forget."

"I guess you're right."

Amos sat with his sister that evening in a silence as vast as the country around them. Juliet napped in her room. Late in the evening, she woke and, wrapping her robe around her, went upstairs to Frances's room.

Amos was asleep in the chair beside Frances's bed. Frances lay in a restless sleep, her legs moving, her hands twitching at the covers, and she mumbled something now and again that Juliet could not catch.

"Amos?" Juliet touched his shoulder lightly, and Amos awoke with a start.

"What?" He sat up straight and looked around in confusion. "Oh. Yes. I forgot where I was."

"How has she been?"

He looked up the bed to Frances's face. "Real quiet. She must have just started that moaning." He sighed. "She hasn't awakened the whole time I've been here."

"I'll spell you for a while. Why don't you get some sleep?"

He nodded. The knowledge lay between them, heavy but unspoken: Frances's death watch had begun. Until last night, when Juliet had fallen asleep at Frances's bedside, they had left her alone through much of the night. But now it seemed important that someone be with her every moment.

Amos arose, giving Juliet his chair, and started to leave. He stopped and turned back. "I—I wanted to thank you."

"Thank me?" Juliet looked surprised. "For what?"

"What you've done for Frances. She's no kin to you, but you couldn't have been kinder to her if you had been family. I know she's appreciated having a woman with her, to help her with, you know, the private things."

"I'm glad to be able to help."

"I think you really mean that."

"Of course I do. Why wouldn't I?"

"I don't know. It's hard. A lot of work and—not pleasant, I know. It's not anything that you've been used to."

Juliet smiled sadly. "Don't be too sure of that. My life hasn't been pampered. I've sat with more than one person who . . ." She trailed off, shrugging. "My father died, and I took care of him for months before that. One thing I am acquainted with is sickrooms."

"Still, you had no obligation to do it. You're a good woman. I misjudged you in the beginning. I'm not real good at saying things, but I want you to know that I realize how wrong I was. And I'm sorry."

His words warmed Juliet, and tears pricked at her eyes. "Thank you. I—I was wrong about you, too. I've seen how much you love your family. You want to protect them."

"And I can't," he added sadly. "That's what's so awful." His big hands clenched in frustration at his sides. "What good am I if I can't even keep them safe?"

"No, don't say that!" Juliet went to him and laid her hand on his arm. "You're a good man. You can't judge yourself for not being able to keep Frances from death. No one can do that. You can't set yourself up against God."

For an instant, Amos covered Juliet's hand with his other hand. His palm against her skin was warm and roughened with calluses; it swallowed her hand. Then abruptly he pulled it away and turned, striding out of the room. Juliet sighed, watching him go. Her heart ached for him. He was so strong, so determined; it must be terrible for him to come up against something that he couldn't fight. She wished that she could help him in some way.

But she was already doing that the only way she knew

how: by taking care of Frances. Juliet turned back to the bed and sat down again in the chair.

The night crawled by. Juliet had to struggle to keep her eyes open. Frances continued to murmur and moan. She began to move her legs restlessly in the bed.

"Ma?" she said once. "Ma, will you walk with me? Come walk with me."

A chill went through Juliet. Frances's voice sounded small and light, like that of a child. Frances held out her hand. Her eyes opened, but she stared fixedly at the ceiling.

"Ma?" she said again. "Take my hand. Come walk."

Juliet put her hand in Frances's, and Frances's fingers closed around hers tightly. Frances smiled. She was quiet after that.

Juliet awoke with a start and realized that she had nodded off in the chair. Her hand was still clasped with Frances's. She looked up at the head of the bed. There was something different about Frances's breathing; that change must have been what awakened her. Juliet stood up, gently pulled her hand from Frances's, and bent over her. She was breathing in an odd, hiccupy way, now and then stopping for an instant.

Juliet was filled with dread. She turned and hurried out of the room and down the hall to Amos's door. She rapped sharply on it.

"Amos? Amos?" When an unintelligible rumble sounded in the room, she went on, "I think you better come."

Then she turned and ran back to Frances's room.

Frances opened her eyes as Juliet came in. "Juliet . . ." Her voice sounded stronger than it had for some time, and her eyes were lucid. Juliet stared, and hope began to rise in her chest. Could it be that she was mistaken, that this change was for the better? Perhaps Frances was rallying.

"Yes. I'm right here." She hurried to the bed and took Frances's hand. Frances's fingers curled around her hand. "Take care of him. Please."

"Amos?"

Frances nodded. "Yes. Promise me you'll take care of him."

"Of course I will. As long as he needs me."

"He needs you."

She squeezed Juliet's hand tightly, then released it. Her eyes closed, and she slid back into unconsciousness. Her breathing was shallow and almost panting. The moment of elation and hope Juliet had felt slipped away.

Amos hurried into the room. He had obviously taken the time only to throw on a pair of overalls. His feet were bare, and under the overalls he wore his undershirt. He had buttoned the sides of his overalls but hadn't bothered to fasten the front bib, and it hung down loosely in front and back.

"What is it?" he asked, frowning with worry.

"I'm not sure," Juliet said, stepping back to let him near his sister. "I just—her breathing changed. She spoke to me for a minute, quite clearly, but now . . ."

Amos looked at his sister lying in the bed, then back at Juliet. Fear lurked in his eyes. He stepped forward and took Frances's hand.

"I'm here, Fanny. It's Amos. Can you hear me?"

"Amos . . ." Frances smiled, but she didn't open her eyes. "Is that the farm ahead?"

"What? Fanny, you're at the farm." He put his other hand on top of their joined hands. He glanced back at Juliet and said, "You better wake up Ethan, too."

She turned to leave the room, but at that moment Ethan came in. "I'm here," he said quietly. "I heard it when you got up, Pa."

He walked over to the bed to stand beside his father. Quietly Juliet eased out of the room, closing the door behind her. This was a time when they should be by themselves, just the family.

But she could not go to bed and sleep. She went downstairs into the kitchen and made a pot of coffee. They could all use a cup or two in the next few hours, she imagined. She sat down in the old rocking chair she had moved into the kitchen a few weeks ago. She liked to sit there and sew or knit while she was waiting for something to cook. Her knitting bag lay beside the chair, as it usually did, so she picked it up and began to work. The long needles flashed silver in the light of the kerosene lamp, and she rocked while the aroma of coffee filled the kitchen.

When the coffee was ready, she took two cups up to the men, then returned to the kitchen. She sipped her own cup of coffee and rocked, closing her eyes. She thought of her father and her mother and the nights they had died. Death always seemed to come and steal people away in the dark. She thought of her sister, Celia, in

Philadelphia. She wished that she could see her again right now.

She returned to her knitting, her mind drifting as her fingers moved swiftly, the needles clicking. The sky was beginning to lighten when she heard Amos's heavy footsteps on the stairs in the hall. Juliet thrust her yarn onto the needles and stuck it back in the bag. She rose to her feet just as Amos came heavily into the room. He looked at her.

"She's gone," he said flatly.

"Oh, Amos." Juliet had known that was what had happened, but it didn't stop the rush of pity and sorrow from sweeping over her. "I'm sorry."

He nodded abruptly and strode past her out the door. Juliet followed him to the door and watched as he walked across the yard to the barn. His head was down, and every line of his body bespoke a weary sadness. Juliet ached for him.

Suddenly she could not bear for him to carry his grief alone. She slipped through the door and hurried after him. When she caught up with him, he was already in the barn, kneeling in front of the large wooden box where he kept his tools. The lid was up and he was pulling out his hammer. He turned at the sound of her entrance.

Juliet said nothing; she didn't know what to say. She only looked at him, her big eyes dark with sympathy.

"I need to build her coffin," he said, his voice rough with unshed tears. Juliet thought she saw a glimmer of wetness in his eyes, and he turned back to the box. He stared down into it for a moment. "I have the wood set by. I didn't even realize I was doing it."

His voice became choked, and he could say nothing else. He braced his hands upon either end of the box, and his head hung lower. Juliet could not see his face; she knew he was struggling not to break down.

"Oh, Amos . . ." Juliet went over to him, her voice soft with compassion. Tears filled her eyes. She bent down and put her hand gently on his bowed back.

The small gesture of consolation undid him. He gave a great, racking sob and whirled around, throwing his arms around her and clutching her to him. Still on his knees, he buried his face in her stomach and wept. His sobs were harsh and tearing, the sounds of a man unused to crying, and his whole body shook against her.

Juliet knew without question that he was probably humiliated at breaking down in front of her, yet he must feel a great release, too, at letting out the pain inside him.

Juliet said nothing, merely held him close and stroked his hair soothingly. She curled over him to press her head to his, murmuring soft, meaningless words of comfort, and her hand smoothed down over his back.

Finally Amos's sobs quieted and his hold on her relaxed. He sat back on his heels, wiping the tears from his face; he avoided her eyes. "I'm sorry."

"Don't be. It's only natural. You wouldn't be human if you didn't grieve."

"I should be stronger. There are things to be done."

"They'll get done," Juliet assured him. "Ethan and I'll do them."

"Poor Ethan." Amos shook his head. "Frances was all the mother he ever knew."

"He's young and resilient. I think it's you who are hit the hardest."

Amos sighed and closed the lid of the box and sat down on it. He rested his elbows on his knees and his forehead on his palms and stared down at the floor. "I loved her," he said dully. "She took care of me and helped me all my life. I never realized until recently how much . . . I loved her." He raised his head and pain glittered in his dark eyes. "I didn't tell her. I never told her how much I loved her. Now it's too late."

"Oh, no." Impulsively Juliet knelt in front of him, laying her hands over his. He turned his hands over and curled his fingers around hers. Her hands felt small inside his. "I'm sure she knows you loved her. You aren't demonstrative people; she probably knew better than anyone how much you felt and didn't show, didn't say."

"I should have told her, though," he insisted. "I wasn't . . . a good enough brother. I took it for granted that she would always be there. I took from her, and I never gave back."

"That's not true. You provided her with a good home, a good life. She told me how you added things to the house to make her life easier, like the pump at the sink. It meant a lot to her, I could tell."

He looked at her almost eagerly. "Do you really think so?"

"Yes. She knew you cared. She knew you didn't want her to have to work as hard as—" Juliet stopped, realizing that she had inadvertently stumbled onto another painful topic.

"As my mother." He nodded. "That's true. And look—she died just as young. This farm's no place for a woman."

"That's not your fault. There was nothing you could do about it. It wasn't hard work or this farm that killed your sister; it was a disease. She could have gotten it and died just as young if she'd lived in town all her life and had servants waiting on her hand and foot."

A faint smile touched his lips. "I can just imagine Frances doing that."

Juliet smiled, too. "She would have hated it. You know that she loved you; she loved this house and farm, just as you do. This is where she wanted to live and what she wanted to do. It's a senseless, tragic thing that she died so young. But it wasn't because you failed her."

"I did fail her. She should have married that Wilson boy and left this farm."

"That wasn't your fault, either. She told me about it; it was your father who kept her from seeing him."

"If I'd been here, I wouldn't have let Pa threaten her like that. But I wasn't here. And she couldn't stand up to him."

"Maybe it would have been different if you had been here. Maybe not." Juliet gave his hand a squeeze to emphasize what she was saying. "You can't change the past. You weren't there when that happened; you couldn't have known it was going to. You couldn't have spent your whole life hanging around here so you could intervene if anything bad happened to your sister. That would have been absurd."

Amos sighed and nodded. "You're right, I guess. But I feel . . . oh, I don't know. That I should have done a better job of protecting her. What use is it, having this size or strength, if you can't help the people you . . . care about?" He closed his eyes. "I couldn't help Frances. I couldn't help my mother."

"You aren't God, Amos," Juliet told him bluntly. "You can't save anyone if it's their time to die."

"I always felt," Amos said almost meditatively, not looking at Juliet, "as if I was in a war with him. My father. And every time someone's taken away from me, he's won a battle. Ethan's the only one I've been able to keep."

Juliet frowned, puzzled. "I don't understand. Your father didn't kill Frances. Or your mother." Her voice unconsciously hesitated over the latter statement. She knew that Amos had blamed his father for his mother's death.

"No," he said reluctantly. "I know he didn't, not really. It was the land. He always said, 'There's no place for the weak out here.' He wanted to make all of us tougher than our mother, even Frances. He—I think he loved Ma, but when she died, he was angry. Almost as if he were furious with her for dying. He lit into me when he caught me crying in bed one night after she died."

"It must have been awful for you." Juliet laid her hand on his arm. "A child should cry for his mother."

Amos shrugged. "I don't know. Pa always figured if you cried, you were weak. I never saw him shed a tear." He sighed. "I reckon it's not the way a man should act. He told me, 'You're twelve and already the size of a man;

you ought to act like one.' I never measured up to what he wanted of me. I didn't want to be like him. And yet, I'm afraid I am."

"No. I don't believe that. You have too much feeling in you."

"Is that good or bad?" He smiled shakily. "See? I'm thirty-six years old, and I'm still not sure what a man should be. Pa would be disgusted."

"Don't worry about him or what he would think," Juliet ordered emphatically. "You're exactly what a man should be like. A mule can be strong and not cry; that's not the criteria for a man. You have a loving heart, and that's what's important. Your father should have been proud to have produced a son like you."

Her voice was fierce, and her eyes stared into his intently. Her face glowed with the fervor of her words. "A lot of other men would have thrown me out when they realized how little I knew about cooking or a farm or taking care of a house. After all, that was what I was hired to do. More than that, I'd lied about it in order to get the position. You would have had every right to turn me out. But you kept me on and suffered through all my mistakes. Maybe not silently," she added honestly, her eyes twinkling with amusement, and he smiled in response. "But you put up with it. You even paid me."

"You caught on; you're clever." He looked away and swallowed. "And you're wrong if you think there aren't a lot of men who would have kept you on."

"I know, but I also know what my position would have been—and where."

A dull flush started in Amos's throat and spread upward at her blunt words. "You shouldn't say that."

"Why not? It's the truth. We both know it. But you didn't press me to be anything but your housekeeper. You never brought my pay to me late at night in my room or 'accidentally' brushed up against me in the hall." Juliet gazed at him steadily. "You behaved like a gentleman. Even though I know you believed my morals were not the highest."

He shifted uncomfortably. "I'm not anyone to judge you."

"A lot of men would have acted toward me as John Sanderson did. Yet you defended me against him."

She remembered the night when he had kissed her and the hot excitement of his mouth, and she colored. She saw the same memory reflected in his eyes. He pulled his gaze away from her.

"I'm not so different from other men," he told her in a low voice. "A man would have to be dead not to want you. You're beautiful. But the fact that a man feels desire doesn't necessarily mean that it's returned. A beautiful woman could hardly want every fool that lusts after her. It's obvious even to a country bumpkin that you are a woman who is moved only by . . . love." His voice stumbled a little over the word. "Not by money or any sort of material comfort."

He stood up and stepped away from her, awkwardness and uncertainty in every line of his body. His voice was rough and so low Juliet had to strain to hear the words as he went on, "God knows, I've thought about offering them to you often enough."

Juliet blinked, jolted by astonishment. There had been that one hungry kiss, but except for that, Amos had seemed indifferent to her, and she had put that single incident down to simple masculine lust, not something aroused specifically by her, but simply by the fact that she was a woman.

Amos cleared his throat. "I'm sorry. I shouldn't be talking about something like this. Forgive me. I—uh, there are things I need to do. Notify Samuel and Henrietta. Make the coffin. I better get to work." He took another step away, then half turned back toward her, still keeping his eyes steadily on the floor. "Thank you."

"You're welcome. What are you thanking me for?"

"For everything you did for Frances. For—" He made a vague gesture with his hand. "For just then, for listening to me and . . . and helping me."

"I'm glad I was here."

He looked at her then. His face was grim, but softer, too, than she had ever seen it.

"I am, too," he said simply, then turned and walked away.

Thirteen

$\mathcal{H}$enrietta Morgan arrived late that afternoon and took charge. Juliet had already washed Frances's body and braided and wound her hair into a neat coronet, as she had always worn it. Then Juliet had laid her out in her best church dress, hands folded on her chest and eyelids weighted down with coins. Amos had sent Ethan into town to tell his brother of Frances's death, as well as the neighbors along the road, and he had returned to the barn to nail the coffin together.

Juliet sat with the body until Henrietta and Samuel arrived just before supper. Then Henrietta took her place, and Juliet went down to the kitchen to heat up some leftover vegetables to serve for supper along with the pot of stew and apple cobbler that Henrietta had brought with her. No one felt much like eating, but they gathered anyway in a listless group around the table and went through the motions of a meal.

In the evening Amos brought in the coffin and set it in the parlor, and Juliet lined it with Frances's favorite quilt, adding a small pillow with an embroidered slipcover for her head. Amos carried his sister's body to the parlor, where she would lie while friends and relatives sat up with her until the funeral. Amos had obviously labored over the casket, which was sanded to a satin smoothness; a twining vine and roses were carved on each side and on the lid. Tears filled Juliet's eyes as she looked at it; Amos's love for his sister, which he hadn't been able to express in words to her, was evident in every detail of the casket.

She left the Morgan family alone in the parlor with the body, feeling that it was not her place to intrude on them. Instead she pitched in working, making sure that the house was spotless and there would be food for the visitors that she knew would soon arrive.

A cousin and two neighboring families came by that evening, bringing covered dishes of food, as was customary. The three wives of the families stayed to spell Henrietta beside the casket throughout the night. Juliet made up the beds in the empty guest room and Ethan's room for the guests. Ethan would move temporarily into his father's room. She also stripped Frances's bed and opened the windows to air out the sickroom, closing the door to the hall so that Amos would not see the reminder of his sister's absence when he walked past.

The next morning she was up before dawn, gathering the eggs for the large breakfast ahead. When she returned to the kitchen, Henrietta was at the stove, an apron tied around her plump waist, frying sausage and directing the other two women about their tasks. Henrietta smiled at Juliet when she came in and immediately assigned her a

task. Good-naturedly Juliet did as she asked. Henrietta
was a bossy soul, but Juliet had long ago become accustomed to dealing with difficult people in the theater, and
at least Henrietta wasn't vain, as some of the actors she'd
dealt with were. Besides, she wouldn't be here for long,
and Juliet enjoyed her company enough to put up with
Henrietta's tendency to take over, at least for a few days.

All day long people arrived in a slow, steady stream.
Each woman brought at least one dish, so there was no
lack of food for the crowd, but Juliet was kept busy trying
to serve it and find places to store it, as well as wash up
the dishes after everyone had eaten.

Some of the men helped Amos dig a grave beside his
mother's in the small family cemetery on the other side
of the knoll behind the house. Late in the afternoon, the
minister came from the church, and they had a quiet
funeral, then lowered Frances's casket into the grave.

Juliet cast a concerned look toward Amos. His face
was the same careful mask it had been all day. She wondered what he was feeling behind it. She was too busy
looking at Amos and worrying about him to see that
Henrietta had followed Juliet's gaze with her small, sharp
eyes. Nor was she aware that that evening Henrietta
watched her carry a tray of food out to the barn, where
Amos had gone not long after the funeral and had
remained ever since.

By the end of the evening most of the visitors had
gone. Only those who had come from far away stayed the
night and left early the next morning. Samuel left the
next morning, catching a ride with another family from

town and leaving Henrietta to follow the next day in their buggy. The daily routine returned to some semblance of normalcy. Ethan and Amos went out to the fields after their morning chores, and Henrietta and Juliet pitched in to clean up the house and get the remaining gifts of food squared away.

After supper that evening, Henrietta announced solemnly, "Juliet, Amos, I need to talk to you."

Ethan glanced up with interest, and Amos cast his sister-in-law a look of dismay. Juliet was simply puzzled. Why would Henrietta want to talk to the two of them in private? Henrietta met Ethan's curious glance with a firm look, and he sighed.

"All right. I realize when I'm not wanted." He sighed exaggeratedly and stood up, carrying his plate to the sink, then ostentatiously went out into the hall and up the stairs to his room.

Amos frowned at Henrietta. "What's this all about?"

Juliet stood and began to pick up the dirty dishes to carry them to the sink, but Henrietta stopped her with a hand on her arm.

"No, dear, let that go. I'll help you clean up later, but right now I need your full, undivided attention."

Juliet experienced a prickle of uneasiness at the other woman's solemn words. She glanced toward Amos, who shrugged.

"Get on with it, Henrietta," he said bluntly.

"All right, then. Amos, I know you're one who believes in plain speaking. So that's what I'm going to do. There's no use beating around the bush. I don't know if you and Juliet have realized it yet, but the fact is, you two are in a precarious position now."

"What?" Juliet felt more confused than before. "I don't understand."

"Then you aren't thinking. It's understandable, considering what's been going on around here the last couple of days. But when I leave tomorrow morning, Juliet, you're going to be alone here with Amos and Ethan."

"And?"

"Surely it's obvious. You, a young and attractive single woman, will be living alone under the same roof with two men, neither of them related to you. As long as Frances was alive, it was all right. There was an older lady here as chaperone, better still, a relative of the men. But you, alone with them—it isn't decent."

"Oh, hogwash!" Amos said crudely.

"But there's Ethan. I mean, he's a child and Amos's son. Doesn't his presence make it all right?"

Henrietta shook her head, sighing at Juliet's naïveté. "He's sixteen, my dear. That's not a child; most people would consider him a man. His being here is worse, if anything. Now, if he were your son it would be different, but . . ."

"Oh. I—I guess you're right." Juliet knew that having lived in the world of the theater all her life, she was less knowledgeable about the moral strictures of society than Henrietta was. And now that Henrietta had explained it, she could see how the situation might cause talk.

"What nonsense!" Amos folded his arms across his

chest and glared at Henrietta. "You're just trying to stir up trouble."

Henrietta glared back at him indignantly. "Why, Amos! How can you say that? When you know I have only your best interest at heart!" She turned toward Juliet. "And yours, too, my dear. You must see that."

"Of course," Juliet agreed. "I'm sure that you want to help."

"Exactly." Henrietta gave a decisive nod of her head and shot a triumphant look at Amos. "You see? She understands. She's a woman, so she knows how important such things are. What is a woman to do if she loses her good name? And that's what will happen. People will gossip about you, of course, but, then, heaven knows, they've been doing that for years. You're a man, so it's not as bad, and, besides, everyone knows that you're, well, different. When it comes down to it, it's Juliet that will be hurt. It is her reputation that will be ripped to shreds. You know what people will say about her, especially since everyone knows what she used to do for a living. She'll be cut dead in town. No one will speak to her. Think of how it will affect Ethan. Why, people already—"

"I know what people think and say about my son," growled Amos with a grimace. "But I agree; Juliet would be harmed by it. So what do you suggest we do?"

"I think it's clear that Juliet will have to leave this house and come back to Steadman with me."

Juliet gasped. "No!"

Amos's face turned to stone, but he said nothing, merely

turned his head away and stared fixedly across the room.

"But I don't want to go back!" Juliet declared. "I want to stay here." She stopped, blushing, realizing how much of her feelings she was revealing, and she glanced hesitantly toward Amos. "I mean, that is, if Amos wants me to. I—it's a good job, and I've finally gotten everything right. It seems silly to quit now. Besides, Amos and Ethan need a housekeeper as much now as ever."

"That's not the point," Amos retorted gruffly, still avoiding her gaze. "The point is that your name would be ruined if you lived out here alone with me. I won't have anyone saying that kind of thing about you."

Juliet smiled, pleased by his concern for her name. "But, don't you see, I don't mind. Really. I mean, how often do I go into town, anyway? I haven't any friends there. No relatives to be hurt by the gossip. I'm used to people having a low opinion of me; after all, I've been in the theater. I know what everyone assumes, and it's never hurt me before."

"That's because before you were always with other people in the theater. You were in a world apart, so to speak. But here you live among the people who would be talking about you," Henrietta pointed out earnestly. "Maybe you are usually alone here on the farm, but you will go into town sometime. You're bound to. How will you feel if people won't speak to you? Or treat you like a common woman of the streets?"

"Henrietta!" Amos roared, glaring at her.

"Well?" Henrietta gazed back at him defiantly. "What I'm saying is nothing compared to how others will treat her, and you know it." She looked solemnly into Juliet's face. "What about the people you go to church with? How will you feel if no one will sit down next to you, or if they get up and move when you sit down beside them?"

Juliet stared back at Henrietta, her eyes rounded with alarm. She hadn't thought about it that way. Henrietta was right; before she had always been in a group, among friends, and the opinion of the outside world had been rather insignificant. But she could imagine how sick she would feel if the women she was used to chatting with after church acted toward her the way Aurica Johnson did. Or if men began to think about her as John Sanderson had.

"It's not only you, either," Henrietta pressed on. "There are Amos and Ethan to be considered. We all know the cross that Ethan has to bear already. I'm sure you don't want to add to that. What parents would let him come calling on their daughter, knowing that he was living here with you and Amos in who knows what kind of arrangement?"

"Henrietta!" Juliet looked shocked. "How can you say that! As if Ethan and Amos and I were involved in—in something wicked!"

"It's not what *I* say. It's what everyone else will be saying. I, of course, would defend you, but who would believe me? After all, Amos is family."

Juliet looked at Amos. His grim face confirmed Henrietta's words. Juliet's heart sank. Amos wouldn't want her to stay. Even if she were willing to face the contempt of the townspeople, she could hardly ask Amos and Ethan to do so, too, just so she could continue to keep their house. She had come to care for Amos over the weeks she'd been here, but to Amos she was merely a housekeeper. He wouldn't allow his son to be ruined by gossip in order to have her cook his food and clean his home.

"I see," Juliet said, her voice faint and her face pale. "Then I suppose that I must leave tomorrow. May I ride back into town with you, Henrietta?"

"Of course." Henrietta reached out and patted Juliet's hand. "I'll do my best to find you another position. I think Mrs. Wheelock, east of town, is looking for a girl to help her."

"Mrs. Wheelock?" Amos glowered at Henrietta. "She's a devil to work for. She'd drive Juliet as if she were a slave. I won't have her going to work for that mean-mouthed old baggage."

"But, Amos, dear, Juliet has proved how well she can get along with difficult employers," Henrietta protested, the trace of a sly smile hovering on her lips.

"Amos isn't difficult," Juliet protested. "I've lo—it's been a very enjoyable time."

Amos's visage turned darker. "I'll give her the money."

Henrietta's mouth dropped open. "What money?"

Amos shrugged. "Whatever it is she needs. To get back East where she can sing, as she likes to, instead of scrubbing people's floors."

Pleasure that Amos would do that for her flooded Juliet, followed immediately by anger that he would pay her off to get rid of the problem. Nothing could have said more clearly that she was, in fact, nothing more than an employee to him. It would be a nuisance to have to find a new housekeeper, but it obviously didn't make his heart twist within his chest, as it did hers.

"Keep your money!" Juliet jumped to her feet. "I don't want it! I can take care of myself perfectly well."

"Don't be foolish." He turned his scowl on Juliet. "Why would you turn down perfectly good money like that? You'll be able to do what you want to do."

"I'm not the mercenary woman you seem to think I am," Juliet replied haughtily. "I can't be bought and sold."

He gaped at her. "I didn't mean that—"

"No?"

"Juliet . . . Amos . . . please." Henrietta spoke in the same tone she used with her children. "Would you kindly stop this foolishness? We have more important things to think about."

"What else?" Amos growled. "You've already turned everything topsy-turvy."

"Really, Amos, if you would only let me finish. What I was about to say was that perhaps we could come up with a solution to your problem."

"A solution?" Juliet looked at her oddly.

"Yes. You see, it would be perfectly acceptable for you to be living here with Amos and Ethan—if you and Amos were married."

All the air went out of Juliet in a rush, and she plopped back down into her chair. *Married!*

"Married!" Amos echoed her thoughts. He gaped first at Henrietta, then at Juliet. Color flooded Juliet's cheeks.

"Henrietta," Juliet protested softly, unable to look into either one's eyes, "surely you aren't serious."

"Of course I am. Why would I say it otherwise? It's the perfect answer to the problem. You'd be able to stay here without scandal. Each of you would benefit. Think about it. You, Juliet, would have security, a home, a husband who can provide for you quite adequately. You'd no longer have to spend your days worrying about money or finding a job or any of those things. You could have children."

The blush rose higher in Juliet's cheeks at her last words, and she couldn't keep from glancing at Amos. Their eyes met, and both of them quickly looked away. Juliet's stomach began to dance with excitement.

"And you, Amos," Henrietta went on pragmatically, "you'd have someone to take care of your house, a pretty wife, a woman who's proved that she's able to get along with you. Every man needs a wife, even you, and I doubt you could find a better one anywhere. No doubt better than you deserve," she added with some asperity.

Amos stared at his sister-in-law, then at Juliet's lowered head. He swung back to Henrietta. "Have you gone mad?"

Henrietta looked affronted. "How can you say such a thing? Of course I haven't. It's an eminently reasonable solution to the problem."

"But it's—that's hardly the way to choose one's spouse," Juliet pointed out. "I mean, what about . . . well, what about love?" Her voice sank almost to a whisper on the last word, and her face flamed scarlet.

Henrietta waved away Juliet's objection. "Stuff and nonsense. The primary consideration is to take care of yourselves. Neither one of you is some moonstruck youth to be searching for 'love.' You're old enough to be sensible. Juliet, do you want to spend the rest of your life taking care of other people's houses? Sewing and cooking for someone else's children? Or perhaps you'd rather spend it singing on stage and traveling all over the country without a home to call your own, living in hotels and having to put up with the lewd propositions of men, never knowing when some manager is going to run off with the money again and leave you stranded in a strange place without a penny to your name! Of course, that is, until you're too old to draw the men in to watch, and then you'll be kicked out without a thought."

Juliet's stomach twisted. "Of course that's not what I want. But . . ."

"But what?"

How could she say that she didn't want to marry Amos for pragmatic reasons? That she didn't want *him* to marry her for pragmatic reasons? She merely shrugged and shook her head.

Henrietta turned her ammunition on Amos. "And what about you? Is that what you're doing? Waiting for love, too?" She invested the words with a wealth of scorn.

"Don't be a fool," Amos snapped, standing up and shoving back his chair. "I don't need a wife."

"Oh, no. No doubt you'd far prefer to have a housekeeper who doesn't care two cents about you. You'd rather live in a cold and loveless house the rest of your life instead of having children and a wife. You'll enjoy living alone after Ethan grows up and marries and moves away. A solitary life is far preferable to being wedded to a beautiful, kind, agreeable female."

Henrietta heaved a huge sigh. "Ah, well, I can see I'm wasting my breath talking to you two. I hate to see it, but I suppose you both deserve the lives you'll get." She turned to Juliet, giving her a last, sad look. "We'll leave after breakfast tomorrow."

Juliet nodded. "All right."

She stayed in her seat, looking down at the table, as Henrietta marched out of the room. Out of the corner of her eye she watched Amos move restlessly to the sink, then over to the cupboard, his head down and his hands in his pockets. He cast a surreptitious glance at her.

"I'm sorry," he said finally. "Once Henrietta gets her mind set on something, she won't let loose."

"I know."

He paused. "It's a foolish idea," he said tentatively.

Juliet nodded. She thought about the life Henrietta had described for her, and she wanted to cry. Henrietta was all too right. But she couldn't marry Amos because it was the most sensible thing to do. She couldn't share a man's bed in order to have a home to call her own. That would make her exactly what everyone thought women of the theater were, wouldn't it?

She stole a look at Amos. He was staring out the window above the sink, lost in thought. For a moment she studied his tall, broad-shouldered form. His chest and arms were thick with muscles; his legs were long and lean. His hands were big, with long, strong fingers, lightly sprinkled with curling black hairs. There was something exciting about his hands; she thought of how they looked that time when she saw him working with his wood, how his fingers curved around the piece, how his muscles flexed. Would he touch her with the same gentleness he used on his carvings? Would he caress her skin in that smooth, almost reverent way?

Juliet closed her eyes, feeling suddenly hot and liquid inside. No doubt this was a sinful way to feel, but she knew that she wouldn't really mind sharing Amos's bed at all. She would like to have him kiss her again as he had that one time after the dance.

Oh, please. Please ask me to stay.

That was the problem, she knew. It wasn't that she didn't want to stay here and marry Amos. It would be hard to think of never again appearing onstage, of not singing before an audience and hearing their applause. She would miss the cities and the life she had grown up in. But she would gladly give all of them up in order to stay here and marry Amos. She no longer cared about getting the money to go back East. She wanted this home, this life. She wanted Amos.

Juliet knew she might as well face the fact: She loved Amos. She had managed to avoid the idea for some time. It was absurd—he was gruff, he was blunt, he was silent, he rarely revealed his feelings. But Juliet had always been a woman who led with her heart, not her head. She had not taken the reasonable path, but had fallen in love with an impossible man. It would tear out her heart tomorrow to leave him.

However, she couldn't stay. Juliet knew that she also had to face the fact that Amos did not want to marry her. He didn't want a woman interfering in his life. He didn't love her.

Juliet stood up. "I—better go pack my things."

Amos looked at her directly for the first time. He nodded shortly, crossing his arms over his chest. Juliet hurried from the room, keeping her eyes turned downward. Amos stood looking after her for a long moment. Then, with a gusty sigh, he turned and walked out of the house.

Amos sat in the darkness, perched on the edge of the huge stump on which he and Ethan chopped their wood, and stared at the house across the yard from him. A light burned dimly in the kitchen for him. He knew that Juliet had left it burning for him; she always did. He had sat on the stump for the past hour, watching Juliet move around in the kitchen until finally she had turned down the wick of the lamp and left the room.

Amos thought about the fact that she would never again do so, and suddenly it was hard to swallow past the lump in his throat. He wasn't sure how he would be able to bear it when Henrietta took Juliet off with her tomorrow morning.

He dropped his head into his hands and pushed his fingers deep into his hair, clenching his fists and pulling as though the pain would somehow stop the ache inside him. He thought of the lonely days ahead of him, of coming into the kitchen in the evening and not having Juliet there to greet him with a smile, of not looking at her across the table, of not hearing her sing as she worked. He thought of the house no longer brightened by the flowers she picked or the ornaments she had put out. He thought of the house, dark and cold again without her presence. Amos cursed softly. What was he going to do now? He wished to God that she had never come. He had accepted his life and grown accustomed to his loneliness. But how could he go back to the way things had been before now that Juliet had brought sunlight into his life?

Of course, he could ask her to marry him, as Henrietta had suggested. For a moment, the idea dangled tantalizingly in his head. He could imagine Juliet as his wife, his ring on her finger, coming to greet him when he returned from the fields, her arms outstretched to him. They would sit together close to the fire in the winter, snug and safe from the cold outside. She would knit or sew, and he would read, or perhaps whittle. Later they would go up to their room together. There would be soft feminine things of hers in his room—ribbons or a perfume bottle, a hand mirror, a silver-backed hairbrush, a cameo, maybe needle-stitched pillows adorning the bed. She would take down her hair and brush it out, and he would watch her. Perhaps he would take the brush from her hand and stroke it through her hair himself until it crackled and curled around his hands like a living thing, red-gold and soft. Then he would bend to kiss her, and she would stretch up to him willingly, linking her arms behind his neck.

He sucked in his breath unconsciously, thinking of her mouth underneath his, warm and inviting. He could smell her sweet scent, feel her skin beneath his hands, almost taste her on his lips. It would be heavenly to kiss her, to sink into her softness.

With a groan, Amos lifted his head and looked up at the sky, dark and distant above him, glittering with hundreds of remote, bright stars. He was a fool to torment himself with thoughts of making love to Juliet. Nothing was going to come of it. It couldn't.

What would Juliet want with a gruff old farmer like him? She was young and fresh and lovely, and she was filled with the romantic dreams of a young woman. She wanted love; she wanted a handsome young man singing her praises. She wanted poetry and flowers. Not some sour man of few words and little patience. Not a clumsy fool who was twelve years older than she.

With a sigh, he got up and walked back to the house. He picked up the lamp in the kitchen and carried it to his room. He was lost in his dark thoughts and so at first he didn't see his sister-in-law sitting like a guard outside his door. Henrietta was in a narrow straight-back chair, wearing her nightshift and dressing gown, her hair hanging down her back in a single long braid. Her arms were crossed stiffly across her chest, and she regarded him with disapproval.

Amos stifled a groan. The last thing he wanted was his bossy sister-in-law telling him what he should do.

"I came here to ask you one question," Henrietta said.

Amos nodded, thinking that that would be the day when Henrietta Morgan said just one thing. He stopped, thrusting his hands in his pocket, and waited.

"Are you unwilling to marry that girl because of what she's been? Do you think she's soiled?" Henrietta asked bluntly.

Amos's head snapped up, and he stared at Henrietta in shock. "No!" Red crept up his neck. "Henrietta! How could you think such a thing about her? Why, anyone can see that she's a lady, even if she did sing for a living. She may have lived around theater people all her life, but she's not loose."

Henrietta rolled her eyes. "I never said she was. But it's possible, you know, for a woman not to be easy and yet to have—" she paused delicately, "—well, experience."

His jaw set mulishly. "She's no more experienced than . . . than Ethan. I'm positive."

Henrietta arched her brows expressively. "You seem awfully sure of that."

His blush spread higher. "I've not tried to seduce her, if that's what you're thinking! If she weren't still a—a maiden, it would only be because someone forced her or took advantage of her loving heart. She hasn't a wicked bone in her body."

"Then why in the Sam Hill won't you marry her?" Henrietta demanded exasperatedly.

"You said you were going to ask me only one thing," Amos reminded her and started past her into his room.

Henrietta put out a restraining hand. "You are the

stubbornest man I ever met. Samuel can't hold a candle to you."

Amos grimaced. It was clear that Henrietta wouldn't let him have any peace until he'd explained everything to her. "For heaven's sake, Henrietta, surely you can see that she wouldn't want to marry an old geezer like me!"

"You talk like you're tottering at the edge of your grave. You're only thirty-six!"

"I'm too old for her. It'd be crazy. She wouldn't have me anyway."

"Well, you could at least ask her before you decided that, couldn't you? I don't know why you think she wouldn't be happy to marry you! You have a good farm, the biggest for miles around. A nice house. You aren't bad-looking, at least when you can bring yourself to smile. And what kind of future does she have if she doesn't marry you?"

"I don't want her to marry me because she doesn't have any other choice!" Amos hissed. "You think I want a woman in my bed just so she can have a decent house and a little money in the bank? Because her only alternative is to be penniless or to accept a wealthy man's favors?"

Henrietta stared at him. "Well, I'll be! You're just as silly and romantic as she is. You're perfectly suited for each other." She shook her head and got up. She started away, then turned back and shook her forefinger at him. "I'll tell you this, Amos Morgan. You're in love with that girl. And you're a worse fool than I thought if you let her get away from you!"

Fourteen

Juliet awoke the next morning with a feeling of dread. It took her a moment to realize why: she was leaving the farm today—unless Amos asked her to marry him, of course. But she knew that that wasn't likely. Sadly she rose and washed, put on her prettiest skirt and bodice, pale blue with black frogging down the front of the bodice and around the hem of the skirt. She brushed her hair until it gleamed and piled it up in a soft pompadour atop her head, something she rarely took the time to do since she'd been living on the farm. She was usually too busy to indulge in such vanity, but she was determined to look her best this morning. *Just let him see what he would be missing!*

Juliet went into the kitchen, where she found Henrietta already bustling about, making biscuits. Bacon was sizzling in the frying pan, and the savory smell of coffee filled the air. A basket of eggs sat on the worktable beside a mixing bowl. Henrietta turned at Juliet's entrance and smiled at her.

"My, how pretty you look."

"Thank you." The smile Juliet gave her didn't reach her eyes.

Henrietta sighed, but said nothing. Instead, she turned back to the counter and resumed cutting the biscuits with even more vigor, shaking her head a little and muttering to herself.

Juliet tied an apron over her clothes and got out a whisk to beat the eggs. The two women worked quickly and efficiently, and for the most part, they said nothing.

Finally, with the air of someone who could no longer hold it in, Henrietta turned to Juliet and said, "He wants you to stay, you know."

Juliet glanced at her, surprised. "Amos?"

"Of course, Amos. Who else would I be talking about?"

Juliet's face turned wistful. "I wish he did. But he's given me no reason to believe that."

Henrietta flapped her hand impatiently, dismissing Juliet's objection. "He won't admit it, but I know that it's true. He's simply too stubborn and scared to tell you."

Juliet smiled faintly. "Amos, scared?"

"Of course he's scared. Just because he's the size of a mountain and doesn't care who he offends doesn't mean he isn't frightened by something like a feeling he can't control or a woman who might say no."

"Surely he must know—" Juliet stopped abruptly, biting her lip, and her face turned pink as she realized what she had been about to reveal.

"That you want to stay as much as he wants you to?" Henrietta hazarded a guess. "No. Amos is smart about some things, but when it comes to people's hearts, his or someone else's, he's a goose." She paused, considering. "No, that's not right. I think—well, I think he was hurt terribly some years ago, probably by Ethan's mother, though no one knows for sure because he won't say a word about it. Anyway, I think he's afraid to trust a woman. He's scared to believe. What if he thinks that you love him and then it turns out that you don't? It'd be disastrous for him if he was wrong. So he clings to what's safe."

Juliet sighed. "Maybe you're right. Frankly, I'm inclined to think that he doesn't care."

"Amos isn't the only one who's afraid of being hurt, I see."

"I can hardly force him to let me remain. I offered to stay without his having to marry me."

"That's out of the question."

"Then what else can I do? I can't say I'll marry him unless he asks me, can I? I can't ask him to marry me!"

"With a man like that, that's about what you have to do," Henrietta muttered. Then she shrugged her shoulders. "I guess you're right. But it's maddening to see two people who want the same thing, and neither one of them will tell the other one."

"I don't imagine Amos wants the same thing I do."

"I wouldn't count on it."

"If he did ask me to marry him, it'd only be because it's more convenient than having to hire a new housekeeper."

"That's not true. I'm certain that—"

Henrietta's words were cut off by the back door opening. Amos came into the room and glanced once, quickly, at Juliet, then did his utmost not to look at her again as he washed up and sat down at the table. Juliet cooked the eggs, just as studiously avoiding Amos. Henrietta cast an eye at first one, then the other, and stifled a sigh.

As Juliet was dishing up the eggs, the door opened again, and Ethan came in. He smiled a little at Juliet, his face sad. "Good morning." He took off his hat and stood for a moment, looking at her and turning the hat around in his hands. "Are—are you still planning to go back to Steadman this morning?"

"I guess so, if Mrs. Morgan is." Juliet looked toward Henrietta.

Henrietta nodded. "Yes. We'll be driving back to town."

"Couldn't you stay a day or two longer, Aunt Henrietta?" Ethan asked hopefully.

Henrietta hesitated, then said, "No. There's no point to it, Ethan. It'll only make the leaving more painful."

"Maybe we could think up some way for Juliet to stay if we had a little longer."

"It's impossible." Amos spoke up for the first time, his voice sharp.

"I don't understand why," Ethan responded.

Amos fixed him with a stern look. "It's been decided, son. Leave the subject alone and come eat your breakfast."

Ethan cast him a sullen look, but he hung his hat on the hook and went over to the washstand to clean his hands. Juliet and Henrietta put the last of the breakfast things on the table, and they sat down to an excruciatingly silent meal. Now and then Ethan glanced at Amos or Juliet in frustrated puzzlement. Henrietta, too, sent them a look or two as she ate, though there was no puzzlement in her eyes, only irritation.

After the meal, Henrietta and Juliet began to carry the dishes from the table. Amos and Ethan remained seated, and Amos couldn't keep his eyes from following Juliet as she moved. This was the last time he would see her do this, he knew. The last time he would watch her in his house, taking care of him. The last time he would be close to her.

Amos found it difficult to breathe this morning. He knew that he and Ethan should get out of the house and start on their chores. But he couldn't bring himself to get up and leave yet. He lingered, watching Juliet. His son watched him.

When the dishes were scraped and set in the sink, Juliet said to no one in particular, "I better finish my packing."

No one said anything in reply. Slowly she walked out of the room. At the sound of her door closing down the hall, Ethan jumped to his feet.

"Why don't you say something?" he exploded, turning to his father. "Why will you let her go like this?"

"I can hardly make her stay, Ethan," Amos pointed out, his voice flat and reasonable. "She's a grown woman; she can go wherever she wants."

"Well, she doesn't *want* to go to Steadman, I can tell you that! You wouldn't have to *make* her stay. All you have to do is ask."

"It wouldn't be a good situation. You heard your aunt; Juliet's reputation would be ruined."

"Not if you married her! Why didn't you ask her to marry you? Aunt Henrietta explained it to me last night, and it makes sense."

"It wouldn't work."

"How do you know? You aren't willing to try. You won't even ask her!"

"Convenience isn't enough to base a marriage on."

"Convenience!" Ethan stared. "That's all it would be? Don't you feel anything for her? Don't you care whether she leaves? Won't you miss her? I already miss her. I love her. She's—she's been like a sister to me. How can you not have any feeling for her?" When his father didn't answer, but continued to stare stonily ahead, Ethan burst out, "Anyone with half a heart would love her!"

He turned and ran out of the room, his work boots clattering loudly on the steps outside. Amos sighed and set his elbows on the table, propping his head in his hands. Henrietta glanced at him but said nothing, continuing to wash the dishes.

Juliet came into the kitchen a few minutes later, carrying her carpetbag and reticule, her bonnet tied on her head. "I'm ready, Henrietta."

"Yes. I am, too." Henrietta turned away from the sink, where she had washed and rinsed the dishes and set them aside. "If you will dry these for me, I'll put on my bonnet."

Juliet obediently went to the sink and dried the dishes. She was very aware of Amos's presence in the room, although he said nothing. She wished he would jump up and come to her, would take her in his arms and beg her not to leave. She wished he wanted to marry her.

Henrietta returned to the kitchen, her own small bag in her hand. "Amos, you'll have to fetch Juliet's trunk, of course. And the buggy will have to be harnessed."

Amos nodded and walked down the hall to Juliet's room. He paused in the doorway, looking around. It was once more bare, robbed of all signs of the life Juliet had brought to it. There were no knickknacks, no ribbons, no feminine articles on the dresser. He felt as if his heart were being squeezed within his chest, but he stoically picked up the trunk and lugged it out the front hallway to the porch.

Then he went to the barn and reluctantly harnessed Henrietta's horse to the small buggy in which she and Samuel had ridden out here. His fingers were clumsy on the leather straps, but eventually he finished the task. He drove the buggy the short distance to the front of the house, where Henrietta and Juliet stood waiting on the porch. Ethan was nowhere in sight. Amos understood how he felt. He, too, would have liked to run away somewhere and hide, and not have to watch Juliet drive out of their lives.

He got out of the buggy and stood to the side. He couldn't bring himself to look at Juliet. But he couldn't bear to leave, either.

"Well, good-bye, Amos," Henrietta said briskly, climbing into the buggy and taking the reins. "I'll advertise for another housekeeper. I'll make sure this time that she's an older woman."

Amos wanted to tell her to forget it, that he didn't want another housekeeper, but that was patently absurd. Of course he would have to have someone to clean and cook. He and Ethan couldn't manage the house, as well as their chores. But everything within him rebelled at the idea of another woman taking Juliet's place in his house. It would be awful. Every time he saw her he would be reminded of Juliet and of how poorly this woman compared to her. Of how much he missed her.

Juliet went around the buggy and climbed up on the other side. She turned toward Amos. "Good-bye."

Her voice wavered on the word, and she clamped her lips shut, unable to say anything else without breaking down and crying. Amos nodded to her briefly, but said nothing. Juliet's eyes filled with tears, and she clenched her fingers tightly around her reticule.

Amos picked up the baggage and loaded it into the back of the buggy. He stepped back and turned toward Juliet. She would be gone in a minute, and he didn't know how he could stand it.

Henrietta clicked to the horse and slapped the reins. "Giddy-up!"

Juliet dug her hands more deeply into the small cloth bag. She didn't dare look back at Amos. *Oh, if only he would call to them to stop! If only he'd ask her to stay!*

Amos watched the buggy pull away from the house and cross the yard. He felt as if something inside of him was being torn out as the buggy moved away. He wanted her to stay. In another minute, he knew she'd be gone. He'd never have her, never know her, never see that smile . . .

"Juliet!" He started running after the buggy. "Wait!"

Juliet's heart leapt in her chest, and she twisted around in her seat to look at Amos. He was running after them! She whirled back around to face the front, her heart pounding inside her chest as if it would leap out at any moment.

Henrietta pulled the horse to a stop, a grin spreading across her face. Carefully she pulled her mouth back down into a neutral expression, and she turned to Amos with only a look of inquiry on her face. "Yes? Did you forget something, Amos?"

He ran up to Juliet's side of the buggy and stopped. His breath was coming in pants from his dash after them. "Wait. Don't go. I—we need to talk about this."

"About what, Amos?" Henrietta asked innocently.

"Not you," he retorted rudely, shooting her a quelling look.

"You want to talk to me?" Juliet prompted. She didn't know what to say, hardly dared breathe, in fact.

"Yes. I—" Amos looked at her. "We—well, maybe it wouldn't be such a bad idea. You know, what Henrietta was talking about. I do need a wife, and you'd be a lot better off married than going back to the theater. It's— Ethan's grown real fond of you, and he's never really had a mother, you see. It'd be good for him to be around a woman, a nice woman. The house needs a woman's touch; it's looked much better since you've been here.

The, you know, curtains and flowers and such."

Juliet listened to his halting speech about the advantages of marrying. She wasn't sure whether to laugh or to cry. He seemed to be leading up to a proposal of marriage, yet his reasons were so mundane, so unromantic. He was talking more about an arrangement of mutual benefit than about wanting to marry her.

"I'd take good care of you; you'd never want for anything," Amos went on, rubbing his palms surreptitiously down the sides of his legs. "I—it's a good house. I have money in the bank and a good farm, one of the best hereabouts—you could ask anybody."

He paused, and Juliet wondered if she was supposed to say something. *But what?* He hadn't asked her a question. "It is a good farm," she agreed inanely. "A good house."

"Oh, for pity's sake," Henrietta grumbled beside her. "You two! I don't think you'd ever come to the point if I wasn't here. Amos, are you trying to ask this girl to marry you?"

Amos looked chagrined, but he admitted, "Well, yes, I guess I am."

"Then ask her!"

A flush rose in his cheeks, but Amos faced Juliet squarely. "Juliet, would you be willing to marry me?"

"Oh, Amos!" Juliet's heart felt like a bird trying to beat its way out of her chest. Tears started in her eyes, and she had to swallow. She couldn't break into tears now!

"Well?" Henrietta turned to Juliet, impatient with her hesitation. "What's your answer?"

"Yes." Juliet's voice was barely more than a whisper.

She cleared her throat and tried again, "Yes, I'll be happy to marry you."

Amos stared at her, stunned. "You will?"

Juliet nodded.

"Don't look so dumbfounded, Amos, or Juliet'll start wondering if she made a mistake," Henrietta advised, smothering a smile.

"I—well, that's—good." A grin began to spread across his face, at odds with his unenthusiastic words.

"It's a miracle, is more like it," Henrietta told him crisply. "When shall we have the ceremony?"

Juliet pulled her eyes away from Amos and glanced at Henrietta. "I don't know. I hadn't thought." She looked back at Amos, wishing that he'd reach up and pull her down from the buggy and plant a kiss on her lips. She wished he'd take her in a bone-cracking hug and tell her how overjoyed he was that she was going to be his wife. She wondered how he felt, deep inside.

"It should be soon," Henrietta decreed. "There's no reason to wait; the house needs a woman quickly. And summer's a busy time." She didn't add that she feared that if they waited, this couple would get cold feet and call it off. "I think two weeks ought to be enough time to get everything ready. A week from Saturday all right with both of you?"

"So soon?" Juliet blinked, but then she nodded. "All right. I guess there's no reason to wait. But what about Frances? It was so recent—"

"Frances'd be the first to wish you well, and you both know it. Nothing would have made her happier than your marrying Amos. She'd be the last to say you should hold off because of mourning for her." She turned to Amos. "Saturday all right with you, too?"

He nodded.

"All right, then, you better stand back and let us go on. We have hundreds of things to do to get ready in time."

Amos stared. "What? You mean, you're leaving? You're taking Juliet with you?"

"Of course. Just because you're getting married doesn't mean it'd look right for her to stay out here for almost two weeks alone with you. There's all the more reason not to cause talk now. You can't have everybody gossiping about your wife and speculating on the reasons for your marriage. Juliet's coming home with me, and we're going to prepare for the ceremony. We'll have it in town."

"Oh. Yes. Certainly." Amos stepped back reluctantly. He looked at Juliet. *His wife!*

"Good-bye, Amos," Juliet offered softly.

"Good-bye."

Henrietta started the buggy again, and they drove off. Amos stood staring after them until at last they disappeared on the horizon. He turned and started slowly back to the house.

He was getting married! Suddenly Amos chuckled. Then it turned into a full laugh. If he'd had his hat with him, he would have tossed it into the air. As it was, he hurried back to the house in great strides, his face glowing with a smile. *Juliet was going to marry him!*

* * *

It seemed to Juliet as if the two weeks would never pass. It wasn't because she had idle time on her hands; there was no such thing as idle time in Henrietta Morgan's house. But as soon as she drove away from the farm, she began to miss it. She missed gathering the eggs in the morning, and she missed watching the calves bound around on their knobby-kneed legs, shying at every sound or movement. She missed Ethan's laugh, and she wondered if he would remember to water her vegetable garden. She couldn't imagine how either he or his father would get along for almost two whole weeks without someone to look after them.

Most of all, she missed Amos. She yearned for his solid presence. The scent of his pipe on the evening air. The rumble of his voice in a nearby room or the rare sight of his smile when she said something that amused him. There were times when she would have sworn she even missed his silence.

There was never a quiet moment at Henrietta's. There were always hotel guests going up or down from their rooms and the clatter of footsteps on the wooden sidewalk out front, the chatter of the maid or the clerk or a customer. Sometimes it seemed as if the whole world passed outside the door of the Morgans' small apartment upstairs. As if that weren't enough, Henrietta herself filled in any blank spaces that there might be, talking nonstop as she worked. When they weren't working, she was dragging Juliet hither and yon—to meet this person or that, to be fitted for her dress at the seamstress's, to find a veil at the millinery shop. The list of things to do was unending. For Juliet, accustomed as she was now to the quiet solitude of the farm, it seemed an unending jumble of noise and people.

There were moments when Juliet suspected Henrietta didn't dare let her out of her sight, for fear she might take off and leave Amos in the lurch. *As if she'd ever do that!* But Juliet was realizing that fond as Henrietta was of her brother-in-law, she couldn't believe, deep down inside, that any woman would really *want* to marry him.

Amos came to call on Juliet the next Saturday afternoon, and they sat stiffly in the Morgans' small parlor, watching each other and saying little. Amos looked uncomfortable and out of place in his best black suit and white shirt, his hands folded awkwardly in his lap. Juliet, who was at ease with most people and had felt at home with Amos in the farmhouse whether there was talk or silence, now felt distinctly awkward. Henrietta and Samuel sat in the room with them, and their presence only added to the awkwardness of the situation. Even Henrietta couldn't carry a conversation entirely on her own and Juliet found herself too tongue-tied to help Henrietta out.

Finally Henrietta remembered an errand that she had to run. "And you better work on those books this afternoon, Samuel," she told her husband.

"What? What books?" Samuel looked at her with a confused expression.

Henrietta raised her eyebrows and shot a pointed

glance at Amos and Juliet. "You know, dear, the hotel's books."

"But I did that yesterday. Besides, Amos is here visiting."

"I know." Henrietta made a series of peculiar faces, nodding her head toward Amos, then Juliet. "But there was a mistake, dear, that you said you had to investigate. Remember?"

"What?"

"Besides, I'm sure that Amos and Juliet will be all right on their own, won't you?"

Dutifully they chorused their assent. Suddenly Samuel's troubled face cleared. "Oh! Oh, I see. Yes, why, yes, of course, the mistake. In the books. Yes, it's most upsetting. I better get to work on it."

Juliet pressed her lips together to keep from smiling. She did not dare glance toward Amos for fear that she would break into laughter. But after the other couple went out of the room, leaving the door discreetly ajar, she hazarded a peek at Amos. His eyes were dancing, and his mouth was twitching dangerously. Juliet burst into laughter, and Amos did the same.

"Thank God!" he exclaimed. "I thought they'd never leave. I didn't know Samuel could be such a dunderhead."

Juliet thought it was more that Samuel was so used to his brother's bachelor status and gruff nature that he couldn't imagine him wanting to be left alone with his fiancée. "It is easier to talk without an audience."

"I don't know how a man ever manages to get through

weeks—months!—of calling on a girl's family."

"Tell me, how's the farm?" Juliet asked, leaning forward and linking her hands around her knees.

"Dirty," Amos answered succinctly. "Ethan and I haven't had a decent meal since you left, either."

Well, it was obvious that he missed her, Juliet thought, even if it was not for very romantic reasons.

"But Henrietta said she'd send out the hotel maids to clean before the wedding, so you won't be returning to a messy house," he went on.

"How thoughtful."

"We've been keeping the weeds out of the vegetable garden," Amos assured her. "Ethan made a snake out of rags to put in the apple tree to scare away the birds. The blackberry thickets down by the creek are full of ripe berries now."

"Good. I can try my hand at preserving them."

Amos had apparently reached the end of his stock of things to say about the farm, and the conversation limped to a halt again. Juliet wondered why she felt so uncomfortable now sitting with him in silence when she had done so many times before at the farm. But, of course, then they hadn't been planning on getting married in a week. Then she hadn't thought about the fact that in only a few more days they would be sharing a bed.

She stared down at her hands, hoping that Amos had no idea where her mind had wandered. Amos shifted in his chair. "Oh! Wait, I brought something for you. I left it outside. Just a minute."

He got up and left the room and returned a moment later carrying a wooden box. As he held it out to Juliet, she recognized it. "Why, Amos! That's your mother's music box!"

He nodded.

"But that's yours. Why are you giving it to me?"

"Actually, it belonged to Frances, and she's the one who told me to give it to you. She wanted you to have it after she died."

Tears filled Juliet's eyes. "How sweet." She reached out and took the box, running her fingers over its rich mahogany surface. "It's so beautiful. I'll treasure it always."

"Open it up."

Puzzled, Juliet obeyed. The familiar tune lilted out of it, reminding Juliet of those evenings in the kitchen when she had danced with Ethan and Amos. She blinked away the tears. There was something else in the box. Lying on the bottom, on top of the plush red velvet lining, was a set of jet earrings and matching necklace. Beside them lay a cameo brooch and another set of earrings made of pearls.

She looked up at Amos, astonished. "I don't understand. What are these? I mean—"

"Some of my mother's jewelry. Her nicer pieces. She gave some to each of us. Henrietta has what Ma left Samuel, and I—well, mine should go to my wife."

How odd, she thought, to hear him call her his wife. It suddenly seemed much more real.

"They're lovely. But are you sure you want me to have

them? I mean, they were your mother's. Wouldn't you want to keep them?"

He shook his head. "No. She would want you to have them; she would have liked you very much. She would have told me how lucky I was." He looked away, suddenly vastly interested in Henrietta's rug. "I know that I am. Lucky. I'm not good at saying things like that. But I feel them."

"Thank you. I'll wear them proudly."

"I have something else for you. I wasn't sure if you'd like it." He pulled a small black cloth bag from his coat pocket and extended it to her.

Curious, Juliet took the bag from his hand and pulled the drawstring open. "Amos!"

Her mouth dropped open, and she reached inside to pull out a strand of gleaming white pearls. "They're beautiful!" Her voice was awestruck. She looked up at him. "Were these your mother's, too?"

He shook his head. "No. I bought them for you. For your bride's gift. I took the train to Omaha a few days ago and went to the jewelers." He looked uncertain. "But when I told Henrietta what I'd got she said pearls were unlucky for a bride."

"Oh, pooh. These are too beautiful to be unlucky for anyone. I've heard that: pearls are tears for a bride or something like that. I don't care." She gazed up at him, her eyes glowing like sapphires. "I can't believe that you did this for me, went to Omaha and everything."

Amos shrugged, looking embarrassed. "Well, you're supposed to get a bride's gift. A betrothal ring seemed pretty foolish when we'll only be betrothed another week. Henrietta didn't leave me much time, so I figured I'd better go to Omaha to get it. When I saw this at the store, I thought it looked like you. So beautiful, I mean, and yet not glittery like other jewels. It seemed rich, you know, like your voice or your hair."

Juliet unfastened the clasp and held the necklace out to him. "Would you help me put it on?"

He nodded, taking the two ends of the necklace between his fingers, and Juliet went over to him, turning her back so that he could fasten the strand from behind. His fingers fumbled with the clasp, but he finally got it to catch. His fingers trailed down across her shoulders, pausing for an instant before they dropped away.

Juliet stepped away and turned. "There. How do they look?"

"Beautiful," he replied simply.

Juliet's smile was like sunshine. "Oh, thank you, thank you. I love them."

Impulsively she reached out her hands and took one of his between hers. His hand was huge and rough against hers, and the feel of his skin sent a little thrill through Juliet. She was reminded once more of the physical intimacy they would soon share, and she felt eager and a little frightened.

"Amos . . . there's something I must tell you."

His face closed, and suspicion flared in his eyes. "What?"

"It's not a subject that I would bring up normally, but I feel you have a right to know, since you're marrying me.

I know that because of my background in the theater and all, you've had some doubts about my . . . well, my virtue in the past. Anyway, I want you to know that I've never been with another man. I'm not a naive sixteen-year-old girl, but I've never been loose, either. I'm coming to you as pure as any other woman."

Amos's hand was suddenly hot between hers, and Juliet could hear the quick indrawn hiss of his breath. "I know that. I told you long ago that I'd realized I was wrong about you."

"I know. You understood that I wasn't a—a 'lady of the night,' but I wasn't sure whether you might be afraid that I was not as, well, that I was laxer in my morals than the women you know. What I want you to know is that I am a virgin."

"You don't have to tell me that. I was certain of it, anyway, and even if you hadn't been, I know it wouldn't have been because you are in any way wicked. Besides, who am I to lecture anyone on morals?"

Juliet smiled up at him. "You're a good man. That's who you are. A good man."

Their wedding day dawned bright and clear, and by afternoon the little town of Steadman was washed in the intense late-June heat. Juliet didn't notice that it was hot; she was so nervous that her hands were as cold as if it were winter, and she could think of nothing else except that in a few hours she would be Mrs. Amos Morgan, irrevocably tied to him for the rest of her life.

They were married at the simple white-washed Methodist church in town, where Henrietta was a ruling force. Juliet felt better when she saw Amos waiting for her at the altar. He looked even more scared than she felt, and she had to bite back a giggle, his obvious nervousness soothing some of her own. When he took her hand, his was as cold as ice. *What if one of them fainted dead away right there at the altar?* Juliet was sure that would be a scandal that would live long in the annals of Steadman.

But neither of them fainted. They managed to say their responses in clear, even voices. Once the ceremony was over and they walked out of the church, Juliet was flooded with relief. The world seemed calm, bright, and sane again. She was still a trifle nervous, but she was certain that she had done the right thing.

She glanced up at Amos and found him looking back down at her. The color was back in his face, and Juliet suspected that the tentatively hopeful expression on his face was probably a duplicate of her own. She relaxed, letting out a chuckle, and Amos grinned back.

"Thank God that's over," he remarked, taking her hand in a firmer grip, and, smiling, they walked down the steps of the church.

Fifteen

$\mathcal{A}$mos cast a sideways glance at Juliet, beside him in the buggy, as they turned onto the path leading from the road to the farmhouse. Feeling his eyes on her, she turned and smiled. She was so beautiful that it made his heart hurt. He returned her smile a little shakily, wishing for the thousandth time in the past two weeks that he knew why she had agreed to marry him and what it would take to make her happy.

It had been tremendously lonely on the farm without her. The days had dragged by, and the bad meals and ever-growing stack of dishes beside the sink had played a miniscule part in his wishing that Juliet were once more in the house.

He had known that he would desire her. He'd been doing that for weeks now, practically since the moment she'd arrived. His nights often had been plagued with hot, yearning dreams about her. Those had continued; he had been certain that they would. But what Amos had not been prepared for was the longing, not physical but emotional, that had sat inside him like a lead weight. His life had suddenly turned bleak, as if the sun had gone permanently behind a cloud. He missed her laugh, her smile, her voice.

That kind of loneliness, he was discovering, was even worse than the sexual ache that had become his almost constant companion. It never went away, and he couldn't be distracted from it even by his carving. He had tried to carve a funny face for her out of part of a limb that had fallen from a cottonwood down by the creek, but he'd been unable to concentrate on it, and he'd found that instead of a merry little wood elf, the figure was turning into a slender, lovely tree nymph, peeking out from behind a birch with a teasing smile, her robes and hair flowing out of the wood. The nymph, of course, had Juliet's face. He wasn't sure whether she would be pleased by that, so he'd left it in the barn, hanging on the wall above his worktable, where he could look at it whenever he glanced up from his hobby.

He realized that asking Juliet to marry him had been the only solution he could have lived with. Without intending to for a second, he had fallen hopelessly, foolishly in love with her, so much so that his youthful infatuation with Ethan's mother now seemed laughable in comparison.

What puzzled him was why Juliet had accepted his proposal. Why would a sophisticated city dweller consent to spend the rest of her life on a farm in Nebraska? Why would a woman as beautiful as Juliet was, who could have had her pick of men anywhere, choose to marry a grouchy bachelor twelve years her senior? If it had been any other woman than Juliet, he would have said cynically that she knew that a man twelve years older would die sooner, leaving her a sizable inheritance of savings and farmland. But not Juliet.

It was tempting to think that maybe she actually wanted to marry him. Perhaps she had fallen in love, too. She had, after all, kissed him back with passion that night after the dance. Maybe she hadn't felt obliged to do so because she worked for him; maybe she had some real feeling for him.

But Amos was scared to let his mind turn that way. Along that road lay destruction. It couldn't possibly be true, and when he found out the real reason, he would be devastated.

Besides, he reasoned, he didn't really have to know why she had agreed to marry him. It was enough that she had. She was his wife. The thought sent a thrill of anticipation through him. It also chilled him to the bone.

Amos pulled the buggy to a stop in front of the porch. He looked up at the house, then at Juliet. She was staring at the house, too, her mouth open in astonishment.

"Oh, Amos!" She looked at him, then back at the porch, as if she couldn't believe her eyes. "I knew I'd be happy to get back here, but this! Flowers?"

Amos grinned, pleased that his surprise had gone over so well. He sent an almost smug glance toward the row of rose bushes planted in front of the porch. Someday, given loving nourishment, they would trail up the porch railing, decorating the house with bright color.

"Do you like them?"

"Like them!" Her smile was like sunshine. "I love them! Oh, thank you!"

She jumped down from the buggy and darted over to the bushes, bending over to inspect each of them.

Amos tied the horse to the rail for the moment and walked around to the back to pull out Juliet's trunk. She ran lightly up the steps to open the front door for him. Amos, carrying the heavy trunk, went inside and up the stairs. Halfway up, he hesitated. He had instinctively headed toward his bedroom with her baggage, but in the midst of doing so it seemed odd. Perhaps it was assuming too much to carry her trunk to his room. She might be appalled at the idea of sharing his bed; she might expect him not to demand his rights as a husband. Or she might at least want some time to adjust to their marriage before she submitted to such intimacy.

On the other hand, Amos didn't know where else to take the trunk. Juliet was his wife now; it would seem ridiculous to put her things in the old guest room where she had lived before they were married.

But Amos couldn't help but think of the implications of her trunk going to his room, and his loins tightened in response to those implications.

He glanced back down the stairs. Juliet was standing at the bottom, looking up at him, waiting. He turned and went up the rest of the steps, not knowing what else to do. When he reached his room, he set the trunk down at the foot of the bed. He looked around at the room. Suddenly it struck him how bare and plain it was.

Juliet's footsteps sounded in the hall behind him, and he turned just as she stepped into the doorway. She was less than a foot away from him. Her beauty was almost overwhelming, and he couldn't keep from thinking about the fact that they were standing in his bedroom. Amos clenched and unclenched his hands. It was difficult to breathe; the air seemed heavy and thick. He wondered what Juliet thought about his putting her things in here.

"I—uh—I guess it's not very pretty." He apologized, making a vague sweep of his arm to indicate the room. "Feel free to do whatever you want, make any changes."

"Thank you."

They stood for a moment, awkwardly looking at each other. Finally Amos said, "Well, ah, I better unhitch the horse. I'll bring your other bag up."

Juliet nodded. Amos left the room and hurried down the stairs. He put the buggy in the barn and unhitched the horse, turning it loose in the pen. He could think of nothing else to do to delay returning to the house, but he was uncertain about going back inside.

Juliet was there, pulling jars and bowls out of a basket. She turned and gave him a bright smile. "Look, Henrietta sent a cold meal for us. Wasn't that nice? Are you ready to eat?"

He agreed, more because it was something for them to do than because he was really hungry. They sat down at the table; it was strange to be there alone, just the two of them. Henrietta had asked Ethan to stay in town for a couple of weeks so that the newlyweds would have some time by themselves. Amos had been grateful, but now he thought that it might be better if Ethan were there; at least he would be able to talk to Juliet. She was probably wondering if she'd married a bump on a log, as silent as he'd been since they left town.

"This is good," he said to break the silence. The truth was, though he'd managed to squeeze down a few bites, he'd hardly tasted it.

"Yes, isn't it?" Juliet agreed. Amos noticed that she had eaten as little as he.

It was almost dark by the time they gave up on the meal. Juliet put the food away, and Amos went out to take a walk around the farmyard. This night he spent longer than usual on his stroll, glancing now and then toward the house, where the window of his bedroom glowed yellow. He thought of Juliet in his room, getting ready for bed, and his heart began to hammer in his chest. He wanted her so much he didn't know whether he *could* leave her alone. However, the idea of her hating him was even worse than a night or two spent in the torments of unfulfilled passion.

Resolutely, Amos squared his shoulders and marched back into the house. When he reached his room, his steps faltered and stopped. Juliet was standing at the window, looking out at the night. The lamp was turned down to a low glow. She whirled around at the sound of his entrance and came forward a few steps.

Amos swallowed, unable to say anything. Juliet was wearing a frilly white nightgown, which, though quite demure, was rendered almost transparent by the light of the lamp behind her. He could plainly see the outline of her torso and legs through the material. Her face, however, was in shadow, and he could not read her expression at all.

"Hello, Amos," she said helpfully when he did not speak, but just stood staring.

There was a faint quiver in her voice that reverberated in Amos's ears. She *was* afraid.

He pulled his eyes away from the delightful view of her body. "Uh . . . I . . . I'm sure you'll be comfortable enough in here. Ah, there are extra blankets in the trunk there beneath the window. But, of course, it shouldn't get that cold tonight."

Amos cursed himself for his stupidity. She must think him a complete idiot, talking about blankets when the day had been in the nineties. Personally, he was so hot he was sweating.

"No, I wouldn't think so," Juliet agreed amicably.

"I'll just—well—" He began to back out into the hall. "I'll be down in Ethan's room, if you need anything."

"Ethan's room?" Juliet repeated blankly.

"Yes, uh, second door down, across the hall."

He retreated farther into the hall, and she followed him a step or two, then stopped. He gestured toward Ethan's room, thinking as he did so that he was making a complete ass of himself. It wouldn't surprise him if she decided he was mad, taking himself off to sleep in another room without any explanation. But he couldn't think of adequate words to explain it to her. He was afraid that to touch on the subject of their conjugal union, even to assure her that he wouldn't press his advances on her, would make him start blushing and stammering like a schoolboy. *How did one talk to a lady about sex?*

"I'm sure it'll be easier—" he began, then stopped.

"That is, you know, if I don't . . . well, at least for a while." His irritation with himself was mushrooming by the second, and he scowled. "Good night," he ended abruptly and turned and walked off down the hall.

Juliet stood where he had left her, astonished. This wasn't how she had envisioned her wedding night. Heaven knows, she had been nervous about it, uncertain and even a bit afraid about taking this tremendous step. But she had been excited, as well, and eager to feel Amos's arms around her, to taste his kiss, to discover the intimate pleasures of sharing his bed. Certainly the last thing she had wanted, or expected, was for Amos to sleep in one room and her in another.

Whatever was the matter? Did Amos find her unappealing?

Forlornly Juliet drifted over to the bed and turned down the covers, then blew out the flame in the oil lamp. She wondered if Amos regretted their impulsive marriage. But if that were true, if he didn't have some feeling for her, then why had he planted the rose bushes? That had obviously been done for her sake, and Amos had looked boyishly pleased that she had enjoyed his surprise. The roses had given her hope; she had felt as if she floated up the stairs.

But everything had changed in an instant. Now she was lying alone in Amos's bed. The room seemed huge and cold without his presence. Tears glittered in her eyes. Juliet felt bereft, abandoned. She didn't know how she could bear it if this was how the rest of her married life was to be.

A fat tear seeped from her eye and plopped onto the pillow. Juliet turned her head into the thick feather pillow and gave way to tears.

The next day Amos and Juliet were tense and awkward with each other. Juliet wondered despairingly if all of her married life was to be like this. Why, they had gotten along far better when she was merely working for him!

But Juliet wasn't one to let such a situation go on long. That night after supper, she waylaid Amos in the kitchen when he returned from his nightly stroll. When he walked in and saw her sitting there, waiting for him, he stopped so abruptly that it would have been comical—if Juliet had been inclined to feel any humor at that moment.

"Oh. Hello. I didn't expect you to still be up."

"I know. That's why I'm here." Juliet rose to her feet. "I—I want to know if this is what you intend for our married life."

"What? I don't know what you mean." His face took on a hunted look.

"I mean, are we going to continue to sleep in separate bedrooms?" A blush rose in Juliet cheeks, but she continued doggedly. "Do you not want to have a . . . a real marriage?"

Amos looked stunned. He stared at her, saying nothing.

Juliet hurried on, "I'm sorry if I seem too bold, but I am a straightforward person. I want to know if I misunderstood your proposal. I can't spend my life wondering and waiting. Do you not want to—to make love to me?"

There, she'd said it. Juliet wiped her sweating palms on her skirt and waited, heart hammering in her chest.

"Juliet! My God, of course I want to! That's not why I slept in Ethan's room last night." Amos sighed and dragged a hand across his face. "Lord, but I'm no good at this. Look." He spread his hands out in front of him in a gesture that asked for understanding. "I want you. I'd like nothing more than to take you to bed." His voice acquired a husky tone. "But yesterday when I carried your trunk to my room, I thought that I might be taking too much for granted. It occurred to me that perhaps you were nervous, even frightened. After all, we don't really know each other."

A warmth spread through Juliet as she realized that Amos had stayed away from her not through lack of desire but because he was sensitive to her feelings.

"I've lived here some time now," she offered softly.

"I know. But that's been in a different way. I mean, you worked for me. We haven't done any of the usual courtship sort of things; you haven't gotten to know me that way. I thought you looked nervous, and I didn't want to push you."

"You're such a sweet man."

Amos's brows rose in amazement at that statement, but he said nothing.

"You were right: I was a little nervous, even scared. It was kind of you to want to ease my mind." She smiled at him. "But I—I don't want to be a stranger to my husband." Her smile grew broader. "Why don't we remedy our lack of a courtship?"

"Can we?" His face looked bleak after her announcement that she was indeed nervous about the marriage act.

"Of course. We'll simply have our courtship now!"

"I don't know how!" Amos growled, glaring at her. "That's the problem. I don't know how to act around women or what to say. I invariably do something clumsy or wrong."

"Nonsense." Juliet's eyes lit up with fun. "I'll teach you. Come here." She held out her hands, motioning to him to come closer.

"Juliet . . ."

"No, no groaning, now. Just come here. First: I open the door." She pantomimed opening a door and broke into a broad smile of welcome. "Why, Mr. Morgan! How very nice to see you."

"*Mister?* You mean we've gone back to that? I'm not sure this is progress."

"You're calling on me; I have to address you as mister or else you might think I was forward."

"Are you sure you know how to do this?"

"Of course I do. Now, I hold out my hand, thusly." She extended her right hand toward him in a languid, elegant gesture. "You take it in your hand." He started to shake her hand, and she grimaced, shaking her head. "No, no, no. Honestly, Amos. This isn't a business meeting. You kiss my hand."

Obediently he raised her hand to his lips, pressing his mouth gently to her skin. A tingle ran up through Juliet's arm at the velvet touch of his lips.

"Very good," she managed to say, though her voice was a trifle breathless. "Now. We go into the parlor and sit down."

She pulled two kitchen chairs to face each other, close together, and they sat down. "Now, you must look soulfully into my eyes, like this." She gave him a comically lovesick look that made him laugh, then made a mock pout at his levity. "Amos, you're not being serious. Pay attention. You have to gaze deeply into my eyes and tell me how lovely I am."

"You're beautiful." His simple, unaffected words were like a finger laid upon her very heart. Juliet's breath caught in her throat, and for a moment she couldn't speak or even think.

"Oh, Amos . . ." Impulsively she leaned over and placed a light kiss on his lips.

His arm wrapped around her shoulders and he stood up, pulling her with him, as his mouth sank into hers, turning the kiss into one of passion, his smoldering desire brought to life by the mere touch of her mouth. Eagerly Juliet threw her arms around his neck, clinging to him. His tongue crept into her mouth, and she answered with her own tongue, not surprised this time by the glorious sensation that rushed through her, but eager to feel more.

Amos groaned deep in his throat, and his hands dug into her. He lifted her up until her feet were dangling off the floor; now her mouth was on a level with his, and he took it in an even deeper kiss. Suddenly, wantonly, Juliet wanted to wrap her legs around his waist and press herself hard against him. She wanted to feel his reaction.

Amos tore his mouth from Juliet's and began to press heated, hungry kisses over her face and down her neck, nuzzling into the neckline of her dress. His lips touched the tops of her breasts, and Juliet gasped, her fingers digging frantically into his back. She had never felt anything like this, never dreamed it. Her breath sounded almost like sobs to her ears as Amos's mouth delved more deeply into the neckline of her dress, nuzzling and kissing her breasts. Her nipples hardened achingly. Juliet was amazed at the sensations pulsing through her, wild and sizzling. She wanted to feel his hands all over her, to have his mouth on her skin, even beneath her clothes. Instinctively she knew that only he could ease the frustrated ache that had sprung up in her.

Abruptly Amos released her and stepped back. His dark eyes glittered wildly, and his chest heaved up and down in labored pants. Juliet stared back at him, shocked by the sensations that were running through her body, as well as by the sudden cessation of the glorious things his lips had been doing to her.

"What—why—" she stammered, too confused to be coherent.

"I'm sorry!" His voice was rough with self-condemnation. "I shouldn't have. I didn't mean to rush you."

"No. It's all right."

He shook his head. "You ought to have a courtship first."

"That was just teasing! We don't have to do those things."

Juliet didn't understand, Amos knew. She probably thought that the marriage act was all like this. She didn't realize that there would be pain for her, and she didn't think about the awkwardness of being naked before him. Of course, she was ready to rush in without thinking. That was Juliet; she always let her emotions rule her head. But he was afraid that those very same ready emotions would turn against him when they reached the final reality of love-making. Then anger and hurt might rise up in her, a feeling of betrayal because he had gone ahead and taken her.

What if he hurt her? The thought plagued him, had for the past day. He was so big and clumsy, and she was so small and delicate. She was young and pure, innocent. He had to be responsible for them both; he had to take care of her and make sure that her first night was something sweet and memorable.

"Juliet, you don't understand . . . ," he began.

"No, I don't. I don't mind, truly I don't. I'd like to go on and—" she hesitated, then drew a deep breath and rushed onward, "I want to make love with you."

A tinge of pink touched her cheeks at the bold words, but she stood her ground, gazing back at him almost defiantly.

Amos swallowed. "I want to, too. Oh, Juliet, believe me, there's nothing that I want more right now. But. . . ." He paused, not knowing what to say. He didn't want to suggest that he might hurt her for fear of frightening her; he didn't want to describe the marital act to her in detail for fear she might be disgusted at his bluntness.

"But what?" Juliet snapped, sounded frustrated.

"I want everything to be right for you," he finished lamely, looking so disconsolate that Juliet's irritation vanished.

She smiled and reached out toward him. "I know you do. You're a terribly nice man. But don't you see? I want it, too. All we're doing by delaying is causing this conflict between us."

That was obvious, Amos thought. And she was right: What good would it do to wait if it made Juliet aggravated with him? Things would get even more awkward, and he'd be even more likely to offend her. It was a hopeless situation.

"All right," he agreed abruptly. "But not this moment." He should at least take a break, bring his throbbing hunger back under some kind of control. He would need to proceed slowly for Juliet's sake, and at the moment he was much too heated for that. "I need a little time to—to cool down, and you'll probably want to"—he made a vague gesture—"get ready for bed and all."

A smile broke across Juliet's face. "Yes, you're right." She would prefer to undress and get into her nightgown outside of Amos's presence. It would avoid a great deal of awkwardness and embarrassment. "It's kind of you to think of it. I'll run upstairs and change."

Juliet started away but turned at the doorway and smiled back over her shoulder at Amos. Her lips were faintly swollen and rosy from their kisses, and desire lingered in her eyes. She looked so utterly delectable that

Amos felt a new flood of yearning pour through him. It was, he realized, going to be damned hard to go slowly.

Amos lingered in the yard as long as he could, until long after he was sure that Juliet must have changed into her nightgown. But he knew that he needed the time worse than she did. He was having a great deal of trouble getting his pulse to slow down when he kept thinking about Juliet upstairs undressing and waiting for him.

Finally, he went back into the house and up the stairs to his room. The door was open and Amos paused just outside it, looking at Juliet. She sat on the bed, her legs curled up under her, her hair girlishly down. The dim glow of the kerosene lamp caressed her face and lit the paler strands of blond in her red-gold hair, so that she seemed to burn with a pale luminescence. She turned her head at his entrance. Her eyes were shadowed, but he could see the smile that curved her lips.

"Hello, Amos." Her voice was a little breathless.

His chest tightened within him, and he couldn't speak. He wanted her so much at that moment that he wasn't sure how he could bear it. He wanted to stroke her warm, soft skin, to crush her vibrant hair between his fingers, to pull her into him and kiss her endlessly. His passion almost frightened him.

Amos walked over to her, struggling to clamp down his desires. "Juliet." Her name was barely a whisper in his mouth. "It's time for bed." The ordinary words thrummed with meaning.

Juliet nodded slightly, her eyes gazing up at him, glowing in a way that shook him to his soul. He wasn't sure how he could live if he couldn't have her. Amos raised his hand and touched her face. His fingertips drifted down her cheek, barely grazing her skin, and his eyes followed the movement of his fingers. His skin was brown against hers, his work-hardened skin rough against her exquisite softness. Juliet, looking up into his eyes, saw the desire in them. She felt it, too, in the heat of his hand and its faint tremor. An answering warmth rose inside her, as it had earlier this evening. As it did whenever Amos touched her.

"You are so lovely," he told her softly. "So delicate and beautiful. I'm afraid I'll hurt you."

"Hurt me?" She echoed in surprise, then smiled. "No. How could you hurt me?"

"Without meaning to. Without wanting to. I'm so big and clumsy." He hadn't meant to reveal his fears to her, but somehow he couldn't seem to stop the words from tumbling out. "You're so fragile; I'm afraid . . ." His hand slid down over her jaw and neck, and slowly, fingers spread, he moved his hand across her shoulder and back up. His eyes followed the course of his fingers, watching in fascination the creamy smoothness of her skin as he felt it beneath his fingertips.

"Afraid of what?" she breathed. His touch excited her, took the air from her lungs and made her heart race. Her skin tingled where he had touched her, and she thought that surely he must see the track of his hand, so different did her skin feel there.

"That I'll break you. Bruise you. Make you fear me. Or hate me."

"Amos! No, how could I hate you? I could never do that." She almost blurted out that she loved him, but she stopped just in time. She knew that he would not want to hear that. Amos might want her, might be gentle and caring, but that didn't mean that he loved her . . . or that he wanted to be burdened with the knowledge of her love for him. He was used to her, and he needed a house-keeper; he found her pleasing enough to want to bed her. None of that meant that he felt the same for her that she did for him. He had married her for convention's sake, for convenience.

"No?" A wry smile twisted his mouth. "There have been times when I think you felt otherwise."

She shot him a worried glance, then saw that he was teasing her. "Oh, Amos! Stop it. You aren't being fair; you know what my temper's like."

"I know. I saw you go after that rattlesnake, remember?"

Juliet giggled. "I fire up sometimes—and you have to admit that it's not hard to fire up at you, either."

"You may have had your reasons."

"But I never hated you, even when I was angry at you. I know that you're a good person. I like you. I admire you."

"I know." He nodded, the serious expression back in his eyes. "That's why I don't want to do anything to ruin that. When I'm close to you, hell, I feel like a big, dumb ox. You're like—" He made a vague gesture with his hands, skimming over her without touching her. He sighed and took a step back. "I don't know. Something so beautiful and foreign. There's nothing dark in you, like there is in me. I want you." His voice shook slightly on the words, and he looked away from her. "I want you so much. But I'm afraid I'll offend you, that I'll say or do the wrong thing."

Juliet took both his hands in hers and brought them up to her chin. "You won't. Trust me." She leaned against his hands for an instant, closing her eyes. Juliet loved the feel of his rougher skin against hers, loved the smell of him; she knew a wild, wanton desire to touch her tongue against his skin and learn the taste of him, too. "I'm not nearly as fragile as you think. I don't know where you got that idea, after seeing me work here every day for I don't know how long."

"You don't have to convince me that you're tough. I know that. At least inside you're tough." He took one of her arms and wrapped his hand around her wrist. His hand was huge; two fingers overlapped around her thin wrist, the skin dark and hard against hers. "But when I look at you . . . and me. It would be so easy for me to hurt you."

"Yes, it would." Juliet gazed up at him with clear, trusting eyes. "But I know you won't. You're a good man, Amos. Kind and gentle, too, no matter how you try to hide it. Perhaps you aren't very experienced with women. Well, neither am I very experienced with men. We'll learn together." She raised her arm where his hand still encircled her wrist and gently laid her lips upon the big bony outcroppings of his knuckles.

Her gesture almost undid him. A shiver of desire so intense that he almost groaned shot through Amos.

"Juliet . . ." he murmured. His hands went to her shoulders, gripping her, lifting her up onto tiptoe, as he bent down to her.

Juliet turned her face up to his, her eyes wide, watching him, waiting, as his face came closer and closer to hers. Her eyes were huge blue fathomless pools, drawing him in, destroying his reason. He couldn't think, only feel, and all he knew at that moment was the creamy beauty of her skin, the beckoning softness of her lips, the yearning that rushed through him like a storm. He kissed her.

Sixteen

At first his kiss was sweet and soft, but then his mouth turned hungry and fierce upon hers, his lips digging into hers as if he could pull from her the sweetness and light and beauty that he craved. His fingers dug into her flesh with a kind of desperation, pressing her body into his.

Juliet wrapped her arms around Amos's neck and clung to him, kissing him back with all the fervor that was suddenly burning in her. Her limbs felt heavy and hot, strangely languid, yet inside she jumped and sizzled with nerves. They clung together, lost in a tumult of sensations, kissing again and again. Her breasts were flattened against his chest, her nipples hard. Even through their clothes, they could feel the heat of the other's body, the curves and hollows and ridges of flesh.

His lips went to her ear; his breath sent shivers down her. Then he took the soft lobe between his teeth, gently worrying it, and Juliet jumped at the sensation. Heat exploded in her abdomen, and an unexpected moisture began to dampen her thighs. She could not hold back a soft moan. The sound made Amos quiver, and his hands curved down over the soft flesh of her hips and back up. Restlessly he stroked her legs and buttocks and back, squeezing the fleshy mounds that enticed him. But it wasn't enough. Taking her hips firmly in his grasp, he rubbed her pelvis against his while his tongue and teeth toyed with her ear.

Juliet felt as if she were melting, and she leaned into him even more, molding herself to his strength. His breath came out in a shudder. His mouth moved down onto the delicate skin of her throat, kissing her over and over as he made his way down to her shoulder and along its hard plane until he was stopped by the ruffle of her nightgown.

Amos groaned and considered ripping the nuisance away from her body, but he retained enough control over his urges to release her and step back. He was determined not to take her with any roughness; nor could it be a hasty, ramshackle coupling, like two animals in heat. Juliet deserved something finer, no matter how much it cost him to hold back.

He began to undress, never taking his eyes from her, and the heat in his gaze kept the fire in Juliet's blood simmering. He looked as if he could consume her whole, and Juliet's heart slammed in her chest, hard and fast, at the thought that she could bring this quiet man to such a fever pitch of feeling. If she had known what to do to stoke his desire, she would have, but since she did not, she simply stood, letting him watch her. Had she known it, her unaffected stance without any attempt to cover herself modestly, was enough to stir Amos's hunger even more. His eyes lingered on the rounded shapes of her breasts beneath her gown, the dark, pointing nipples visible through the thin white cloth.

Finally Amos had torn free of his clothes and stood before her naked. Juliet's eyes traveled involuntarily down his body, taking in the heavy musculature of his chest and arms, the dark curling hair that covered his torso, the long powerful legs. But it was his masculinity, heavy and thrusting, that caught and held her fascinated gaze. She had never seen a naked man before, certainly not one in a state of arousal. He looked huge and primitively male, but the sight of him brought up in her not fear, but a heavy, throbbing ache in her own loins.

Amos saw the slight slackening of her mouth, the glaze of hunger that came over her eyes, and the evidence that she found him arousing sent an even fiercer bolt of passion through him. He came toward her, meaning to sweep the nightgown off her, but Juliet was too quick for him. She reached down and pulled it up and off over her head so that she matched him in nakedness.

He stopped, and his eyes moved over her slowly, taking in every sweet, white, intriguing inch of her skin. Her breasts were plump, high and rosy-tipped, the nipples hard and pointing. Her waist was narrow and flowed out into enticingly curved hips. She was small but beautifully proportioned, her legs shapely. His eyes went to the juncture of her legs and the triangular patch there, bright golden red, slightly darker than the hair on her head.

Amos swallowed hard and reached out his hand. Like a man mesmerized, his hand touched her chest and trailed slowly, lightly down her body. He touched her with only his fingertips in a mere breath of a caress, traveling over the pillowy softness of one breast and the contrasting hardness of its nipple, down onto her flat stomach, until finally his finger stopped at the edge of the fiery tangle of hair.

Juliet sucked in her breath, trembling beneath the pleasure his hand brought her. She wanted more; she wanted to feel his hands all over her. It was probably wanton of her, but she didn't care; the wild yearning inside her was too strong to be suppressed by propriety. She moved forward slightly, so that his hand was pressed against her. A tremor shook him, and Amos closed his eyes, as if the pleasure was almost unbearable. Juliet was close enough now to touch Amos, too, and her hands moved without shyness over his shoulders and arms and onto his chest. Her fingers tangled in the curling hairs of his chest and scraped over the small, hard, masculine nipples. She moved downward, exploring the hard texture of his stomach muscles, one fingertip delving into the shallow well of his navel.

Amos groaned. He could take no more. Swiftly he swept her up in his arms and carried her to the bed. Laying her down on the high, massive bed, he bent and kissed each berrylike nipple. Juliet smiled, her eyelids drifting closed, and moved restlessly on the bed.

"Please," she whispered.

Her word was like a white-hot spur to his passion, and he pulled one nipple into his mouth and began to suckle it. His mouth was hot and wet, and each movement of his lips sent fierce ripples of desire shooting through her. Juliet writhed beneath the onslaught, and unconsciously her legs moved apart. Amos stretched out on the bed beside her, his mouth moving to consume the other breast, and his hand slid down her body to accept the invitation she had offered.

She was slick and hot, and his fingers stroked her gently. Juliet's hips came up off the bed at the unexpected touch of his hand, and Amos went still. But then she moved impatiently beneath him, and his fingers resumed their teasing exploration. He opened up her silken folds, easing into her secret feminine heat. He found the small nub that nestled there and stroked it with infinite care.

Juliet shuddered and moaned, driven almost wild by the supremely delicate caresses. She dug her heels into the bed, arching up toward him, urging him onward—to what, she wasn't sure, but she knew that she wanted it, wanted *him* desperately. But Amos took his time, knowing better than she how much higher she could go, how much more she could experience. He was so hard now he thought he would explode, but he was determined that she feel everything he could possibly give her.

Finally he moved between her legs, unable to wait any longer, and he pushed gently into the entrance of her womanhood. When he met resistance, his hand clenched in the sheets and he plunged deep inside her in a single powerful thrust, wanting to make her pain brief. Her small choked cry tore at him even through the haze of his lust, and he paused. She was so tight and hot around him that it was all he could do not to race to his finish right then, but he held off sternly, waiting until he felt her relax around him.

Then he began to stroke inside her in smooth, even movements, building the fire of his passion to almost unbearable limits. Juliet moaned and writhed beneath him, wrapping and unwrapping her legs around him restlessly, and her fingers dug into his arms and back. Soon she was moving in rhythm with him, and the tiny gasping sounds she made threatened to undo him. Suddenly her fingernails dug hard into his skin, and she let out a tiny noise of surprised delight. She tightened around him, and the movement sparked the thunder of his own release. He shuddered, groaning, as his life seed pumped into her.

They collapsed together, wrapped in a tangle of arms and legs. Drenched with sweat, they lay stunned and silent, still caught in the wild, sweet beauty of that moment when they had been united, no longer separate. They were without strength, without words, and they lay together in mute harmony as they slid into sleep.

If ever any two people were happy, it was Amos and Juliet that summer. They worked hard every day, but the work seemed light because of their inner joy. Alone in the house, they spent their evenings talking, laughing, and making love. Uninhibitedly they tried everything that came into their minds, even making love in the parlor one evening, lying on a quilt on the floor and giggling over the unseemliness of their behavior.

They went blackberrying, strolling along the creek and plucking the thick, juicy berries from the bushes and dropping them in their buckets. Sometimes they ate the berries instead, and other times they playfully fed them to each other, until their lips were stinging and stained with the dark red juice. They had brought along a picnic basket, and they spread out a blanket underneath a cottonwood tree and ate a hearty lunch upon it. Afterward they dozed, lazy in the midday heat, and when they awoke they made languid love, with the sunlight through the leaves dappling their bodies and the tinkling rush of the creek sounding in their ears.

Sometimes Juliet strolled out to the barn after she finished the evening's dishes and sat there, watching Amos work on his wood carvings. He showed her, somewhat reluctantly, the wood nymph that he had carved and which Juliet realized resembled her. She threw her arms around him and hugged and kissed him. Exclaiming over the carving she was filled with pride that he had represented her as such a beautiful being. After that, he drew out another piece of wood, which appeared to be a glum-faced dwarfish creature crawling up out of the ground. They were a pair, he told her, and Juliet knew that the grim gnome was meant to be Amos himself, paired with her light and lovely nymph. She was awed by his talent and insisted on bringing them both up to their bedroom and installing them on the dresser. Everytime she saw them, it was an affirmation that she and Amos would always be together.

All that was missing in Juliet's life was an avowal of

love from Amos, but she told herself that that, too, would come someday. He desired her, and that was enough for now. Later there would be children and a family and a strong enduring love that wouldn't end until they died. And she smiled, thankful that her life had taken the bizarre turn it had when Westfield ran off with their earnings in Steadman, Nebraska.

Ethan came home after three weeks. The summer was drawing to a close, and it would soon be time to harvest. Many of the vegetables had already matured during the summer, and Juliet and Amos had picked them. Juliet had spent most of her time since she returned to the farm canning and preserving, following the detailed instructions that Frances had written down for Juliet in the weeks before she died. Sometimes, as Juliet struggled in the steaming-hot kitchen with the jars and vegetables, she would turn again to the pages of directions, and as she looked at the shaky lines of writing, she would think of Frances sitting there at the table and writing them down, despite her pain. Then her eyes would fill with tears, and she would cry again for the loss of her friend.

The larder and the shelves on the wall of the root cellar were now fully stocked with jams, jellies, pickles, and jar after jar of canned carrots, corn, and squash. There was a large barrel on the floor of the root cellar full of cabbage packed in brine that would turn into sauerkraut for winter. The peas and beans had been carefully dried, sacked, and stored away. Onions hung in bunches from the low rafters of the cellar. Later Amos and Ethan would dig up the potatoes and most of the remaining space in the cellar would be given over to them, except for the corner reserved for the pumpkins and fall squashes.

Juliet, surveying her domain, felt like the picture-perfect housewife. She had worked hard, half the time afraid that she would ruin the food through her ignorance, but it had been worth it. She enjoyed the life she was leading, and it seemed as if it grew better with each passing day.

The harvest crews came through and camped out on the Morgans' land, working their way with their great threshing machine through the fields of wheat. Juliet, surprised to see that there was a woman or two with the crew, noticed that one of them called and waved to Amos. He waved back half-heartedly, and that evening Juliet glanced out the kitchen window to see Amos standing in the yard talking to the same woman. After a time, she left, giving him a smile that Juliet thought looked downhearted. She was a handsome enough woman, though several years older than Juliet and built along sturdy, buxom lines far different from Juliet's own small frame. Juliet knew somehow that Amos and this woman had been lovers. She started to ask him about it, but decided that it was better left alone. After all, that had been in the past, long before she came to the farm.

She never saw them together again, and Juliet was positive that her husband was far too busy with her in bed to have any time or interest in seeing another woman. A little smugly, she smiled to herself. Whatever any other woman might have been to Amos in the past, *she* was his wife, and she had his full attention.

The weather turned cooler. The last of the crops were hauled in to the root cellar, including the big, bright pumpkins, some of which had to be put in the kitchen because there was no more room in the cellar. The fire in the kitchen stove was a welcome thing in the early morning and late at night. Juliet needed her cape when she went out to feed the chickens and gather the eggs. October was hog-killing time, Amos said, and he and Ethan butchered one of the hogs and hung the meat in the smokehouse to season. Ethan began to tease Juliet about living through a Nebraska winter, telling her stories about the depth of the drifts and the fierceness of the blizzards, until Juliet wasn't sure how much of his tales were tall and how much real.

One morning there was a light snow on the ground when they woke up, but by the end of the day it had melted in the sun, and after that the weather continued cold, but sunny. Juliet, smiling to herself, was certain that she wouldn't find the winter boring, even if she was snowbound much of the time in the house. If her suspicions were right, she would have plenty of work to do, knitting little blankets and sweaters and sewing tiny garments. Afraid that she was wrong, Juliet did not tell Amos, but hugged the news to herself. Her life, she thought, would be perfect if only Amos would tell her that he loved her.

There had been many times when Juliet had wanted to tell him how much she loved him, but always she had stopped the words before they came out. She told herself that she didn't want to make Amos feel obliged to say the words just because she had said them, but, deep down inside, she knew that the truth was that she was afraid that she would declare her love, only to be met with blank silence from Amos.

Still, her life was as wonderful as she could wish it—until their visitor arrived.

It was a bright, crisp November morning when Juliet heard the jingle of a harness in the yard and realized that someone had come to visit. She looked out the window over the sink, but she couldn't see anything. A man's voice sounded, and then a horse whinnied. Setting down the glass she had just rinsed, Juliet wiped off her hands on her apron and started toward the front of the house.

When she was halfway down the hall, there was a short, loud tapping of the door knocker against the door. Juliet wondered who it could be, feeling the uplift of curiosity and excitement that attended any visit on a lonely farm. She hoped it would be Henrietta.

Juliet opened the door, a smile already formed on her lips. A woman whom she had never seen before stood on the small porch in front of her. "Oh," Juliet said, nonplussed. "I—hello. Can I help you?"

She glanced curiously past the woman to where a buggy loaded down with trunks stood in the farmyard. It was driven by an older man whom she vaguely remembered having seen before. He tipped his hat to her. "Morning."

Juliet gave him a nod. "Good morning."

Her gaze came back to her visitor. She was a stunning

woman, tall and statuesque, with blond hair swept up under a wide hat gloriously bedecked with flowers. A thick, long black cape was wrapped around her, fastened with black braided frogs in the front. The wide hat shadowed her face, concealing the color of her eyes and softening her skin, but Juliet could see her well enough to tell that she was older than Juliet and quite lovely.

The woman stared back at Juliet, her eyes making a quick survey of her. Then she said, "I'm here to see Amos Morgan."

So she hadn't made a mistake; that had been Juliet's first thought. "This is his farm. But I'm afraid he's down by the creek working now. He won't be in until noon."

"Oh." The woman glanced around. "I see. Well . . ."

Juliet hesitated. The normally courteous thing to do would be to invite the woman in to wait for Amos. But Juliet sensed something a little wrong about this woman. There was a flamboyant quality to her; her good looks were too florid and overblown. Juliet suspected that the color in her cheeks was not entirely natural. Juliet had been in the world enough that she was certain that this woman was not a lady. She also couldn't imagine why on earth she would be asking for Amos. It wouldn't surprise her if Amos was upset with her for letting the woman in. On the other hand, she could not in good conscience make the woman wait outside on a cold November day until Amos returned; that would simply be too rude.

"Would you like to come inside and wait for him?" she asked finally, thinking that Amos would simply have to handle the problem himself. She couldn't turn the woman away.

"Yes, I would." The visitor swept through the door into the hallway.

Juliet glanced toward the buggy outside. "Wouldn't your, uh, husband like to come in, also?"

The woman laughed. "My husband! Oh, my no. Dear child, he's only the driver who brought me out from town. Dreadful little place, Steadman." She turned and called back to the man, "Unload my trunks. Just leave them here in the hall."

Juliet's mouth dropped open. *She was intending to stay!* Juliet floundered, searching for something to say. She wanted to protest the woman's bold assumption that she was going to stay. It seemed outrageous, and Juliet couldn't imagine Amos allowing it. But she also knew that hospitality was the rule in the West, where it was so far between towns and even between houses. Friends and relatives often came for visits of several days, even weeks, and lodging was given ungrudgingly to strangers who were overtaken by bad weather or had misjudged their time or were simply struck by the bad luck of a broken axle or wheel.

What if the woman turned out to be one of Amos's relatives or the wife of a dear friend? Juliet wouldn't want Amos to think her rude or ungracious or—yes, admit it, jealous, for she had to acknowledge that part of what stirred inside her chest was a twinge of jealousy at the thought of a woman this beautiful coming to live with them, even for a short time.

So Juliet held her tongue regarding the other's presumption and asked politely, "Could I offer you something? Some coffee, perhaps?"

"Yes. All right. Frankly," she said, pressing one gloved hand to her stomach, "I'm starved. Do you have anything to eat?"

"Yes, of course. How rude of me not to have thought. No doubt you rose early today and had breakfast long ago."

"I didn't have anything." She shuddered expressively. "I can't eat at that hour of the morning."

The woman unfastened her cloak and took it off, handing it to Juliet. The dress she wore beneath the cloak was a vivid green trimmed with black braid and fringe. Several loops of jet black beads were hung around her neck and jet earrings dangled from her ears. Her clothes were obviously expensive and pretty, but, as with her style of looks, it seemed too much, overdressed.

Her visitor unpinned her wide hat and handed that to Juliet, too. Juliet's temper began to simmer up. *The woman was treating her like a maid!* However, she held her anger in check and hung the garments on the oak hat rack in the hall. Then she showed her visitor into the front parlor and hurried into the dining room to take out some of the best dishes from the china cabinet. Somehow she felt the need to present the best front possible to this woman. In the kitchen, she cut up an apple and a pear in a bowl and sliced a piece from the pound cake she had made the day before. She set the bowl and small plate on her best silver serving tray and filled the silver coffeepot, then added two cups and the creamer and sugar bowl to the tray. Last, she whisked off her apron and laid it on the back of a chair. Picking up the tray, Juliet returned to the front parlor.

"Here we are," she said cheerfully as she came into the room, offering the visitor her best smile. She set the tray down on the low table in front of the sofa, where the woman sat.

Juliet herself sat down in the chair at right angles to the sofa and picked up the coffeepot. "Would you care for cream or sugar?"

"Yes. Both." The woman gave her a speculative glance as Juliet prepared the cup and handed it to her.

Juliet poured herself a cup, as well, and added cream to it. She sipped at her cup as she watched the other woman eat, and all the while she racked her brain for a polite way to find out what the woman wanted here.

"I hope your trip wasn't too difficult," she began.

The other woman shrugged. "Boring, of course, and miserably cold. But I suppose it was all right."

"That's good." Juliet paused. She couldn't think of anything to talk about, let alone a clever question to ferret out the reason for her visit. She cleared her throat. "I should have asked your driver if he wanted something to eat or drink, too. He should wait in the kitchen; it's too cold to sit outside." Juliet started to stand up.

The other woman waved lazily at her to sit down. "Don't worry. I sent him back while you were in the kitchen. I don't need him anymore."

Juliet stared. She had sent him back? Without even

being invited to spend the night? Juliet could not understand her gall. Could it be that she had already written to Amos, informing him that she was coming to visit, and he hadn't told Juliet?

"I—uh—I'm sorry, but I'm afraid I don't know your name."

"Helen Bangston," the other woman supplied.

"How do you do? I'm Juliet Morgan, Amos's wife."

Her visitor's eyes widened, and she looked suddenly taken aback. "Oh . . . uh . . . yes, nice to meet you."

"We were recently married," Juliet explained, seeing the surprise in the other woman's face.

"I see. Congratulations." The woman set down the small plate of cake which she had been holding and took another sip of coffee. When she looked up again, she managed a smile at Juliet. "You startled me. You see, I had decided that Amos would never get married. He's been a bachelor so long now."

Juliet nodded. "I think it surprised quite a few people." Her smile flashed in her face, lighting it up. "Perhaps even Amos himself."

Helen looked back at her blankly, not answering her smile with one of her own. Juliet felt suddenly foolish. Color stained her cheeks, and she glanced away.

"How is . . . Amos's son?" Helen asked.

"Ethan?" Juliet's face brightened. "You know Ethan?"

"Yes, of course. I'm . . . an old friend of Amos's."

"I see." Thank heavens she had invited her in and hadn't taken her up for her rudeness earlier. "Ethan is fine, most of the time. Lately he's had a little trouble with girls—you know how young men are. But he's a good boy, kind and generous. Of course you know that, since you know Ethan."

"Of course." Helen echoed her words, plainly bored. "Perhaps—if you'd show me to my room, I think I would like to lie down for a while. I'm beginning to feel a little tired from my trip."

"Certainly." Again her calm assumption that she would be staying sent a ripple of resentment through Juliet. Helen Bangston acted as if she belonged here. She hadn't asked Juliet if her visit was all right with her. She hadn't even thanked her for letting her stay there. *Why hadn't Amos told her about Mrs. Bangston's arrival?* Juliet wasn't sure which one of the two she was more irritated with— this bold-seeming woman with her overblown good looks or her own husband. She intended to give Amos a piece of her mind about it when he did come strolling in. She must look like a fool to this woman, so obviously unaware of her visit or even who she was.

Juliet led Helen down the hall to the room where she had lived before she married Amos, relieved that she had kept clean sheets on the bed and had dusted it only a few days ago. She would have been embarrassed to let a guest see a room that was not in order even if it wasn't normally used.

After she left Helen in her room, Juliet returned to the kitchen and hastily upgraded her noontime meal. When she had made the kitchen as neat and tidy and the food as good as she could, she sat down at the table to wait for Amos and Ethan to appear.

Finally she caught a glimpse through the south window of Ethan coming into the farmyard, and she jumped up and hurried to the door. Sure enough, there was Amos, too, walking in front of Ethan. He glanced up and saw Juliet and smiled.

Juliet was tempted to smile back, but she sternly refused to let herself be led off track just because Amos's smile did funny things to her insides. Grabbing her cape from the hook by the door, she threw it around her shoulders and ran lightly down the steps toward her husband. Amos's steps slowed and he cast her a wary glance when he saw the expression on Juliet's face.

"Why didn't you tell me?" Juliet asked before she even reached him.

"Tell you what?" Amos stopped, facing her. His hands started automatically toward her, but he stopped himself and instead balled them on his hips. "What's wrong?"

"What's wrong?" Juliet asked with dreadful irony. "An old friend of yours arrives this morning, trunks and all, obviously coming for a long visit, and I know nothing about it! And you ask what's wrong?"

"Wait. Slow down. What are you talking about? What old friend?"

"Mrs. Bangston!" Juliet retorted irritably. "Who else is coming here to visit?"

"Mrs. Bangston." He gazed at her blankly. "Maybe I've been out in the sun too long this morning, but I haven't a clue what you're talking about. Who is Mrs. Bangston?"

Now it was Juliet's turn to stare at him. "You mean to tell me you don't know her?"

"Know who?"

"The woman sleeping in my bed!" Juliet exclaimed, making a sweeping gesture back toward the house.

"What!"

"My old bed, I mean. The bedroom on the bottom floor."

"There's a strange woman in our guest room?"

"Well, she's certainly strange to me! But she said she knew you. She knew Ethan."

His brow furrowed. "But who—you said her name was Babcock?"

"Bangston. Helen Bangston." Juliet was beginning to feel alarmed. "If you don't know her, who could she be? What's she doing here?"

"Helen Bangston," he repeated thoughtfully. "Helen Ban—"

Suddenly the color drained from his face. "Oh, my God, it couldn't be."

"Amos?" Juliet reached a hand out toward him, but he backed away, shaking his head slightly.

"Where is she?"

"I told you: lying down in the guest bedroom."

He turned and walked rapidly toward the house, almost running, leaving Juliet staring after him.

Seventeen

Ethan, who had been standing watching Amos and Juliet, gazed after his father in surprise as he rushed into the house. Ethan turned toward Juliet, perplexed.

"What's the matter?"

"I haven't the slightest idea." Juliet wasn't sure whether to be vexed or scared. "Some woman has come visiting and seems to intend to stay with us."

Ethan stared. "Does Pa know this woman?"

"He didn't seem to, but then all of a sudden he turned white and rushed off to see her. Have you ever heard of a woman named Helen?"

Ethan shrugged. "There's Helen Shaw who lives in town; she lives with her sister, Dorothy Gilbern, and her husband."

"No. I think this must be someone you knew in the past, someone who moved away, maybe. She inquired after you."

Ethan's eyes sparkled with curiosity. "Why's she here?"

"I don't know," Juliet replied slowly as she and Ethan started toward the house. "But I think she plans to stay awhile." She described the woman's actions this morning. Going over them again—and considering Amos's strange reaction—the things the woman had done seemed even more bizarre.

By the time Juliet had their dinner on the table, and Ethan had washed up, the two of them were agog with curiosity. As they rattled around in the kitchen, they could hear Amos's voice raised in anger down the hall and the answering sharp staccato of a woman's voice, but Amos and the visitor were inside her room with the door closed, and they could not understand the words.

Finally, when Juliet was beginning to wonder if she should put the food back in its pans to reheat or if she and Ethan should go ahead and eat without Amos, the door down the hall banged open and Amos came striding out of it. He marched into the kitchen, his face like thunder, yanked out his chair, and plopped down into it. Much more languidly, Helen Bangston followed him down the hall.

She paused, framed in the doorway. Juliet suspected that she had practiced the pose frequently. Then she came forward into the room to the only empty chair at the table. Ethan popped politely up out of his chair when she entered the room and watched her walk to the table. Juliet could almost see him quivering with curiosity. She was only slightly less curious herself. She longed to know what had been said behind that closed door. Whatever it was, it appeared that Mrs. Bangston had won the argument. Her face was placid, the look in her eyes smug, whereas Amos looked as if he could eat nails.

"Amos?" Helen said in a prodding voice. "Aren't you going to introduce us?"

Since Juliet had already met her, she must be talking about Ethan, Juliet thought. Amos looked directly at Mrs. Bangston for the first time since she had walked into the kitchen; the gaze he directed at her was so fierce that it made Juliet shiver. She would not like to be the recipient of that stare.

"Ethan," he said through clenched teeth, "this is Helen Bangston. Mrs. Bangston, this is my son Ethan. She's going to be staying with us for a few days."

Juliet barely managed not to gasp. Mrs. Bangston most certainly had won their argument! Amos looked as if he wished her as far away as he could send her, yet he had obviously agreed to let her stay. What had she said that had made him give in to her?

"How do you do?" Ethan greeted their visitor politely.

"I'm so happy to meet you, Ethan. I've been longing to for years."

"You have?"

"Yes, of course. I've often thought about you."

Juliet saw Amos's hand tighten into a fist on the table. She glanced up at his face; he was looking at Helen, and his eyes were deadly. Juliet swallowed, sure that he was about to explode into a rage.

But all he said was, "I doubt that Ethan wants to hear about such old stuff."

"Sure I do, Pa," Ethan said cheerfully. His eyes were on their visitor and he didn't see his father's grim expression. "How come you knew about me?"

"Your father and I knew each other long ago." Helen smiled and glanced over at Amos in a smug way that plainly said she knew how furious she was making him and that she delighted in it.

"Really? Did you use to live here?"

Helen laughed merrily. "Mercy, no. I lived in Omaha when I knew your father." She paused and turned her head toward Juliet. "Be a dear, uh, Julia, is it? Pass me the potatoes, please."

"Juliet," Juliet corrected quietly, thinking that she would like to tell the woman to call her Mrs. Morgan.

"Of course. Juliet. Such an unusual name."

Juliet silently handed her the bowl of potatoes.

"I didn't know you ever lived in Omaha, Pa." Ethan turned toward his father.

"Briefly. When I was a few years older than you. I was trying to earn a little money during the fall and winter in the packing plants."

"Oh. Gosh, that sounds interesting. How come you never told me that before?"

Amos shrugged. "I didn't think it was important."

"But, Amos, dear," Helen interjected in a sweet voice, "that's where you met Ethan's mother."

Everyone at the table froze, except Helen, of course, who calmly began to eat her potatoes. Ethan's face went pale, then pink. Juliet looked at him, then at Amos. Amos stared at the plate in front of him, steadfastly refusing to meet anyone's eyes.

Juliet began to have a glimmer of understanding. This must have something to do with Ethan's mother. That was why Amos was allowing this pushy woman to stay here. Juliet looked at Helen. She disliked the woman more every second.

"You—you knew my mother?" Ethan asked finally in a strangled voice.

Helen gave a secretive smile. "Yes, I knew your mother. Quite well, in fact."

Juliet could see that Ethan longed to ask more about his mother, but after one swift glance at his father, he swallowed his curiosity.

When Ethan said nothing more, Helen offered, "We'll have to talk more about her sometime."

"All right." Ethan's voice couldn't hide his eagerness.

Juliet picked up the closest thing to her on the table, a dish of butter, and thrust it close to Helen. "Would you care for some butter, Mrs. Bangston?" she asked, her voice falsely sweet. At the moment, she would have liked nothing better than to ram the dish down the woman's throat.

Helen cast a startled look at the butter dish held practically under her nose, then glanced at Juliet with amusement, as though to say she knew precisely what Juliet was thinking. "Why, yes, thank you. My goodness, did you make this butter yourself?"

"Yes."

"And everything else on the table, too? My, how talented you are." There was a faint touch of mockery in her eyes that told Juliet that Helen thought exactly the opposite of what she was saying.

"Thank you," Juliet returned blandly. She didn't care

if the woman shot darts at her; her main concern at the moment was to turn the conversation away from Ethan's mother and thus ease some of Amos's anger. "Tell me, Mrs. Bangston, do you still live in Omaha?"

"No, I moved to Chicago some time ago."

"Really? How interesting. I've visited Chicago a few times myself." Juliet began to talk about the city, keeping the conversation steered down a safe, boring path.

They managed to get through the meal without any more tense moments arising. Amos was silent throughout the meal. He ate quickly, and when he was through, he stood up and said, "Time to get back to work, Ethan."

"But, Pa, I'm not finished!" Ethan looked up in protest.

"Better hurry, then. There's still plenty of deadfall at the creek to saw up."

"Yessir." Ethan knew his father well enough to know when it was useless to argue with him. He swallowed the last of his milk in one long drink, grabbed two pieces of bread to eat as he went, and followed his father. At the door, as he took his hat off the hook, he turned toward the table and smiled shyly. "Good afternoon, Mrs. Bangston. I'll see you this evening. Bye, Julie."

"Good-bye, Ethan." Juliet fondly watched him as he went out the door.

Helen stood up, too. "I'm afraid I'm not particularly hungry after that snack I had this morning. Perhaps I'll get something later this afternoon."

She walked out of the kitchen and down the hall to her bedroom. Juliet shook her head in amazement. The woman hadn't offered to help, or even thanked Juliet! Juliet didn't think she had ever met a woman that impolite. One simply did not eat at another woman's table, then leave her to do the cleaning up, without even offering to help with the dishes. The most basic courtesy required a thank-you. Grimacing, Juliet stood up and began to clear off the table.

Helen Bangston made no further appearance the rest of the afternoon. Juliet went about her chores, but her mind was churning as she did the familiar tasks. She thought about Helen and Amos and his reaction to her, and she thought about what Helen had said to Ethan. She didn't understand precisely what was going on, but she certainly intended to find out. As soon as she got Amos alone she would make sure he told her the entire story!

As it turned out, she had no opportunity to talk to her husband alone until late that evening when they went to their room to go to bed. As soon as Amos closed the door behind them, Juliet plunged into her questions, "Amos, who *is* that woman? And why did she come here? It's obvious that you know her, but it's equally obvious that you are no friend of hers. Why didn't you send her on her way?"

Amos shook his head tiredly. "Don't, Juliet. I don't want to talk about it."

"Don't want to talk about it!" Juliet shot him a disbelieving look as she reached up and began to pull the pins from her hair. "How can you not talk about it? Don't you think I have a right to know who is visiting in my own house? Who I am cooking and cleaning for—and why?"

He rubbed his hands across his face, then turned away from her and sat down on the side of the bed to untie his shoes. "I know she's a burden to you. I'm sorry. But I can't send her away. Just be patient for a few days. She'll leave. I know her. It will be too boring for her. She'll start wanting to get back to where there's lots of lights and dancing and men."

"I certainly hope so," Juliet agreed fervently.

He finished untying one shoe and pulled it off, tossing it onto the floor in a frustrated, angry gesture. "Damn her! After all these years, why'd she have to show up now?"

Juliet gazed at him with concern and pity. He looked so weary that it tugged at her heart. She went over to the bed and knelt on it behind him and began to rub his shoulders.

"Ahhhh . . ." He released a long sigh of pleasure, letting his head roll forward loosely. "You're too good to me."

Juliet chuckled. "I try my best to make you think so."

"I know." He reached back and took one of her hands and brought it to his lips. He pressed a gentle kiss into her palm.

With an upswell of emotion in her heart, Juliet bent down and laid her cheek against his head. "Oh, Amos . . . I know this hurts you."

"It's Ethan I'm worried about."

"She's his mother, isn't she?"

Juliet felt the shock go through Amos, and he released her hand, twisting around to look at her. "How did you know? Did that witch tell you?"

Juliet shook her head. "No. I guessed it. I thought about it all afternoon, wondering why you'd let her stay when it obviously upset you so much. I figured that had to be the answer; she had to have an important claim on you."

Juliet swallowed. Her voice had grown shaky at the end of her speech. She didn't want Amos to know that she was upset or worried. But she couldn't keep from feeling a frisson of fear when she thought about Helen and the prior claim she had on Amos. Juliet remembered all too well what Amos had told her about Ethan's mother that day when John Sanderson had told Ethan not to call on Ellie anymore. Amos had been desperately in love with her, had worshipped her, as he'd put it. He had wanted to marry her and the only reason he hadn't was because she refused him.

Amos was angry with her now, of course. But what other feelings for her remained under that anger? Bitterness, hurt . . . and, at the wellspring of it all, his tremendous love for her. Juliet couldn't help but be concerned about what might happen if Amos was around the woman every day. Helen was older, certainly, but she was still beautiful. And Juliet would have bet her last penny that she knew all sorts of feminine wiles that Juliet had never even dreamed of.

Juliet was sure that Helen had returned to try to recapture Amos's love. She was getting older and she was probably beginning to worry about what she would do in a few years when she was no longer attractive. She had regretted the decision she had made years ago when Amos asked her to marry him, and she had decided to come back and marry him. That was why she had looked startled when Juliet said that she was Mrs. Morgan.

What chance did Amos's practical, loveless marriage in middle age stand against the sweet memory of his youthful passion? Juliet didn't fool herself. Amos felt affection and desire for her; he'd shown that amply since their marriage. But that wasn't the same thing as a love that burned like fire within him.

Juliet could see her marriage, the sweet and happy life she had built up, crumbling into dust around her. She felt like crying. But she could not let Amos see that.

Amos let out a grunt of disgust. "Claim! That woman has no claim on me. She's nothing to me. Hell, what kind of claim could she have? I asked her to marry me, and she refused." His mouth twisted. "She doesn't even have a claim on Ethan. She deserted him. She was going to Chicago with some man she'd met; she wanted to have fun, not take care of a baby."

"How could she do that?" Juliet asked, amazed. Though she had heard this story before, she still found it difficult to believe. "I don't understand. How could any woman walk off and leave her own child?"

"She has no heart. All she thinks about is herself, and her sole method of judging things is by whether or not they give her fun. A child didn't. A salesman from Chicago with money to spend would. She told me she didn't want to be tied down all her life, certainly not by my bastard son."

"Oh, Amos!" Juliet's heart was wrung with pity for him.

He shrugged. "By then, it didn't hurt. I'd gotten over her. I was happy to see her go. But, of course, there was the boy. I wasn't even sure that he was my son."

"What!" Juliet's hands stilled in shock. "You mean that Ethan might not be your child?"

"Maybe. I don't know. He seemed awfully big to be the age she said he was. I couldn't see anything in his face that looked like me or my family. But it didn't matter. I had to take him in. I couldn't leave him with a woman like that, could I?"

"No, of course not. But, oh, Amos, to pass off her baby as your son if he wasn't! How could she be that cruel?"

"I don't know that Helen even knows what cruel is. She doesn't think about things like that, only about what she wants and what will get her what she wants. Good or bad, cruelty, kindness—nothing like that comes into it. Anyway, it doesn't matter anymore. Ethan *is* my son now. I raised him. I fed him and took care of him when he was sick and tried to teach him what he needed to know. He's my son more than he ever was hers. And I'll do anything to protect him from being hurt. *She* knows that."

"What do you mean?"

"That's why she's here—to threaten to tell Ethan who she is. She said she thought he'd like to meet his mother, might even like to go live with her for a while."

"No! But Ethan would never do that!"

"Wouldn't he? I can't be sure. If he found out that I'd lied to him, that I had told him his mother was dead when all these years she was alive, he might hate me for it. You don't know how Helen can twist things, how she can make you believe something that isn't true. If she told him that I'd forced her to give him to me and painted some pitiful picture of herself, if she told him he wasn't even mine . . ." He shook his head. "I don't want to risk it. I want her out of my life. And she knows it! She wants me to pay her to keep my secret."

"You mean she asked you for money? Threatened to tell Ethan the truth if you didn't give it to her?"

"Of course she did. Why else would she come here? She hates being anywhere but a city. She's been living in Chicago ever since she left Ethan, and she wouldn't have left it for my farm except to get money."

"Oh. I thought maybe as she got older she realized what a mistake she made, that she was hoping she could come back here and marry you."

Amos let out a bark of laughter. "Not likely. She lost her latest 'male protector' and she's having trouble finding another, I'll bet. She's getting too old; there are lots of other, younger women competing for the rich old men. She ran out of money, and she was desperate, so she thought about me and Ethan and figured she could rest up here for a few days and get some money to start again in Chicago."

"Are you going to pay her?"

"No." He set his jaw. "She's getting nothing from me.

If I gave her money, she'd keep coming back with the same threat every time she needed more cash. I figured the only way to get rid of her was to let her stew here a few days until she got so bored she'd leave. It shouldn't take long."

"I hope you're right."

"Me, too." Amos sighed and stood up, unbuttoning his shirt and pulling it out of his trousers. He stopped and turned back toward Juliet, his face troubled. "Juliet . . ."

"What?"

"I'm sorry about her being here. You shouldn't have to associate with someone like her. I know it probably seems like an insult to you. I didn't know what else to do."

Juliet smiled. "It's all right. I've been around women like Helen before—and worse. I'm not offended because you have to put her up for a few days; I understand. I just hate to think of it hurting you or Ethan." Her smile turned into a teasing grin. "Anyway, as I remember, you used to say that *I* was a woman like her."

"All right." One eyebrow rose, but the bubble of laughter in his voice turned the sternness into mockery. "No holding up my past misjudgments to me. All my stupidities before I married you have to be forgotten."

"They do? Where is that written, I'd like to know?"

"It's the only fair thing. A man can't be expected to think clearly when he's met the woman he's going to marry."

"Ha! As if you knew then that we were going to get married!"

He smiled, the slow, almost sweet smile that always melted Juliet's heart. "Ah, but I did." He hooked his thumbs in his suspenders and pulled them down and off, then peeled his shirt back, all the while walking slowly toward where Juliet sat on the bed.

Juliet sat back on her heels, her heart speeding up in excitement, loving the light of mischief and desire that had lit in her normally sober husband's gaze. It was wonderful to see Amos tease, to see him emerge from the rigid cocoon of his austere upbringing. "I'll bet," she retorted, egging him on, her eyes dancing with glee, her mouth widening in an unconscious sensual invitation.

"Didn't you wonder why I fought you so hard?" he asked in a low voice, coming to a stop beside the bed. He loomed over her, hard and powerful, gazing down at her with heat in his eyes.

Juliet's breath began to come more rapidly as she looked up at him, anticipating his touch, his kiss. His nearness was almost overwhelming. She was barely able to keep track of what they were saying. "To get rid of me, I thought."

He shook his head. "I was scared. 'Cause I knew, deep down, what you could do to me."

"Do to you?" Juliet asked in a mockly innocent way, opening her eyes wide. "You mean, things like this?"

She put her hands on his stomach and slid them up his chest, coming up onto her knees as she did so.

"Yeah," he agreed shakily.

"And this?" She unbuttoned the top two buttons of his shirt and pressed her lips against his bare chest.

"Oh, yes, especially that," he growled. Tilting her head back, his mouth seized hers in a long, deep kiss, and together they fell back on the bed, all thoughts of Helen Bangston fled.

Eighteen

$\mathcal{A}$mos's hopes that Helen Bangston would soon grow bored and return to Chicago were proved wrong. Certainly, she was bored enough. She spent most of her time in the small, informal parlor, staring out the window or perusing a fashion book she had brought with her. She didn't do any housework. She didn't occupy her hands with sewing or knitting, even for herself. She seemed completely at a loss for anything to do, often getting up and wandering around the house, sighing gustily, and complaining about the lack of sophistication and any sort of pleasures in Nebraska. But she did not announce that she was returning to Chicago.

The longer she stayed, the more frayed Juliet's nerves became. The woman was a nuisance. Worse than a nuisance. Before she was there, with little work to do on the farm, Amos had spent much of his time indoors, often sitting in the kitchen to read or whittle. Ethan joined them many times, and the room was filled with talk and laughter. Now, with Helen constantly in the house, Amos seized every opportunity to get out of it. As soon as breakfast was done, he disappeared to the barn, and he stayed there the rest of the day, coming in only to eat. When he was in the house, he was obviously ill at ease and irritated, so there was little conversing with him.

Being the cause of Amos's absence was bad enough, but Helen was also personally annoying. She arose late and demanded breakfast when she sauntered into the kitchen, long after Juliet had cleaned up the breakfast dishes and started on the day's tasks. She never thanked Juliet or offered to take on her share of the workload. She added her clothes to Juliet's laundry, expecting her to clean them, too, and not a word of thanks. But worst of all, she whined. Morning, noon, and night she found something to complain about. She was too cold, so a fire had to be built in the small parlor; she didn't want to sit in the kitchen where it was warm because the chairs were uncomfortable. She hated the quiet of the country, the lack of entertainment, the absence of people. She mourned the fact that she could not go shopping for a new hat. She deplored the coldness of the wind and the ugly barrenness of the landscape. At first Ethan had stayed around Helen, talking to her, eager for new company and even more eager to hear something about his mother. But soon he, too, sought refuge in the barn with his father, unable to bear her complaints.

It seemed that only *she*, Juliet thought angrily, could not get away from the woman.

At first Juliet tried her best to be nice. After all, any guest deserved courtesy. Besides, Amos was afraid that Helen would tell his son the truth, so it seemed imperative that Juliet try to stay on Helen's good side. She didn't want Helen revealing the truth to Ethan because she was mad at Juliet. But as the days passed, it became harder and harder for Juliet to remain gracious. Juliet was not feeling well these days, which made it even more difficult to do extra things for the interloper, and she was more than usually snappish, so that the woman's whining frayed her nerves worse than ever. Juliet was constantly tired and often queasy, and she was more and more convinced that she was pregnant. However, she still hadn't told Amos now because Helen was in the house. It was silly, she supposed, but she didn't think she could bear to have Helen intruding on their private moment of joy.

She would tell Amos after Helen left, she decided, thinking how she would make a special dinner and then give him the news after supper. But Juliet was beginning to wonder if that event was ever going to take place. Helen seemed to have become permanently entrenched in their home, and Juliet wondered if anything could blast her out of there.

One afternoon when Helen complained about the lack of heat in the small parlor, clearly expecting Juliet to come build up the fire for her, Juliet surprised them both by bursting into tears and hurrying from the room. She went straight up to her bedroom and flung herself across the bed, giving way to a storm of tears.

Finally, exhausted, she took a nap. She awoke with a new calm and sense of purpose. She had reached the end of her patience. There was no way she would continue to put up with that woman in her home. Juliet washed her face and pulled her hair back into order as her mind worked on the best way of getting rid of Helen. An idea came to her, and she smiled at herself in the mirror, wondering why she hadn't thought of it earlier. With a new-found air of tranquility she swept from the room and down the stairs to the kitchen.

Supper was of necessity a thrown-together affair, since Juliet had spent much of the afternoon napping instead of working, but Juliet was secretly glad. She was certain that Helen would bring that fact up—and that she could use it to set her own plan in motion.

Just as she had expected, when they were seated at the table, Helen glanced over the sparsely laden table and said, "Why, what a nice little supper you managed to throw together, Julie." Helen had taken to calling Juliet the nickname that Ethan often used, and it grated on Juliet every time. "I was afraid that after this afternoon, you wouldn't be able to cook at all."

Amos looked up at that remark, his eyes going to his wife; he frowned. "What? What happened this afternoon?"

"I was quite concerned about you," Helen went on with a falsely sweet smile, looking at Juliet. "I mean, for you to fall into hysterics like that . . . well, it was most astounding."

"Hysterics!" Amos looked dumbfounded. "Juliet, what the devil is she talking about?"

Prepared, Juliet gave him a reassuring smile. "Now, Amos, don't worry. It was nothing. I was a little over-tired, and I began to cry."

"About what?" Amos glanced suspiciously toward Helen.

"I scarcely remember." Juliet turned toward Helen, giving her back the same sort of sweet smile Helen employed with her. "But I confess, I must be overextending myself. I don't usually overreact so. I mean, it's obviously silly to get upset. After all, it wouldn't have been much trouble for me to bring in more firewood for you, now, would it?"

Helen's smile froze on her face. Ethan glanced at Juliet in astonishment. "You mean, she asked *you* to bring in wood for her?"

Quickly Helen put in, "Julie dear, you must have misunderstood." It was clear that Helen at least wanted to maintain some illusion of a good nature with Ethan. "I wouldn't think of asking you to put yourself out for me. You are already so busy, scrubbing floors and all that. Of course, if I *knew* about such things, I'd be happy to help you. Unfortunately, I was never raised to do housework."

"That's all right," Juliet put in quickly. Helen had played right into her hands. "I'll be happy to teach you. It's kind of you to offer to help with the housework. I'm sure it will make everything much easier."

Helen blinked at her, stunned into silence.

"We can start right after supper," Juliet went on. "You can help me clear the table and wash the dishes."

"You mean you haven't been helping Juliet?" Amos swung his head toward Helen, his expression turning black.

"Why, Amos," Helen tried a little twitter of laughter. "You know how terrible I am at such things. I knew it would be even more of a burden on Juliet to have her try to teach me."

"Worse than doing everything for you?" Amos exuded skepticism. His eyes were cold with anger. He turned toward Juliet. "Why didn't you tell me?"

Juliet shrugged. "I didn't see any need to bother you with it."

Helen began to justify her actions, "Of course, I offered to help poor Juliet, but she is such a wizard in the kitchen that it was absurd to offer my humble abilities."

A crack of laughter escaped Ethan. "A wizard!" His eyes dancing with mirth, he looked at Juliet. "You should have seen that first meal she cooked!"

Juliet smiled back at him, then turned toward Helen and said smoothly, "Yes, that's why I'm certain that I can teach you how to do it, too. No one could have been a more hopeless case than I, I'm afraid."

Helen opened her mouth, then closed it, looking remarkably like a fish, Juliet thought. "It was so nice of you to offer," Juliet went on. "I'm sure we'll have lots of fun doing the housework, won't we?"

Helen's smile was a trifle sickly. "Of course."

Helen tried to slip out of the kitchen as soon as the meal was over, but Juliet had been expecting that and was too quick for her. She reached over and grabbed Helen's arm as she started to leave the table, saying, "First thing you need to do, dear, is clean the table. See, pick up the dirty plates and carry them over to the sink."

She pointed helpfully toward the sink. Helen glanced about, then said, struck by inspiration, "I better run to my room first and change so that I won't get this dress dirty. It's silk, of course, and so easily stained."

"Why, that's no problem," Juliet said, holding fast to the other woman's arm and smiling determinedly. "I have several aprons right here that you can put on, so you won't do any damage to your lovely dress."

Helen shot her a dark look, but went with Juliet over to the cabinet, from which Juliet drew a full-length apron. Since Juliet maintained her firm hold on Helen's arm, she had no other choice. Once she had the apron tied on firmly, Juliet set Helen to work clearing the table. Amos sat back, taking out his pipe and lighting it, as though he were settling down to enjoy a show. Since everyone else stayed, Ethan remained, also. Juliet knew that it was Ethan's presence most of all that kept Helen there. She couldn't afford to alienate him completely when her threat rested on his believing her.

The women worked in silence, broken only by Juliet's instructions to her helper. Once the dishes were cleared from the table and the table wiped, Juliet suggested that Helen wash the dishes and she would dry them. Helen gaped at her.

"You mean put my hands in that soapy water?" She gestured toward the sink, where Juliet had pumped a washbasin full of water.

"Yes. It's nice and warm," Juliet responded cheerfully, giving her a nudge toward the sink.

Something sparked in Helen's eyes, and Juliet thought for a moment that she was going to let fly with a few choice words, but Helen drew a breath, pasted on a smile, and went to the sink. Gingerly she dipped her rag in the water, trying to avoid getting her hands wet but not succeeding, and washed the first plate, grimly handing it over to Juliet to rinse and dry.

Juliet kept the same pleasant smile on her face throughout the dishwashing session. It wasn't difficult, since she was deriving a great deal of pleasure from the disgusted expression on her companion's face. It took twice as long to get the dishes done, of course, since Helen moved with agonizing slowness (in the hopes of getting out of the job, Juliet suspected) and also had to rewash several things, but Juliet was determined to see that Helen did the entire job.

When Helen was finally through washing and pulled her hands out of the water, she gasped and exclaimed, "Oh! Look at my hands! They're so wrinkled and red!"

Juliet nodded. "Yes. Isn't it terrible what housework does to them? Why, I can remember how proud I used to be of my hands. But washing clothes is even worse—oh, that lye soap!" She shook her head and heaved a sigh, then brightened, "But at least we won't do that until Thursday."

With that parting sally, Juliet put down her towel and sailed out of the kitchen, leaving Helen staring after her with a thunderous face.

The next morning when Juliet came downstairs to start breakfast, she pounded on Helen's door. "Rise and shine!" she called out, smothering a giggle as she remembered how she had hated being awakened so early when she first came to the farm.

There was a drowsy murmur on the other side of the door, and Juliet banged on it again. "Helen! Time to get up! We have to fix breakfast. First we need to gather the eggs."

Inside the room there was a sharp, "What!" After another moment, the door opened a crack to reveal Helen in her nightgown. Uncorseted and without makeup, she looked older and even blowzier. "What time is it?" she croaked, leaning her forehead against the door, struggling to open her eyelids.

"Almost six o'clock. Now that it's getting cold, we don't get up as early as we used to."

Helen managed to open an eye long enough to fix Juliet with an icy stare. "Have you gone completely mad?"

"I don't believe so."

"I'm not going out to pluck eggs from under chickens!" Helen snapped. "Now go away!"

"Oh," Juliet sympathized, pulling her mouth down comically. "I'm sorry you're feeling too poorly to go out. You're probably too sick to eat, either. Well, that's all right; you just stay in bed all morning. I'll bring you some nice hot broth for lunch."

"Damn it! I am not sick!" Helen screeched. "I don't want to go out to the goddamn chicken yard and find any goddamn eggs!"

"My goodness, what a thing to say," Juliet responded, looking both innocent and grave. She reached out to touch Helen's forehead, as if she were taking her temperature. "You must be feeling very bad to talk that way. So unlike a lady."

"I am not—" Helen started to scream, then stopped. She glanced beyond Juliet into the hall and pulled a smile onto her mouth. Juliet glanced behind them and nearly chuckled with glee. Ethan had come into the hall; she couldn't have planned it to happen any more neatly. Helen effected not to have seen Ethan. "That is to say, perhaps you *are* right. I am feeling a trifle down. I ought to stay in bed and rest."

"I'm sorry," Ethan said, joining in the conversation. "Are you sick?"

"I'm afraid so." Helen offered him a courageous, but weak, smile.

"Yes, she probably has a temperature," Juliet added mendaciously. "My guess is she has a stomach ailment. Won't be able to hold down any solid foods."

She moved away, and Ethan went with her. Behind them, Helen closed her door with a thud that reverberated down the hall. Juliet snickered, and Ethan glanced down at her in shared amusement.

"I think you might have taken the wind out of *her* sails," Ethan joked.

Juliet looked at him in surprise. "I thought you liked her."

Ethan grimaced. "I thought so, too, at first. But how could I keep on liking her the way she acts? She treats you like a servant. I don't know why Pa lets her stay."

"Perhaps he feels sorry for her."

"That's just like you to make excuses for him. But I think he's been acting mighty strange ever since she came. Nothing's the same anymore. Why, he doesn't even notice the way Mrs. Bangston treats you!"

"I'm sure he has other things on his mind," Juliet demurred.

"Like what?"

Thus challenged, Juliet could do nothing but shrug. *Lord, what an impossible situation! If Amos wasn't careful, he was going to create a rift with his son just by having Helen in the house!* Juliet was more determined than ever to get rid of her now.

Helen did not emerge from her room all day. Juliet carried her a bowl of chicken broth for both dinner and supper. When she handed the tray to Helen the second time, she thought that Helen was going to hurl the tray, soup and all, at her head. But with a visible effort, she restrained herself. No doubt, Juliet thought, she realized that after her grand gesture, she would have nothing left to eat.

The next morning when Juliet pounded on Helen's door, the woman shouted back an annoyed, "All right! Give me a minute!"

Helen dragged into the kitchen fifteen minutes later, looking heavy-eyed and yawning and wearing a sulky expression. "All right," she said sullenly. "Let's go."

It took three days of housework to break Helen. The first day Juliet taught her how to scrub the floors, and the second day she gave her experience in laundering clothes in a huge tub over a fire in the yard. The third day, they baked bread. Not long before the noon meal on that day, as Helen, red-faced and irritable, reached into the oven to pull out the last loaf, her hand slipped on the hot pad, and her finger touched the pan.

She let out a shriek and dropped the pan. The golden loaf fell out of the pan and went skidding across the floor. Juliet watched the bread on its way, and a ripple of laughter came out of her. Helen glared at her, sucking the offended finger.

"I'm sorry," Juliet said and clapped her hand over her mouth to suppress another giggle, though her eyes still twinkled merrily.

"No, you're not!" Helen shot back. She planted her fists on her hips and glared at Juliet. "You're not the least bit sorry. This is what you want!"

"Not for you to burn your hand. Come here, and we'll put some salve on it."

"You don't care! You hate me!" Helen cried childishly.

"What do you expect? You think I should like you when you're doing your best to hurt my husband and his son?"

"I'm not trying to hurt Ethan. Or Amos, either. I just want what I deserve."

"I doubt that," Juliet retorted dryly. "I don't think you'd enjoy what you deserve at all."

"I bore his child! Doesn't that entitle me to something? And I'm going to get it. I'm not going anywhere until he gives me my money."

"You abandoned your son, and you think that Amos should pay you for that? It's not enough that you left him like an old rag, you want to sell his happiness now?" Fury rose up in Juliet.

"Stop it!" Helen shrieked. "You have no right! You have no right to judge me! You're no better than I am! You're just some tramp from the stage who managed to worm her way in here! Oh, yes, Ethan told me you used to act. Seemed quite proud of you, too, foolish boy. Well, I know what actresses are like, so you needn't give yourself airs. You want a piece of this pie, too, don't tell me. And now that you're carrying his child, you'll use that to your advantage. You'll try to push my son right out of here and take the whole thing for your brat!"

Juliet gasped and her hands went instinctively to her belly as though to protect her unborn baby. "How did you—"

"Please, I'm not a fool. I've been around plenty of women foolish enough to get pregnant." She paused, and her gaze turned speculative. "He doesn't know yet, does he? You haven't told Amos. Why, I wonder?"

Juliet's hands curled up into fists, her nails biting into her palms, and she took a step toward Helen, her protective instincts rising in her. "Because you've been here, that's why, and you could spoil anything, even that!" she spat out.

"Oh, really? I wonder if Amos would believe that? If I were to let your little secret slip—"

"Don't you dare threaten me. You try to hurt Amos or Ethan or my baby, and I'll make your life a living hell. That's a promise. What you've been doing the past few days will seem like fun in comparison."

Unconsciously Helen stepped back in the face of the younger, slighter woman's fury, but she thrust her chin out defiantly. "What's the reason, 'sweet little Juliet'? Perfect little Juliet. Is the baby some other man's bastard? Or did you have second thoughts—maybe even a big farm isn't worth the pain, so you'll get rid of it quietly before—"

With an outraged cry, Juliet lashed out, slapping the other woman hard across her face. "You vicious, filthy-minded—"

Helen staggered back with a shriek, but she was both taller and heavier than Juliet and, unlike Juliet, had come to blows with another person before. She quickly recovered her balance and reached out, grabbing Juliet's hair and yanking so hard that it came loose, sending hairpins flying. Juliet struggled to get out of her grasp, while behind them there was the sound of loud footsteps on the porch and then the door was flung open, crashing against the wall.

Juliet and Helen whirled around, their arms falling to their sides. Amos stood in the doorway, astonishment stamped on his face, staring at them.

"What the devil is going on?" he demanded. "I heard Juliet scream."

Juliet blushed, embarrassed at being caught in such a situation, and she looked away, trying futilely to pull her hair back into some kind of order. She couldn't meet her husband's eyes, let alone answer him.

But Helen had no such problem. "That woman attacked me!" she accused, pointing toward Juliet in a picture of outrage.

"Attacked you!" Amos rolled his eyes. "Really, Helen."

"It's true!" Helen retorted, outraged. "I asked her a question, and she screeched like a banshee and threw herself at me, hitting and clawing and kicking. Naturally I defended myself."

"Juliet?" Amos looked at her, his voice gentling. "What really happened?"

Tears filled Juliet's eyes. "Oh, Amos," she gulped. "I'm so sorry. I did slap her. I did. Suddenly I couldn't bear it anymore." She began to cry and raised her hands to her face as if to hide her shame.

"Juliet, no, don't cry," Amos said tenderly and started across the room toward her.

Helen, watching this interaction with a jaundiced eye, put in acidly, "Well, I suppose I shouldn't have been surprised. Women who are expecting often have hysterics, so I've been told."

It took a second for her words to sink in. Amos stopped and stared at Helen. "What? What did you say?"

Helen repeated her words blandly. Juliet whirled and glared at her fiercely. "How could you!" she hissed. "Haven't you caused enough damage already?"

Amos swung back to Juliet. "Expecting? Julie, is this true?"

Miserably Juliet nodded her head. He would be angry with her now, she thought, for not telling him. He would want to know why Helen knew and he did not. Was it possible that he might even think those awful things that Helen had tossed at her?

The amazement on Amos's face gave way to tenderness. He reached out to pull his wife gently to him. "But, sweetheart, why didn't you tell me? You've been working too hard for someone in your condition. Oh, Lord, and taking on this extra burden of having her here. You should have told me."

"I wanted to, but at first I wasn't sure, and then she was here, and I couldn't bear to tell you with her around. I wanted it to be private and special." Juliet began to cry again, more quietly now, and she rested her head against Amos's substantial chest, as if she could draw strength from it.

"It is, sweetheart, it is," Amos reassured her lovingly, cradling her to his chest and bending his head to kiss the top of hers. "It doesn't matter who's here. This *is* special. There couldn't be anything more special."

He held her tightly for a moment, his eyes closed. Helen grimaced at his reaction, so different from what she had hoped when she revealed Juliet's secret.

"For pity's sake, Amos, you're as big a fool now as you ever were," Helen snapped. Amos raised his head and focused his gaze on her, scowling. But Helen refused to back down before his obvious anger. "Don't glare at me like a wounded bear. I'm not the one who's leading you down the garden path; it's that little miss right there. Oh, she's got the innocent act down good, but she's dross underneath that gold, just like the rest of us."

"Juliet is nothing like you. Thank God." Amos gazed at Helen evenly across the top of his wife's head. His voice was calm and emotionless. "It's time for you to leave. I want you out of here. I won't allow Juliet to take on the extra work at a time like this, nor does she need any more upsets. I'll drive you into town first thing in the morning."

Helen drew herself to her full height. "You think so? Then I believe that I'll tell your son about his mother, shall I? Unless, of course, you'd like to give me that small loan we discussed."

"It wasn't small, and it wasn't a loan. What you're doing is called blackmail, and I won't go along with it. If you choose to hurt Ethan by telling him that you're his mother and that you chose not to marry me, that you abandoned him to run off to Chicago with a man, then go ahead. I can't stop you."

Helen's eyes blazed with fury. "Damn you! You're so smug and self-righteous, so concerned about your little wife. As if she was china and would break. You don't know anything. Let me give you a piece of news: your precious Ethan isn't even your son! I left him with you because you were the most gullible fool I could think of. I knew you'd have to keep him; you're too 'noble' not to. But he wasn't yours; all these years he wasn't yours."

There was a gasp from the doorway. Everyone froze. Slowly Amos turned in the direction from which the gasp had come. Ethan stood there, blank horror written all over him.

Nineteen

"Oh, Lord," Amos breathed, and his body slumped, as if all the energy had been drained out of him.

Ethan saw Amos's reaction, which spoke more clearly than words. "Then it's true? I'm not your son? She's my mother? My mother didn't die? She was a whore who abandoned me!"

"She is your mother," Amos began heavily.

"Sweet Jesus." Ethan ran his hands back into his hair, clamping his fingertips down as if he could hold in the horrible thoughts flying around inside. His expression was confused and stunned.

"Ethan, it's not how you think." Amos took a tentative step toward his son.

"No?" Ethan stopped him with a fierce look. "Then how was it? How else could it be? I'm a bastard! I don't even have the right to your name!" A new idea dawned on his face. "That was why Sanderson didn't want me around, isn't it? He knew I was a bastard, and he didn't want somebody like me marrying Ellie. And he didn't even know the worst; at least he thought I was your son, even if on the wrong side of the sheets. But I don't even know who my father is! The only parent I have is—" He swung toward Helen, and disgust was clear on his face. "Oh, God!"

He turned and ran out of the kitchen. Amos watched him, his expression anguished. He pivoted back to face Helen, and hatred burned out of his eyes. "Pack your bags. I'm driving you to town this afternoon."

Helen started to speak, but Amos held up his hand, shaking his head sharply. "No! Don't even try it. You've said enough. You burned your bridges; you have nothing left to bargain with." He turned to Juliet. "Make sure she takes everything. I don't want any reminder of her here. If she refuses to pack, do it for her. I'm going to try to talk to Ethan."

Juliet nodded, and Amos walked out the door, following Ethan toward the barn. Juliet turned back to Helen, who crossed her arms and stared at Juliet defiantly.

"Well, how was I supposed to know the boy was listening? I didn't see him come up."

Juliet swept past her without answering. With a theatrical sigh, Helen followed her. They went to Helen's room, where Helen hauled her trunk out from the corner and began to fill it. She was so slow that Juliet joined in, emptying the drawers at a much faster rate. At least, Juliet thought grimly, it would be the last time she would do any work for Helen Bangston.

When they were finished, Juliet dished up a bowl of hot stew for Helen to eat, knowing that she would feel guilty if she sent anyone, even Helen Bangston, on a cold ride back to town without anything warm in her stomach. But she didn't have to stay with her while she ate it, Juliet thought, and she threw on her cape and walked out to the barn. She found Amos there, finishing harnessing the horses to the wagon. The look on his face was grim, and when he saw her, he didn't smile as he usually did.

"What happened?" Juliet asked with dread.

Amos shook his head. "Nothing. He wouldn't listen to me. Kept insisting that he was not my son and that it didn't matter what I said. Finally he ran off back to the house. He was furious with me for lying to him all these years." Pain twisted Amos's face. "But what was I supposed to do? Tell him that he's illegitimate, that he might not even be mine? All I ever meant to do was save him pain. Now look what's happened."

Juliet sighed and placed her hand on Amos's arm. "Don't worry. He'll calm down. He's young; he acts first and thinks later. But he'll come around. You'll see."

"I don't know. I never have been good at talking with him. How do you make someone believe that you love them as if he was your own son? Hell, he may be, for all I know; Helen certainly wouldn't be averse to lying. But even if he's not, it doesn't matter to me. He won't believe that, though. He looks at me as if I were a stranger."

Wounded by the pain she saw on his face, Juliet put her arms around Amos and hugged him. "It'll be all right," she assured him. "You'll see. Give it time. Without Helen here, things will work out."

Amos squeezed her tightly. "Thank you. Maybe you're

right." With a sigh, he released her and stepped back. He cleared his throat. "Anyway, I better get going. Her things all packed?"

"Yes. I oversaw it myself."

"Good." Amos glanced out the open barn doors at the sky, which was becoming increasingly gray and sullen. "Looks like there's a norther going to blow in. We better get started before it hits."

Juliet walked with him as he led the horses to the back porch. Amos loaded up Helen's trunks and bags and pointedly directed Helen to sit in the back of the wagon, as far away from him as she could get. Then he gave a wave and a half-hearted smile to Juliet and drove out of the farmyard. Juliet watched them until the pathway ended at the road. She shivered—Amos was right; it was turning colder already—and hurried into the house.

She didn't feel like eating; her stomach was easily upset these days. She forced down a bit of bread, then dipped out a bowl of stew and placed it on a tray to carry up to Ethan's room.

His door was closed, so Juliet set the tray down on the floor and knocked. "Ethan? It's me, Juliet. I've brought you some lunch. May I bring it in?"

There was no reply, and after a moment Juliet shrugged and walked away. At least he knew where it was, if he should become hungry. She went downstairs and busied herself cleaning up the kitchen. When she was through, she returned to her bedroom and took a short nap, something she was doing more and more often these days. It seemed as if she was always sleepy.

Afterward, as she left her bedroom, she noticed that the tray was outside Ethan's door again, empty of food. She went to pick up the tray and on impulse knocked on the door. "Ethan? Won't you talk to me?"

He didn't answer. Juliet tapped once more, then turned the doorknob and pushed. To her surprise, it opened readily. She had expected it to be locked against visitors. She peeped inside, but there was no sign of Ethan. She opened the door all the way and stepped in. There was no one there.

Juliet let out a disgruntled noise. She'd been talking to a door and nothing else. She walked over to the window and glanced out to get a view of the fields beyond the house. The sky was massed with gray clouds, and a wind swept across the fields, kicking up bits of chaff and dirt. There was no Ethan anywhere in sight. She wondered where he could be.

Juliet turned away from the window and started toward the door, when an opened drawer caught her eye. She went over automatically to close it, and she saw that it was empty. *That was odd.* Quickly she opened another drawer, then another. One drawer was empty, and the other held only a few garments. Juliet went to the oak wardrobe cabinet and opened its doors. Several sets of clothes were there, but Juliet was certain that it wasn't Ethan's entire wardrobe. The closet looked too empty. She glanced down at the bottom. A pair of shoes was gone, too, from the looks of the empty spot beside an old pair of work boots.

Just to make sure, Juliet rattled through all the drawers and doors again. *It was true*. She couldn't deny it; Ethan had left, taking a good many of his clothes. He had run away! Sometime while she was taking her nap, he had packed a few clothes and sneaked out with his bag.

Fear swept through her heart. She tried to imagine what Amos would say, how he would feel. He would be heartbroken, she was sure. He would blame himself for not telling Ethan the truth years earlier. And what about Ethan? What kind of trouble might he get into, lonely and bitter and far away from his home?

A new fear occurred to her. It was cold outside and getting colder all the time, yet Ethan had set out on foot. Amos had said a norther was blowing in, which she had taken to mean that it would get colder still soon. If Ethan were caught outside tonight, he might freeze to death. The foolish boy!

She went to the window and looked out again, worried. The view was the same as it had been. She tried to calculate how long it would be before Amos got home from town, so she could tell him that Ethan was missing. It would be at least another hour, she thought, and since it was already almost the middle of the afternoon, there would not be much daylight left in which to search for Ethan. It occurred to her that she ought to go out to look for him herself, but she knew that she couldn't hope to catch up to Ethan on foot, and Amos had taken both the horses to pull the wagon.

Worriedly, she drifted from room to room upstairs, scanning the horizon from every window. From Frances's room, she could see the trees that bordered the creek and between them and the house, the small family cemetery. As she watched, something moved beside one of the graves. It took a moment for the movement to register. She leaned forward, squinting. The movement came again, and she saw that it was a tall, thin person, who had been squatting beside a grave and had now stood up. Ethan!

Of course! That made sense. He was planning to leave the farm, so he had stopped by Frances's grave to say his farewell. Juliet grinned. She could still catch him!

She ran into her room and grabbed her heavy wool cape with a hood that pulled up over her head. She wrapped a wool scarf around her throat and put on gloves, then threw the cape on over it all. She didn't want to endanger the baby she carried, so she had to make sure she was warm as she trekked out to the cemetery.

She ran down the stairs and out the front door, striding as quickly as she could toward the cemetery. The wind was much colder now than it had been before, and the thick gray clouds were hanging ominously low above them. Halfway to the cemetery, Juliet realized how foolishly sanguine her expectations of not being cold were. There was no way to completely cut off this chill, even bundled up as she was. She wrapped the scarf higher, covering the bottom half of her face, and pulled the hood forward all the way.

When she reached the cemetery, she found, much to her disappointment, that Ethan had already left. However, he hadn't been gone long, for she spotted him entering the trees down by the creek.

"Ethan! Ethan, wait!" Juliet called and hurried after him, but he didn't give any sign of having heard her. She almost ran down the slight rise on which the cemetery sat. As she grew closer to the trees, she called to Ethan again.

A moment later, he came back out of the trees and stared at her. "Juliet! What are you doing here? It's too cold for you to be out."

Panting, Juliet hurried the last few yards to where he stood. "I might ask you the same question."

He shrugged. "I'm used to it; you aren't. Besides, you're, well, you know, in the family way and all." When Juliet stared at him in astonishment, he blushed and shrugged, saying, "I heard that, too. Anyway, you shouldn't be running around out here, especially in this weather."

"I couldn't let you run off, could I?"

Ethan's face closed down and he started back into the trees. "Juliet, don't—"

"Don't what? Stop you from doing something you'll always regret?" Juliet followed him into the trees. It was a little warmer here—or perhaps she should say, a little less cold—for the trees blocked much of the wind. "Ethan, you can't leave now. It would break Amos's heart."

He shook his head. "No. He's got you and the new baby on the way. It will really be his child. He'll be fine."

"*You* really are his child, too. And the fact that he'll have another baby won't make up for losing his son. Ethan, he loves you. He doesn't want you to leave."

"I can't stay," Ethan insisted, his face closed. "I don't belong. I'm not really his son. I'm *hers*. God!" His voice was laced with disgust. "It's no wonder Mr. Sanderson didn't want me around his daughter. What if I'm like her? And who knows what my real father was like?"

A snowflake landed wetly on Juliet's face and melted. She looked up in surprise. Sure enough, there were delicate white snowflakes beginning to drift down. She looked out beyond the trees. The snowfall was heavier there, with no shelter from the trees, and the wind was blowing it at a steep slant. Juliet shivered. She couldn't spend much time here arguing with Ethan. They needed to get back inside where it was warm and dry. Already her feet and hands were tingling with cold.

Juliet turned around and faced Ethan pugnaciously. "Stop feeling sorry for yourself! There are thousands of orphans who would have given anything to have had the father you did, to have been raised in a good, clean home by a parent who loved them, even if it was only one. Besides, who's to say that you aren't Amos's son? You only have Helen's word for that, and I'd say she's as likely to lie as not. Your coloring is different, it's true, but there are definite similarities in your jaw and nose. And look at your size. When I first saw you and Amos, I thought that you resembled your father. I doubt Samuel or Henrietta or anyone around here thinks that you're not his son. It's only you and your father who are too close to the situation to see it realistically. Go home and look hard in a mirror and then tell me that you're sure you aren't his son."

Doubt showed on Ethan's face. "Do you think so?"

"Yes. And even if you don't share a drop of his blood, he is still your father. He's raised you, cared for you, loved you. I think it's far more wonderful of him to have raised you as his son when he wasn't sure you were his than it would have been if he was positive you were. How much more love could a man have shown?"

"Oh, it *was* wonderful of him," Ethan agreed in a choked voice. "He is good. But I'm not like that. What if I'm like her? I've heard people say that 'bad blood will out.' What if I turn out to be bad? What if I'm an embarrassment to Pa? And you."

"Why should you suddenly turn bad? I've never seen you act like anything but a good young man, the kind of son any man would be proud of. Why would you change?"

"I don't know. It's just that—I don't know who I am anymore!" He burst out. Snowflakes had begun to gather on his hair and shoulders, giving him an odd, fairy-tale look. Impatiently he brushed them away from his face. "All my life I've known who I was and where I belonged. I was Amos Morgan's son, a farmer. I lived in that house; I went to a certain church. I—now it's as if the whole foundation of my life has vanished! I'm not Amos Morgan's son. My mother didn't die when I was born, like I'd always thought. All my life I've been living a lie, and *he's* been living one right along with me. I don't know if I can believe what he says, if I can trust that he does love me. Could he really consider me his son? Could he really love me when he knows what my mother is like? And who am

I, if all the things I believed are no longer true?"

"Your whole life isn't a lie," Juliet countered fiercely. "Amos may not have told you the truth about one or two things. They were important things, I grant you. But what would you have had him do? Tell a child? Or would it have been better when you were twelve? or fourteen? or sixteen? When would be the right time to tell you? He only wanted to protect you, not to hurt you. You know Amos; he's an honest man. It hurts him to lie, and I'm sure he hated it every time he had to lie to you. But he didn't know what else to do! Can't you forgive him for that? You have to know, deep down, that he wasn't lying about anything else. He loves you; you're his son. It will hurt him terribly if you leave this way."

Ethan hesitated and glanced away.

"Please?" Juliet urged, extending a hand to him.

Finally, he gave a short nod and took her hand. They turned and started out of the trees. Juliet gasped, startled, when they stepped out of the protective cover of the trees and the full force of the wind struck her. Under the relative protection of the trees and in the intensity of her conversation, she had not noticed how much worse the snowstorm had become. In just the minutes they had been talking, the wind had grown much fiercer, and the snowflakes, bigger now, were falling in a steady white curtain, whirled by the wind. Juliet shivered and walked faster. Ethan was walking even more quickly than she, his long legs eating up the ground, so that Juliet almost had to trot to keep up with him. And she had to keep up with him, since he still held her hand in his grasp.

Juliet would have liked to tell him to slow down. She was cold, but it wasn't *that* far to the house, and the walking would keep her blood circulating. However, she was soon too out of breath to tell him anything.

"There's the cemetery," Ethan said, and Juliet heard an emotion in his voice that sounded strangely like relief.

She had been walking with her head down, eyes on the ground, to ease the sting of cold wind and snow on her face, but now she raised her head to look at the cemetery. For a moment, she saw nothing but white whirling snow. Then she was able to make out the iron railings that surrounded the small group of graves.

The wind whipped around her, almost ripping off her cape, and she had to grab it from inside to keep it on. It did knock back her hood. She let go of the cape to pull the hood back over her head, and the cape twisted around her, exposing half her body to the chilling elements. Juliet grabbed at the cape, pulling it back around her, and immediately the hood was blown off. Following Ethan as he wound his way through the graves to the other side of the cemetery, she clumsily pulled her long wool scarf up over her head before she twined it around her lower face and her neck. That left her hand free to hold the cape together.

Ethan ushered her through the gate on the house side of the cemetery. He stopped and looked around him for a long moment. Juliet followed his gaze. It seemed as if the wind and driving snow were growing worse by the second. Juliet realized in dismay that she couldn't see anything in the swirling whiteness, not even the looming shape of the farmhouse in the distance. Now she knew why Ethan had been hurrying. He was more familiar with these Nebraska storms, and he probably had realized that soon they would be able to see only a few feet in front of them.

"Damn!" he muttered, moving his eyes slowly across the horizon. "I can't see a thing."

"But we know where the house is from the cemetery," Juliet reminded him, having to raise her voice almost to a shout to be heard over the wind. "Why can't we just go in that direction?"

"A blizzard distorts your sense of direction," Ethan told her, cupping his hand over her ear to make himself heard. "We could end up walking around and around in circles, not even knowing it. You can't see any landmarks."

He was certainly right about that. It was terrifyingly white out here. Fear clutched at Juliet's stomach. How were they going to make it to the house? They obviously couldn't stay here. Already her hands and feet felt numb, and her face stung. Before much longer, she'd have to begin worrying about frostbite. She cast a sideways glance at Ethan.

He looked down at her, then took a deep breath. "It's that direction," he told her, pointing. "We better try for it. We can't stay out here all night."

Juliet nodded. She couldn't think of any other alternative. Ethan linked his arm firmly with hers, and they walked along the outside of the cemetery fence until they reached the post. Ethan put his back against the post and turned to face where the house would be if they could see it. Then, gripping Juliet's arm tightly, he began to stride purposefully in that direction. Juliet marched along with him, praying that they would be able to stay on the right path. It seemed to her as if they walked forever, while all around them the blizzard worsened. The snow grew deeper beneath their feet. Juliet was so cold that her teeth were chattering, but after awhile she no longer felt the cold. She felt only tired and sleepy. She wished they could take a rest.

She tugged at Ethan's arm, but he pulled her along ruthlessly. "No!" he shouted into her ear. "We can't stop. That's certain death. We have to keep going."

It seemed to Juliet that they should have reached the house by now, even walking against the strong wind, and from the worried look on Ethan's face, she knew that she was right. Somehow they must have missed the house. If that was true, they were doomed. Juliet thought of the baby growing inside her and choked back a sob. She couldn't let her baby die!

With renewed determination, she struggled through the snow. Suddenly she caught sight of something in front of them. She nudged Ethan and pointed. Squinting to see through the blinding snow, they trudged toward it. As they grew closer, they could see that it was thin and straight, and finally it took shape as a tree trunk. They reached it, and Juliet sagged against it in relief, wrapping her arms around it.

"It's the hickory!" Ethan shouted. "The one south of the house."

At least they were not far from the house, Juliet thought, gathering her strength for the final push. She tried not to think what would have happened if they had missed the relatively narrow tree. By reaching it instead of the house, they had obviously been walking at the wrong angle and would not have come upon the house.

"But how"—Juliet panted, "how do we know which way to walk from the tree?" They could as easily walk directly away from the house as toward it.

Ethan grimaced and leaned his forehead against the tree trunk defeatedly. Then his head popped up and he grinned. He squatted down on the ground and peered at the tree trunk closely, duck-walking around it until he found what he was looking for. "There!" He pointed to an old wound near the base of the tree that had healed years ago.

He stood, orienting himself with the scar, and pointed to his left. "That way!"

Juliet wished she could share his confidence. She was so tired and sleepy that all she wanted to do was to sit down against the tree and close her eyes for a few minutes. Her eyes must have drifted shut, for suddenly she was aware of Ethan shaking her hard.

"We have to go!" he shouted, his face close to hers. She could see the deadly signs of sleepiness in his eyes, too. She was afraid that it wouldn't be long before neither of them would want to go another step. How could they be so sleepy? So tired? They hadn't been walking *that* long, even if it had been hard walking against the strong wind.

They started off again, stumbling in the direction of the house. Juliet tried to keep her baby in her mind and think of nothing else. She had to get back for the baby's sake. And for Amos's. *Oh, God, what if he had gotten caught out in this storm, too?*

The sudden fear gave her the impetus for a few more steps. Her legs were feeling weaker, and she could no longer feel her feet. It was as if she were hovering over the ground, moving without steps. A giggle escaped her at that thought, and she wondered what was the matter with her.

Suddenly Ethan stiffened beside her, pulling her up short. He stood, listening, his whole body tense. Juliet imitated his pose, straining to hear something.

"There! Did you hear it?"

Juliet nodded. She thought she had heard a voice in the midst of the wind noise, but she couldn't be sure. It could have been only a change in the pitch of the wind's whine. But Ethan cupped his hands around his mouth and called out, "Help!"

They waited, hearing nothing, and Ethan shouted again. Afterward, there was another noise like the one they had heard before, but louder. Ethan and Juliet glanced at each other, hope welling up in them. They both yelled back and waited.

This time, the sound came loud enough that they could distinguish a word, "Juliet!"

"Pa!" Ethan screamed at the top of his lungs. "Pa, we're over here!"

"Ethan!" The voice was clearer now, though strangely muffled by the snow. "Juliet! Where are you?"

They continued to shout back and forth, and all the time Amos's voice came closer. Finally an odd yellow light appeared not far from them, and, still calling to Amos, Ethan and Juliet started toward it. The odd image resolved itself into a glowing lantern, and then they could make out the arm carrying it and the man's face.

"Amos!" Juliet cried and ran to him, throwing herself against his chest.

"Oh, Juliet! Juliet!" He wrapped his arms tightly around her and leaned his head against hers. "Thank God!"

He clung to her so tightly she could hardly breathe, but Juliet didn't mind. She could have stayed this way forever. Finally Amos shifted, lifting his head and looking over his shoulder. Juliet pulled away slightly to look at him and then at Ethan, still standing a few feet from them. Keeping one arm tightly around her, Amos held out his free arm to Ethan. Ethan hesitated for a moment, then came to Amos. Amos flung his arm around his son, and Ethan hugged him back tightly. For a moment all three of them clung to each other, wrapped in a cocoon of warmth and love.

Juliet snuggled more deeply into the bed, the feather pillows plumped behind her back. A hot water bottle warmed her feet beneath the bed covers, and for the first time that evening she was completely warm. She looked across the bedroom to Amos, who was standing beside the fireplace, poking at its logs and encouraging them to flame.

They had been back in the house for some time now, having followed the rope that Amos had cleverly tied around his waist and to the post of the porch. Amos had brought her and Ethan blankets, and they had sat in the warmth of the kitchen, away from the direct heat of the stove fire, while their numbed hands and feet warmed up gradually. Amos had held Juliet's feet and hands between his hands for a time, then wrapped them in warm towels, and before long her fingers and toes had come painfully, tinglingly alive.

Amos had dished up warm stew for them all, and they ate hungrily while he told how he had come home through the beginning of the blizzard, finally having to get out and walk the horses the last few hundred yards, following the ruts of the driveway. He had gone inside the house and found his wife and son missing, and then he had searched the farmyard and outbuildings for them, becoming more and more frantic with each passing moment. Finally he had tied the rope around himself, attaching the other end to the porch post, so that he would not get lost in the storm and had gone out in ever-widening arcs, calling to them. He had been on the verge of despair when at last he found them.

Afterward, Ethan and Juliet had told their stories, and Amos and his son had made their stumbling amends to each other. They hadn't completely healed the rift caused by Helen's words, but at least they had made a start—and Juliet fully intended to see that they talked it out again, at length.

By that time, Juliet's hands and feet had regained their normal feeling and she had finally stopped shivering. Amos had carried her upstairs to their bedroom, silencing her protests with a look. In truth, Juliet had not minded his carrying her. It was wonderful to put her arms around his neck and lean her head upon his chest, feeling cozy and protected. Only an hour or two earlier, she had been afraid that she would never see him again.

Amos turned toward Juliet and smiled when he found her watching him. He walked over to the bed and sat down beside her.

"Don't you ever do something like that again," he told her, trying to sound stern, but his relief and concern were too obvious to sustain that pose.

"I won't," Juliet answered with heartfelt agreement. "I had no idea what was going to happen! How could a storm get so bad so quickly?"

"Blizzards are like that. It's why they're dangerous." He paused, then took her hand and looked seriously into her face. "I was scared to death when I came home and couldn't find you. I thought for sure I had lost you forever. I—I've never told you this; I guess I'm too much of a coward. But this afternoon, I was so scared, and I was sorry that I'd never told you before. I promised myself that if I found you I would." He drew a deep breath, his expression one of someone facing a firing squad. "Juliet . . . I love you. I love you more than anyone or anything in the world. When I thought you might be dead, I didn't want to live myself. My whole world would have crashed to the ground without you. I'm no good without you, never have been; I just didn't know what was missing all that time. Please, promise me you won't ever leave me."

"Oh, Amos!" Tears choked Juliet's throat, and she flung her arms around him. "I won't leave you. I couldn't! I love you, too. I love you desperately."

"You do?" His voice sounded shocked, and he pulled back to look down into her face. "You love me?"

"Of course I do!" she retorted, wiping at the wayward tears that were streaming down her cheeks. "Why do you think I married you?"

"I don't know. I thought—well, it was because of those things that Henrietta said. You know, security and all that."

Juliet shook her head, smiling. "No, silly, it was because I loved you and wanted to marry you. I wanted to so much I was willing to take that kind of bargain from you. It was you who didn't love me, who just needed a housekeeper."

"Housekeeper be damned! That's not why I married you. I married you because I love you."

Joy swelled in Juliet's heart, but she had to ask another question. "And . . . are you glad about . . . about the baby?"

"Of course I am." His voice thickened. "Nothing could make me happier than for you to bear my child."

"I'm sorry I didn't tell you earlier. I was upset because Helen was here, and I didn't want to tell you with her around."

"I understand. I'm not mad at you for not telling me."

Juliet pulled back and gazed up into his eyes. "Oh, Amos! I'm so happy. I could fly right out of my skin."

He smiled. "I'd rather you stayed in it. I happen to like your skin . . . quite a bit."

Juliet giggled, and Amos bent to capture her mouth in a long kiss. Juliet sighed with pleasure and curled her arms around his neck, kissing him back. At last she had come home.

Epilogue

$\mathcal{E}$than bounded up the steps and into the kitchen. "Surrey's waiting," he announced.

Juliet looked up. "Then I guess we better go. We don't want to be late to your sister's christening."

She glanced at Amos, sitting beside her at the kitchen table, and smiled. He held their daughter, one month old now, in his arms and was bent over her, gazing raptly down into her face while she gurgled and blinked. Her tightly curled fists waved wildly in the air, and Amos chuckled.

"You're ready to take on the world, aren't you?" he cooed. "Feisty little thing. Just like your mama." He looked up at Juliet and grinned.

"Her mama?" Juliet repeated sardonically. "I wouldn't say that's where she got her fight from."

"Now, who else?" Amos asked innocently. "You know her father is the mildest of men."

"The biggest of fibbers," Juliet retorted with a chuckle, leaning down to plant a kiss on his forehead. "Come on, Papa, let's go."

"I'll carry her out," Ethan offered, coming forward with outstretched hands.

Amos wrapped a light blanket around the baby and handed her over to his son. "Be careful on the steps."

Ethan rolled his eyes toward Juliet comically and singsonged, "Yes, Pa, I'll be careful." He walked out the door, looking down at the baby. "Well, you ready for your christening, Frances Amelia Morgan? Hmmm? I just bet you show everybody up. Isn't that right?"

The door closed behind him, cutting off his voice. Juliet shook her head, chuckling, and reached over to pick up the bag of extra diapers she was taking along for the baby. "You two," she said with mock exasperation. "I don't know which of you is worse about spoiling her."

"Oh, we'll do it in equal measure," Amos replied cheerfully, wearing the grin that had once been so infrequent upon his face but that now was often there. "Wait."

He reached out a hand to take Juliet's arm, and she looked up at him questioningly.

"I wanted to give you something first."

"Give me something?"

"Yes. It's a christening present."

"Christening presents are supposed to be for the baby," she protested, smiling.

"Well, this one's for the mother. I ordered it when Fanny was born, but it took this long to get here; I had to order it from Chicago." He reached into the pocket of his jacket and withdrew a box, carefully wrapped in white tissue paper and tied with a pink ribbon.

"Chicago! My, my . . . ," Juliet remarked teasingly as she tore the wrapping paper and ribbon from the package. She lifted the lid of the box and sucked in a breath.

"Amos! It's beautiful!"

Inside the box, on cotton batting, lay a delicate blue Jasperware box, decorated with raised white Grecian figures. Juliet reached in and withdrew it carefully, holding it up to look at it.

"Not half as beautiful as you," Amos said seriously.

"Oh, darling!" Tears sprang into Juliet's eyes and she turned to him, wrapping her arms around him and hugging him tightly.

"I thought you needed something of your own to add to Mama's collection of heirlooms."

"Our own," Juliet corrected and kissed him lightly. "You're so sweet. So good. But you shouldn't have. This is so expensive."

"It doesn't even begin to be enough. I am the luckiest man alive, to have you and Ethan and now Frances. I would never have believed I would say that to anyone. But you changed my life. You changed me."

"No." Juliet leaned back to gaze up into his face, her eyes glowing with love. "I didn't change you. You were always there inside, just as you are now. There was always so much love inside you, so much goodness. It was just that you'd been hurt until you were afraid of what you felt."

"Not any longer. Not with you."

"Good. Because no matter what, I'll always love you."

"I know," he whispered and bent down to kiss her.

Finally Amos raised his head and gazed down into his wife's radiant face. "Come on. We better go. Our family's waiting."

Juliet took his hand, and together they walked out the door.

AVAILABLE NOW

INDIGO BLUE by Catherine Anderson

The long-awaited final installment of the Comanche trilogy. Indigo Blue Wolf, a quarter-breed Comanche, has vowed never to marry and become the property of any white man. When tall, dark, and handsome Jake Rand comes to Wolf's Landing, Indigo senses he will somehow take over her life.

THE LEGACY by Patricia Simpson

A mesmerizing love story in the tradition of the movie *Ghost*. Jessica Ward returns to her childhood home near Seattle to help her ailing father. There, she meets again an old friend, the man she's secretly loved since she was a teenager.

EMERALD QUEEN by Karen Jones Delk

An exciting historical romance that sweeps from the French Quarter of Antebellum New Orleans to the magnificent steamboat *The Emerald Queen*.

THE STARS BURN ON by Denise Robertson

A moving chronicle of the life and loves of eight friends, who come of age in the decadent and turbulent '80s.

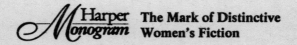

Harper Monogram **The Mark of Distinctive Women's Fiction**